P9-DXT-943

"A TALE WHOSE PLOT MOVES AT WARP SPEED ...

Expect to be entertained ... You'll have a hard time paying attention to anything or anyone else until you've finished it."
—*Winston Salem Journal*

"Frey gives the reader an in–depth look at high finance, politics, and the inner sanctums of inherited wealth and power of an American family with fierce ambitions in every field."
—*Abilene Reporter-News*

"Suspenseful ... [A] high–octane conspiracy thriller ... Real–life financier Frey cleverly incorporates the workings of Wall Street, global economics, and the wired world into his plot."
—*Publishers Weekly*

"Readers will keep turning the pages ... [of] this fast–paced novel."
—*Booklist*

Also by Stephen Frey

THE TAKEOVER
THE VULTURE FUND
THE INNER SANCTUM
THE LEGACY
THE INSIDER

TRUST
FUND

Stephen Frey

FAWCETT BOOKS • NEW YORK
Ballantine Books

This book contains an excerpt from the hardcover edition of *The Day Trader* by Stephen Frey. This excerpt has been set for this edition only and may not reflect the final content of the forthcoming edition.

Published by The Ballantine Publishing Group
Copyright © 2001 by Stephen Frey

Excerpt from *The Day Trader* by Stephen Frey copyright © 2002 by Stephen Frey

All rights reserved under International and Pan-American Copyright Conventions. Published in the United States by The Ballantine Publishing Group, a division of Random House, Inc., New York, and simultaneously in Canada by Random House of Canada Limited, Toronto.

Ballantine is a registered trademark and the Ballantine colophon is a trademark of Random House, Inc.

www.ballantinebooks.com

ISBN 0-345-42830-7

Manufactured in the United States of America

First Ballantine Books Hardcover Edition: January 2001
First Ballantine Books Mass Market Edition: January 2002

10   9   8   7   6   5   4   3   2   1

To Lillian, Christina and Ashley,
forever

ACKNOWLEDGMENTS

Many thanks to the following people for their wonderful support of *Trust Fund*:

Cynthia Manson, Peter Borland and Gina Centrello, Steve and Julie Watson, Kevin and Nancy Erdman, Matthew and Kristin Malone, Pat and Terry Lynch, Bob Wieczorek, Mike and Barbara Pocalyko, Barbara Fertig, Alex Fisher, Louise Burke, Andy and Chris Brusman, Dr. Teo Dagi, Bart Begley, Arthur Manson, Jeff Faville, Rich and Kathy Luczak, Brian and Lois Williams, Scott Andrews, Marvin Bush, Julie Plaza, Walter Frey, Rick Slocum, Jim and Anmarie Galowski, Gerry Barton, Mark Tavani, Robert and Missy Carpenter, Chris Tesoriero, Gordon Eadon and Sir Cody Blake.

CHAPTER 1

APRIL 1984

"Give me more," the young woman murmured.

Bo Hancock smiled in his measured way, the hint of emotion veiled by midnight. He was enjoying the multitude of bright stars filling a moonless sky, the scent of Melissa's perfume blending with the sweet smells of spring, and the absolute serenity of this place he dearly loved. They might have been the only two people on earth, but that was the estate's charm. It made him feel safe.

Bo had grown up here, exploring every corner of the estate's vast forest as a child. He knew it better than anyone. He'd played touch football on the great lawn in front of the playhouse with his father, brothers, uncles, and cousins before Thanksgiving dinner each year, the soft grass blanketed thinly by snow some Novembers, bathed in warm sunshine others. He'd canoed and swum in the cold, clear lake in summer and played hockey on its ice in winter. And he had experienced his first kiss beside the lake at fifteen, hidden with the girl in a grove of sweet-smelling cedar trees.

"What do you mean, Melissa?" Bo asked, his gravelly voice made even rougher by his fondness for alcohol and

1

tobacco. "Give you more what?" He knew exactly what she meant.

The young woman brushed against him as they stood on the smooth granite of the mansion's back veranda. "More of your words-to-live-by," she answered, mesmerized by his voice. It was gruff for a young man, but oddly reassuring too. Like a shovel scraping rock and a cat purring at the same time.

"Oh, I see," Bo said, drawing his words out. He took a drag on his cigarette before beginning. "The best relationship you ever know will be the one in which you love each other for your faults—not despite them."

"That's nice," Melissa said as his words dispersed slowly in the stillness of the evening, her voice all at once as raspy as his.

Bo chuckled softly. He had finally broken through her veneer of detachment. He understood why she needed that barrier, but it had gotten in the way of any meaningful conversation between them. He looked away from the many points of light suspended above them to admire her silhouette. She was tall and statuesque, with long, jet-black hair and eyes as dark and mysterious as the surrounding woods. "You weren't expecting anything quite so romantic," he said. "Were you?"

"I don't know," she answered, trying to sound indifferent.

"How about this one?" Bo suggested, his tone lighter. He realized that he had caught her off guard and that she needed a lifeline. Saving people was one of the two things he enjoyed most in life, particularly when he had introduced the danger. And that was the other.

He took a swallow of scotch. "Make certain you approach both love and cooking with reckless abandon."

Melissa's laugh was genuine. "What on earth does that mean?"

"It means I'm willing to risk burning down the kitchen in pursuit of the perfect meal," he answered, a wry smile on his full lips.

Melissa tried to suppress her answering smile, but couldn't help herself.

He liked the way her eyes caught the starlight, and the way her long black hair shimmered down her back. She was a beautiful woman, and on one level he understood his brother's need for her. "It means approach every day as if it's your last. Never second-guess, never look back." Again Bo's words resonated in the silence of the night. "It's all those things."

Melissa tried to regain her composure, but Bo had a way about him. She wanted to confide in him, to feel his powerful arms wrapped around her. She sensed that he would understand her anguish. But none of that was possible.

Bo took another sip of scotch. "You like me, don't you?" he asked, leaning forward to catch her eye.

"I don't like anyone," Melissa replied curtly, annoyed with herself for entertaining the fantasy. They had known each other casually for almost a year, but tonight was the first time they had been alone.

"Yes, you do. Come on, admit it."

"You're so damn sure of yourself, aren't you, Bo Hancock? You think you know everything. Well, you don't."

"I know you were the one who sent Paul off to make his phone calls."

Melissa shut her eyes tightly, regretting the fact that she had asked Bo to come out here on the veranda alone with her. She found herself drawn to him, which wasn't good.

"Admit it." A confident smile played across his lips. "You like me."

"Maybe," she said quietly.

From where they stood on the edge of the veranda a neatly manicured lawn sloped gently down to the lake. Melissa gazed steadily at the reflections in the black water, then turned to face Bo. Although he was only in his midtwenties, his natural sophistication and charm—benefits of a monied upbringing, she assumed—made him seem older and more insightful than a man just a few years removed from the ivy of Yale. He was about six feet tall, with broad shoulders, a barrel chest, and the forearms of a blacksmith. His handsome face was wide and strong, dominated by an imposing forehead with a small scar above one brow and piercing sapphire eyes. He kept his short dark hair neatly parted to one side, and tonight, as usual, wore a casual shirt and old jeans. She had rarely seen him in anything else.

"Are you seeing anyone?" Melissa asked, trying to move the conversation to safer ground.

Bo nodded. "Yes. A woman named Meg Richards."

"What company does her daddy own?" Melissa asked sarcastically, regaining her hard edge. "How many millions does she bring to the table?"

"She doesn't. Meg's a middle-class girl from Long Island," he answered, rattling the ice cubes in his glass. "Her father is a high school principal who's depending on his pension for retirement."

"How did you meet her?"

"At Yale. She was there on an academic scholarship. I fell for her the moment I saw her walk into my political science class first year." Bo's voice took on a distant tone as he relived the moment. "I didn't get up the nerve to

ask her out until second year, but then we were insepa-
rable for six months. We were out of touch for a while
after graduation, but I never lost that feeling I had the
first time I saw her. That's how I knew she was the one.
About a year ago I tracked her down and we picked right
back up." Using the resources at his disposal, he had
asked the Hazeltine Security people to locate Meg.
Hazeltine handled sensitive business projects for Bo's father, James "Jimmy Lee" Hancock, and, on occasion,
helped the family with personal matters that required
discretion. "I haven't thought about anyone but her
since."

"Sounds serious," Melissa observed, a shard of jealousy entering her voice. She took a sip of wine.

"I think it is."

"But you aren't sure."

"I'm sure, I just don't know if she is. I don't know
what she'll say when I open the black velvet box."

"Give me a break," Melissa groaned. "What's any
middle-class girl going to say to a Hancock son offering
her five carats?" She glanced over her shoulder. "Is she
really going to turn down all of this?"

The huge structure rising behind them stood at the
center of the Hancock family's secluded thousand-acre
compound in Connecticut's rolling woodlands, forty
miles northeast of New York City. On the estate were
stables for thoroughbred horses, miles of riding trails
weaving through the dense forest, a nine-hole golf course,
tennis courts, the twenty-acre man-made lake stretching
out before them, a boathouse on the far side of the lake,
as well as five other mansions in addition to the playhouse, in the shadow of which Bo and Melissa now
stood. Inside the playhouse were two more tennis courts,

a pool, a fifty-seat movie theater, a formal dining hall, a billiard room, and several guest suites. Surrounding the entire compound was a tall chain-link fence topped by razor wire, obscured by the trees and constantly patrolled by a full-time security force, never seen but always present. Every bit of it was available to Bo, his older brothers Teddy and Paul, and their sister Catherine, whenever they wanted it. It also belonged to Bo's younger sister, Ashley, but she seemed to have no interest in enjoying it. She had moved to Europe after finishing Harvard three years ago and had yet to return.

"Meg doesn't care much about material things," Bo finally answered. "If she did, I wouldn't care about her so much."

Of course you wouldn't, Melissa thought. It only made sense that of the three Hancock brothers, Bo would be the one to marry for love. "How did your family get so rich?" she asked.

Bo flicked an ash from his cigarette and watched it streak to the granite, where it glowed red hot for a few moments. He was thinking about Ashley. They had been close growing up, but after college she had rebelled against the money and their father's need for control. He understood her desire to escape, but it didn't make her absence any easier. "Oil and railroads back in the eighteen-hundreds," he said hesitantly. He'd always been self-conscious about the money. "More recently the stock market, now that it's going up again."

Melissa fanned her face. It was an unusually warm night for April. The heat of the evening, combined with the wine she'd drunk, was making her cheeks feel flushed. "How much are you worth, Bo?"

"Why do you want to know?" he responded instinctively. He'd been trained by Jimmy Lee from an early age to answer that question with this one. The training had come in handy because so many people wanted to know.

"I just do." Most people recognized the roadblock and continued no further, but Melissa had worked for everything she'd ever gotten in life, including information.

Bo inhaled deeply. The scotch was filling him with that familiar glow. "Why don't you tell me about yourself," he said, trying to turn the conversation in a different direction.

"I will if you will."

He nodded. He understood the quid pro quo, and there were questions he wanted to ask. "A billion dollars, give or take twenty to thirty million depending on the day and the Dow." He sensed her awe. A billion dollars was a figure most people couldn't comprehend—there were simply too many zeros. "Now you," he said, uncomfortable about having revealed the amount. He had broken one of Jimmy Lee's cardinal commandments. Never give an outsider the number. Never give an outsider anything that might make the family vulnerable.

"What do you want to know?" she asked defensively.

"I've been impressed with you tonight," he answered. "You've obviously been to college."

"Yes, I graduated from St. John's in three and a half years with a double major in English and economics. And a minor in American history," she added, proud of how hard she had worked.

Bo extinguished his cigarette in an ashtray set atop the low stone wall that ran along one side of the veranda. He was trying to think of the best way to ask what he really wanted to know. As usual, he chose to be direct. "Then why this line of work?"

For some reason men had to know why a woman would turn to prostitution. They all wanted it to be the result of heightened sexual desire—which excited them immeasurably—and her practical answer never pleased them. "My parents are poor, I had thirty thousand dollars' worth of school loans when I graduated from St. John's, and the Wall Street men in their expensive suits and fancy suspenders weren't impressed with my résumé."

"So this job is just a money thing?"

"That's all."

"No fulfilling a fantasy?" he asked, digging a handful of sunflower seeds from a pocket and sprinkling them on the veranda for three black squirrels that had appeared from the shadows. "No didn't-get-along-with-Daddy-while-you-were-growing-up complex? No lurking need-to-control-men-as-a-result issues? Nothing sordid or fascinating like that?"

"Hardly," she replied indignantly.

"Oh well."

"You sound disappointed," she said, watching Bo make certain that each squirrel got its share of seeds.

"Maybe a little," he admitted.

"Why?"

"It's a guy thing." Bo thought for a moment. "I bet you get that question a lot."

"I do."

"Damn. I hate being predictable."

"It's like offering candy to a hungry child," she said quietly. "Most men can't do without sex and I simply take advantage of their weakness."

Bo groaned in mock torment. "It really isn't our fault, Melissa. We're born with this sex drive that makes hurricanes seem like spring breezes. It gets us into so much trouble."

She laughed and he squeezed her arm gently. In his touch she could feel an undeniable physical strength.

"Hello down there!"

Bo and Melissa turned and looked up in the direction of the voice, shading their eyes against glaring spotlights that had just been turned on. Paul, the second-oldest Hancock brother, stood above them on a balcony drinking brandy from a Baccarat snifter. Paul was tall, blond, startlingly handsome, and at the young age of thirty already a Connecticut state senator.

"What are you two doing?" Paul asked suspiciously, slurring his words slightly. He usually didn't drink, but tonight he was celebrating his thirtieth birthday.

"Just talking," Bo answered.

"You're trying to steal Melissa away from me, aren't you, little brother?"

"Maybe." Bo touched Melissa's arm again, making certain that Paul noticed.

"It wasn't any accident that you intruded on our evening, was it?" Paul asked, irritation in his tone.

"No accident at all, brother," Bo answered pleasantly. "I've been planning this coup for weeks." Bo hadn't had any idea that he would stumble upon Paul and Melissa having a quiet dinner for two in the playhouse. But when Melissa had asked him to join them, he couldn't resist the temptation to cause his brother angst. "I've come to find that Melissa is quite a woman."

"You've clearly been plying her with more of your words-to-live-by. Probably a good deal of wine too. Or maybe she just likes those rugged looks of yours." Paul put a hand to his mouth and pretended to speak only to

Melissa. "It makes Bo feel better when we say that. It's always been hard for him to admit that Teddy and I are the good-looking sons."

"So true, brother," Bo said, forcing a smile.

"Well, I've got a few more calls to make, Melissa," Paul announced, "then I'll be down to rescue you."

"Don't hurry on my account," she said quietly as he disappeared from the balcony.

Bo took a long swallow of scotch, considering his next question. It was crude, but she had entered into the quid pro quo as well. "Do you ever enjoy it?"

"No," Melissa said curtly, her mood darkening as she thought of what lay ahead tonight. "It's a job and that's all. In two years I've paid off all my school loans and saved twenty-five thousand dollars," she said defiantly. "Now Wall Street calls me."

"I'm sure. The I-bankers rarely care whose money it is as long as they can take their crumb."

Her chin quivered slightly. "I've hated every minute of it."

"We all make choices, Melissa. And there are challenges down every path."

She rolled her eyes. "With a billion dollars, what challenges could you possibly have?"

He took a deep breath. "From the time I was a child, I've never known why someone wanted to be my friend. Was it me, or what we have? Nine times out of ten they were using me. It took a while for me to figure that out, but once I did, I was better off." He heard her low, unimpressed groan. "Money changes the rules, Melissa, and not always for the better. Until I graduated from Yale, I had a chaperon wherever I went. My parents called him a bodyguard, but he was really there to watch me and make sure I didn't take liberties with the family name. A girl had to be screened carefully before I could see her."

"We all know that the elite must stick together," Melissa said sarcastically. "God help us if there were ever a mixing of the gene pools."

"Hey, I didn't say I liked it," Bo countered quickly. "My parents were preoccupied with maintaining our family's good reputation in society as well as in the press. Actually, *obsessed* is a more accurate description."

"Why did they care so much?"

"The press is always looking to trash prominent families. Always after the blood of the rich and famous because our scandals sell more copies. You know that."

"So your parents were obsessed with maintaining the family's good reputation, but I'm the reality. A woman kept in the shadows." Melissa's eyes narrowed. "Does Paul's wife know about me?"

Betty Tweed Hancock, Paul's wife, was a plain, pale-skinned woman whose father was the managing partner of one of Manhattan's most prominent law firms. He had many valuable contacts inside the Washington beltway, and those contacts would prove invaluable to Paul as he progressed onto the national political stage. As a bit of political maneuvering, Paul and Betty's marriage was a triumph. In the bedroom, however, it was less than satisfying. So a year ago Melissa had entered the equation. Paul made it a point to see Melissa at least once a week. Sometimes for fifteen minutes, sometimes, when he could arrange it, all night.

Bo shook his head, thinking about the fact that Betty was less than a mile away in Paul's mansion just over the hill from the playhouse. "Betty has no idea about you. She thinks Paul is attending a political function in another part of the state tonight. Paul has his staff well trained."

"Your family is so concerned about the public image, but the reality is much darker."

"It wasn't when my mother was alive," Bo answered. "Ida Warfield Hancock ran a tight ship. Without her around things have been different."

"When did she pass away?"

"About a year ago," Bo said softly.

They were silent for several minutes before she spoke up again, trying to recapture their earlier mood. "So, do you have a day job, Bo?"

"I'm one of those Wall Street guys who weren't impressed with your résumé. I work in Goldman Sachs's corporate finance group. In a few years I'll be brought in-house to run Warfield Capital, the family investment fund." Bo took another swallow of scotch. "I'm the blocking-and-tackling guy of the family. Paul is the quarterback. The one everyone is watching."

"Does that bother you?"

Bo's posture stiffened. "No."

"Is Paul worried that you'll tell his wife about me?" she asked. "Is that why he seemed upset when you showed up tonight?"

"He isn't worried about that at all. He knows I won't say a word. My father would disown me if I did anything to hurt Paul's image or reputation. My father believes Paul can be president."

"Of the United States?" She sounded incredulous.

Bo nodded. "Look around you, Melissa. Paul is as connected as anyone, he has tremendous firepower behind him and he can sell ice cubes to Eskimos. He can make people believe anything he wants, whether it's in person or in front of a camera. He's part movie star and part cult leader. It's a helluva combination."

"I know," Melissa agreed.

"Once it became clear—when Paul was still a teenager—that he would be a natural leader, that he possessed that unique power of persuasion and the looks to boot, the Hancock machine went into action."

"What do you mean?"

"Paul is just thirty years old and he's met and been photographed with everyone who counts in the political, business, entertainment, and sports worlds. He's been the chairman of several important charities and been given full credit for their successes in the press, even though he has no more appreciation for what the charities do than he does for how hard the common man works every day. He's gone to the finest schools and traveled around the world." Bo's expression hardened. "And he won his state senate seat virtually unopposed. His next objective is to be governor of Connecticut."

"Governor?"

"Yep. And my father will make it happen. Jimmy Lee's influence is remarkable. He has a lot of friends who owe him favors."

Paul's voice interrupted them. "Melissa, I'm ready."

Bo and Melissa turned around quickly.

Paul stood in the veranda doorway. "I've finished the calls I needed to make," he announced. "Come on."

"I'll be right there," she answered, wondering how long he had been standing there.

"What are you waiting for?"

"I want to say good night to Bo," she said hesitantly, aware that she risked facing his considerable wrath by not being immediately obedient. But she wasn't ready to leave Bo yet.

Paul eyed Bo. "Don't be long," he warned Melissa. "I'll be inside, by the pool."

When he was gone, she touched Bo's hand. "I enjoyed this."

"So did I." Bo had a feeling that she wanted to say more.

"Well, good night," she finally said, and started toward the door.

"Good night, Melissa." Bo reached into his shirt pocket and pulled out another cigarette. "You asked me why Paul was upset when I ran into you two tonight inside the playhouse."

Melissa turned back to face him. "Yes?"

"He really was afraid that I'd try to steal you," Bo said, lighting the cigarette.

Melissa hesitated. "Did it ever cross your mind?"

"What?"

"Stealing me."

Bo inhaled, sucking smoke deep into his lungs. "I love Meg."

"But you're tempted."

"Any man with a pulse would be, Melissa."

"Isn't wanting as bad as doing?"

"No."

"Why not?"

"Thoughts come and go. The key is controlling your actions."

Melissa gazed at him for a long time, then moved to the doorway, where she stopped and turned around once more. "Bo."

He looked up. "Yes?"

"Remember that all things done in the dark eventually come to light." Then she was gone.

For a few moments Bo stared at the empty doorway. Finally he dropped the cigarette, stepped on it, and moved to the door. Down a long corridor leading to the indoor pool, he could hear Paul, obviously drunk, talking loudly. Bo put his empty scotch glass down on a coffee table and collapsed into an easy chair, exhausted. Paul's laughter rang in his ears as he drifted off to sleep.

"Bo. Bo!"

Bo's eyes flashed open. The expression on Paul's face was one of intense panic. "What's the problem?" Bo asked blearily, coming slowly out of a nightmare.

"I . . . I don't . . . I mean—" Paul swallowed his words and held out his hands as if giving himself up.

Bo rose unsteadily, still anchored in the terrible dream. "Tell me what the hell's going on," he demanded, shaking his head to clear it.

"The girl."

"Melissa?"

"Yes . . . I suppose," Paul said, his expression blank. "Was that her name?"

"Yes," Bo snapped, realizing with a chill that Paul had referred to Melissa in the past tense. "Tell me what's going on!" Paul was drifting slowly toward the veranda door. He seemed detached, only vaguely connected to reality, as if he'd suffered a blow to the head.

"She's . . . I saw her, but . . . but I couldn't . . . ."

They stepped out onto the veranda together. "Where is she?" Bo roared, grabbing Paul by the shirt and shaking him. "Where is she?"

Paul gestured toward the lake. "Down there."

Bo sprinted down the slope, guided by the spotlights illuminating the playhouse. When he reached the shoreline, he spotted Melissa. She lay facedown in the black water, nude, arms outstretched. "Jesus Christ!" He plowed into the water up to his knees, sending a foamy wake into the darkness. He grabbed one of her arms, pulled her to the sandy beach, and rolled her onto her back, dropping beside her and touching her soft neck. His fingers urgently searched for a pulse.

He lifted her neck, leaned down, and pressed his lips to hers, forcing air into her lungs, then pumped her chest several times with his hands. "Breathe," he urged, certain that he had felt a heartbeat. "Come on, Melissa. Stay with me, sweetheart. Breathe! Please!"

For five minutes he labored over her limp form, trying desperately to revive her. Finally he fell back on the sand, exhausted, staring at her delicate face in the dim light. Her dark eyes were wide open, but they saw nothing. The heartbeat he had felt had been her last.

Bo's head dropped and he put his face in his hands. "You bastard."

CHAPTER 2

APRIL 1999

"What the hell do you think you're doing?"

Bo looked up from behind an array of computer monitors stacked three wide and two high on his immense wooden desk at Warfield Capital. His brother Teddy, oldest of the five Hancock siblings, stood in the office doorway. Tall, blond, and still boyishly handsome despite his forty-seven years, Teddy had a strong physical resemblance to Paul. Teddy's facial features were rounder and less defined than Paul's, and he carried a slight paunch and a double chin, but there was no mistaking the fact that he and Paul were brothers. "What are you talking about?" Bo asked, irritated at the intrusion.

Teddy stepped into the office and slammed the door, hard enough that a picture atop the credenza behind Bo's desk tumbled to the floor. "The damn gold thing," he snarled. "That's what I'm talking about."

"What gold thing?"

Teddy jammed his hands in his pockets and stalked past Bo's desk to a window overlooking Park Avenue forty floors below. "You know exactly what gold thing," he said, furious.

Bo leaned down over the arm of his chair and picked up the fallen picture. It was a panoramic shot of the beach in front of the playhouse, taken from the top of a hill across the lake. "I'm involved with billions of dollars' worth of transactions a day here, Teddy," he said. "Work with me. I know you only like to deal with the wide-angle view from thirty thousand feet, but for my sake dig into the details for a second."

"The guys on the commodities trading floor tell me you're taking a mammoth risk with a ton of our capital in the gold markets."

As if on cue, an intercom on the front right corner of Bo's desk buzzed.

"Yeah?"

"It's Fritz."

"I know who it is," Bo said calmly. The console lights on the intercom were marked by name. "What do you want?"

Fritz Peterson was head of commodity trading at Warfield Capital, the primary Hancock family investment vehicle. Fritz was responsible for buying and selling huge amounts of everything from gold and platinum to oil and cattle. Warfield Capital also operated several massive stock portfolios, an equity arbitrage department, a huge foreign exchange desk, a government and a corporate bond desk, and a private equity operation through which the firm purchased large stakes in nonpublic corporations involved in everything from furniture manufacturing to the latest Internet technology.

All of these groups, including the commodity trading group run by Fritz, reported directly to Bo, the firm's chief operating officer. Teddy, Warfield's chief executive officer, was a figurehead, rarely at the firm more than a few hours a week. Warfield was Bo's life, and despite the massive size and breadth of the firm's investment portfolio, he knew what was in it like he knew what was in his wallet.

"I got a report from a reliable friend that several French banks are going to be aggressively selling gold at the European open in a few hours," Fritz shouted through the box, the roar of the trading floor audible in the background. "The latest consumer price index report is out tomorrow morning here in the States. The frogs must have gotten a peek at that report ahead of schedule, and they've found out that the CPI is going to be down, so they're selling ahead of its release. We could get stung big on this thing, Bo."

Investors bought gold largely as a hedge against inflation, so if the CPI—a widely used gauge of inflation at the retail level—was down, the price of gold would likely fall as investors perceived the threat of inflation to be low. Warfield had a huge gold investment, so even a tiny per-ounce drop would cost the firm millions.

"How reliable is your friend?" Bo asked calmly, checking his watch. It was six-thirty in the evening.

"Very reliable," Fritz answered. "He's inside the foreign exchange group at one of the Paris banks. Do you want me to trim our position?"

"No."

"In the next few hours I can dump a good chunk of it without anyone in the market noticing."

"No," Bo replied again, cutting off the connection abruptly.

Teddy moved from the window to the front of Bo's desk. "We pay Fritz a great deal of money to manage our commodities desk," he said, his fair skin becoming flushed.

"That we do," Bo agreed, grinning slightly. He knew Teddy hated that grin.

"Fritz is in constant contact with market insiders, and he knows what's going on." Teddy was grinding his teeth, as he always did when he was angry. "Why are you disregarding his recommendation?"

Bo shrugged. "Just a feeling."

"Sell!" Teddy demanded.

"Pound sand, brother."

"I mean it!"

"No."

Teddy slammed the desk with his fist. "Wipe that God-damned smirk off your face, Bo, before I do it for you."

Bo rose to his feet.

He was five inches shorter than Teddy, but Teddy still took an instinctive and unsteady step back.

"I'd like you to try," Bo said quietly. "I really would."

"Exactly how big a gold position do we have?" Teddy asked, ignoring the invitation. Once provoked, Bo was like a wolverine. He didn't stop until the other man was down and defenseless. Bo had been a star hockey player at Yale, and from the stands Teddy had watched him single-handedly and simultaneously take out three opposing players in an all-out brawl one night. "How much do we have?" Teddy repeated. But his voice was subdued as he recalled how Bo had been in uniform the next night for another game despite the loss of blood and two bruised ribs. "Or don't you know?"

Bo stared at the perfect knot in Teddy's Ferragamo tie,

then at his perfect hair, not one strand of which, it seemed, was ever out of place, even when Teddy was zipping around Connecticut in his Porsche with the top down. Chief executive officer of Warfield Capital, Bo thought to himself. A bigger joke he'd like to hear. Teddy wouldn't know an interest rate collar from a dog collar, yet Jimmy Lee still gave the oldest brother ultimate authority over Warfield Capital.

Their father had formed Warfield twenty years before to hold the lion's share of the Hancock family fortune. Since then the firm had grown from a billion dollars in assets to a hundred-billion-dollar fund that used the Hancocks' eleven-billion-dollar net worth—and four billion more from other wealthy families with close ties to the Hancocks—as its deep capital. On top of that fifteen billion dollars of combined family net worth, Warfield Capital borrowed eighty-five billion from insurance companies, pension funds, and other long-term lenders to leverage the deep capital and generate tremendous returns for the Hancocks and their associates.

It was a risky structure. If the aggregate value of the investment portfolio dropped, the families could quickly suffer substantial losses because their money would be used to cover margin calls. However, in the last ten years—since Bo had joined the firm after spending several years at Goldman Sachs—Warfield had enjoyed outstanding results. The financial strategies Bo had employed had worked to perfection and the Hancocks' net worth had grown exponentially.

As CEO, Teddy received most of the credit in *The Wall Street Journal* and *The New York Times* for Warfield's success, but Bo was the mastermind, the wizard behind the curtain. Finance came as naturally to Bo as breathing.

"Answer me," Teddy demanded, regaining his confidence. He was fairly certain Bo would never physically confront anyone here at Warfield. That would get back to Jimmy Lee quickly, and then there would be hell to pay. Not even Bo would dare to cross Jimmy Lee. Now in his midseventies, their father maintained his absolute power. "Or don't you know how big our gold position is? Maybe that's the problem, Bo. You're always so damn certain of exactly what's in the portfolio. Has that steel-trap mind let you down this once?"

Bo checked one of the computer screens and quickly performed the calculation. "At this moment the market value of our gold position is five hundred forty-two million, seven hundred and nine thousand dollars."

"How do I know you're telling me the truth?"

"You don't," Bo retorted, "and that's the problem. You've got no idea what's going on here at Warfield, but you don't mind taking the credit for its success."

The intercom buzzed again. "What now, Fritz?" Bo watched Teddy pull out a cell phone.

"I got another report from a friend in Moscow confirming what my guy in France said about the European open tomorrow," Fritz answered, his voice urgent.

"You're full of reports this evening, aren't you? The big question is whether you're full of crap too."

"The reports are accurate," Fritz replied firmly.

Bo watched Teddy finish his call, noticing the furtive way in which Teddy had made certain to cover his mouth and speak softly. Fritz's voice continued like a foghorn through the intercom.

"Does the guy in Moscow know the guy in France?" Bo asked.

Fritz hesitated. "I don't know."

"Find out," Bo ordered, and cut off the connection once more. "Teddy, who did you just call?"

"Tom Bristow."

Tom Bristow was Bo and Teddy's brother-in-law, married to their sister Catherine. A wisp of a man with a receding hairline who always wore tortoiseshell glasses and his club or college tie, Tom came from a prominent Boston family who a decade earlier had invested a hundred million into Warfield Capital alongside the Hancocks as part of the firm's deep capital. In return for the investment, Bristow senior had required that Tom be provided a job at Warfield, and, as further insurance over the well-being of the investment, had also required that Jimmy Lee pledge Catherine as collateral. Ten years ago a hundred million had been a meaningful amount to the Hancocks, enough to secure Warfield the additional loans with which to leverage its equity and reap huge incremental profits. So Jimmy Lee had consented to the union. Tom and Catherine were married on a lovely spring day. The grand ceremony took place on a beautiful lawn overlooking the Charles River. Since then Tom had managed Warfield's overnight cash investments. A job, as Bo put it, that could have been handled by a chimp.

"Why did you call Tom?" Bo asked.

"I want his advice on this gold thing. I've asked him to come down here from his office."

Bo's face contorted. "Tom doesn't know anything about the gold markets."

"Just the same, I want his advice," Teddy replied. "I've come to find that Tom is a very useful man."

"Tom is weak."

"Not everyone is a warrior, Bo."

"Which is a damn shame," Bo retorted, grabbing his desk phone and punching out a number. "Warriors are loyal. They follow a code."

Teddy rolled his eyes. "Spare me."

"They stand up for themselves too," Bo continued. "They don't spend their lives kissing their father's ass even when he's wrong. They think for themselves."

"Shut up." Teddy bit his lower lip as if he'd been about to say something else, then thought better of it. "And get a haircut," he said, noting that Bo's dark hair was down to the bottom of his shirt collar in the back, "and wear a suit once in a while." Teddy pointed disparagingly at the flannel shirt Bo was wearing. "People here would have more respect for you. You are COO after all."

"People here have plenty of respect for me."

"Do something about this office too," Teddy went on, kicking at the frayed carpet. "It's dreary as hell in here. It should look more like the office of someone with money. We have a certain image we need to maintain at Warfield Capital."

Bo didn't care about decoration. Things in his life were functional, not aesthetic. He liked his office to look worked-in, as he liked his living room at the estate to look lived-in. He reached for the phone and punched in a number. "You touch my office and I'll cut off your— hello." The person at the other end of the line had picked up. Bo rotated the chair so his back was to Teddy. Ten seconds later the conversation was over.

"Who was that?" Teddy demanded.

"You don't want to know." Bo pressed a button on the intercom. "Fritz."

"Yeah," Fritz's voice crackled back.

In the background Bo could hear people yelling.

Warfield's trading floors operated at a frenetic pace twenty-four hours a day. "Buy more gold. Every ounce you can get your hands on. Increase our position!"

"What?"

"You heard what I said."

"But, Bo, like I told you, the French banks are going to be selling heavily in a few hours," Fritz protested. "It's going to cause a panic and we've got to sell ahead of them. Otherwise we'll get our lunch handed to us."

"Buy everything you can get your hands on up to our internal limit price of this morning," Bo ordered calmly. "Do it quietly, but do it." He cut off the connection before Fritz could object.

"Who did you call just now?" Teddy asked again, nodding at the phone.

"I already told you. You don't want to know."

"Yes, I—"

"No, you don't!" Bo slammed the desk and glared at Teddy fiercely. "You, Paul, and Dad have always wanted me to do the dirty work so you don't have to be down in the trenches where things get nasty. You and Paul get the glory while my uniform is always dirty, and I've accepted that." Bo leaned over the desk. "But do me a favor, brother. Don't get in my way while I'm trying to do my job. Stay out of my world. You can't handle it."

"I can handle anything you can, Bo. I'm as tough as you."

"Tough for you is playing a golf course that won't let you ride a cart," Bo scoffed. "You and Paul have had everything handed to you your entire lives."

"Like you've had it so rough. I've never seen you headed off to the coal mines with a lunch pail in your hand."

"I've worked seventy hours a week here at Warfield for the last ten years. I can count on one hand the number of vacations Meg and I have taken while you and Paul have been joyriding around the globe. I've built Warfield into what it is today. I've faced panics in more financial markets than you even know exist, and you have the nerve to come into my office and tell me what to do with our gold position."

"I can say what I want to anyone, including you. I'm the chief executive officer."

"In name only. Everyone knows that."

"Then why doesn't Dad make *you* CEO?" Teddy asked, a wry smile coming to his thin lips. He knew he had cut to the quick.

For several moments the room was still. "We both know he'll never do that," Bo finally admitted, his gravelly voice subdued. Paul and Teddy could do no wrong in Jimmy Lee's eyes. Bo could never do enough. It had always been that way.

Teddy's smile grew meaner. "How has it felt to be the black sheep all these years?"

Bo clenched his fists. "You son-of—"

"What a surprise. Bo and Teddy, at it again."

Both men's eyes flashed to the office doorway where their sister stood, looking like a runway model in her couture Chanel suit.

"Can't you two ever get along?" Catherine asked.

Bo moved out from behind the desk, took his sister's slender, aristocratic fingers in his strong hands, and kissed her gently on the cheek. "Everything's fine," he assured her. Catherine was tall and had Paul and Teddy's fair coloring. A year older than Bo, they had always shared a special bond. Bo still looked after her, keeping an eye on Tom Bristow. "We were just having a little disagreement."

"If you call World War Three a little disagreement." She sighed, giving him a hug. "Hello, Teddy," she called over Bo's shoulder.

"Hello," Teddy answered, making no move toward his sister.

"What are you doing here?" Bo asked.

"Meeting some friends for dinner in the city." She hesitated. "I have a favor to ask you."

Bo chuckled. "I should have known. Tell me what you need."

"My girlfriends and I want to go to dinner tonight at that new Italian place down in the Village. You know, Georgiano's. The food is to die for and we heard De Niro was going to be there. You know how much I love Bobby. I met him that one time in Los Angeles and we really hit it off. I called the restaurant, but I couldn't get in. They told me they were booked solid." She looked at Bo sheepishly. "I know you're busy, but could you help? I was sure I could get us in. Now I don't want to look . . ." Her voice trailed off.

". . . like you aren't a player?" Bo finished the thought.

"It's pure vanity, I admit."

The intercom buzzed again. "Bo!" Fritz's voice held a note of panic this time. "The price of gold is weakening. It's down a buck and a half an ounce in the last few minutes. I think the early birds in Tokyo picked up on the frog rumor. If we're gonna get out, we've got to do it *now*."

"It's an opportunity. Buy more."

"Have you lost your mind?" Teddy broke in. "We've got to *sell*."

Bo took a breath, trying to control his temper. He didn't want to let loose in front of Catherine. "Go home, Teddy."

Teddy's eyes flashed to the intercom. "I could order Fritz to sell," he said, but his voice wavered. He knew Bo was rarely wrong when it came to investing.

"Be my guest," Bo said, gesturing toward the office door. "Go out on the trading floor and give the word. But be ready to explain to Dad"—his tone turned vicious—"why we lost forty million dollars, which is about what the damage will be if you lose your nerve now. Fritz can't dump a position as big as ours quickly. We'll take a big hit and Dad will be livid. He'll be even more pissed off when he checks gold prices in the morning and figures out that we could have *made* forty million if we'd just showed some guts and held on. And I assure you the price will be up in the morning."

"Listen to Bo," Catherine urged. "He knows what he's doing—"

"Quiet, Catherine!" Teddy shouted. "This is between Bo and me."

"Don't talk to her that way," Bo warned.

"Sell the position, Bo," Teddy ordered.

"Like you said, brother. You're the CEO. You make the call. You tell Fritz to dump."

"Hey, the guys on the gold desk are going crazy!" Tom Bristow said, rushing into Bo's office. "Catherine. Hello. What are you doing here?"

"Hello, Tom," Catherine answered coolly. "Will you be home when I get back to the estate tonight?" she asked, an unpleasant edge in her voice. She was fairly certain she already knew the answer.

Tom avoided her eyes. "Well, I—"

"Catherine, you'd better get going," Bo urged, not wanting to see his sister's unhappiness laid bare. "How many people will there be in your group tonight?"

"Five, including me," she answered, glaring at Tom.

Bo took her by the hand and walked with her to the door. "I have a friend who knows the restaurant's owner," he said soothingly. "We'll get you in. You'll have a reservation for five at eight o'clock."

"Thanks, Bo," she said gratefully, hugging him. "You're always so good to me."

"You're my big sister. I'll always take care of you."

"Sorry you had to witness that, Bo," she whispered.

"I know. Now get going, we've got business to attend to." When she was gone, Bo turned to face Tom. "Are you cheating on my sister?" he asked bluntly.

"What?"

"Are you cheating on Catherine?"

Tom shifted nervously from foot to foot. "No."

Teddy glanced up curiously. "What's all this about?"

"Nothing," Tom replied curtly. "Nothing at all."

"Why are you spending so many nights away from the estate?" Bo wanted to know. "Catherine misses you. She needs your help raising the children."

"I've been working late a lot the past few months," Tom explained.

Teddy nodded vigorously. "I can vouch for that. I've talked to Tom several times from my car in the past couple of weeks when he's still been in his office late at night. Right, Tom?"

"Yes," he answered hesitantly.

"So let's stop being distracted from the issues at hand," Teddy said firmly. "Sell the gold, Bo."

Bo folded his arms across his chest. "We're not selling."

Teddy took a deep breath and seemed to resign himself to the situation. "Dammit, Bo, you'd better be right on this. Come on, Tom, let's get some dinner."

When they were gone, Bo returned to his desk, sat down, and closed his eyes. He was exhausted.

A knock on his door made Bo look up. Frank Ramsey stood in the office doorway. "What is this tonight, Grand Central Station?" Bo said.

Ramsey was thirty-four, handsome in a manicured kind of way, and nattily attired in a dark blue pinstripe shirt, charcoal suit pants, and a bright red tie, which matched his suspenders. Six months ago Jimmy Lee had hired Ramsey away from Morgan Stanley, a bulge-bracket Wall Street investment firm, to be Teddy's special assistant. He'd given him a huge salary without allowing Bo to interview him. Without even telling Bo that Ramsey was being hired.

So Bo had gotten the lowdown on Ramsey from acquaintances at Morgan Stanley. From what he could gather, the man was a master trader who never lost his nerve under fire. A man who pulled a hair trigger on massive trades when he believed the odds were stacked in his favor, whether that belief was based on significant research or simply gut feeling. A man who didn't flinch when he had a bad streak—as all traders did at some point—because he was supremely confident his luck would turn around quickly. Which it always had.

"How are you feeling?" Ramsey asked, moving into

Bo's office. It was the first they'd seen of each other today.

"Fine," Bo answered quickly. He knew why Ramsey was asking.

Ramsey grinned. "You had a lot to drink last night."

"I didn't have that much," Bo protested. He and Ramsey had eaten dinner together at a restaurant close to the office, then taken a cab to an Upper East Side bar famous for its selection of rare liquor.

Ramsey's smile grew wider. "Not that much? You drank almost a whole bottle of scotch yourself."

"No, I—"

"Oh yeah, you did. Otherwise you wouldn't have climbed up on the bar and started belting out Mick Jagger songs. By the way, that little redhead you were dancing with at the end of the evening knew exactly who you were and what the Hancocks are worth. You're usually a little more discreet, Bo, if I know you as well as I think I do. It's the scotch that makes you tell family secrets to opportunists like that redhead, Bo."

Bo watched Ramsey blink slowly, as if it were a conscious effort each time. "You don't know me at all," he retorted. "And the redhead was nice. I liked her."

"I could tell. Everybody in the place could. If I hadn't dragged you out of the bar when I did and taken you back to my place for the night, you would have ended up going back to Brooklyn or Queens or wherever the hell she lived and spending the night with her."

"I don't do that. I love Meg," Bo asserted firmly. "I'm faithful to my wife."

"Sure you are." Ramsey's expression soured. "But you've got to cut this stuff out. It's going to catch up with you."

"Careful, Frank," Bo warned. "You have no right to speak to me that way. You are not a member of the family. Remember that. I told you, I love Meg and I wouldn't do anything to hurt her. I just need to blow off steam once in a while. There's nothing wrong with that. I would never put myself or my family in a compromising position."

"Jimmy Lee isn't amused. I can tell you that."

"My father can go to hell." Bo's head was killing him again. "I've made Jimmy Lee and the rest of the family a grotesque amount of money here at Warfield."

"He's worried."

"What about?"

"Your drinking. The fact that you seem to enjoy the company of women other than your wife."

Bo's eyes narrowed. "And who's been feeding him those lies?"

Ramsey shrugged. "I don't know, but Jimmy Lee is worried that the stories about you might negatively affect Paul's campaign. There are people trying to dig up dirt on Paul, and your father is wary of your growing reputation for gravitating toward the seamier side of life. Afraid that Paul might be found guilty by association."

"That's crap."

"Your father is upset. You better watch it or you might find yourself out of a job," Ramsey warned. "You might find that your services are no longer required at your beloved Warfield Capital."

Bo waved a hand in front of his face. "My father needs me here."

Ramsey raised one eyebrow. "He needs someone *like* you here."

"Teddy can't do it," Bo retorted. "You and I both know that."

"I wasn't talking about Teddy."

"You aren't family, Frank," Bo said, understanding his meaning. "My father would never turn this place over to an outsider."

"If you say so."

"I do say so."

Ramsey hesitated, then said, "If you go out tonight, don't come knocking on my door looking for a place to stay. I'm beat. I'm going to bed early."

"I'm not going out tonight, I'm going home."

"That's what you think now, but give yourself an hour. Like you always say, 'The hair of the dog is the best cure for a hangover.'"

"Give me a break," Bo said, rubbing his eyes.

"I'm trying to help."

"I know what you're trying to do, Frank, and by God if I ever find out that you are going behind my back, I swear to Christ I'll make you wish your mother and father had never met. Now, what do you want, Frank? Why did you come into my office?"

"To establish the fact that you were alive. I had to just about carry you from the taxi to my apartment last night. You weren't in my guest room this morning when I woke up and I figured you might have gone searching for your dance partner."

"We've established that I'm fine, so—"

"And I've come in to talk to you about the gold situation."

Bo rolled his eyes. Teddy had no stomach for taking final responsibility, but he was a relentless operator behind the scenes. Ramsey had obviously been sent in as a second assault force. "What about it?"

"Teddy and Fritz are concerned," Ramsey said matter-of-factly.

"So what?"

"If Teddy is concerned, I'm concerned. I'm his right-hand man."

"I thought you traded *bonds* at Morgan Stanley."

"Among other things. What's your point?"

"I don't recall seeing anything on your résumé about trading gold."

"Trading is trading," Ramsey said calmly, "no matter the asset."

The intercom buzzed again. "Off three bucks an ounce!" Fritz shouted.

"Enough." Bo pulled the plug on the intercom. "Get out of here, Frank. Now."

Ramsey stalked from the room.

Again Bo allowed his eyes to fall shut.

"Bo."

"Jesus Christ!"

This time Fritz stood in the doorway, his shaggy hair tousled, tie-knot halfway to his belt buckle, white shirt wrinkled and stained with coffee, a lighted cigarette hanging from his mouth.

"We've got to sell, Bo. Please," Fritz begged. "Teddy's called me three times in the last five minutes. He was going ballistic. He thinks you're trying to tank the family fortune with one deal."

Bo smiled thinly. "Does he, now?"

"Yes."

"After all I've done for him."

"I suppose."

"Why doesn't he give you the order to sell?"

"You know he won't do that, Bo. He doesn't want to be held accountable."

"Of course not." Bo glared at Fritz for a full thirty seconds, then walked to the office doorway and pulled the cigarette from Fritz's mouth. "No smoking at Warfield Capital." He slammed the door in Fritz's face and headed back to the desk, sucking on the cigarette. Smoke curling up into his eyes, he yanked open the bottom drawer of his credenza, grabbed a half-full bottle of scotch from between two files, and took a long swig.

It was three o'clock in the morning when Bo emerged from a taxi and stumbled into the small lobby of a three-story walk-up apartment building somewhere in Greenwich Village. He was no longer intoxicated, simply spent to the point of exhaustion. The woman he had met only an hour earlier at a SoHo nightclub and whose swaying hips he was following had promised him sex. He suspected she was well aware of who he was and how much his family was worth. But all he wanted was sleep.

He hadn't been home in two nights, he realized as he watched her climb the narrow stairway. He kept extra shirts in his closet at the office, but tomorrow would be the third day in a row for this suit. How had a few drinks in a bar turned into this? he thought to himself.

The woman stopped and looked back over her shoulder, aware that he wasn't following her. "What's wrong?" she asked.

Bo gazed at her for several moments, then turned around and headed for the door.

CHAPTER 3

Bo sank wearily into a leather club chair beside the wide bay window of his father's study. Jimmy Lee's impressive mansion sprawled across a grassy rise overlooking the lake's boathouse, and from here Bo had a panoramic view of the distant playhouse and its perfectly manicured lawn leading to the beach where he had discovered Melissa's body fifteen years before, floating in the pitch-black water. He shut his eyes tightly against that unwelcome memory—and against a brutal hangover.

The study's heavy wooden door creaked on its hinges.

"Wake up, Bolling."

Bo felt his blood pressure spike. Meetings hastily called by his father always unsettled him. Bo was forty-two now and a man of power in his own right, a man Wall Street revered, yet Jimmy Lee still intimidated him. Just as he always had.

"Bolling!"

Bo sat up straight. Jimmy Lee had taken a seat behind his immaculately organized platform desk and was scanning a computer screen littered with blinking stock quotes. "I'm awake," Bo said.

Jimmy Lee continued to check the computer screen as

he worked his way through a coughing spell. "Barely, I'm sure," he gasped.

"Are you all right, Dad?" Bo asked, ignoring the remark. Jimmy Lee claimed to have given up cigarettes years ago, but Bo suspected that his father still snuck one now and then.

"I'm fine."

Bo watched his father labor to catch his breath. "Why don't you loosen your tie a little?" Jimmy Lee still wore a suit and tie every day, even though he had stopped commuting to Warfield Capital several years before. "That would help."

"It's just a damn cold," Jimmy Lee retorted, peering at his son over reading glasses. "Why don't you *wear* a tie for once?" He nodded at Bo's open collar.

Again, Bo ignored the comment.

"You were out late last night," Jimmy Lee said.

"I beg your pardon?"

"You were out at a Manhattan steak house until midnight," Jimmy Lee continued. "Then you and some people went to a nightclub in SoHo. People I don't like you hanging around with."

Bo stared at Jimmy Lee for several moments, struck by how the physical characteristics of the bloodline had been passed directly to the first three children. Jimmy Lee was tall, fair-skinned, and physically striking, just like Teddy, Paul, and Catherine. He was a little gaunt after seventy-four years and his hair had turned from lifeguard blond to sterling silver, but he was still an impressive man. Bo was broad and dark, resembling a distant cousin his mother had shown him a picture of a few weeks before her death. Ashley, two years younger than Bo, was small-boned and petite.

"Were the Hazeltine people watching me last night?" Bo asked uncomfortably. Jimmy Lee's lack of response gave Bo his answer. "I thought that all stopped after college."

"Get serious," Jimmy Lee snapped. "You're responsible for a hundred billion dollars at Warfield. I need to know where you are and who you're with every second of the day."

"At my age," Bo said, his voice steely, "I don't need my father having me followed. You have my cell phone number. I'm ten digits away anytime you need me. Why do you have to do it? I've proven what I can do and I've proven my loyalty. I've done a damn good job with Warfield."

Jimmy Lee checked the computer screen once more. The price of a stock Bo had taken a large position in last week had popped, netting Warfield a six-day profit of over twenty-two million dollars. A pittance of that profit would go to the insurance companies and Warfield's other long-term lenders to pay interest and a little bit of an incentive kicker. The Hancocks and their friends would keep the rest.

Jimmy Lee's eyes lingered on the screen a moment longer, as if admiring a beautiful woman, watching the stock tick up another quarter point. No one else on Wall Street had been bullish on the company, which was involved in gold and silver mining, with the majority of its operations in Canada. In fact, for the last month most of the Street's all-American analysts had been panning the company, urging their clients to sell its shares. Bo had gone against the tide, and won huge. Now the investment banks were jumping on the Warfield bandwagon, imploring investors to buy. Warfield would ride the hype for a few more days, then jettison the stock through a series of discreet transactions, leaving the latecomers holding the bag. Jimmy Lee would see to that himself.

"You're a master investor, Bolling," Jimmy Lee admitted, still watching the stock price rise, making him millions. "Stocks, bonds, real estate, foreign exchange, gold, and oil. You've made us a fortune in all of those and more. I've never seen anyone better, and I've seen them all."

That was more like it, Bo thought, allowing himself to relax a little.

"You never doubt yourself when it comes to the financial world," Jimmy Lee continued. "You have incredible discipline even in the face of others' panic, which is one of the secrets of your success."

Bo clenched his jaw to keep from grinning. The old man had never been generous with accolades. With Teddy and Paul all the time, but not with him.

"Hell, I watched that whole gold thing yesterday afternoon right here in my office," Jimmy Lee said, scrolling the screen to a new page to check commodity prices. "I saw the price drop off the table yesterday evening around seven. I'm sure Fritz was upset."

Bo nodded, remembering Fritz's panicked expression as the office door slammed in his face. "He wasn't happy."

"But around ten the price started heading up. They were buying the hell out of gold in Tokyo before I went to bed." Jimmy Lee tapped the screen where the gold quote was blinking. "It's way up this morning," he said, smiling. "The CPI number that came out a few hours ago was high, much higher than expected. All of a sudden people are worried about inflation again."

Bo nodded, thinking about how Fritz's contact inside the French bank had been so certain that the CPI number would be down this morning.

"Fritz got snagged, didn't he?" Jimmy Lee asked curiously.

"Yes. An informant of his claimed that a couple of French banks had gotten their hands on the CPI report early and were going to be dumping Fort Knox at the European open because the report would supposedly indicate that inflation was low," Bo explained. "Someone inside one of the banks. Then somebody from Moscow called to confirm all of that. It was too convenient, too neatly packaged."

"Your instinct was that Fritz was being worked."

"There's an element out there that always wants to hurt the Hancocks. They hate our success. You know that, Dad."

"Yes, I do, but how did you figure out the rumor was false so quickly?"

"I called one of *my* informants."

"Not going to tell me which one, are you?" Jimmy Lee asked, a faint smile touching the deep creases in his cheeks.

"You said you never wanted to know."

"Very good, Bolling. That's another key to your success. You don't have that compulsion to relay secrets the way most human beings do. You're a helluva businessman, son."

"Thanks, but I—"

"It's just too damn bad you can't conduct your personal life with the same discipline." Jimmy Lee seethed as he remembered the report he had received from the Hazeltine people a few hours before.

"What are you talking about?"

"You were out until three o'clock this morning," Jimmy Lee said. "A few hours ago you were running around Manhattan like a fraternity kid, just like you were the night before. The difference is, two nights ago you had Frank Ramsey to watch over you. Last night you were on your own." He hesitated. "Where were you when I talked to you on your cell phone this morning?"

Bo tried to swallow but his mouth had gone dry. "Some dive in the Village." Bo was certain Jimmy Lee already knew all that had—and hadn't—happened, but he'd play the game if that was what was required.

"With a woman," Jimmy Lee stated.

"No!"

"You picked her up at a SoHo nightclub and took her home to her place," Jimmy Lee continued angrily.

"I dropped her off," Bo retorted, shaking his head, "then I checked into the first hotel I came to."

That was the thing about Bo. He told the truth or said nothing, but he never lied. Which was the problem and why they had to do this to him, Jimmy Lee thought to himself. "I know you did," he agreed solemnly, his tone turning less confrontational. "But it's the *appearance* of what you did. You put the family in a vulnerable position. What if that woman got herself pregnant by someone else, then came after you? I'll bet she's just the type who would do something like that. An opportunist with money problems. Even though her story would be completely false, it would have teeth for a while. People might have seen you leave the nightclub with her, or go into her apartment building lobby." Jimmy Lee rapped on his desk. "Why the hell didn't you get yourself to our suite at the Four Seasons?"

"I—"

"Or call one of our drivers who would have gotten your ass home to your wife where it belongs."

"I—"

"Christ, it smells like a distillery in here," Jimmy Lee said scornfully. "How much did you drink last night?"

"A little. It was no big deal."

"You have a problem, Bolling," Jimmy Lee said firmly.

"No I don't."

"What do you tell Meg when you stay out all night like that?" he asked. "She called here around midnight looking for you."

Bo looked down. Before leaving the office last night, he had called Meg to say that he was going to stay in the city at the Four Seasons suite the Hancock family leased year-round, and he'd had every intention of doing that. However, at three o'clock in the morning he'd been so tired he just wanted to find the nearest port in the storm. He'd fallen asleep in the taxi the woman had hailed outside the SoHo nightclub, and the next thing he knew they were at her apartment building.

"I told her that—"

A sharp knock on the study door interrupted Bo.

"Come in," Jimmy Lee called.

The door opened and Paul strode confidently into the room, bronzed after a week in the Caribbean sun at the family's compound on St. John. Without acknowledging Bo, he moved to where Jimmy Lee sat. "Hello, Father," he said, his voice booming through the study.

Jimmy Lee stood up, a proud smile spreading across his face. "Good morning, Governor."

Paul Hancock was in his second term as governor of Connecticut. The first election had been close, but he had won the second in a landslide and now he had turned his sights on the ultimate prize. The presidential election was a year and a half off, but the Hancock machine had already kicked into high gear.

Bo looked away as Paul and Jimmy Lee embraced. Finally Paul acknowledged Bo with a curt nod. "Hello."

"Hello yourself." Bo made certain his voice yielded no emotion.

"How are things at Warfield?" Paul's interest in Warfield Capital was focused on two things: the fund's value and how much of that value he was ultimately going to receive. "Is the fund doing well?"

"Very well," Bo replied. "We bought a fairly large position in—"

"Do we know yet who will be running against you in the primaries?" Jimmy Lee interrupted.

Paul gave Bo a quick smile. Jimmy Lee was much more interested in Paul's campaign than in Bo's stock purchases. "Ron Baker and Reggie Duncan. There will be others, but the people at party headquarters believe those will be the only serious challengers."

Jimmy Lee chuckled. "I don't think either one of them will be a threat. Baker maybe. Ultimately, it won't matter anyway."

There was another rap on the study door.

"Come in."

Teddy entered the study. He too embraced Jimmy Lee, then embraced Paul, and finally nodded stiffly at Bo. "What the hell happened to you? You look terrible." Teddy was more direct than e-mail, which explained why he hadn't gone into politics. "Like shit reheated."

"Thanks for your concern."

"Well, we made a great deal of money in the gold pits

yesterday," Teddy announced loudly. "I'm glad I doubled down on our position."

"*You* doubled down?" Bo asked incredulously. "You—"

"It's all right, Bolling." Jimmy Lee held up a hand. "We can work through all of that later. Right now we have something more important to discuss." He pointed toward three chairs facing Bo's. Paul and Teddy sat down obediently, the empty chair between them.

Bo searched their faces for clues, then glanced at his father, trying to figure out what was going on.

"You're going to take a vacation, Bolling," Jimmy Lee announced, like a judge pronouncing sentence.

"A vacation?" Bo's fingers gripped the arms of the club chair.

"Out west," Paul added, "where no one can find you."

"In fact, I've already purchased a ranch in Montana through one of our holding companies," Jimmy Lee went on. "Where you won't be able to associate with gamblers and whores."

"What!"

"Where you won't get into trouble," he continued.

"Not the kind of trouble the New York press will care about anyway," Teddy seconded.

"Wait a minute," Bo protested, trying to defend himself against the tag-team assault. "What do you mean, 'vacation'?"

"Time away from New York," Paul explained.

"And Warfield Capital," Jimmy Lee added.

"I don't understand."

"You've become a major liability to Paul," Jimmy Lee said firmly. "The national election is still some time off, but I'm sure Paul will be asked to run for president by our party leaders. His keynote speech at the convention last time around and his popular social programs here in Connecticut have made him an early favorite with some very influential people. They believe this could be Paul's time, and so do I."

Social programs put in place by others and about which Paul could barely give the average Joe even the barest details, Bo thought to himself. "I'm glad for Paul, but what the hell does that have to do with me?"

The other men exchanged uncomfortable glances.

"We have learned that a newspaper which is less than friendly to the party, and particularly to our family, has taken an interest in your late-night activities," Paul answered. "Where you've been going and with whom. They've become interested in knowing more about the women you've been seen around town with and on bets you've been laying down with some pretty seedy characters. You're on the tabloid radar screen. You could ruin my chance to win the nomination if the rags start writing about this stuff. I can't have you falling down drunk all around New York City, associating with whores and gamblers."

"Falling down drunk? Whores and ga—"

Jimmy Lee broke in. "A high-class madam on the Upper East Side had a visit from a reporter who was asking about you. We found out about this from a friend who uses the madam's services on occasion. The reporter wanted to talk to a woman he claimed was draped all over you one night last week at Elaine's. A woman who works for the madam." Jimmy Lee looked as if he'd just taken a full bite of a lemon. "We can't have that kind of behavior. In this day and age one or two nasty articles about our family and Paul might not even have the chance to run. Guilt by association and all of that crap. Rumors of drugs and the like. We know that there are those in the press who would like to see our family take a fall. Some members of the press will do anything to screw us. I don't intend to give them ammunition at this critical time."

"I wasn't *with* that woman at Elaine's the other night," Bo argued. "She was throwing herself at me." He spotted Paul rolling his eyes. "I'm not kidding!"

"I don't believe you," Paul retorted bluntly. "And we've got to put a stop to all of this right away."

"It's starting to affect you at Warfield too," Teddy said, jumping in like a lion at the kill. "You've made some bad decisions in the last few months because you've been hung over or tired. It's just a damn good thing I've been there to catch you."

"What the hell are you—"

"Absolutely," Jimmy Lee cut in. "You've always had a weakness for scotch, Bolling. Women too."

"That's not true! Someone's been feeding you very bad—"

"We can't tolerate it any longer," Jimmy Lee interrupted again. "Remember what I've always told you. The family must come first. We have a chance to put one of our own in the White House, for God's sake. You must do what is necessary. You must be a team player. I won't have it any other way. I won't have you running around on your wife with prostitutes."

"This is crazy!"

"Really?" Jimmy Lee asked cynically, nodding subtly in Teddy's direction. "Then why don't we get some objective testimony."

" 'Testimony,' " Bo said. He watched Teddy walk dutifully to the study door. "What, am I on trial now?"

"We are all constantly on trial," Jimmy Lee snapped as Frank Ramsey followed Teddy into the room. "Sorry to interrupt your day, Frank. I know how busy you are at Warfield."

"No problem," Ramsey answered respectfully, taking a seat between Teddy and Paul.

"I want to hear about what happened two nights ago, Frank," Jimmy Lee demanded.

Bo tried to catch Ramsey's eye, but Ramsey kept his focus on Jimmy Lee.

"Bo and I went out to dinner," Ramsey began, his voice hushed, acting as if it troubled him deeply to have to answer the question.

"Then?"

"Then we went to a bar not far from my apartment on the Upper East Side. Bo drank quite a bit of—"

"I don't understand what this is supposed to accomplish," Bo cut in.

"Let him finish!" Paul shouted. "Go on, Frank."

"Bo's got quite a way with the ladies," Ramsey went on, shaking his head in mock admiration.

"Careful, Frank. You're going to have to face yourself every morning in the mirror. Is it really worth the lie?"

"Quiet, Bo!" Jimmy Lee ordered.

"He and this little redhead were getting very friendly in a dark corner," Ramsey went on, his voice becoming louder. "She had her hands down his—"

"That's a lie!" Bo yelled. The bastard was willing to say anything to get his chance to run Warfield.

"Go on," Paul urged.

"Then they went outside to a limousine I had called for Bo."

"That's another lie, Dad. I never went outside the bar until we left for good, and there was no limousine. We took cabs all night. You can check."

"About ten minutes later," Ramsey continued, his voice rising, "I went outside. The limousine driver was leaning against the building smoking a cigarette. He told me that Bo had ordered him out of the car. I opened the back door and"—he gestured at Bo—"Bo and this woman were going at it on the backseat. There were clothes everywhere except on their bodies. Hell, they were both so drunk they didn't even realize I was there until I pulled Bo off the woman and made her put her clothes back on."

"This is incredible," Bo muttered.

"This is the problem, Dad," Paul said. "This kind of behavior is exactly what I'm worried about. It could kill me in the press during the campaign. The reporters will make me out to be like Bo and try to claim that I'll be as irresponsible as he is if I'm elected."

Jimmy Lee nodded, worry clouding his face.

Bo held up his hands. "I'll admit that I take a drink too many once in a while. Maybe place a bet on the ponies or a ball game every so often just to relieve the tension of my day. God knows I shouldn't feel any pressure. I'm only dealing with billions of our dollars on a second-by-second basis, not to mention the money of the other families and the institutions."

Jimmy Lee pointed a gnarled finger at Bo. "We all have our crosses to bear, Bolling. I too have—"

"I'm sorry," Bo interrupted, immediately ruing his attempt to evoke sympathy. "But Frank is lying. I never touched that woman and she never touched me. We never left the bar."

"You have a track record," Teddy sneered.

"I do not," Bo said adamantly. "Those stories about me are just rumors fabricated by jealous people."

"Drink makes a man weak," Jimmy Lee said.

"I'll control my drinking from now on, Dad. I'll come back to the estate every night by seven and work from my home office in the evening."

"No," Paul interrupted, not giving Bo the slightest opening. "You'd still go out, and our family is too well known. You'd be recognized in Manhattan before your shoes hit the pavement."

"I'll be fine," Bo assured them. "I'll punch a time clock in the guardhouse," he promised, trying to ease the tension. So much of his self-esteem was tied to his success at running Warfield Capital, and he could feel it all slipping away. "I will make that promise to you, Paul," he vowed, adopting a respectful tone. It was difficult to do, but necessary at this point, he realized.

"You might behave for a while," Paul conceded, "but then one night you'd slip up and do something dangerous."

"*I'd* do something dangerous?" Bo asked, and watched Paul shift uncomfortably in his chair. "Me?" As far as Bo knew, Jimmy Lee had no idea what had happened to Melissa that night fifteen years ago. Bo had taken care of it for Paul. Taken care of it for the family, as his father had preached all these years. Kept the drowning a secret and shouldered the guilt alone. He had never told Paul that he had buried Melissa in a remote corner of the estate, and Paul had never asked.

"You might very well do something dangerous—or at least unwise," Jimmy Lee asserted. "You don't display the same discipline in your personal life as you do in selecting investments. For that reason I have taken steps to address the situation. You and Meg will leave Connecticut tomorrow for the West."

"You weren't serious about Montana, were you?" Bo asked.

"Absolutely."

"What about Warfield?" Bo's mind was racing, trying to understand how a father could turn so quickly against a son who had done exactly what had been asked of him all these years, and done it well. He tried to bring the situation down to money, a factor he believed his father would relate to. "Let's be honest here, I'm the driving force at Warfield." He glanced at his oldest brother. "Teddy couldn't begin to tell us what's in our portfolio. How am I going to manage Warfield from a remote location like Montana? Telephones and the Internet are fine, but you know I need to be at the office to manage the people. I can't just—"

"Bolling, for as long as you are in Montana you will have no contact with anyone at Warfield Capital," Jimmy Lee interrupted coldly. "None at all."

Bo's voice was hushed. "You can't mean that."

"Frank will take over your position," Jimmy Lee said, nodding at Ramsey. "He will become executive vice president and chief operating officer and be responsible for Warfield's day-to-day operations. He'll continue to report to Teddy, who will remain chief executive officer."

Bo stared at Jimmy Lee, cursing himself for not paying more attention to Ramsey's hire. He should have seen something coming, but there were only so many hours in a day to manage the fund. But why *should* he have expected anything like this? Warfield was performing better than it ever had. There was no need for a change. "Frank is an outsider. Making him chief operating officer violates everything you've ever taught me. Never give an outsider any control, let alone hand him the reins of the family business. How many times have you said that to me, Dad?"

"There are exceptions to every rule," Jimmy Lee said calmly, "particularly in extraordinary times. We must prioritize. We must put Paul's needs above yours. Besides, Teddy will be spending more hours at Warfield now. He will keep a close eye on what's going on."

"Frank will lose Teddy at the first turn and never look back. You can't trust him," Bo urged, pointing directly at Ramsey.

Ramsey moved forward in his chair. "Hey, I—"

"What about our investors?" Bo asked, cutting Ramsey off. "The insurance companies and the pension funds will scream bloody murder if I leave. They'll smell something rotten. They might even pull out of the fund."

"Leave the investors to me," Jimmy Lee replied. "I'll take care of them. Besides, they have confidence in Frank. I've already spoken to several of our largest partners about this situation and they have given their blessing."

Bo looked blankly at Jimmy Lee, a helpless feeling sinking in. The bastard had already gone to the lead investors, working in the shadows, and prepared them for the transition. It was a done deal. He had nothing left to negotiate with and his father knew it. "I . . . I won't leave."

"You have no choice," Jimmy Lee said firmly. "I've often counseled you about the need to put the family's goals above your own, about sacrifice and duty."

"What if I—"

Jimmy Lee held up a hand. "There will be no more discussion. The decision is made. You brought this on yourself, Bo. This is your day of reckoning. You may be in your forties, but you can still learn from your mistakes. Remember what I've always told you, Bolling. When you lose, don't lose the lesson."

"Please, Dad," Bo said quietly. "Don't do this to me."

"And I warn you," Jimmy Lee added, "don't call some two-bit reporter and tell him about this. When they try to contact you, don't answer. We stand together. The outside world will detect no dissension within our family. Am I clear?"

Bo said nothing. He was numb.

"Bolling, am I clear?"

"Yes, sir."

A few minutes later Bo stood on the hillside in front of the mansion, hands jammed in his pockets, gazing down at the beach where Melissa had died.

"Don't take it so badly."

Bo whipped around. Paul stood on the brick path leading from one of the mansion's side doors to a driveway where his limousine was parked.

"How am I supposed to take it?" Bo asked softly.

Paul glanced at his driver, who was leaning against the vehicle reading a magazine, then moved across the lawn to where Bo stood. He put a hand on Bo's shoulder and smiled broadly, as if working a fund-raiser. "You want to see me succeed, don't you, Bo? You want to see me in the Oval Office."

Bo pressed his lips together tightly.

"Of course you do," Paul continued. "So think of your stay in Montana as a tiny contribution to my opportunity."

"I'd say it's a big contribution. More like taking a bullet than a trivial inconvenience."

Paul thought for a moment. "I suppose it is."

Bo gestured at the beach below. "When do people stop taking bullets for you?"

"What's that supposed to mean?" Paul snapped.

Bo's eyes narrowed. "What happened on the beach that night, Paul?" He'd been waiting fifteen years to ask the question. "What really happened?"

Paul rarely lost his composure, but now he flinched, as if he'd been struck in the face. It was the first time either of them had spoken of the incident since that night.

"Tell me what happened to Melissa," Bo demanded, rage gripping him. "I want to know."

"She drowned," Paul muttered. "You know that. It was her own damn idea to go down to the lake. She was drunk and she drowned. That's all there was to it. She was already dead when I found her in the water."

"Why the hell didn't you pull her to the beach? Wouldn't that have been the natural reaction?"

"I was scared out of my mind, and blind drunk. I didn't know what was going on, thanks to you. Thanks to all of that alcohol you made me drink."

"There were bruises on Melissa's neck," Bo said, remembering her blood-filled corneas as well.

"We had sex. She begged me to give it to her rough. Said she liked it that way. Then she went down to the lake alone to take a swim." Paul shook his head regretfully.

"I don't buy that. I don't think she liked it rough. In fact, I don't think she liked it at all."

Paul shrugged. "I don't really care what you think."

"Why would she take a swim in the lake? The water would have been ice cold in April, just like it is now.

There's a pool inside the playhouse. Why wouldn't she have gone swimming there?"

Paul moved to where Bo stood. "I don't know why she chose to swim in the lake instead of the playhouse pool," he hissed, towering several inches over Bo and jabbing one finger into his chest. "And I don't care. All I care about is getting you as far away from here as possible so I can win an election and not have to worry about you screwing things up."

In their years growing up they had never had a physical confrontation, and the question of who would win still lingered in Bo's mind. Paul was bigger, but Bo had always sensed that Paul lacked the stomach for a real fight. Paul would wage war in the political world, working deftly behind the scenes to destroy an opponent, but his appetite for a fistfight was minimal. It might mar that pretty face. "That's what this is really about, isn't it?" Bo said, shoving Paul's hand away.

"What are you talking about?"

"You just don't want me around." Bo watched Paul's left hand clench and unclench. There was a large brown birthmark covering the third knuckle. "You've never wanted me around. I've always known that."

"You don't know anything," Paul said loudly, jabbing Bo's chest again.

Bo grabbed Paul by the lapels of his suit coat, lifted him into the air, then threw him to the ground.

Paul scrambled to his feet quickly and took a step toward Bo as if to attack, then stopped. He realized that his younger brother wouldn't back down. He could have been Goliath and Bo wouldn't have backed down. He forced himself to smile. "This just isn't worth it," he said.

Bo smiled back. He'd been right after all. Paul was

willing to wage political war, but was unwilling to put his body at risk. "You know something?"

"What?" Paul asked, through gritted teeth.

"All things done in the dark eventually come to light."

"More words-to-live-by?" Paul had regained his composure. "You never stop with those asinine things, do you?"

"This time the words aren't mine," Bo said.

"Whose are they?"

"It isn't important, not to you anyway." Bo took a deep breath. "I once loved this estate so much," he said, turning toward the lake. "You ruined that for me, Paul, and I'll never forgive you."

"Get over it, little—"

"More important," Bo interrupted, "a woman died down there on that beach. Someday I'll find out what really happened to her. I owe Melissa that much."

Joseph Scully eyed the man seated on the other side of the café's outdoor table. Jim Whitacre was the second-highest-ranking executive at Global Media, the largest information technology company in the world. Global Media's operations included local, long-distance, and wireless communication systems as well as satellite operations. It operated the largest cable television footprint in the United States, was a dominant Internet service provider, and owned a cutting-edge software developer. Whitacre was a high-profile corporate officer, easily recognizable in the United States and Europe, but not here in Korea. Which was exactly why Scully had chosen to meet at this out-of-the-way place on the outskirts of Seoul.

"What are we going to talk about tonight, Mr. Scully?"

Whitacre asked. He had known Scully for six months and liked him even less now than he had the first time they'd met. "What is so urgent that you have to come find me during the middle of a very important week of meetings in Asia?"

Whitacre was too sure of himself for a man who had never put himself at risk in the name of a cause, Scully thought. Scully had spent his career in the intelligence shadows, constantly one small misstep away from being spirited off to an enemy interrogation camp and certain torture. Scully was the type of man the United States government would never acknowledge knowing if he found himself in hot water. He had sacrificed family, friends, and monetary gain for his country. He was certain the only cause Whitacre had ever sacrificed anything for had its roots firmly planted in the dollar.

"We're going to talk about something near and dear to your heart," Scully said. "The money."

Whitacre snuffed out his cigarette in a dirty porcelain ashtray. He liked coming to Asia because you could smoke whenever and wherever you chose. "What about it?"

"It's time to move it."

"Is the infrastructure ready?"

"Yes." Scully was aware of Whitacre's disdain for him, but it didn't bother him at all. The feeling was mutual. He had expressed his displeasure at the prospect of working with Whitacre to the higher-ups, but the decision to use Whitacre for the operation was final.

"Have we decided which pocket the money will come from?"

"Yes."

"How much will be transferred?"

"A billion initially, then another billion later. It's a lot, but thanks to our contacts no one will ever realize what's happened."

"And the destination is no problem?"

"The final details have been worked out," Scully said proudly. He had been proposing this plan for years, but until recently no one had paid attention. Eighteen months ago the higher-ups had finally understood the incredible opportunity. Predictably, they were now claiming the idea as their own, but he didn't care. He derived an immense amount of satisfaction because he knew down deep who was responsible, and he was patriotic to a fault. "Everything is ready."

Whitacre lit another cigarette. "The reach of this thing seems to grow every day."

Scully leaned over the table. "Does that scare you?"

"No," Whitacre replied hesitantly. What scared him was Scully.

"Good," Scully said, checking his watch. "Your CEO will be here in a few minutes, according to our people."

"Right," Whitacre muttered. He felt a pain in the pit of his stomach. At least he was capable of remorse, he thought to himself. He knew Scully had none.

"Have you ever been under fire, Mr. Whitacre?" Scully asked, a thin smile on his lips. "Ever had someone attack you brandishing a deadly weapon with the intent to kill?"

Whitacre shook his head. "No," he said. "Why?"

"Just curious." Scully pointed at a dark window above a grocery store across the street. "I'll be right up there."

Whitacre realized the cigarette between his fingers was

shaking and he quickly placed it in the ashtray. "It's going to happen here?" he asked, swallowing hard.

"Yes."

"But there are so many people around," Whitacre protested. It was well past sundown, but the thoroughfare remained crowded with pedestrians.

"Don't worry about them. They'll be fine."

"Why not do it back at the hotel?"

"It has to look as if you were *both* targets."

Whitacre put the cigarette to his lips again and drew on it deeply to calm his nerves. "I suppose," he agreed.

"In a few minutes everything will be fine," Scully assured him. "It will all be over and you'll be the new chief executive officer of the largest information technology company in the world."

Whitacre watched Scully slink away. "James Whitacre, CEO of Global Media," he said to himself quietly. He liked the sound of it.

A few minutes later Whitacre spotted Richard Randolph, Global's CEO, lumbering up the street toward the café lugging a bag filled with gifts for his wife and children back in the United States. Randolph was a bear of a man—six and a half feet tall—with a grand vision for Global Media and the determination and courage to make the vision become reality. In three years he had assembled the company with an adept string of mergers and a hard-nosed attitude. Randolph believed he had done the public a favor by bringing such an incredible array of technology together in one package. Randolph had no idea what he had really done, Whitacre thought to himself as he rose from his chair and shook Randolph's hand.

The instant their hands met, Whitacre heard the first

crack of the rifle, felt Randolph's grip loosen, and watched the huge man topple to the pavement before him with a muted groan, presents tumbling from the bags as he collapsed. Then Whitacre felt a searing pain and he too crumpled to the street.

Bo sat in a wicker chair on the playhouse veranda, smoking a cigarette as he watched darkness yield to dawn over the lake. He'd spent the night out here, staring into the darkness, attempting to understand how flesh and blood could be so cruel. He had tried to talk to Jimmy Lee one-on-one several times since the confrontation in the study yesterday morning, but had been unable to gain an audience. The decision had been made. Paul was the victor. That was the reality. So was Montana.

"Bo."

He turned slowly in the direction of the voice, suddenly aware of how tired he was.

Bruce Laird nodded as he sat down in the chair beside Bo's. "Morning."

Bruce Laird was Jimmy Lee's personal attorney. A man who knew more about Jimmy Lee's dealings, both business and personal, than anyone else. Jimmy Lee had lured Laird away from the white-shoe firm of Davis Polk seven years ago to be his point man. Bo and Teddy were privy to all issues concerning Warfield Capital; Paul had been introduced to all of Jimmy Lee's many political contacts; and certain nonfamily insiders ran or had access to other specific areas of information within the Hancock empire. But Laird had access to everything.

Laird was only five six and a hundred forty pounds, but he made up for his lack of physical stature with a steel-trap mind that never forgot a name, a face, a place, or a document. He had a take-no-prisoners attitude when it came to negotiation, whether that negotiation had to do with a piece of beachfront property Jimmy Lee wanted to purchase or the price of a cup of coffee from a street vendor. Price tags and suggested legal language were starting points to Laird, and with the Hancock name behind him, he rarely caved to anyone on the other side of the table concerning either issue.

As Laird sat down it occurred to Bo that he knew very little about the man even though he was an integral part of the family team. All Bo knew was that Laird was a workaholic who rarely had time for his wife and two small children who lived with him in a sprawling Park Avenue penthouse; that Laird had little respect for Teddy or Paul; and that he was brusque with everyone, even the formidable Jimmy Lee.

"How are you, Counselor?" Bo asked. Jimmy Lee had addressed Laird as such from the beginning and now everyone inside the family called him by that title. And in return only Laird dared to call Jimmy Lee by the nickname J. L.

"Oh, I'm fine." Laird frowned at Bo's cigarette. He was a health nut who ran five miles a day and didn't drink or smoke. "You're the one in the hot seat, Bo. When are you leaving?"

News traveled fast. "Why do you ask, Counselor? What part of my life has my father promised you?"

"Don't be emotional, Bo." Laird was only a year older than Bo, but he dispensed paternal advice to all three Hancock brothers with regularity. "There is no place for emotion in business."

Bo counted to ten quietly, refraining from his first-instinct response. Laird was a powerful man within the empire and Bo needed every ally he could get. "I like numbers, but I can't be purely analytical like you. I can't accept what my father did to me yesterday."

"You'll be back," Laird said quietly.

Bo looked up at this small but encouraging comment. "You think so?"

"You're too valuable. J. L. knows that."

"Thanks for saying so."

"When are you leaving?"

"Jesus, Counselor, I—"

"J. L. has asked me to make certain arrangements to facilitate your transition away from Connecticut. I simply want to know how long I have."

Bo exhaled heavily. "I thought at first that it was going to be today," he answered, watching the sun's first rays glaze the lake's surface. "But I've been given a one-day reprieve. Meg and I have until tomorrow to leave."

As Laird rose to go he dropped a copy of the *Daily News* on Bo's lap. "You'll be interested to read about your exploits of the other night in the Society section on page fifty-two."

Bo pushed the newspaper off his lap onto the ground. "So nice of you to stop by, Counselor."

Laird stopped when he reached the veranda door. "For what it's worth, Bo, I told J. L. I thought it was a bad idea to turn Warfield over to Frank Ramsey." Laird sidestepped Dale Stephenson, who was coming out onto the veranda, then ducked inside.

"Hi, Bo." Dale Stephenson ran Warfield Capital's private equity operation and reported directly to Bo. The private equity group negotiated the purchase of significant stakes in large nonpublic companies and bought divisions of Fortune 1000 companies usually in partnership with those divisions' management teams. Over the last five years the private equity group had been one of Warfield's most successful entities, consistently selling its investments at five to ten times the initial purchase price.

Bo gestured for Stephenson to take the seat Laird had just vacated. "Thanks for coming out on such short notice." Bo had awakened Stephenson at his Short Hills, New Jersey, home with a 4:00 A.M. telephone call. "Sorry for waking you up at such an ungodly hour."

"No problem." Stephenson was accustomed to Bo's relentless work ethic. He assumed that Bo had identified another attractive investment opportunity for the private equity group. Bo's referral network was immense and he was constantly sourcing opportunities before other investment groups did. In the private equity world you had to move quickly because the other groups had their networks as well and would ultimately find what you had found. The trick to the business was striking a deal with the management team or the young Internet entrepreneur before the other people arrived. "Got another deal for us?"

Bo kicked at the early edition of the *Daily News*. "I wish."

Stephenson heard Bo's dejection. "What's wrong?"

"I'm going away for a while, Dale."

"Away?"

Bo shut his eyes. "I'm 'taking a vacation,' as Jimmy Lee so eloquently put it. He and Paul have decided that I've become a liability to Paul's campaign."

Stephenson had heard rumors to this effect since last week—Ramsey had been dropping hints—but he hadn't believed that they could be true. Bo was a hard drinker, there was no denying that, but he was the mastermind and without him Warfield would be rudderless. "I can't believe it."

"It's true." Bo dropped his cigarette to the granite, then glanced at Stephenson, a pasty-faced man who could structure a massive leveraged buyout on the back of a napkin. "Meg and I leave tomorrow for a ranch Jimmy Lee bought in Montana. I don't know when I'll be back."

"Who will—"

"Frank Ramsey," Bo cut in, anticipating the question.

"That's ridiculous. We can't trust that—"

"What's done is done." Bo checked the veranda door to make certain no one was listening. "I need your help, Dale," he said, lowering his voice.

Stephenson nodded. Bo had made him a multimillionaire over the last few years. More important, he liked the man. "What do you need?"

"Jimmy Lee has forbidden me to have contact with anyone at Warfield. I told him I needed to close the loop with you this morning on the transactions that are currently in process and he agreed to let me see you, but after this meeting I am officially exiled."

"Bastard."

"I have to stay in touch with someone about what's going on at Warfield, Dale. I can't just walk away from what we've built and trust that Ramsey will take care of it while I'm gone."

"I agree," Stephenson said hesitantly. He knew what was coming and it scared him. You didn't disobey a direct order from Jimmy Lee without considerable deliberation, because you knew that the punishment upon discovery would be swift and severe, and he'd become accustomed to earning his millions from Warfield Capital.

"You and I will maintain contact, Dale."

Stephenson grimaced.

"We'll keep it very quiet," Bo assured the other man, taking note of the reluctance in his eyes. "We'll work out a system of communication that doesn't make you vulnerable."

Stephenson took a deep breath. "You're a good friend, Bo, and you've made me a wealthy man. My family and I owe you a great deal. Jimmy Lee scares me, I'll be honest." He paused. "But of course I'll do what you want."

CHAPTER 4

APRIL 2000

"Been drinking tonight, Bo?"

Bo reclined against the side of the Jeep, massive forearms folded over his barrel chest. "No more than usual, Sheriff Blackburn."

John Blackburn aimed his flashlight into the Jeep. "There's no need to be so formal."

Emergency lights blazed across Bo's three-day stubble. "Just the same, Sheriff."

"Where's your wife?" Blackburn asked, concerned. "Where's Meg?"

Blackburn was a wiry man of medium height with curly red hair and a bushy mustache that looked too big for his angular face. He never carried his service revolver on his hip, but kept it back in the patrol car. He was a commonsense lawman who was more concerned with taking care of his townspeople than intimidating them.

"Where's *your* wife?" Bo retorted. "Where's Katie?" Meg and Katie had become good friends over the last year, during the Hancocks' exile in Montana.

"At home," Blackburn said calmly, keeping his

annoyance in check, recognizing that Bo wasn't himself. "Now where's—"

"Meg's back East seeing her family," Bo answered.

"Who's that in the passenger seat?"

Blackburn's only problem was that he asked too many questions. "A friend."

"I don't recognize her."

Bo knew better than to engage a police officer in conversation during a traffic stop, even an officer as good-natured as Blackburn, but he couldn't resist the temptation to start something. As a child he'd always been the one to stir up trouble. Always the one to hurl a rock at a hornets' nest or commandeer a canoe out onto the lake without adult supervision. "Do you have to know everyone, Sheriff?" he asked.

"Libby, Montana, is a small town," Blackburn said evenly. He was aware of what Bo was trying to do. They'd played enough poker last winter to understand each other very well. "I like to know everyone."

"Even visitors?"

Blackburn aimed the flashlight at the woman. "Especially visitors." He turned the flashlight beam into Bo's bloodshot eyes, inspecting the crimson road maps leading to sapphire irises. "What's her name?"

Bo shielded his face. "Tiffany."

"Where's she from?"

"Missoula."

"What's she doing in Libby?"

"Participating in the local service economy."

"What do you mean?"

"She's working."

"Doing what?"

"Guiding on the Kootenai River," Bo replied, getting annoyed at the third degree.

Blackburn snickered. "I doubt she even knows what a fly rod is." He aimed the light into the Jeep again. "Judging from those red high heels, that skirt, or more accurately the lack of it, and that pallid skin, I'd say she's active in another sector of the service economy."

"What's your point?"

"Are you and the boys at it again in the back room of Little Lolo's?" Blackburn asked, chewing on a toothpick.

"Now, Sheriff," Bo answered cordially, "you shut us down for the fishing season, remember?"

"Uh-huh." Blackburn gestured at his patrol car. "Why don't you take a quick walk with me?"

"Am I under arrest?" Tonight was the third time Blackburn had pulled Bo over in the last month. Bo had avoided arrest on each occasion.

"You must be drinking vodka, Bo, because I can't smell a thing on your breath."

"Am I under arrest?" Bo repeated.

"And if I say yes, what then?"

"You know the drill. I'll request consultation with my attorney. Once I make that request you can't do anything to me until he arrives. That is my right."

Blackburn kicked at a pebble. "I suppose it'll take him a few hours to get here from Kalispell."

"At least a few."

"You'll be stone sober by then, won't you?"

"Give me a little credit, Sheriff. That's a trick question. I'm not going to incriminate myself." Bo watched Blackburn exhale heavily. At this point Blackburn had to arrest him without administering a test, or let him go.

"It's just a damn good thing most people aren't as familiar with the law as you." Blackburn patted Bo on the shoulder. "All right, you can go, but be careful and watch your speed. Slow and steady."

"The speed limit in Montana is 'reasonable and prudent,'" Bo replied, hauling himself behind the steering wheel.

"Not anymore," Blackburn corrected, leaning into the Jeep through the open window, looking for a bottle or a gun, both of which lay concealed beneath the seat. "We changed that."

"All right, all right. Seventy-five."

"Sixty at night."

Bo squinted at the sun, half hidden by mountain peaks on the west side of the valley. "It isn't dark yet."

"I mean it," Blackburn said firmly. "Take it easy."

"Yeah, yeah."

Blackburn took a deep breath. "When you first got out here to Montana a year ago, you were a model citizen. I never saw you take a drink, let alone get behind the wheel of a vehicle with alcohol in your system. Now I hear things."

"Oh, you hear things, do you?"

"Yes."

"Do you have spies out there checking on me?"

"People talk and I can't help but overhear them. You can throw a stone from one side of this town to the other."

"What do you hear?" Bo asked impatiently.

Blackburn knew about the Hancock family wealth. The rest of Libby's natives thought Bo was just an everyday Wall Streeter who had come to Montana looking for something ethereal they knew he'd never find, and who would go home after the second or third winter. They assumed, as they did about most Easterners who lived in large houses in the middle of huge tracts of land, that Bo was rich, but they had no idea how rich. Blackburn knew because he'd done his research on the Internet, and because he'd been cautioned by an anonymous telephone call that the long arm of the Hancock family could easily reach Montana if Blackburn was too much of a pain in Bo's ass. Then there'd be a new sheriff of Libby, Montana, the caller had warned. Still, Blackburn was a man of honor and he had a duty to the citizens of Libby to uphold the law, and a duty to protect a man from himself—at least one he liked.

"They say you've been drinking," Blackburn said. "Drinking a lot."

"Your spies are misinformed," Bo countered defiantly.

Blackburn spat his toothpick to the ground. "I don't think so," he said confidently.

"I'm *telling* you so."

The sun had almost disappeared behind the mountains now and Blackburn had accomplished his goal. Bo would be forced to obey the sixty-miles-an-hour limit or risk being pulled over again. "Bo, besides being small, this town is poor. There isn't much of a tax base in our county, especially since the paper mill shut down last year. So when that new community center went up in the fall, I was surprised and I did some digging. I found out who donated the money for its construction. You did a good job of covering your financial tracks, but I figured out what had happened with some help from a banker friend of mine in Bozeman."

"You're crazy."

"And I know what you did for the Schmidt family

when their daughter was diagnosed with cancer. If that little girl hadn't made it to the Mayo Clinic when she did, she wouldn't be with us any longer. I know how generous you've been."

"You don't know—"

"Ease up, Bo." It was noble that the man didn't want any credit for his acts of kindness, but Blackburn knew with certainty about the two donations, as well as a dozen others Bo had made over the last year. "I'm trying to help."

"Can I go?"

Blackburn was still tempted to haul Bo into town—for his own good, and the woman's—but he was the only officer on duty tonight, and he needed to be out on patrol in case there were emergencies. And though Bo had clearly been drinking, his ability to drive didn't appear to be impaired. "Yes," Blackburn said. He glanced at the young woman and touched the brim of his hat. "Evening, ma'am," he said, stepping back.

Bo shoved the Jeep in gear, then looked up and smiled. "Bring Katie and the kids over to the ranch for dinner one night this week," he called after Blackburn, revving the Jeep's engine. "I've got a saddle I want to give you. It'll be perfect for your older boy."

Blackburn laughed despite his frustration. Bo had that way about him. You liked him even when you wanted to kick his ass. "You know what, Bo?"

"What?"

"Dealing with you is like trying to herd rabbits. Now get the hell out of here before I change my mind about running you in." Blackburn turned away as he heard a call coming in over the patrol car's two-way radio.

"Goodnight, Sheriff!" Bo shouted as he raced off,

spewing gravel at the patrol car. He was dying for another taste of vodka.

"You seem to know that cop pretty well," Tiffany observed. She was a tall platinum blond with a mole above her upper lip.

Bo glanced over at her. She had high cheek bones just like Melissa's, he noticed, studying her by the greenish glow of the dashboard lights. He checked the rearview mirror. Blackburn had extinguished the patrol car's cherry-tops, but Bo could see the vehicle's headlights pacing them several hundred yards back. "Yeah, I know him. We've been friends for a while. He's a good man, but he's got a den-mother complex. He feels like everybody in town is his personal responsibility."

Bo retrieved the vodka bottle from beneath his seat and held it up, considering what Blackburn had said about too much drinking. "Screw it," he muttered and took a long, defiant swig, then handed the bottle to Tiffany. "He thinks that being a law enforcement officer gives him the right to intrude without restraint."

"I hate it when the government sticks its nose into our lives," she said indignantly, grabbing the bottle. "We shouldn't have to worry about them digging into our private affairs all the time."

"Amen, sister." Bo wiped his mouth with the back of his hand, watching bubbles rise in the bottle as Tiffany drank. She was pretty, in a hard-edged way, but there was a desperate look about her too. Like life had dealt her more than a few bad hands and there weren't many chips left on her side of the table.

She gasped as the liquor hit her hard. "You don't go long without a drink, do you, Bo?"

"Well," he drawled, "some people say I'm an alcoholic, but I think they're just jealous."

Tiffany laughed. She had met many men in her line of work, but never one like Bo Hancock. "It's pretty up here," she said, gazing through the twilight at the scenery.

To their right was the Kootenai, a wide, fast river that cascaded out of British Columbia into northwest Montana, then turned around and retreated as if it hadn't found the United States to its liking. Majestic pine-covered peaks rose from both banks of the river, and the virgin forests were inhabited by elk and moose, as well as the mountain lions, wolves, and grizzly bears that hunted them. Towns in these parts were isolated and small.

"Very pretty," she repeated, hoping that the tiny, needlelike microphone she had attached to the dashboard during the traffic stop was transmitting. She had followed her instructions to the letter.

"Yes, it is."

"What kind of name is 'Bo' anyway?" she asked.

"It's short for Bolling."

"Oh." Tiffany gave the bottle back to him, then put her hand on his thigh and squeezed. "I'm chilly," she said, shivering.

Bo flipped on the heat. It was early April, and when the sun went down there was still a bite in the air. Winter hadn't released its grip on the territory yet.

"Are you from Montana?" she asked, knowing the answer.

"No."

"Where, then?"

"Out East," he answered evasively. Even after a year out here the instinct to protect still kicked in automatically.

"You know, getting an answer out of you is like paddling upstream on that river over there," she said, pointing into the darkness. "Will the tips be good tonight?"

"Should be." He thought he saw her look of desperation deepen. "Ought to be quite a crew there."

Sheriff Blackburn had sized up the situation precisely during the traffic stop. They were heading for Little Lolo's, a tavern located in a lonely spot fifteen miles east of town beside a long bend in the river. Tiffany would be the entertainment in the back room this evening—as long as Blackburn didn't show up and spoil the fun. The sheriff had put a stop to exotic dancing at Lolo's last week.

Each summer, fishermen traveled to Libby from around the world, and Blackburn didn't want his quaint Montana town developing a nasty reputation on the Internet as a rowdy place full of seamy strip bars. However, the boys—an eclectic group of locals Bo had befriended last fall—were already starved for female entertainment. Bo had picked Tiffany up this afternoon from a strip bar in Missoula, promising her a thousand dollars plus tips in return for the hundred-mile journey to Libby and a Saturday night performance.

Bo patted Tiffany's icy fingers reassuringly. "Don't worry," he said gently. He could see she was scared. "You'll be fine. I'll take care of you. I'll drive you back to Missoula tonight when you're finished," he promised. "I won't let anything happen to you."

"Thanks." Tiffany smiled. She had been impressed with Bo's nonchalance in the face of arrest. "So, what do you do?"

It was nice to be in a part of the country where people had no idea who he or the Hancock family was. "I'm semiretired," Bo answered. Though not for much longer, he thought. He'd had enough of Montana—Paul's campaign be damned.

"You don't look old enough to be retired."

He chuckled. Tiffany was young, and forty-three would sound ancient to her. "I don't feel old enough either."

"What did you do before you retired?"

"I was a farmer."

"A farmer?" she repeated, surprised.

"I grew money," he explained, laughing.

"So you're good with numbers."

"Yes."

"Real good?"

"Try me."

"What's seventy-two times thirty-nine?" she blurted out.

"Two thousand eight hundred and eight," he answered immediately.

Tiffany closed her eyes and did the calculation slowly. "Hey, that's right," she said. "At least I think it is. How did you do that so quickly?"

"I've had the ability ever since I was young."

"Can you do that every time?" she asked, sounding impressed.

"Every time. You see, numbers are one of the best things in life, Tiffany." He checked the rearview mirror. Blackburn was still back there pacing the Jeep. "They can tell you almost anything you want to know and they're completely dependable. They never lie, unlike people."

"Why did you stop working?"

"I needed time off."

"Will you go back?"

He hesitated. "Why do you want to know?"

She slid her hand along his leg and squeezed. "Because I like you. I don't want you to go back East—I'd never see you again." She moved her hand higher on his leg so that her fingers disappeared beneath his baggy khaki shorts. "You're thinking about going back, aren't you?"

"Maybe."

"What did you say?" she asked. "I couldn't hear you over the engine."

"I'm thinking about it," he said in a louder voice. "Montana is nice, but I love the financial world. New York City is where I belong."

"What's keeping you here?"

"It's a long story."

"I've got time."

Bo peered out into the darkness.

"Tell me about your family," she said, removing her hand from his leg and tugging at the hem of her miniskirt.

"Why do you want to know?"

"I was just making conversation," she said softly. "I didn't mean to pry."

"I'm sorry." He shook his head, embarrassed. He'd been thinking about how difficult it was going to be to defy Jimmy Lee.

"Do you have brothers and sisters?"

"Two brothers and two sisters."

Tiffany brightened. "So do I. What are their names?"

"My brothers are Teddy and Paul and my sisters are Catherine and Ashley."

"Are you close to them?"

"Catherine and I have always gotten along pretty well," he answered, "and I was very close to Ashley when she and I were young, but after college she went to Europe and never came back. That was almost twenty years ago."

Tiffany's eyes widened. "You haven't seen your sister in twenty years?"

"I've seen her a few times," he said. "When I was traveling over there. Not for very long when I did though."

"Why did she leave?"

Bo jerked the steering wheel to the left to avoid the carcass of a rabbit killed by a passing car. "I think it was because she couldn't stand my father, but we've never really talked about it."

Tiffany nodded as if the explanation had struck a nerve. "Why were you close to her and not the others?"

Bo hesitated. "I guess because we were the two youngest."

"Do you miss Ashley?"

"What?" He'd been a thousand miles away, thinking about why he and Ashley had been that close growing up. It wasn't simply because they were the youngest. They'd shared a deep bond that he'd never been able to explain. "What did you say?"

"Do you miss her?"

"Yes," he admitted quietly.

"Maybe you could help me invest my money." Tiffany sensed that she had struck a nerve and that it might be best to change the subject. "I've built up a nest egg to—"

"Uh-oh," Bo interrupted. In the rearview mirror he saw the patrol car's emergency lights go on. He shoved the vodka bottle beneath the seat as Blackburn raced toward them. "Here comes trouble."

"What's wrong?"

"The sheriff must have decided to run me in after all."
The boys at Little Lolo's were going to be disappointed.
Blackburn would undoubtedly force Tiffany to go to
town as well and miss her performance.

But the patrol car tore past them, siren blaring, and
disappeared around a curve.

"What was that all about?"

Bo shook his head. "No telling."

A few miles down the narrow, twisting road they
came upon several emergency vehicles, red lights flashing. Bo slowed down and guided the Jeep cautiously past
burning flares, Blackburn's patrol car parked at an angle
to the side of the road and an ambulance parked the
same way. At the center of the cluster was a late-model
sedan, upside down, roof flattened into the passenger
area. Extending from the driver's side of the car was a
limp, bloody arm. The entire scene was brightly lighted
by the high-beams of the emergency vehicles.

"Is it bad?" Tiffany leaned forward, trying to catch a
glimpse of the wreckage.

"No." Bo pushed her back into her seat, then took one
more look as they passed within several feet of the
wreckage.

"I hope the people were all right," Tiffany said softly.
"My little brother was killed in a car accident."

"I'm sorry." Anyone inside the wreckage was dead.
Blackburn wouldn't be coming to Little Lolo's. He'd be
filing fatality reports.

They rode in silence for several minutes, then Bo
turned off the state road onto a gravel lane cutting
through a thick patch of tall cedar trees. It was pitch-
black in here and he flicked on the Jeep's high-beams.

"Pull over," Tiffany directed suddenly.

"What?"

"Here." She grabbed the steering wheel and aimed the Jeep at the trees lining the lane.

"Hey!" Bo slammed on the brakes and the vehicle skidded to a halt, the front bumper inches from a thick trunk. "What are you doing?"

"I want some time alone with you before we go in."

"Huh?" Bo glanced at Little Lolo's a hundred yards ahead of them. Music was blaring from inside and there were already a few cars parked out front.

Tiffany leaned toward him until their lips were close. "I like you, and I need to get warmed up before I go in there."

Bo felt her fingers sliding inside his shorts again. "What do you mean, 'warmed up'?"

"Before I go onstage, I need to be ready." She kissed his jutting chin. "You know what I mean."

Bo smelled her perfume. It was cheap, but somehow that seemed appropriate and his excitement intensified. "I can't do this," he mumbled, thinking of Meg. "I—I can't."

Tiffany pulled back, laughing confidently as she undid her halter top. "You can and you will." She pulled the top away and her breasts spilled out.

Bo gazed at them in the dashboard light. They were large and firm. As he stared, she cupped them in her hands and brought one nipple to her mouth, running her tongue around it. He felt himself losing control. "Please don't."

She reached over, undid his shorts, then leaned down and carefully pulled him out.

Instantly he could feel her hot breath on him and excitement surged through his body. A moment longer and it would be too late. "Tiffany, stop!" He grabbed a fistful of her blond hair and pulled her head up violently.

At the same moment the Jeep's door flew open and a camouflage-clad man burst into the vehicle, clamped a damp rag over Bo's face, forcing it against his nostrils and deep into his mouth, and pinned him to the seat.

Blind, Bo reached beneath the seat, desperately grasping for the gun as he struggled against his attacker. He could feel himself weakening as he inhaled the awful odor of the substance soaking the rag. His fingers closed around the 9 mm pistol lying beside the near-empty vodka bottle, but it was too late. His eyes flickered shut and the last thought that went through his mind as his fingers went slack around the gun was that he hadn't heard Tiffany scream.

Up to this point it had been an easy assignment, his easiest yet in his four years as a Hazeltine employee. Move to the tiny town of Libby, Montana; keep a casual eye on Bo Hancock for the people back East; report in once a week. Nothing tricky, just don't screw up and let Bo figure out who you are or what you're doing. Those had been the orders. With all of his expenses paid for, ample free time, and no superior on-site to answer to, things couldn't have been much better for him—until tonight.

Hands and feet tightly bound behind his back, he was powerless to defend himself as the three men forced his head beneath the river's icy surface and into the muddy bottom of the shallows. He screamed into the black water out of instinct, not because he believed they would take pity on him. He knew better.

When they were certain he was dead, they pulled his limp body out of the water, onto the bank, and up into the cover of the thick forest. Here they were hidden from any prying eyes, though the precaution was hardly necessary. They were three miles from the nearest farmhouse, and at this late hour there were no fishing boats on the Kootenai.

"What do we do with him?"

The leader nodded into the darkness. "Carry him halfway up the side of this mountain and bury him. No one will ever find him out here."

CHAPTER 5

"How do you feel?"

Bo brought his hands slowly to his face.

"You don't look so good," the voice continued.

Bo tried to sit up but fell back on the couch with a loud groan. "Where am I?" he mumbled, trying desperately to clear his head. "What's going on?"

"That's what I want to know."

Bo took a deep breath and made another painful attempt to lift up, managing this time to pull himself to a sitting position. It was all coming back to him. A wild struggle in the Jeep, viselike hands smothering his face with a foul-smelling rag, then darkness.

"Are you all right?"

Vaguely aware that his hands and feet weren't bound, Bo tried to stand, hoping that whoever had brought him here wouldn't expect him to run so quickly. Once more his body failed him and he tumbled back on the couch, head spinning.

"I wouldn't advise moving so fast just yet. Give yourself some more time. Apparently you've been through a very difficult experience."

Through the dense fog dulling his senses, Bo recognized Michael Mendoza's distinctive voice. It was deep and melodic, still faintly tinged with an accent acquired during early childhood in Castro's Cuba. Bo relaxed and let out a relieved breath. Somehow he had been rescued. Mendoza was an old friend.

"Should I request medical assistance?" Mendoza asked, his baritone laugh filling the room. He was well aware of Bo's fondness for scotch. He was also aware of how unhappy Bo had been during his exile in Montana and how the drinking had spun out of control in the last few months. Jimmy Lee had communicated with Bo only twice since sending him far away from the spotlight a year ago, but he'd kept close tabs on his son with constant reports from a Hazeltine employee who had quietly taken up residence in Libby to watch over Bo from the shadows. Mendoza had spoken to Jimmy Lee on several occasions over the past month and received detailed updates on Bo's activities in Montana.

Bo managed to pry his eyes open slightly, but the world was lost inside a kaleidoscope. "Where am I, Michael?"

"In a hotel room."

"I mean, where—"

"Jackson Hole, Wyoming. I'm in town for an international trade summit."

"How did I get to Jackson Hole, Wyoming, from Libby, Montana?"

"A couple of my aides brought you down here to me," Mendoza explained. "I found out at the last minute that I was going to be the summit's keynote speaker because the senator who was supposed to speak fell ill suddenly. Anyway, I knew you were out here, so I tried to call as I was leaving Washington yesterday. Since we haven't seen each other since you left for Montana, I thought it would be nice to get together. I've missed you. Your cell phone went straight to voice mail every time I tried to make contact, so I sent a couple of my people ahead looking for you. I was worried."

"Uh-huh."

"Looks like the bottle got the better of you last night, Bo. I'm surprised. Usually you're tougher," he teased.

"I'll be all right," Bo said, rubbing his eyes. "Where did you find me?"

"In a dump of a motel on the edge of town," Mendoza replied, his voice turning judgmental. "When my aides couldn't find you at the ranch, they started looking around Libby and located your Jeep in the motel parking lot. What were you doing there?"

"How in the hell did your aides know what my Jeep looked like?" Bo demanded suspiciously, searching his brain for a memory of anything after the attack and ignoring Mendoza's pointed inquiry.

"Your father gave me details. Color, make, everything. Right down to the license plate number."

Bo tried to swallow. His mouth felt full and prickly, as if it were stuffed with cotton balls. "When did you talk to Jimmy Lee?" he asked, trying to generate saliva.

"Yesterday. He called me on the plane while I was waiting to take off from Reagan National in Washington. I talk to your father every few days or so. Right now, I'm advising him on Paul's campaign."

"How did my father know what my Jeep looked like? I've never told him about it. Jesus, I've only talked to him twice since he banished me to this place and neither call lasted more than a minute."

Mendoza smiled and shook his head. "Bo, you and I have both known your father for more than forty years. He keeps close track of anything he holds dear."

"Don't give me that crap, Michael. My father doesn't hold me dear, he just keeps track of me."

"You're wrong."

"All I've ever been is a hardworking, loyal son and he sent me out here like he sent me to boarding school when I was twelve. To get rid of me because I'd become a nuisance and he didn't want to have to deal with me anymore. It's Teddy and Paul he cares about," Bo said bitterly, "mostly Paul."

"Jimmy Lee wants to see Paul become president," Mendoza argued gently. "You can't blame him for that. My God, it's an incredible opportunity. It's natural for a father to take every action and every precaution necessary to see his son achieve that goal. President, for Christ's sake. Think about it, Bo. Don't blame Jimmy Lee for doing everything in his power to keep Paul's campaign headed in the right direction. A campaign that is going very well, I might add. Your father is a very savvy man."

"You too?" Bo asked accusingly. "We've known each other for so long, and now you're turning on me as well."

"You drink too much," Mendoza said matter-of-factly.

"I have fun."

"And look what that fun does to you." Mendoza gestured at Bo, who was still sloppily clad in the untucked denim shirt, dirty khaki shorts, and sandals he'd been wearing in the Jeep. "You haven't shaved in days, your hair is down to your shoulders, and you stink of liquor. Your father is worried about you, and from what I can see, he has every right to be."

"I'm fine," Bo retorted. "I'm a survivor."

"I'll give you that. If you survived last night, you can survive anything."

"What do you mean by that?"

"There was an empty vodka bottle *and* an empty scotch bottle on the motel floor, as well as some other incriminating evidence spread around the place," Mendoza answered in a low voice. "You drank enough to kill two men last night but you're sitting here in front of me a few hours later and you're reasonably alert."

Bo hesitated. "I was attacked, Michael. My condition has nothing to do with alcohol."

Mendoza leaned forward in his chair. "What?"

"I was on my way to see some friends and I had pulled the Jeep over to the side of the road to check directions." Bo didn't want to tell Mendoza about Tiffany. They had been close friends since Bo's childhood, but Mendoza would still be suspicious if he knew there was a woman in the vehicle and it wasn't Meg. Bo didn't need the fact that he'd been alone in the Jeep with another woman getting back to Jimmy Lee—or Meg. "All of a sudden I've got this rag that smells like a hospital jammed up my nostrils. The next thing I know I'm here on this couch."

Mendoza's eyes narrowed. "Come on, Bo, do you really expect me to believe that?"

"I don't care what you believe," Bo retorted, spying a wet bar in a far corner of the suite's living room. He stood up and almost fell over from a sudden knife-in-the-eye pain searing through his head. The residual effects of the drug that had rendered him unconscious caused the world to blur once more, but he staggered to the bar. "I'm telling you the truth."

Mendoza rose from his chair and followed. "You're telling me you don't remember anything about being at a motel?" he asked.

"Nothing."

"That's hard to believe."

Bo held up the shot glass of scotch he'd poured himself, then consumed it in one gulp. "Hair of the dog, Michael," he gasped.

Mendoza chuckled. "You're incredible."

Bo poured himself another shot. "Have you ever known me to lie, Michael?"

Mendoza shook his head solemnly. Bo Hancock would stretch the truth on trivial issues every once in a while, but when it came down to things that really mattered, Bo was the most honest man Mendoza had ever known. "No. There's always a new rumor about you doing something crazy, but you've never lied to me about anything important. As far as I know anyway," he added quietly.

"Then believe me now." Bo sucked down the second shot. "Somebody attacked me last night while I was in my Jeep, knocked me out cold with a drug, and must have taken me to the motel where your people found me."

"Was anyone with you in the Jeep when you were attacked?"

Bo grimaced. "Yes," he admitted.

"Who?"

"A woman."

Mendoza raised one eyebrow. "Not Meg?"

"Meg is back East visiting her family on Long Island. I'm sure you already knew that." If he knew about the Jeep, he probably knew about Meg, Bo figured.

"Jesus, Bo." Mendoza slammed the bar with his fist. "You're out of control."

"It was nothing, Michael, I swear."

"Who the hell was the woman?"

Bo took a deep breath. He knew how this was going to sound. "A stripper."

"A stripper," Mendoza repeated incredulously. "A stripper in your Jeep and you say it was nothing."

"I was bringing her up to Libby from Missoula. She was the boys' entertainment for the evening."

"The boys?"

"Some locals I've become friends with up in Libby."

"What are you doing hanging around with locals?"

"Who am I supposed to hang around with out here?" Bo asked angrily. "You know me, Michael. I like people. I don't like to be alone. They're salt-of-the-earth guys who've provided me with companionship over the last twelve months when I've needed it."

"They've let you pay for their drinks."

Bo nodded. He knew there was some truth to that. "And let me bring them entertainment, but so what?"

Mendoza held up his hands. "All right, all right." He could see how difficult the last year had been on Bo. "I guess I can't relate to what you've been through."

"No, you can't."

"I believe you," he said softly after a few moments. "About the attack and the fact that the woman wasn't anyone you were involved with. I know how much you love Meg." He smiled. "What the hell? I wouldn't be here if it weren't for you anyway. I owe you my life."

Bo poured himself another shot. "Don't start with that again. It was nothing."

"Nothing my ass," Mendoza protested loudly. Years ago they had been climbing together in the Swiss Alps when Mendoza's safety rope had snapped. "You were still in high school at the time. It was over your Christmas vacation from Deerfield, right?"

"Something like that."

"I was literally hanging by my fingernails and you free-climbed across a sheer rock face to save me. Another few seconds and I would have fallen. I had nothing left when you got to me." Mendoza shook his head, remembering the mortal fear, which had remained vivid in his mind all these years. He'd been dangling a thousand feet above certain death. When Bo had reached him and secured him firmly to his rope so that he knew he was safe again, Mendoza had hugged Bo and cried uncontrollably. "Our guides said they'd never seen anything like it," Mendoza whispered, the intense terror of the incident rushing back to him. "You could have been killed so easily, Bo. One misstep and you would have gone down. I'll never be able to repay you."

"I had to save you, Michael," Bo said. "I needed you. You were always there for me when I was growing up. When Jimmy Lee would yell at me for something Teddy or Paul had done, you'd be there. It was a purely selfish act on my part." Michael Mendoza had been more of an older brother to Bo than Teddy or Paul ever had. He'd been someone Bo could confide in about personal matters during his youth when the others didn't care. "Tell me why you sent people all the way up to Libby to find me."

"I already explained. I wanted to see you, and I was worried when I couldn't get in touch with you."

Bo took a slow sip of scotch. The first two shots had produced the desired effect and now there was no need to rush. "I appreciate the sentiment, but I think there's more to it than that. You're as close a friend as I have in the world, and I know you too well. There's another agenda here. Tell me," Bo prodded. "Come on, Senator."

Mendoza brought his hands together in front of his

face and bowed his head, as if he were about to pray. Now fifty-five, Mendoza was tall, trim, and honey-skinned, with perfect silver hair, a prominent nose, and a calm, confident demeanor. He was in his twentieth year as a United States senator from Connecticut and he owed everything to Jimmy Lee and Ida Hancock. As one of their many philanthropic projects, they had rescued Mendoza from a juvenile home in Brooklyn when he was twelve, placed him in private school, and funded his up-bringing. Now he walked the halls of the Senate as an influential member of several powerful committees. He had attended Harvard and Georgetown along the way—all paid for by the Hancocks—and become an extremely influential man. An unlikely outcome for the child of a woman who had washed up on a Florida beach after a harrowing trip from Cuba in a leaky wooden boat, pen-niless and unable to speak a word of English, already carrying the unborn baby in her womb. Mendoza had spent the summers of his high school and college years at the estate with the Hancocks. Despite their age dif-ference, he and Bo had developed a strong bond. Jimmy Lee had guided Mendoza's first campaign and his rise to prominence within the Senate. For a time Mendoza's name had been bandied about as a possible presidential candidate, but that dream had never become reality and now his time had passed.

"Michael."

"Okay." Mendoza smiled sheepishly. "You always have been able to read me like an open book."

"My father sent you, didn't he?"

"We were talking about Paul's campaign as I was waiting to take off in D.C., and I told him I was headed out to Wyoming for the summit," Mendoza explained. "He thought it would be a good idea for me to see you."

"I knew it," Bo said triumphantly.

"He's concerned about you," Mendoza added quickly.

"If he's so damn concerned, why didn't he come himself, and what am I still doing here?"

Mendoza hesitated. "Paul's campaign is progressing well and Jimmy Lee—"

"Paul, always Paul," Bo said disgustedly. He threw back the rest of the scotch. "I'm going home, Michael. I can't stay out here any longer. It'll kill me. I've got to get back to the East."

Mendoza held up his hands. "That's not a good idea, Bo," he warned. "You know they don't want you coming back with the convention getting close."

"I don't give a damn what they want."

"Let Paul sew up the nomination first," Mendoza urged.

"Then what?" Bo asked bitterly. "You think they'll let me come back then? Not a chance. They'll tell me I have to stay out here until the election is over. When that's over, they'll think up another reason for me to stay. I've been permanently edited out of the family script, my friend. The only option for me is to fight my way back in."

"Bo, don't go back East yet," Mendoza pleaded. "It'll cause so much trouble. Give it a little more time. I know you're going stir-crazy, I know it's been hell for you and Meg, but it won't be long. I'll work out something with Jimmy Lee when I get home, I promise. Give it a few more months."

"It's not just the boredom, Michael." Bo hesitated. "There's something else."

Mendoza glanced up. "What?"

Bo didn't answer right away.

"Come on, Bo."

"You have to promise me you won't say anything to Jimmy Lee."

Mendoza hesitated, considering the pledge he was about to make. Jimmy Lee was his mentor and a man he found it difficult to keep anything from. "All right."

"I have to get back to Warfield Capital," Bo said quietly.

"Why?"

"There's trouble at the firm."

"What are you talking about?"

"Dad hired a guy named Frank Ramsey a few months before kicking me out."

"Sure, I've met him a few times. Seemed like a good man and from what I could tell, very intelligent."

"Ramsey's a prick, Michael. When I was booted out here, he got my job. From everything I hear, he has been taking liberties with the portfolio he shouldn't be taking. He can't be trusted."

Mendoza sighed. "Are you sure this isn't a case of misplaced resentment? Isn't it your father who deserves your bitterness?"

"Frank Ramsey is out of control."

"How do you know?" Mendoza demanded.

"I've kept in touch with someone at Warfield since I've been out here," Bo admitted, thinking just how important a link Dale Stephenson had become.

"I thought Jimmy Lee had forbidden you to talk to anybody at Warfield."

"There are still people at Warfield who are loyal to me."

"I'm sure," Mendoza said. His expression turned

serious. "What is Ramsey doing with the portfolio that is so wrong?"

"Apparently he's invested a great deal of money in some very risky ventures." Bo didn't want to reveal too much, not even to Mendoza. If Jimmy Lee ever found out who had been feeding Bo information, that individual would find himself in immediate peril. As it was, Stephenson had missed a scheduled call and Bo was concerned. "I need to get in there and see what's going on."

"Isn't Teddy there?"

Bo rolled his eyes. "You and I both know that Ramsey could have transferred half the portfolio to Switzerland and Teddy would never know."

Mendoza nodded. "Maybe you're right. Teddy doesn't much care for work. But I think you're wrong about Ramsey."

"I hate Frank Ramsey." Bo reached for the scotch bottle again, but Mendoza grabbed it first.

"That's enough," Mendoza said firmly.

"Don't treat me like a child, Michael. What's your problem?"

Mendoza put the bottle down and pulled a Polaroid print from his pocket. "This is my problem," he said, placing the photograph on the bar.

Bo gazed at the picture. He saw himself lying on a bed, naked. Tiffany, straddling him, was also naked. "That can't be." His voice was barely audible. "You can't really see my face," he protested lamely, glancing up into Mendoza's judgmental eyes. There was no mistaking who was in the picture. Meg certainly wouldn't have any doubt if she got a look. "I don't know what this is all—"

"Here," Mendoza interrupted, holding out a wallet and a set of keys. "These were beside the photograph on the nightstand of room seventeen at the Hilltop Inn. Your Jeep is still parked outside the door."

Bo shook his head. "That's impossible."

"And this was in a pocket of your shorts." Mendoza reached into his coat and placed Bo's wedding band on the bar.

Bo picked it up slowly. It was the band Meg had placed on his finger so many years ago.

"Bolling," Mendoza said paternally, "you need to get control of yourself. Meg would be destroyed if she ever saw that picture. I care very deeply about the two of you. I know how much you love her and how much she loves you. I understand that sometimes people stray, but—"

"I didn't stray," Bo said flatly.

"Then explain the photograph."

"I was set up. I was drugged." Bo gritted his teeth. "If I had strayed, do you think I'd let someone take a picture of me like this?"

"Maybe you didn't know you were being watched." Mendoza locked onto Bo's eyes until Bo looked away. "Look, I don't—" A telephone on the bar rang, interrupting Mendoza, and he picked up the receiver.

Bo saw Mendoza's expression change. "What is it, Michael?" he asked as Mendoza hung up the phone. "Michael."

"It's your father. He's sick, Bo," Mendoza said quietly. "He collapsed at the estate yesterday evening. He's in the ICU at St. Luke's Hospital in New York. His condition is critical."

Scully eyed the man moving through the night toward him. This was the target. He glanced around to make certain that the Georgetown side street was deserted.

"Excuse me," Scully said quietly as they came together on the dark sidewalk.

The man stopped and looked up. "Yes?"

"I need to find K Street."

"It's three blocks that way." The man jabbed a thumb over his shoulder. "Can't miss it."

"Thanks. Oh, one more thing," Scully said quickly.

"What?" the man said, irritated at the imposition.

"I know what you did in Denver last month."

The man's eyes flashed to Scully's. "What did you say?"

Scully suppressed a smile. He had heard panic in the other man's voice and seen his posture stiffen, even through the gloom. "I know all about Denver, and about your rendezvous at the motel near the airport with a woman named Sharon Jones."

"I . . . I don't know what you're . . ." The other man's voice trailed off.

"You were supposed to be downtown at the Brown Palace. In fact you checked into your room, but you didn't sleep there. You see, you couldn't, because there were four other people from your company on the trip with you, and all of you were staying on the same floor. They might have seen Mrs. Jones going into your room." Scully paused. "What would your wife and three children have thought?"

"I'm not going to listen to any more of this." The man brushed past Scully and began walking away.

"You better listen," Scully snarled. "Or your wife and Mrs. Jones's husband will find out everything. As will your boss."

The man cringed and stopped short.

"I'll make certain they both receive copies of the e-mails

you've been sending Mrs. Jones from your office computer. They'll both enjoy the explicit content. I know I did."

The man whirled around. "Who are you?" he yelled.

"I believe you and Mrs. Jones are planning another get-together next month in St. Louis," Scully went on calmly. "She has a client there and you have a supplier. How convenient."

The man removed his glasses and rubbed his eyes. "What do you want?" he whined.

"One simple thing." Scully walked to where the man stood. "Your silence."

"I don't understand."

"You are a senior executive of a large defense contractor."

The man gazed down at the sidewalk, his brain pounding. He was still amazed and frightened at how much the other man knew. "Yeah, so?"

"You've come to Washington from Boston to testify," Scully continued. "You're going to tell the Senate Armed Services Committee all about significant overbilling on a new attack submarine project. Code name, Tiger Shark."

"How did you find out?" the man asked, his voice hoarse. "That project is classified top secret."

"The prototypes are almost complete and in preliminary tests the subs have performed even better than expected," Scully said, ignoring the man's questions. "You testify and the entire project will grind to a halt only a few months from the finish line."

The man's eyes darted around, searching for the people who were supposed to be protecting him.

"That can't happen," Scully said firmly. "The United States needs that submarine. It's light years ahead of what any other country has."

"I still don't understand what you want," the man said lamely. Doves in high places were counting on his testimony tomorrow. In return he was to receive a large sum in cash.

"Tomorrow morning you will go to Union Station instead of the Capitol. At the station you'll board a Metroliner and return to Boston. If any word of the overbilling ever officially reaches anyone on the committee, I'll hold you personally responsible. Your wife will find out all about your affair. Your children too. Every sordid detail. How you and Mrs. Jones occasionally pay other people to be involved in your trysts."

The man stared straight ahead, his mouth open.

"Women and men."

"All right, all right." The man held up his hands as if he were being arrested, petrified at the prospect of his secret life being laid bare for all to see.

"Don't underestimate me," Scully warned, his voice rising.

"I won't," the other man answered meekly.

"Get back to your hotel and never mention this encounter to anyone. If you do, I'll know." Scully watched the man slink away and a smile came to his lips. RANSACK had gone operational.

CHAPTER 6

"Sir!"

Bo stopped, his hand on the doorknob. A sturdy-legged nurse pressing a clipboard to her chest was hustling down the linoleum-tiled corridor toward him, rubber soles squeaking on the freshly waxed floor. "Yes?"

"That's a private room," she called, still several doors away. "No visitors allowed."

"Yes, but I'm—"

"No exceptions."

Bo smiled reassuringly and tried again. "I'm Mr. Hancock's son."

"You could be the son of God," the nurse snapped, "but I have my instructions."

"Look, I'm going in to see my father," Bo said firmly. "That's all there is to it."

"I'll call security," the nurse warned.

"It's all right." A short, dark-skinned man emerged from a doorway across the corridor. He was dressed in a white shirt, rumpled blue tie, dark pants, and a long white coat. "Bo can go in. He's family. Don't give him a difficult time."

"Oh, I'm sorry, Dr. Silwa." The nurse smiled nervously, then scurried away.

Bo shook Silwa's hand. "Hi, Doc." Silwa had been Jimmy Lee's physician for as long as Bo could remember.

"Hello, Bo," Silwa said, his naturally sad gaze taking in Bo's appearance. "You look terrible."

"Thanks a lot."

Silwa forced a smile. "Perhaps I should be attending to you as well."

"I'm fine." Bo avoided medicine, doctors, and hospitals whenever possible. The smells reminded him too much of death—from somewhere in his past, though he couldn't have said precisely where. "I haven't had much sleep since yesterday," he explained. "I flew here to New York as soon as I got word of my father's condition, and I came to the hospital straight from the airport."

"You were in Montana, right?"

"Yes." Everyone seemed to know about his exile. "So how is my father?"

Since last night Bo had been unable to get any information concerning his father's condition other than the fact that Jimmy Lee had collapsed a few minutes after eating dinner. Meg, visiting her parents on Long Island, wouldn't have known about the emergency because she wasn't close to any of his siblings. For some reason the Hancock family hadn't taken to her. Bo had told her the news himself when he'd talked to her from the Gulfstream IV he had chartered out of Jackson Hole just before midnight. His sister Catherine would have been a mess and unable to provide any reliable details, so he hadn't called her at all. And, as usual, Paul and Teddy hadn't bothered to return any of several voice-mail messages he had left.

Silwa's expression turned grim. He clasped Bo's elbow, as was his custom when he was about to deliver difficult news to a patient's family. "I'm going to be blunt." Silwa was speaking in a low voice even though there was no one else in the corridor. It was quarter to six in the morning and the hospital was just beginning to stir. "Your father has a malignant tumor in the left frontal lobe of his brain. The tumor is inoperable."

"A brain tumor," Bo said in a hushed voice.

"Yes," Silwa said with an air of gentle but firm finality.

"But—"

"Your father was complaining of a migraine headache and blurred vision to his valet after dinner Saturday evening," Silwa said, letting go of Bo's elbow. "Fifteen minutes later, the valet found Jimmy Lee in his study chair, slumped over his desk. He had suffered a massive hemorrhage into the tumor. We located the mass in the left frontal lobe after performing a CAT scan late Saturday evening." Silwa pointed to the left side of his own forehead with a pencil he'd taken from the top pocket of his hospital coat. "Last night I ordered an MRI, and we found three more tumors that hadn't shown up on the CAT scan." He hesitated. "Your father is on steroids and diuretics. The situation turned critical this morning. I alerted Catherine and your brothers a half hour ago. They are on the way to the hospital now. I'm sorry to have to tell you all of this, but it's better that you know the truth."

"Of course I want the truth," Bo murmured.

"One thing." Silwa took Bo by the elbow again.

"Yes?"

"He may say things he doesn't mean while you're in there with him, what with the drugs we have administered. He isn't lucid."

"I understand," Bo said, still numbed by the terrible news.

He slipped from the hallway into a dim, windowless room, lighted only by a low-wattage lamp on a corner table and a bluish hue coming through a long glass partition, behind which he saw a nurse in the next room carefully monitoring several computer screens. He shivered as he looked around. It felt cold as hell in here.

He took slow, hesitant steps toward the bed, and as he neared it, felt his stomach churn. The man lying before him was his father, yet he wasn't. During Bo's year in Montana, Jimmy Lee had deteriorated from a vibrant being into a frail old man. His hair had faded from its distinguished silver to a dull gray. His cheeks were sunken, his neck was covered with ugly brown spots, and his teeth were crooked and yellow. He was no longer the strong patriarch Bo had locked horns with so often since childhood. For several moments Bo stood beside the bed without moving, hating the fact that he and his father had never found common ground, not even through Warfield Capital. Despising the fact that Paul and Teddy had allowed Jimmy Lee to wither away without calling him in Montana.

"Paul." Jimmy Lee's voice was barely audible. "Is that you?"

Bo glanced down. His father's eyes were mere slits etched into wrinkled skin above parched lips. "No, it's Bolling."

"Come closer," Jimmy Lee moaned, reaching for Bo with a gnarled hand.

Bo sank into a chair beside the bed and took his father's cold fingers. "I'm here, Dad."

"It is you, Bolling." Jimmy Lee was able to speak only

a word or two at a time before gasping for his next breath. "I always recognized your hand." He tried to smile. "It's so much rougher than Paul or Teddy's. They never were ones to get their hands dirty, were they? But you always would. You are a good son."

Bo felt tears flood his eyes and he looked up at the lights.

"I don't have much time, Bolling."

"You're fine, Dad," Bo said comfortingly.

Jimmy Lee squeezed Bo's fingers hard. "No, I'm not, God dammit. Don't patronize me."

"Save your strength," Bo urged.

Jimmy Lee began coughing, a deep grinding hack. "Listen to me"—he was struggling to get the words out— "please."

Jimmy Lee would fight to the last breath, Bo thought. That was the attitude that had bound his parents together. Never give in, fight to the last. Thank God he had inherited that trait. "I'm listening, Dad."

Jimmy Lee tried to rise to a sitting position, then collapsed back onto the pillows, exhausted by even this small effort.

"Dad, take it easy."

"Dammit!"

"What's wrong?"

"I've lost my sight again."

"What?"

"I can't—" Jimmy Lee's coughing intensified. "It happens from time to time. My eyesight comes and goes since I had the attack Friday night."

Bo checked the nurse's station behind the window. Silwa was standing beside the woman now, studying the computer monitors intently. The attack had occurred

Saturday night, according to the doctor. As Silwa had warned, Jimmy Lee was confused, Bo reasoned. "Should I get Dr. Silwa?"

"He can't help me."

Bo watched his father's eyes slowly close and felt his grip weaken. "Jesus Christ!"

"Bolling," Jimmy Lee gasped, tugging at his son's hand with a sudden burst of strength. "Don't leave me."

"You need help."

"Don't go."

"All right, all right." Bo sank back into the chair. "I'm here, Dad."

Jimmy Lee patted the back of his son's hand gently. "Thank God you got the message."

Bo looked up from the floor. "The message?"

"About getting back here."

"Yes, Michael Mendoza was—"

"Michael Mendoza?"

"That's what you meant about a message, wasn't it? Michael was out West this weekend and told me about your attack when he got the call." Bo hesitated. He'd spent most of the flight back this morning thinking about the two men who had dragged him from the Jeep at Little Lolo's. And about how Mendoza had claimed that aides had found him in a nasty motel with Tiffany just outside the Libby town limits, when he had no memory of the motel at all. But there was the Polaroid shot that proved he had been there. He shook his head. He'd been set up, plain and simple. "I would never have known about your condition if Michael hadn't told me."

"What?" Jimmy Lee struggled for breath. "I don't know what you're talking about. I haven't spoken to Michael in a week."

Despite Silwa's warning that the drugs could cause confusion, Jimmy Lee seemed lucid enough.

"I had a Hazeltine operative in the area," Jimmy Lee continued. "He was supposed to—" He shut his eyes tightly and groaned, arching his back as a sharp pain shot through his head.

"Dad!"

"I'll be all right in a minute," Jimmy Lee moaned, clutching Bo's fingers tightly. "It'll pass." Slowly the pain began to ease.

"You were saying that you had a—"

"I've never told you how much I care about Meg," Jimmy Lee interrupted, opening his eyes. "She's a wonderful woman, Bolling. I know I didn't make her feel comfortable at times, but then, I didn't do a lot of things I should have. I didn't say some things I should have said either. You hold her close, Bo. Never let her go."

"Yes, sir."

Jimmy Lee hesitated, aware of what he wanted to say, but not sure how to say it. "I know you always felt that Paul and Teddy were my favorites. I know I was always harder on you. I'm sorry. I've appreciated your work at Warfield. I've appreciated your contributions." He hesitated again. "I know I didn't spend enough time with you while you were growing up. I've always regretted that."

"It's all right, Dad."

"Remember that fishing trip to Canada when you were twelve?" Jimmy Lee asked, a faint smile coming to his face. "Just you and me. Remember what a wonderful time we had?"

Bo could remember the trip as if it were yesterday. It

was the only time he and Jimmy Lee had ever spent an extended period of time alone together.

"I love you, son."

Bo shut his eyes tightly. He'd waited a lifetime to hear those words.

"Bolling."

Bo felt the tears poised at the edges of his eyelids. "Yes, Dad."

Jimmy Lee licked his dry lips. "I just wanted to make sure you hadn't left me."

"I won't leave you."

"Where are Paul and Teddy?"

"On their way."

"And Catherine?"

"She's coming too."

"I wish Ashley were coming. But I suppose she isn't."

"I don't know." Bo could find no other words. He had tried to call Ashley in Europe from the G-IV, but had only reached her answering machine. It hadn't even been Ashley's voice at the other end of the line, just a computer-generated greeting.

Jimmy Lee gazed at a glass of water on the nightstand. He didn't have the strength to reach for it. "Bo, you must take care of the family after I'm gone. Take care of Paul, Teddy, and Catherine. Ashley too, but especially Paul."

Bo recognized his father's need and brought the water glass carefully to Jimmy Lee's chapped lips. "Of course I will. Though I think that out of all of them, Paul is the one who can probably take care of himself."

Jimmy Lee sipped the water, then pushed the glass away, spilling some of it on the white sheet. "No," he gasped. "You must take special care of Paul. Promise me that you will, Bo."

Bo said nothing.

"Bolling, please."

"I will."

Jimmy Lee touched Bo's hand once more. "I treated you terribly by sending you to Montana. I let myself get swept up in the election and Paul's opportunity. Swept up in a nightmare. I didn't see what was really happening."

Bo leaned forward. "What do you mean, Dad?"

"There are those who would destroy Paul."

"Of course there are," Bo agreed. "Any man in Paul's position has enemies." A long coughing spell shook Jimmy Lee. Out of the corner of his eye, Bo saw the nurse in the next room stand and point to something on one of the monitors. "Deep down, I know you were right to send me away. I was losing control. I was drinking too much. I really might have done something to damage Paul's campaign." He was rattling on, he knew. But these were the last few moments—somehow Bo understood that—and there was so much to say. "You were right. You were simply looking out for the family."

Jimmy Lee reached up with one hand and grabbed Bo's shirt. "You must go back to Warfield, Bolling. You must take charge of the family's affairs."

"I will, Dad." Bo's mind was reeling. On his deathbed Jimmy Lee had reversed his decision. Now he wanted Bo back at Warfield's helm.

"You must return to Warfield as soon as possible. Teddy can't run the place. I realize that now. And Frank Ramsey is— Oh, God!" Jimmy Lee let go of Bo and collapsed onto the mattress, then arched his back as pain knifed through his skull once more.

"Jesus, Dad, let me get the nurse."

Jimmy Lee grabbed Bo's shirt again, pulling him down

with a death grip. He was trying to say something, but Bo couldn't make out what it was. With his dry lips close to Bo's ear, Jimmy Lee whispered the word again as Silwa and the nurse burst into the room. Then the nurse grabbed Bo by the wrist and dragged him into the corridor. Bo's final image of his father was Silwa administering something into one of Jimmy Lee's limp arms from a long syringe.

"What the hell's happening?"

Paul was sprinting down the corridor, several steps ahead of two bodyguards in dark suits.

"Dad had a seizure," Bo explained as Paul came near. "Dr. Silwa is in there with him."

Paul glared at Bo for a moment, then tried to push past the nurse, who wouldn't yield. "Get out of my way!" he roared.

"You can't do anything for him at this point," Bo said quietly. "Dad's unconscious. Dr. Silwa gave him something. He was in a great deal of pain."

"I can at least see him."

"No." The nurse was emphatic. "You can't."

"God dammit, I'm going in there." Paul pushed the woman roughly to the side.

Before Paul could enter the room, Bo grabbed him and threw him against the wall beside the door.

"Get off me!" Paul shouted, pushing Bo back with both hands.

The dark-suited bodyguards approached the brothers hesitantly, uncertain of how to handle the situation. Then Teddy appeared, pushing past the bodyguards, but he stopped short as well.

"Don't be an idiot, Paul," Bo muttered. "Let the

medical staff do their job. Just stay out of the damn way for once."

"I'm going in there."

"You'll have to get past me," Bo said defiantly. Paul made a quick move for the door but Bo hurled him back again.

"Stop it, you two!" Teddy's voice was trembling. "This is no time to fight."

"You've already seen him and you don't want me to have the chance. That's what's going on here," Paul hissed at Bo. "You want to be able to say that you were the last to see Jimmy Lee."

"Shut up."

"Who the hell gave you permission to come back from Montana anyway?"

"I didn't need anyone's permission."

"Who told you Dad was sick?"

"Why do you want to know?"

Paul's eyes narrowed. "Dad taught you well, didn't he? Always answer a question you don't like with that one." He leaned down so that their faces were very close. "Who told you?" he demanded again. "I bet it was that asshole Mendoza. You and he always did have a cozy relationship."

"Why do you want to know?" Bo repeated.

Paul's upper lip curled evilly. "I've been waiting a long time to tell you this, Bo," he said. "Dad wouldn't want me to, but, what the hell, he isn't going to be with us much longer."

"Tell me what?" Bo had heard a strange, triumphant tone in Paul's voice.

"Didn't you ever wonder why you don't resemble Catherine, Teddy, or me?"

"What?" Insecurity multiplied inside Bo faster than Ebola in a hot zone.

"Haven't you ever been curious about why you don't look like a Hancock?"

"What are you talking about?" Bo asked. "I look like that cousin on Mother's side. The man in the picture she showed me just before she died."

"So you look like a man in a picture," Paul scoffed. "So what?"

"I don't understand," Bo said, his voice wavering.

"That wasn't a picture of her cousin. It was just a picture she found somewhere of a guy that vaguely resembled you. It was her way of throwing you a security blanket as she was dying, just in case you ever had doubts."

"Doubts?"

Paul laughed harshly and gave Teddy a victory glance. "You never knew, did you?"

Bo swallowed hard.

"You're adopted, you idiot," Paul sneered. "They got you when you were a year old. Your mother died in childbirth. Adopting you was Dad's way of feeling good about himself. His way of giving something more back to society. He must have been going through his midlife crisis. That's the only answer I can come up with for why he'd want *you*."

Bo's gaze flickered from Paul to Teddy, then he edged slowly backward until the wall stopped him. "It's not possible," he gasped.

"It's fact, Bo," Paul said.

"When we were young," Teddy chimed in, "we used to take turns drawing what we thought your real father looked like. We'd use the bums in Central Park as our models."

Bo clenched his fists. He could feel rage building as it had only a few times in his life. Building to the point that he knew he would not be able to control himself if he let go.

"Paul!"

Bo's head snapped toward the voice. Catherine was racing down the corridor toward them, her long blond hair streaming behind. Tom Bristow loped after her.

She pushed her way past Teddy and the bodyguards, then rushed into Paul's arms. "What's going on?" she cried. "I got a message from the hospital telling me that I needed to get here right away." Her face was streaked with tears. "What's happened?"

"Everything will be fine, Catherine," Paul said. "It's just . . ." His voice trailed off as the door to Jimmy Lee's room opened slowly and Silwa emerged.

"I'm sorry to have to tell all of you this," Silwa said quietly, "but your father is dead."

CHAPTER 7

Raindrops spattered the windshield as the taxi sliced through heavy traffic on Park Avenue. When it had skidded to a halt at the curb, Bo shoved a ten-dollar bill into the driver's hand and thrust open the door. He sprinted through the spring downpour toward the Warfield Capital building, a copy of *The Wall Street Journal* over his head as he darted across the sidewalk, dodging umbrellas. After leaving the hospital Bo had gone to the Yale Club, where he showered, shaved, and had his hair cut—leaving the ponytail he'd worn in Montana on the tiled floor of the club's barbershop—then caught a short nap on a secluded couch in a reading room. Refreshed, he was ready to take on Frank Ramsey.

At the building's revolving doors, Bo glanced back over his shoulder through the rain and noticed a woman standing on the sidewalk a short distance away. She was wearing a yellow top and had stark blond hair. Standing absolutely still beneath her umbrella while everything around her moved, she seemed to be gazing straight at him. Bo strained to keep sight of her as he was jostled into the doorway. When he had cleared the doors, he pushed past two men and sprinted to a tall window overlooking the street, but the blond woman had disappeared.

He tossed his soaked newspaper into a trash can. She had looked so much like Tiffany.

Five minutes later he stood in Warfield Capital's lobby. "I'm here to see Frank Ramsey," he announced to the receptionist, who wore a headset with a thin silver microphone curling in front of her lips.

The woman raised her hand to indicate that she was talking to someone at the other end of the line. "Do you have an appointment with Mr. Ramsey?" she finally asked, after redirecting the call.

It seemed strange to Bo to have to wait in the lobby of Warfield Capital for someone to come and escort him. "Frank is expecting me," Bo assured her. He had called Ramsey that morning from the Yale Club and demanded the meeting. Ramsey had tried to avoid the confrontation, but Bo had insisted, citing Ramsey's fiduciary duty to family members.

"What is your name, sir?" the receptionist asked.

"Bo Hancock."

She looked up from her pad, recognizing the name. "I'll let Mr. Ramsey know you're here," she said respectfully, gesturing toward a sofa and chairs in one corner of the lobby. "Please have a seat over there, Mr. Hancock."

Bo watched the woman turn to the side, push a button, and speak softly into her microphone. She was new to the firm—at least she'd arrived since he had been exiled to the West—just as the Warfield Capital logo hanging on the wall behind her desk was new. Everything about the place seemed sleeker and shinier than the day he had been forced out, and this made him uncomfortable. Sleek and shine usually meant you were hiding something. "One more thing," he said.

The receptionist covered the microphone with her hand. "Yes?"

"Is Dale Stephenson in today?" Bo had been unable to reach Stephenson since the night Stephenson had relayed news that Ramsey was taking unacceptable risks with the private equity portfolio. He hoped it was simply because of the strict precautions they both took to keep their communication secret. Stephenson had been on a mobile phone that last night they'd spoken. As Bo thought back to the conversation, he recalled that Stephenson had sounded anxious, almost scared.

"Dale Stephenson," the woman repeated slowly. "I don't believe I know him."

"Don't know him?" Bo asked incredulously, an eerie sensation crawling up his spine. "Dale runs the private equity group. He's a senior executive here at Warfield."

"Well, I've only been at the firm a few days," she explained apologetically. "Maybe he's on vacation."

"You haven't seen his name on anything? No mail, no memos?"

"No, I haven't. I, well, I . . ."

"What is it?" Bo said. "Go on."

"I don't want to alarm you, Mr. Hancock."

"What were you going to say?"

"I know that a senior person at the firm just died in an accident," she said quietly. "I don't know who it was, though. I heard the name but I don't remember. People haven't talked about it much."

The receptionist blurred before Bo's eyes as he processed her words. The awful car wreck he and Tiffany had driven past in Montana only a couple of nights ago flashed back to him. "I see."

"I don't know any more about the situation."

"I'll speak to Mr. Ramsey about it."

"I think that would be best," she agreed.

Bo walked unsteadily across the lobby, worried that Stephenson was the senior executive who had died, and that his death had not been accidental. Worried that their communication had been discovered and that somehow there was a connection between that and Stephenson's death. But that was crazy, Bo told himself. Not even Jimmy Lee would go that far.

Bo shook his head. It was the episode in the Jeep that had him unnerved enough to make him consider such extreme possibilities. That, and the thought that there were compromising pictures of him somewhere out there. It occurred to Bo as he sat down and picked up a magazine from the coffee table that Frank Ramsey would pay dearly to have those pictures.

The blond woman on the magazine cover reminded Bo of the woman downstairs. It couldn't have been Tiffany, he told himself. He had tried to contact her in Missoula several times, but no one at the strip bar where he had met her could say they had seen her since Saturday afternoon—around the time he had picked her up in front of the place.

He leaned back and rubbed his eyes. This morning he'd lost the man he had believed was his father. He'd found out that his name wasn't really Hancock, at least not by birth. And he'd been told all of that by people he had thought for more than forty years were his brothers. Paul and Teddy had probably known about the adoption since childhood—judging by Teddy's remark about using bums as their image of his father—but had been under strict instructions to say nothing. With Ida and Jimmy Lee gone, they'd enjoyed letting loose with the secret.

If there really was a secret. Bo realized that Paul was a

master manipulator who might say anything to gain an advantage. He and Teddy would stand united to keep Bo out of Warfield and New York City. What better way to get him to back off than to make him feel he wasn't really part of the family. Bo let out a long, slow breath, trying to relax. Jimmy Lee's death would spark a flurry of activity as people battled for position, and there would be snakes in the grass everywhere.

"Good morning, Bo."

"Hello, Frank." Bo stood up and shook Ramsey's hand. It was a forced, uncomfortable greeting. They were like two local political combatants warily acknowledging each other for the cameras before a town hall debate.

"Follow me," Ramsey directed, shoving his hands in his pockets and ambling confidently past the receptionist's desk.

"This was my office before I left," Bo remarked as he followed Ramsey into the large room overlooking Park Avenue.

"Yeah, and it looks a lot better now. As you can see, I've had a lot of work done to it." The furniture had been upgraded, expensive antiques adorned the tables, and Monets hung from the walls, which were now paneled in dark wood, far different from the dull gray painted wallboard of before. "Do you want any coffee?"

"No," Bo answered as he sat down at a round, dark wood table positioned in one corner of the room.

Ramsey whispered something to his executive assistant, then shut the door after the young man had darted away. "Maybe I should have instructed my assistant to bring you something with a kick to it," he said, taking a seat across the table from Bo.

"What's that supposed to mean?"

"You know what it means, Bo. It's nine o'clock in the morning." Ramsey tapped the crystal of his Rolex. "Remember what you told me once? Never drink alcohol before eight in the morning and never screw a woman who lives within fifty miles of your wife. The eight-by-fifty rule."

Bo silently rued the fact that he'd been friendly with Ramsey when the man had first come to Warfield. The remark, made after several drinks, had been intended only to evoke a response—to see if Ramsey agreed or disagreed. "Things have changed."

"Sure they have," Ramsey retorted sarcastically. "I guess the temperature outside must have dropped a few degrees since I came in," he said. "You've got some real color in your cheeks, or maybe that's the 'changed' scotch you've already been sipping this morning."

Bo forced himself to remain calm. "We need to talk." He watched Ramsey blink very slowly, the habit he'd always detested.

"Talk away." Ramsey made a sweeping gesture, letting Bo know who was in charge. "I can give you a few minutes before my next meeting."

"You'll give me as much time as I require."

Ramsey said nothing.

"As you know, I haven't made contact with anyone at Warfield Capital in more than a year," Bo began, wondering if Ramsey knew about his weekly telephone updates from Stephenson.

"And I believe your decision to be hands-off during that period has benefited the firm tremendously," Ramsey said. "We've made great progress since you've been away."

"Warfield was already performing extremely well when I left."

"I've taken the firm to a higher level," Ramsey countered. "When you left last year, Warfield had a hundred billion dollars under management. Now we've got almost two hundred billion."

Bo's eyes narrowed. Two hundred billion. During their last telephone call Stephenson had guessed that the figure was a hundred and fifty billion. "Where has the money come from?" Bo asked curiously.

"Insurance companies and commercial banks, mostly."

"More cheap money."

"Yes," Ramsey said. "I had high-level contacts at those institutions before I came to Warfield."

"All loans? We didn't have to give up any equity in the firm?" Bo asked.

Ramsey hesitated.

"Because if you've added another hundred billion dollars of debt on top of what we already had at Warfield without adding any equity," Bo continued, "I'd have a huge problem with that. That structure would be far too risky. That would be too much leverage."

Ramsey shifted in his seat. "There's some new equity," he said. "But it was all done with your father's and Teddy's approval," he added quickly. "I didn't do anything unilaterally."

"I didn't say you did, Frank," Bo replied politely. "Where did the equity come from?"

Again Ramsey hesitated. "Europe, I think."

"You think?"

"I know," he said firmly.

Bo scratched his head. "It doesn't make sense that Europeans would invest equity money into a U.S. hedge fund."

"Oh?"

"The tax consequences would be terrible. Foreigners typically invest in offshore vehicles, which Warfield isn't." Bo pointed at Ramsey. "You should know that."

"Well now I do," Ramsey said curtly. "The lawyers blessed it. That's all that matters." He checked his watch for the third time since they'd sat down. "What do you want, Bo? Why did you come here?"

"Where is Dale Stephenson?"

Ramsey's eyes shot to Bo's, then a gloomy expression clouded his sharp-featured face. "Unfortunately, Dale has died," he answered solemnly.

Bo's pulse jumped. Here was confirmation of the receptionist's speculation. "Died?"

"Yes. It was a terrible loss," Ramsey said sadly, running his thumbs up the underside of his suspenders. "We were all devastated."

"I'll bet."

"What do you mean by that?" Ramsey snapped.

"How did Dale die?"

"He drowned. He was on a fishing trip out West."

"Where out West?"

"Colorado, I think. You can check the police records."

"Why would I do that?"

Ramsey smoothed his tie, choosing his words carefully before speaking. "You wouldn't," he answered calmly. "It's just that there was some question initially about the possibility of foul play. But the police in Boulder have since ruled that Dale's fall out of the guide's raft was purely accidental. That's all."

Foul play. The words echoed in Bo's brain. "Have we taken care of Dale's wife?"

Ramsey nodded. "Warfield held a standard million-dollar policy for him with his wife as beneficiary, and we have made further arrangements. She'll never have to worry about money." Ramsey raised one eyebrow. "I noticed that you paid him very well."

"Dale deserved what he got. He made Warfield a great deal of cash as head of the private equity operation." Bo paused. "Who is running the operation now?"

"I am."

"You have no experience with private equity investing."

"I'll do fine, as I've done fine running the entire firm over the past year. I've got confidence in several of Dale's lieutenants in the private equity group. They can tell me what I need to know, and I'll make all final decisions based upon the information they provide me." Bo tried to interrupt, but Ramsey kept going. "Now, did you come all the way from Montana to ask me about Dale Stephenson?"

"No."

Ramsey crossed his arms. "Then what do you want to talk about?"

"My father died a few hours ago."

Ramsey blinked several times, even more slowly than normal. "I know. Teddy called to tell me. I'm sorry. I should have said so before." Ramsey checked his watch once more. "But that still doesn't explain what you're doing here."

"I'm coming back to Warfield full-time, Frank," Bo said bluntly. He saw Ramsey's jaw clench. It was the only visible sign of how vile the other man found this piece of information. "I will return as executive vice president and chief operating officer now that my father has died. You will assume your former duties as special assistant to Teddy."

"Has Teddy approved your return to Warfield?"

"Teddy's input is irrelevant."

"It was my understanding that he and Paul were calling the shots for the family now," Ramsey argued. "Including any and all decisions having to do with Warfield Capital."

"I'm needed around here, especially with Jimmy Lee gone. The sharks on the Street will start circling this place because they'll figure we'll be weak without him. Warfield will need my contacts, and my judgment."

"I'm here. I can take care of everything."

"That's exactly what I'm worried about."

"Hey, listen, I—"

"Shut up, Frank." On the way to Warfield Bo had questioned his right to be involved in family affairs any longer—if what Paul had said about his adoption was true. But whether or not it was true, Jimmy Lee had squeezed his hand at the very end and pleaded, with the little strength he had remaining, that Bo take charge. Bo might not be a Hancock by birth, but he was one in every other way, and he was going to act like it. "During this transition period I must be very careful with my family's investments. *I* have to make the important decisions, not an outsider," Bo hesitated, interested to see Ramsey's re-action to what he was about to say. "As it is, I'll be fasci-nated to see what I find in Warfield's portfolio when I drill down into it. Fascinated to see what you've done."

Ramsey drew a slow circle on the tabletop with his fingertip. "Yes, well, I—"

"You haven't been taking any undue risks with my family's money, have you, Frank?"

"No more than usual."

"You haven't been putting an irresponsible amount of our money into some tiny Internet start-ups, have you?"

Ramsey glanced up. "What are you driving at, Bo? Who have you been talking to?"

"I understand that lots of people think these Internet start-ups will all be worth tens of billions someday, but I believe we ought to be more conservative and take a wait-and-see attitude on that industry. That's all."

"Teddy and I have been very conservative about our investments in that sector," Ramsey assured Bo. "There's nothing for you to worry about."

"Just the same, I'll take a hard look at the portfolio and judge for myself."

"Suit yourself, but Teddy has been fully briefed on what I've done." Ramsey pointed at Bo. "You don't give Teddy enough credit. He's very sharp."

"Teddy is easy for you to manipulate, which is why you like him," Bo answered. "Paul doesn't much care for numbers, though he could handle the big-picture issues and figure out if we were being misled by one of our senior employees."

Ramsey understood the inference clearly. "Hey, I won't stand for that kind of—"

"But Paul's only concern at this point has to be his campaign," Bo said loudly, cutting Ramsey off again. "Paul is in a tight race to win the party's nomination. A race that's going to go down to the wire, but one I believe he'll ultimately win. When he does, the road will only get tougher, because then he'll have to focus on the general election. My point is, he doesn't have time for Warfield, but I do. My focus can be completely on Warfield Capital. Of the three brothers, I am most qualified to do the job."

"If you consider yourself a brother."

Bo stared at Ramsey, thinking about how he could tear the skinny little bastard apart with one hand.

"Go back to Montana," Ramsey said rudely. "You're a liability to Paul here in New York. Teddy and I can take care of Warfield."

"You don't know what the hell you're talking about."

"Forget what you could do to ruin Paul's chances in the election." Ramsey kept going, undeterred. "You need to stay away from here at all costs for another reason."

"Other than the obvious selfish reasons, and because I always enjoy a good laugh, why do you say that?"

Ramsey leaned over the table. "Because the pressure of running Warfield Capital is immense. The fund has over two hundred billion dollars in assets now. At some point the pressure of running that much money would break you. Maybe on a day when the markets are gyrating like hell, maybe out of nowhere on a quiet day, but it would happen. It's inevitable. You and I both know that." He paused. "Just like it happened last time."

"You're full of—"

"Remember that morning I found you?" Ramsey pointed at the floor by the desk. "Right over there, curled up and shivering like a baby just out of the womb, arms wrapped around a bottle of scotch like a life preserver."

"I was sick."

"You certainly were."

"I mean physically sick. The doctors thought I had pneumonia. I had been working too hard. Sixteen-hour days, seven days a week."

"You'll need something to help get you through the day," Ramsey continued, "just like you did last time. And Manhattan is out there with a bar on every corner, open all the time, with lots of women inside. You'll cave in to the pressure and the temptations to run to the bottle. What would your wife say if she found out that you were crawling around nightclubs at three in the morning again? What would Warfield's investors say if they knew you were coming in here on half a bottle of Glenlivet after a night with some woman you'd never laid eyes on until fifteen minutes before last call?"

"I don't need your—"

"What would your father say?" Ramsey interrupted, his voice rising. "I didn't want to have to tell you this, Bo, but he made it clear to me several times over the past year that he didn't want you back in here. I have a great deal of respect for your father. I want to honor his wishes."

"Thanks so much for your heartfelt concern," Bo snapped, aware that Ramsey was bludgeoning him with everything in the hope that he'd slink back to Montana. Aware that it wouldn't do any good to tell Ramsey of Jimmy Lee's dying words because he wouldn't believe them. Bo would have fired Ramsey on the spot, but he'd found out that Ramsey had been smart enough to negotiate a five-year, no-cut contract with Jimmy Lee when he'd come to Warfield. A contract that included an equity interest in the fund, for which Ramsey hadn't paid a dime. There were still three and a half years left on the contract. "I'm coming back to Warfield, Frank. There will be no further discussion on that point."

"The newspapers will find out all about you this time," Ramsey warned, continuing the assault. "All of those high-class friends of yours up in Connecticut will read about you closing bars down at dawn and going home with whores. The press will get hold of the story this time and our investors will pull their money out. You'll blow Paul's chance to get to the Oval Office, just like your father thought you would. I won't be able to save you like I did before."

"You didn't save me, and I've never cheated on my wife."

"I saved your ass many times," Ramsey argued. "I dragged you to my apartment once a week and sobered you up with coffee and a cold shower. I answered calls from your wife and the investors while you were hunched over the toilet puking your guts up. I won't do that again."

"I'm clean."

"Go back to Montana," Ramsey urged. "Back to the strippers who think five bucks is a fair price for a lap dance and a screw. Back to a place where no one cares if you're falling-down drunk on the ranch all day long."

"I'm coming back to run Warfield Capital!" Bo shouted, slamming the table.

"I could take this to Warfield's advisory board. I could tell them all about you, confirm to them that the rumors are true."

"They won't believe you, and in the final analysis they are powerless anyway," Bo said defiantly. "They can rattle their sabers, but my family controls this firm. What I say goes. I run the family business now."

"Teddy and Paul run it."

"Wrong."

"As long as Teddy and Paul are united, you don't have a chance of taking control here."

"Watch me."

"You'll get yours."

"What's that supposed to mean?"

"Wait and see." Ramsey met Bo's gaze across the table. "I'll walk out of here and leave you in this thing alone. I'll take the big institutional investors with me," he threatened. "The ones who lend us all that money at dirt-cheap rates. The ones who allow you and your family to make so much money. They are loyal to me now. Warfield Capital will crash and burn without me, especially if I go to *The Wall Street Journal* and tell them how many shots of scotch you need to make an investment decision. You'd be all over the front page. Your family's dirty laundry will be hung out for all to see. The rest of the press corps will jump onboard. It'll be a feeding frenzy."

"You won't do that," Bo said evenly.

"What makes you so damn sure?"

"Your equity stake."

Ramsey looked up, surprised. "You know about that?"

"All about it. It's less than one percent of profits," Bo shot back, pleased at the look of shock on Ramsey's face. "There are ways to make the value of a small stake like that evaporate over time if you aren't on-site to protect it. Don't doubt that for a second," Bo warned.

"I have a no-cut contract as well," Ramsey said defiantly.

"For the next three and a half years," Bo acknowledged. "I have to concede that, for better or worse—mostly worse—we're partners." His voice turned steely. "You can stick around because legally I have no way of getting rid of you, but understand this and understand it very well. You will no longer be involved in major decisions at Warfield Capital. I'm running the show now."

Ramsey tugged on his upper lip with his thumb and

forefinger, blinking slowly. "I need to talk to Teddy and Paul."

"You can talk to them all you want, but I'll be in here first thing tomorrow morning," Bo said firmly. "Between now and then, I want you to get all of your crap out of *my* office."

The two men stared at each other silently for several moments. Finally, Ramsey nodded. "Fine. I'll have my things moved back into my old office by the end of the day. But don't think for a second that this thing is over." His lips formed a tight smile. "It's a good bet that by the end of the week this office will look just as it does now. Teddy and Paul aren't going to let you return to Warfield." Ramsey broke into a full grin. "In fact, I believe you'll be back on a plane to Montana by tonight. You might be tied to your seat, but you'll be on the plane."

Bo clenched his right hand, then slowly let it relax. "Get out of my sight," he snarled.

"I suppose I should say welcome back," Ramsey said, pushing back the chair so it rolled against the wall as he stood up. "But I won't." He stalked toward the door.

"Frank!"

Ramsey whipped back around. "What?"

"If you ever lie about me again the way you did to my father about the redhead at the bar, I'll take matters into my own hands."

"I did that for the good of the family."

Bo stood up slowly. "Do you understand what I'm saying? About taking matters into my own hands? Do you understand that?"

Ramsey smiled nervously. "You wouldn't dare."

"Try me."

Ramsey stepped back, bumping into the side of the doorway, startling himself.

"Now get out of here!" Bo shouted.

Ramsey turned and darted into the hallway.

Bo exhaled heavily. He needed a drink.

So he got one. And then another. At a hole-in-the-wall joint on Forty-eighth Street, a few blocks from Warfield Capital. At least the scotch was mixed with a splash of water, he thought grimly as he sat on the stool, elbows resting on the bar. It wasn't pure poison. As if that were some great victory.

"I'll need another one of these," Bo called to a hefty man behind the bar. "As soon as possible."

The bartender finished drying a shot glass as he sauntered over to where Bo sat. "That'll be your third in less than a half hour."

"I can see you didn't miss many math classes." Bo felt the alcohol coursing through his system. Jimmy Lee's death and the confrontation with Ramsey had taken more of a toll on him than he'd thought. He tapped the glass. "Again."

"It's not even two o'clock yet," the bartender protested.

"Thanks, Big Ben."

The bartender smiled good-naturedly. "How about a glass of water first?"

Bo reached into his shirt pocket. "How about I give you this fifty-dollar bill and tell you I don't need change?"

"Never let me be accused of getting in the way of progress," the bartender answered quickly, mixing the drink and putting the glass down in front of Bo in a matter of seconds.

"That's a good man." The bartender reached for the fifty, but Bo snatched it away at the last second, satisfied that his reflexes hadn't yet been affected by the alcohol. "Remember that your character is your destiny," he said quietly, then stuffed the bill in the man's hand and raised the glass. "Hair of the dog." Just as Jimmy Lee had always professed, everything was for sale.

"Hello."

Bo glanced to his left. The woman was tall, with dark hair and long legs. Pretty, though not pretty enough to have escaped the business world, she was dressed in a chalk-striped suit and a frilly-down-the-front, out-of-style blouse. "Hello, yourself."

The woman picked up her wineglass and moved to the stool next to Bo's. "You shouldn't be drinking alone."

"I'm not," he said with a wry smile.

"What do you mean?"

"Mr. Glenlivet keeps me company." Bo pointed at the glass. "He's the best kind of company there is. He never has to say a word to put me in a good mood." He could feel the alcohol taking control. God, he loved the sensation. Words flowed smoothly from his mouth, pressures and inhibitions disappeared, and he was left with nothing but a warm, secure feeling. "Best of all, I don't have to say anything to him."

The woman smiled uncertainly. "I'm Sara."

"Bo." He ran his finger around the rim of the glass. He hated to admit it, but Ramsey was right. It would be so damn easy to fall into the trap, and this was the first day back. "What are you doing in New York, Sara?" It was obvious that she wasn't from the city. From the accent, he was guessing the Midwest, probably Chicago.

"I'm here for a medical conference. I work at the Mayo Clinic in Rochester, Minnesota."

She was from halfway across the country, which more than complied with the eight-by-fifty rule. He took a long swallow, cursing silently. Ramsey's words again.

"Where are you from?" Sara asked.

"Around here."

"The city?"

"Connecticut."

"I see." She finished her wine and nodded to the bartender, indicating that she wanted another. "I'm in this bar having a drink because I couldn't listen to one more bore-me-to-tears presentation about scalpels and surgical staples. What's your excuse?"

"I don't have one," Bo admitted.

"Then why don't you take me to lunch and afterwards show me the sights? We could have fun. A lot more than we will alone."

He shook his head. "I'm not big on the tourist thing."

"I don't mean those sights." She smiled provocatively and leaned closer to him.

Bo gazed at her for a moment, then shook his head. "I can't."

When he had made it through the door and into the raw mist outside, he stopped and leaned over, hands on his knees. "No more drinking," he muttered to himself. "No more." His expression turned grim as he headed toward Grand Central Station. He'd made that promise to himself so many times before.

Reggie Duncan, an African American radio talk show host, beamed as he stood behind the podium, waving to a sea of well-wishers stretching out before him on the

Harlem street as far as he could see. His unlikely grassroots campaign for president had picked up considerable momentum in the past few weeks, not only among his traditional minority listener base but also among suburban whites. He spoke the truth with a direct no-nonsense style that was playing well with more and more Americans. They were warming to his relaxed manner, his ability to poke fun at everyone, including himself, and his willingness to answer all questions with a straightforward response that had nothing to do with what he thought his audience wanted to hear.

With just a few months until the convention, Duncan was far behind the two leading candidates, Paul Hancock and Ronald Baker, in terms of polls and funding. However, with the help of the Internet and a small but determined volunteer staff, money was beginning to pour in and people were suddenly paying attention to his message.

As Duncan deftly entertained the mass of humanity stretching before him with a story about the punishment he had endured as a child for believing that he could fool his omniscient mother—who stood beside him now on the raised platform, smiling proudly—one face in the crowd did not smile along with her. A couple of nights before, this man had murdered a Hazeltine Security employee who had been watching Bo Hancock in Montana. Working with two accomplices, he had drowned him in the Kootenai River. Then he had pulled his gun and killed his accomplices, burying them in the same grave with the Hazeltine employee. You could never have more than one witness to a murder and expect to maintain secrecy. He knew that very well.

As he watched Duncan speak, the man marveled at the

candidate's ability to connect with the crowd. And he marveled at Duncan's ability to lure whites—there were many in the crowd—from other parts of Manhattan into this mostly black neighborhood. Almost overnight, Reggie Duncan had become a force.

Three thousand miles away from the streets of Harlem, Ronald Baker sat high above the streets of Los Angeles in his huge office on the top floor of a glittering, glass-encased office building. Feet up on his desk, he was reviewing the information his chief of staff had just handed him. Baker was a West Coast businessman who had risen from meager beginnings to become a successful real estate investor, amassing a fifty-million-dollar fortune over the last six years.

"These numbers stink," Baker complained to his aide, who sat on the other side of the desk, munching on a turkey sandwich. "Duncan is going to cost me the nomination." He scanned up the page to Paul Hancock's figures, tapping the paper anxiously. "With most of the primaries over, I'm neck and neck with our fair-haired, silver-spoon boy from the East in terms of delegates. But the information here indicates that Paul Hancock will pick up Reggie Duncan's delegates when it becomes clear that Reggie can't win the nomination. How can that be?" Baker demanded. "How can a rich white boy like Paul Hancock be in a position to pick up the minority vote?"

"The Hancock machine is incredible," the aide offered, after swallowing a mouthful of the sandwich. "They are well financed and well organized."

"But that doesn't explain how they can get the black vote." Baker tapped his chest. "I came from nothing and we've advertised that fact. Shouldn't minorities relate to me?"

The aide nodded. "Of course they should, but our information is that the Hancock people have made a deal with Duncan. Duncan will have a position high up in a Hancock administration."

"We'll make the same deal," Baker bellowed.

"There's something else," the aide said. He put what remained of the sandwich down on a paper plate in his lap. "Through a series of discreet transactions, Duncan will become a wealthy man. The Hancocks will essentially buy him a network of radio stations so that he can get his message out twenty-four hours a day all across the country."

Baker's eyes narrowed. "What?"

"Yes."

"How much will that cost them?" Baker asked quietly.

"Four hundred million, conservatively." The aide shook his head, aware that four hundred million was eight times Baker's entire net worth, but a drop in the bucket to the Hancocks. "They'll arrange the whole transaction skillfully and quietly through one of their investment vehicles so that no one can ever scream conflict."

Baker slammed his feet on the floor. "What you're telling me is that without something shaking up this campaign, I don't have a chance."

The aide hesitated. Baker had always claimed that he wanted straight talk, not lies, but you never knew. People said a lot of things, but when confronted with the truth, they often shot the messenger. "That's exactly what I'm telling you."

Baker was not a man who accepted defeat. He was a man who steadfastly believed he could always find a way to win at anything. "Then it's time to pull out all the stops."

"What are you saying?" the aide asked hesitantly.

Baker grinned, thinking about the tidbit of information he had come upon through friends he still had on the seamier side of life. "It's time to start playing dirty."

The aide grinned back. Up to this point, despite strong advice to the contrary, Baker had refused to run a negative campaign. "You mean—"

"Yeah, napalm."

CHAPTER 8

"Why did you want me to come to this meeting?" Tom Bristow asked. Manhattan had disappeared behind them fifteen minutes ago as Teddy's Porsche sped west into northern New Jersey. The terrain was becoming more rural by the mile and the change of scenery was making Tom uncomfortable. "Teddy."

Teddy didn't answer. He was thinking about Jimmy Lee's death, and how much the stakes had been raised for him as a result. Paul had always been the dominant sibling. But suddenly, for the first time in their lives, Paul had become dependent on him. From what Jimmy Lee had told him, he was now the only link to those of influence working in the shadows. The potential rewards and the opportunity to consolidate power were immense, but the risks were immeasurably greater as well. Secrets he had been able to keep hidden might be revealed as the level of scrutiny intensified. As a result, the man in the passenger seat made him vulnerable. Very vulnerable.

"Teddy!" Tom said loudly.

"What?"

"Why am I going with you?" Tom repeated.

"I told you already," Teddy answered, irritated at the interruption. "This meeting is with three senior officials of a large insurance company that is considering a significant investment in Warfield Capital, a loan of several billion dollars without any equity kickers. It's dirt-cheap money, and that is the kind we love." He lifted his hand from the stick shift and patted Tom's arm reassuringly. "I wanted to have another senior Warfield person with me who can continue the meeting in case I'm overcome with grief."

Tom Bristow had never considered himself a senior Warfield person. He'd always assumed that his money-desk job was simply a throwaway. One of the terms and conditions his father had negotiated in return for the hundred-million-dollar investment the family had made in Warfield years ago.

Perhaps Jimmy Lee's death was going to present an opportunity, Tom realized. Friends at the country club were beginning to ask when he would be moving up at Warfield. It didn't impress them anymore that he simply worked at the firm. "I want to tell you again how sorry I am about your father, Teddy," Tom offered respectfully. "He was a great man."

"Yes, he was." Teddy took a deep breath, remembering the swirl of emotions he had experienced as Silwa had emerged from Jimmy Lee's hospital room a few hours ago to announce their father's passing. Sadness at the loss, and at the same time exhilaration at the opportunity to make his own mark on the Hancock empire. "Dad would have wanted me to keep this meeting," he said quietly. "He was a businessman first, and we've been negotiating with these people for months. It would have been weeks before I could have rescheduled this thing." Teddy darted into the left lane to pass a slow-moving truck. "How's Catherine?" he asked, changing the subject. Tom had just ended a short call with Catherine on his cell phone.

Tom flinched as the Porsche barely missed the truck's rear fender. "All right, I guess."

"She was pretty broken up at the hospital."

"Yeah, well."

Teddy snickered and patted Tom's arm again. He sensed that Tom was feeling sorry for her. "Don't tell me you really give a rat's ass about Catherine?"

Tom put the cell phone back in his pocket and gazed out the passenger-side window at the housing subdivisions that had replaced the factories along the road as they traveled farther away from New York City. "She is my wife."

"In name only. Your marriage was arranged by two money lords as a means of keeping an eye on each other," Teddy sneered. "Nothing more. You and I have agreed on that many times."

"Catherine and I have two children."

"You had them for appearances only. My God, you haven't had sex with her in five years."

Tom noted that patches of trees were beginning to separate the subdivisions and that the homes were moving farther back from the road. Teddy was right. It had been five years since he and Catherine had made love, and he didn't miss it at all.

"Better that she's with Paul if she's upset," Teddy continued. Paul had agreed to stay with Catherine when Teddy asked Tom to accompany him to the meeting. "She's always turned to Paul in a crisis."

"And to Bo," Tom remarked.

"No," Teddy said. "When we were growing up Catherine would run to Paul. She seems sweet and sincere, but when it comes down to crunch time she's drawn to power and influence. Like the rest of us," he added with a chuckle.

"She wasn't as upset as she seemed in the hospital corridor this morning," Tom said evenly.

Teddy took his eyes off the road for a moment. "Huh?"

"Catherine has always hated the fact that Jimmy Lee made her marry me."

"You're giving her too much credit," Teddy said. "She's not smart enough to figure out what was really going on there. Besides, she likes being told what to do."

"You're wrong, Teddy. She detested Jimmy Lee for using her to gain financially. She knew exactly what was happening and she's never forgiven him for it."

"Nah."

"You don't know Catherine as well as you think you do."

Teddy gunned the engine and accelerated to eighty-five. There were very few cars on the road now. "The hell with her," he muttered. "She's useless."

"She hasn't been sitting on the sidelines either."

"What do you mean by that?" Teddy asked.

Tom removed his tortoiseshell glasses and cleaned them. "I'm convinced she's seeing someone."

"No way. We would have been alerted by the Hazeltine people."

"Are they watching her?"

"Yes."

"Do they watch everyone all the time?"

Teddy shrugged. "I don't know. That was always Jimmy Lee's department. And Bruce Laird's," he added.

Tom grimaced. "That guy Laird scares me. He's a cold man."

"He serves his purpose."

"Do the Hazeltine people keep files on the two of us?" Tom asked fearfully. "Do they know?"

Teddy shook his head. "No."

"How can you be sure?" Tom asked, replacing the glasses on the bridge of his patrician nose.

"Certain people within the Hancock empire are exempt. Paul and I fall into that category." Teddy paused. "I put you on the exempt list as well, but we've always watched Catherine."

"Why?"

"She's stupid, and Paul and I have never trusted her. Stupid and untrustworthy is a bad combination."

"My God," Tom exclaimed under his breath. "You have your own sister watched."

"So you can understand now why I don't think she's been seeing anyone." Teddy chose to ignore Tom's quiet remark. It made no difference now what Tom thought.

"Have you noticed that Catherine has been sporting a new hairstyle lately?" Tom asked. "That she's been wearing a new perfume? And that she's dropped ten pounds by hiring a personal trainer?"

"You think she's doing the trainer?"

"No, Catherine doesn't care about sex for sex's sake. She needs to be mentally stimulated as well. I met her trainer once out at the estate. I said hello to him and he was stumped for an answer. I guarantee you that she isn't seeing him."

"Who, then?"

"I don't know."

Teddy made a mental note to call Bruce Laird. He was certain Tom was wrong, but it never hurt to check out a hunch, especially at such a critical time. You never knew who might be using Catherine to get to the fortune.

"How do you feel about Bo coming back from Montana?" Tom asked.

"It doesn't matter how I feel because he won't be staying long."

"How do you know?"

"I just do."

Tom wiped condensation from the window with his palm. "I never understood why you all sent him away. He's a good man."

"I don't know why you'd care. He always said we could have hired a chimp to do your job at Warfield."

"I know." Tom glanced down into his lap. "But he worked his ass off."

"He's a drunk."

"Come on, you and I both know that isn't true. He went on benders every once in a while, but he's different from you and Paul. It was terrible the way you guys kicked him out—"

"Hey, whose side are you on?"

"Not Frank Ramsey's. I understand he engineered Bo's ouster by lying to your father about Bo."

"That isn't true," Teddy said quietly. "Besides, Bo does chase women every chance he gets."

"I don't know about that, Teddy. I think a lot of that is crap. I do know that Frank Ramsey is a slimy prick."

"He serves his purpose, just like Laird."

They drove in silence for a while. Finally Tom smiled and put his hand on Teddy's. "I realize Jimmy Lee's death has been difficult for you, but it should make things easier for us. We won't have to sneak around so much anymore."

The touch of the other man's hand surged through Teddy's body, igniting desires he had tried to ignore as a younger man but to which he had ultimately yielded. He cursed silently. It would have been so much safer to use hustlers all these years. He moved his hand from the stick shift to the steering wheel so that Tom's hand fell away.

"Why didn't you bring Frank Ramsey?" Tom asked, wondering why Teddy was being so cold. "Wouldn't he have been a more appropriate Warfield repesentative?"

"Frank had another meeting he had to attend," Teddy answered gruffly, slowing to sixty. He had no wish to attract police attention. "Besides, Paul and I want you to become more involved in high-level decisions at Warfield. We're impressed with your results on the money desk. We also want you to get your father to work more closely with the people on Paul's campaign staff. We believe he could be very helpful to Paul in Massachusetts."

"I'm sure my father would be glad to help Paul in any way he can with the campaign. He's very close to the governor and several senior state senators."

"And to be honest, Tom, Paul and I aren't that impressed with Frank Ramsey," Teddy continued. "We agree with you that he isn't always forthright. We are thinking about making some changes at Warfield. You will be part of those changes. We're planning to give you added responsibility and take some of Frank's power away."

"Really?" Tom asked excitedly. Perhaps he had mis-judged the situation. After all, he had made the money desk extremely profitable, even if it had been with minimal effort. He started to ask another question, then hesitated. He knew he should let the sleeping dog lie, that his suspicions were probably way off base, but a little alarm in his brain wouldn't stop ringing. "What's the name of the insurance company we're visiting today? I know you mentioned it to me earlier, but I can't re-member now."

Teddy tapped his thigh, annoyed at Tom's persistence. "Cambridge Assurance, or something."

"Right, Cambridge." Tom paused. "You know, I checked that name Cambridge in Best's directory of in-surance companies before we left, but there wasn't a company listed by that name in northern New Jersey."

"It must be under another name then," Teddy an-swered nonchalantly. "It's probably listed under a hold-ing company or something."

"I just figured that since you said you'd been talking to them for several months you'd remember their name."

"It's difficult to keep everything straight on a day like today, you know? I'm just distracted."

"Sure you are." Tom waited a moment. "So what is it then?"

"What's what?"

"The insurance company's name. What is it?"

"I'm embarrassed," Teddy answered, keeping his anger in check. "I simply can't remember. I'm only forty-eight and already I'm suffering from Alzheimer's." He groaned, trying to make light of the situation. "Every-thing is in my briefcase. The file on the company and all my notes. We can look at the stuff right before we go into the meeting."

"Can I review the file now?" Tom asked, checking the backseat.

"It's in the trunk," Teddy said, "and I don't want to stop. We're late as it is."

"I need to at least do a little prep work before I go into a meeting with senior executives."

"You'll be fine," Teddy said calmly. "This is one of those high-level things where the dogs just want to sniff each others' asses before signing on the dotted line. There won't be any specifics discussed. But, like I told you, you can look at the information before we go in if you really feel the need."

"But you said we were late. How will I have time to review any information if we're late?"

"Give me a break, will you!" Teddy exploded, checking the mileage marker on the side of the road as they zipped past it.

Tom noticed that there was nothing but an unbroken line of trees on either side of the road now. "How do you know where you're going?"

"What are you talking about?"

"You can't remember the name of the company, but you know exactly where you're going?"

"I've been out here several times," Teddy answered. "I told you, we've been negotiating this deal for months."

"It seems strange that the company would have their headquarters way out here in the country."

"The CEO has a home out here. The headquarters is in Newark."

"But you said—"

"Christ, will you shut up!"

Tom swallowed hard. "I need to take a leak," he spoke up, suddenly panic-stricken. "I could get your brief-case and the file out of the trunk when we stop."

"It would take too long," Teddy said. "We'd have to pull off at an exit and find a gas station or something. That would really put us back time-wise."

"Just pull over here," Tom suggested.

"On the side of the road?"

"I've got to go real bad."

"Hold it in," Teddy ordered as another mile marker flashed by.

"Please."

"All right, all right. God, you're a pain sometimes," Teddy muttered, checking the rearview mirror. When the Porsche came to a stop a mile later, he nodded toward the thick woods. "Go on."

Tom peered nervously into the woods. Perhaps it was simply his imagination running away with him, but it seemed as if Teddy had chosen this spot specifically. It seemed as if he had been looking for landmarks. "The rain is coming down pretty hard. Maybe I can hold it in after all."

"Go," Teddy ordered.

Tom glanced out the window again. He could see only a few feet inside the tree line. Past that the woods obscured everything. They'd been together too long. "All right, I'll be back in a minute. You'll get the file from the trunk while I'm gone, right? I know you said I didn't need to see it, but I'd like to review the information anyway."

"Yeah, sure."

Tom pushed open the Porsche's door and stepped onto the side of the highway. He paused for a moment to allow a pickup truck that seemed to be moving very slowly to pass, then he hurried up a gently sloping, grassy embankment. He moved a few yards into the woods, stepped behind a broad tree, and unzipped his pants.

As the pressure in his bladder eased, he took a deep breath. It was decision time. Return to the Porsche or run? He would look awfully foolish if all of this was simply in his mind and he took off blindly into the woods. But these were the Hancocks, and last week he'd overheard Teddy and Paul plotting. They'd had no idea that he was outside the door. If they could do it to someone else, he reasoned, they could do it to him.

When he'd zipped up again, he took several steps deeper into the woods. It might be a strenuous hike, but this was New Jersey, for Christ's sake. It could be only so far before he'd run into some kind of civilization.

This was stupid, Tom thought to himself, peering into the gloom. He hadn't overheard them plotting against him specifically, and why would they? Teddy would never hurt him.

He turned to head back to the highway and found himself staring at a pistol and, behind the pistol, a face he didn't recognize. He stumbled backward, instinctively bringing his hands to his face. "Please don't," he gasped.

"On your knees," the man ordered mercilessly.

Tom sank to the ground obediently. "Don't hurt me. I beg you."

The man moved behind Tom, replaced the pistol in his shoulder holster, removed a short piece of rope from his belt, then wrapped it around Tom's neck and twisted. Death from a bullet might leave a clue for the authorities even though the body would be burned far beyond recognition. Rope marks would disappear in the intense fire.

Tom Bristow fought violently, but he was no match for the power of the killing machine choking his life away. Moments later he collapsed face first into the leaves, dead.

Teddy sat in the Porsche waiting for the assassin to appear at the edge of the woods to signal him that Tom Bristow was dead. The murder had been Teddy's first official act as leader of the family. People thought he was soft and unable to be ruthless, but they had no idea what he was capable of.

Teddy tapped the car horn when he saw the assassin appear momentarily from the underbrush, then melt back into the forest. The exhilaration was intense. He hadn't wanted to do this to Tom, he had needed to do it. People would be digging more fiercely than ever into his affairs, and he could not afford baggage. He would miss Tom, but Tom could have caused massive problems. He had to rid himself of anyone or anything that could make him vulnerable. And Tom could be replaced. It was that simple.

Teddy glanced into the rearview mirror as he restarted the engine and felt his mouth go dry. "Dammit!" A New Jersey state police cruiser was easing to a stop behind him. Two uniformed troopers emerged from the vehicle and moved up cautiously on both sides of the Porsche.

Teddy's first impulse was to run, but that would be stupid. He would probably be caught, and even if he managed to escape, they had his license number by now and would track him down through DMV records. Besides, all he had to do was remain calm, he told himself.

Tom's body would be well back in the woods. The officers had no reason to go back there. As long as he stayed cool, everything would be fine.

He lowered his window as the policeman on his side of the car reached the door. "Hello, officer. Is there a problem?"

The officer gazed sternly at Teddy for several seconds, checked the highway once more to make certain there were no cars approaching, then quickly drew his weapon and slammed Teddy on the forehead viciously with the butt of the gun.

Frank Ramsey checked the corridor in both directions, then tapped lightly on the door.

"Who is it?"

"Ramsey." Instantly he heard a drawer open, then quickly shut.

"Come in."

Ramsey entered the sparsely furnished office and closed the door behind him.

"What is it?" Scully snapped, annoyed at the interruption.

Only a few people in the world intimidated Ramsey. Joseph Scully was one of them. "Bo Hancock was in my office this morning," Ramsey explained nervously. Scully's office was in the building directly across Park Avenue from Warfield Capital.

"And?"

Perhaps it was Scully's physical appearance that caused Ramsey such discomfort. The closely set dark eyes beneath thick black brows, the closely cropped hair, the multiple scars slicing his face. Or maybe it was the throat-slitter demeanor, which Ramsey suspected wasn't an act. "He's coming back to Warfield."

Scully looked up slowly from the memo he'd been reading.

"He claims he's going to return to his position as executive vice president and chief operating officer." Ramsey always felt the need to keep talking when Scully stared at him that way. "I'll be demoted to Teddy's assistant." Scully was still staring. "I tried to call Teddy and Paul but I couldn't reach either one of them."

"All right."

"Somehow he found out about equity money coming into Warfield from Europe too."

"What! Did you tell him?"

"Of course not," Ramsey lied. "I don't know how he found out, but I thought you ought to be informed about all of this as soon as possible."

Scully ran his hands over his crew cut, then looked up at the ceiling. "Bo sees his father's death as a chance to get out of Montana and take control of Warfield. He's been waiting a year for an opportunity."

"We can't have him take control of Warfield. We can't have him poking around in the portfolio. For obvious reasons," Ramsey added. "I mean, I'm not—"

"When does he intend to start?" Scully asked, running the memo he had been reading through the shredder beneath his desk.

"First thing tomorrow. But Teddy won't let Bo come back," Ramsey said, more to reassure himself than anything. "He and Paul will have Bo physically removed from the office if he tries to come in."

"I sincerely doubt Teddy will be able to do that."

Ramsey could tell Scully was holding something back. "What do you mean?"

Scully pulled out a pack of cigarettes from his shirt pocket and lit one. "Theodore Hancock is dead."

"Dead?" Ramsey felt a heat wave rip through his body.

"Yes." Scully inhaled deeply. "Teddy and Tom Bristow died in a one-car accident in northern New Jersey early this afternoon. The official story is that Teddy lost control of his Porsche on wet pavement, veered off the road, and plunged down a three-hundred-foot ravine to the bottom of a rock quarry. The car exploded on impact, and the fireball was so intense they were literally burnt to a crisp." Scully leaned back in his chair and exhaled. He loved the little buzz cigarettes gave him. "I believe they found a finger bone."

"But how can they be sure that—"

"Tom's wedding band. It was inscribed."

"My God."

Scully nodded. "Yes, it would appear that someone wanted to make certain there was nothing left of them to analyze."

"You don't think it was an accident?" Ramsey asked.

Scully smiled thinly. "I'm a suspicious person by nature, but it's awfully strange timing, what with Jimmy Lee's death this morning."

"Are the authorities—"

"They've ruled it an accident," Scully interrupted. "At least initially. But I don't buy that."

"But who would have killed them?" Ramsey glanced anxiously at the closed office door. He knew Scully had the ability to lock it with a switch beneath his desk and it crossed his mind that Scully was probably more capable than most of causing a vehicle to plunge three hundred feet off a cliff.

"That's the sixty-four-thousand-dollar question," Scully agreed. "I've always found that the best place to start with something like this is to try to understand the agendas of the parties involved. Who has the most to gain from Teddy's death, or the most to lose if he remains alive?"

The answer stuck in Ramsey's throat for a moment. "Bo?"

"Absolutely," Scully agreed.

"I can't believe that. Other than the drinking, he's the straightest arrow around. Everyone knows that."

"This is his chance to take control of the family," Scully countered. "People will go to extremes when they've been pushed to the breaking point, even good people. Remember, Bo didn't want to go to Montana." Scully took a drag off the cigarette. "I've been studying him. He's smart enough to pull something like this off, tough enough too. Deep down, he hates Teddy and Paul, has for a long time."

"That's hard for me to accept." Ramsey shook his head, more convinced that the man sitting in front of him could have engineered Teddy Hancock's death. "I do know that this situation puts us in a difficult position. What the hell are we going to do about Bo coming back to Warfield?"

Scully thought for a moment. "I want you to welcome Bo back to Warfield with open arms," he answered. "Tell him, what with everything that has happened, it's a good thing that he has returned."

"We can't have that. He'll—"

Scully held up his hand and Ramsey fell silent. "Just do it. Leave the rest to me."

Bo moved along the platform, bucking the flow of people into the main terminal of Penn Station. He strained to catch a glimpse of her getting off the train before she saw him. "Meg!" he shouted, spotting her in the crowd.

"Hi," she called, waving excitedly. They hadn't seen each other in a week and, as always, the sight of him pleased her.

Bo swallowed what remained of the third breath mint he'd consumed since leaving the bar, then jogged toward her praying the smell of alcohol had been camouflaged. As they came together, he grabbed Meg's thin waist and hoisted her high into the air.

"Oh, God," she shrieked, holding on tightly to his wide shoulders and laughing. "Put me down, you brute."

"No." He gazed up at her. He had missed her terribly.

"People are watching." She giggled, throwing her head back.

"Let 'em."

Meg was his age, forty-three, but she looked no different to him than she had the day they were married, fifteen years ago. She was tall, blond, blue-eyed, fair-skinned, and slim, with a country-girl innocence in her countenance and an effervescence in her relaxed manner that easily brightened even this drab dungeon of New York City. Though not catwalk gorgeous, men were naturally drawn to Meg's sweetness, charm, and seeming fragility. Bo could leave her for only a brief moment at a party and return to find that she had attracted a crowd of admirers, despite the diamond wedding band he had slipped on her finger so many years before.

In their early married days her ability to attract men so easily had bothered him. Not because he doubted her fidelity—he'd never seen her look with desire at another man—but because he feared that the wolves of his sex might take advantage of her innocence. But he had come to learn that Meg was far from naïve. She was independent and intelligent and so comfortable with herself that she didn't need to convince others of her value. Though she didn't seek attention, she wasn't uncomfortable with it either, and this made her an ideal companion. He could focus on Warfield while she handled a busy social calendar.

She hadn't fallen in love with the immense Hancock wealth either. It amused him to watch her scour the Sunday *New York Times* for sales as she sat sipping her morning coffee on the sun porch of their huge mansion. She hadn't gravitated to Fifth Avenue's designer clothes the way Paul's wife had, or insisted on redecorating their home every couple of years. The only endeavors to which she had committed a substantial piece of the Hancock fortune, and much of her own time, were several children's charities she had established in New York City. Unable to conceive children of her own, Meg seemed to channel all her maternal instincts into these worthy institutions.

Bo had known about her infertility prior to their marriage, but it hadn't lessened his desire to spend the rest of his life with her. They had discussed adoption several times, but had not yet followed through on their plans. Bo had never given her a direct answer as to why he hadn't embraced her desire to take children in because he was ashamed of his answer. He had doubted that his family would accept children who were not blood relatives.

Bo looked up at Meg's smiling face. She would make a wonderful mother, and he cursed whatever greater power might exist for not giving her the chance to bear children. Though she rarely complained about her infertility, he knew it was the greatest disappointment of her life.

"Let me down," she begged, squeezing his shoulders. "People are staring."

"Something as beautiful as you should be stared at."

"You're just saying that."

He let her down gently and their lips came together. "I missed you."

She nuzzled his neck. "I missed you too. So much, Bo."

He felt her tears on his face and shut his eyes tightly, embarrassed that he had even made conversation with the woman in the bar. He had never cheated on Meg and never would.

"I'm sorry about your father."

Bo nodded. "I know you two were never close, but it means a lot for me to hear you say that." Jimmy Lee hadn't objected to their wedding, but he had never gone out of his way to develop a relationship with Meg. Teddy, Paul, and Catherine hadn't either. Bo hadn't been able to figure out his family's indifference to her until Michael Mendoza explained, just before the wedding, that Jimmy Lee had expected him to marry a woman of equal wealth. His father's attitude had only strengthened Bo's love for Meg.

They embraced a few moments longer, then Bo took her by the hand and led her toward the main terminal.

"Where did you go after the hospital this morning?" she asked.

"The Yale Club. I called you from there to tell you about Jimmy Lee."

"I meant after that."

"What are you talking about?" he asked innocently.

"I called back a few minutes later, but the man who answered the phone at the club said you were gone. That was more than five hours ago."

"I met with our personal banker at J. P. Morgan." He hated misleading Meg, but the news that he was going back to Warfield would upset her terribly. He wanted time to ease her into that idea.

She had heard all of the rumors about his late-night exploits from insensitive family members, mainly Teddy, and from acquaintances who detested her unwavering faith in Bo. Only once had Meg ever confronted him about the rumors, after an anonymous caller claimed to have seen Bo going into a room at the Waldorf with another woman. In fact, Bo had been working late at Warfield that night with Dale Stephenson, who'd made a point of calling Meg to confirm the fact. The next morning Bo and Meg had talked for hours, and he had finally come to realize that what Meg really hated was Warfield. As she had said, a woman would be a temporary dalliance, but Warfield was an obsession, and she strongly believed that the pressure of running such a massive fund was what had made him turn so constantly to alcohol.

"You know how you hate to have to deal with all of that money stuff," he said, hoping she wouldn't press the issue.

"Who did you really meet with?" Meg persisted as they moved through the main terminal. She knew he wasn't telling her everything. "Bo, talk to me," she pleaded.

Bo said nothing.

As they stepped out onto Thirty-fourth Street, Meg stopped and pulled on Bo's arm. "Tell me who you were seeing," she demanded.

He looked away into the afternoon mist. The street was crowded with the early shift of homeward-bound commuters.

"Oh, God." Meg brought her hands to her mouth, suddenly understanding his silence. "You're going back to Warfield."

He had wanted to have her alone when he broke the news so he could deal with her reaction privately, not here in the street with hundreds of people rushing past. "It'll be fine. We'll be fine."

She shook her head. "I know this is such a difficult day, with your father's death, and I'm sorry to be this way, but you know how I feel."

"I'm needed at Warfield now that Dad is gone."

"Your father didn't want you to go back. He knew what it could do to you."

"He changed his mind, Meg. He told me just before he died that I had to go back to Warfield." Bo hesitated. "He said some very nice things about you too."

"What?" she asked, surprised.

"He told me to never let you go, but then I already knew that."

Meg put a hand over her heart. "That's nice," she said softly.

"I've got to go back to Warfield, Meg. I have to."

She looked away. She knew how much he had missed the wheeling and dealing over the last year. She knew how it had killed him to sit in Montana, so far from the action. "I worry about you, Bo. As much as Montana was the middle of nowhere, I had you mostly to myself."

"It's going to be different this time," he vowed, taking her in his arms. "I promise."

"You can't promise. There's so much pressure, billions of dollars, people screaming at you to make decisions every second. It will drive you to an early grave."

"You have to understand that things have changed at Warfield," he said quietly. "It's imperative that I return to the firm."

"For whose sake?"

"What do you mean?"

"Imperative for Warfield, or for you? You've missed Warfield this past year more than you've ever missed me." She pressed against him, instantly ruing the remark. "I'm sorry. That was an awful thing to say and I didn't mean it. I know that isn't really true. I'm just scared." She caressed his cheek. "I love you so much."

"Meg, I love—"

"Please don't go back to Warfield," she interrupted, pulling back and looking up at him. "I have a terrible feeling about this, I really do."

"Meg, I've never seen you—"

"I know," she said, pressing two fingers to his lips.

Bo pulled her to him, bringing her face to his chest. "I have a wonderful evening planned for us," he said. "An early dinner at the River Club and a sail around Manhattan on the yacht. It'll be romantic. I've got it all set up. I've been looking forward to it so much. It will help take my mind off of Dad."

"Have you spoken to Michael Mendoza about going back to Warfield?" She knew Bo consulted Mendoza on almost every major decision.

"Yes."

"And?"

"He was against me returning too."

"You see."

"That was before he knew about Dad's death."

"I'm not sure Michael always has your best interests at heart, but in this case he's right."

Bo slipped his hands onto Meg's cheeks and tilted her head back, but she looked away. "How in the world can you say that Michael doesn't have my best interests at heart?"

"Please don't go back," she pleaded, avoiding his question.

"Bo!"

For an instant Bo wasn't certain that he had really heard his name called out over the noise of vehicles streaming in both directions on Thirty-fourth Street.

"Bo!"

He wheeled around and searched the street, scanning the pedestrians, cabs, and cars flashing past. Then he saw the blond woman standing on the other side of the wide street, beckoning, wearing jeans and a yellow top. The same yellow top he'd seen this morning when he'd passed through the revolving doors at the Warfield Capital building. It was Tiffany.

"I've got to talk to you!" she yelled above the roar of the street, waving frantically.

"Who is that?" Meg asked. She hadn't heard Tiffany yell Bo's name. "Who is she calling to?"

"I don't know." Bo had convinced himself that the woman he'd spotted outside the Warfield Capital building this morning hadn't been Tiffany, just his mind playing tricks on him. But there she was, just across the street, motioning to him. She could answer so many questions. Like what had happened after the men had drugged him, and, more important, who was behind the attack. He moved across the sidewalk and stepped off the curb into traffic as if in a trance, his eyes fixed on her.

"Bo!" Meg called, terrified that he would be hit by a bus that was barreling toward him. "Look out!" she yelled frantically, following him across the sidewalk.

Out of the corner of his eye, Bo noticed a man sprinting down the other side of the street toward Tiffany. The figure disappeared behind a truck, then reappeared quickly, only a hundred feet away from her.

Tiffany spotted the man too, took one last look at Bo, clutched the bag hanging from her shoulder, and ran.

Bo lunged forward as the bus bore down on him, horn blaring.

"Bo!" Meg stepped off the curb into the street, vaguely aware of someone coming up behind her, then felt a rough push. She tumbled forward, landing on her hands and knees in the path of an oncoming taxi. As Meg tried to make it to her feet she caught a glimpse of a man slipping back into the crowd.

Halted on the double yellow line in the middle of the street, Bo turned back for an instant and saw that Meg was down, and saw the cab bearing down on her. He dashed in front of a pickup truck, grabbed Meg by the arm, and dragged her back toward the curb. They tumbled onto the sidewalk together as the cab flashed by, grazing Bo's knee. Not noticing the pain, he scrambled to his feet and for a fleeting second glimpsed Tiffany and the man who had been racing toward her standing side by side, looking back at him from the corner half a block away. Then a truck rolled in front of the pair. When it had passed, they were gone.

It was after ten o'clock when Paul, guided by the faint beam of a flashlight he had taken from his study, slipped into a darkened tack room of the estate's large stable. He disliked horses, as he did most animals, but he loved the sweet smells of grain and hay that surrounded them. Paul played the flashlight beam about the room and found what he was looking for. "Hello, Scully," he said. Joseph Scully was leaning against a cobwebbed wall, exactly where he'd said he would be.

"Hello, Mr. Hancock."

"I trust no one saw you come in," Paul said in a low voice.

"No one."

"Good." Until now, Paul had allowed Teddy to handle this end of the arrangement. Allowed Teddy to believe he was the only link to the people behind the scenes. As of this afternoon, that was no longer possible. Still, he had to be very careful and keep these meetings to a minimum.

"I assume you called me because of your brother's accident," Scully spoke up.

Paul nodded. "You and I will have to communicate directly from now on," he said, hanging the flashlight on a nail protruding from one wall. It cast a dull glow on the room. "But no one is ever to see us together," he warned, moving to where Scully stood.

"I understand."

"What do you have?"

Scully searched Paul's face for any hint of sadness at the loss of a father and brother, but found nothing. "Ron Baker is about to launch an all-out assault on you," he answered.

"What do you mean?"

"He has possession of certain compromising information about you."

"What kind of information?"

"Information regarding a three-month affair you had with a young prostitute last year."

"What exactly does he have?" Paul asked impassively.

"The girl."

"I see," Paul said calmly. "Then it's time to use what we have uncovered about Mr. Baker through our northern Virginia operation."

"That's why I came all the way out here. To make certain that you wanted me to follow through on that."

"Absolutely."

"I'll take care of it then."

Paul took a step toward the flashlight hanging on the wall, then turned back. "I want to ask you a question."

"What?"

"Do you think it was really an accident this afternoon?"

"You mean what happened to Teddy?"

"Of course that's what I mean."

Scully was certain that the episode had been no accident, but he wanted to figure out why Paul was asking. "I don't know."

"Come on, Scully," Paul said tersely. "I'm sure you and your people have already checked out what happened very thoroughly."

"I think he was murdered," Scully said. "What do you think?"

Paul hesitated. "The same. The question is, who did it?"

"Who do you think?"

Paul pulled the flashlight down from the nail on the wall. "I don't know who actually killed Tom and Teddy," he said, raising one eyebrow, "but I believe Bo engineered it."

CHAPTER 9

"Good evening, Counselor."

"Bo." Laird answered with his typical brusqueness. "Meg." He nodded stiffly in Meg's direction without offering his hand to her either.

They hadn't seen each other in a year, Bo reflected, and there was no enthusiasm in Laird's voice or manner. Not a "welcome home," not even a "sorry about your father."

"I appreciate you seeing me so late in the evening, Bruce," Bo offered politely. It was after eleven o'clock. After their close call on the street, he and Meg had enjoyed a wonderful evening cruise on the family's yacht. Now they'd stopped at Laird's Upper East Side apartment on the way out of the city, back up to the estate. "I hope we aren't disturbing you."

"It is late," he said. "Fortunately the children are already asleep. Come in."

Bo and Meg stepped from the foyer into the living room of the apartment as Laird shut the door behind them. Bo had never been here, and he noticed as they came inside that the furnishings were stark and impersonal. There weren't even pictures of the children on the tables.

"Hi, Cindy." Smiling, Meg hugged Laird's wife, who had appeared from a hallway leading to the bedrooms.

"Hello, Meg." Cindy Laird's personality was only marginally warmer than her husband's. As Bo and Meg had agreed in the past, it was a match made in heaven—or hell. The Lairds rarely made an appearance at Hancock social functions, though they were always invited. When they did come, they hardly said anything to anyone, preferring to stay off in a corner by themselves. "We're sorry about Jimmy Lee," Cindy said quietly.

"Thank you," Bo answered.

"Bo, let's talk in the study." Laird gestured toward a hallway opposite the one from which Cindy had appeared.

"I won't be long, sweetheart." Bo kissed Meg on the cheek, then followed Laird down the corridor.

Laird sat down behind a dark, marble-topped platform desk, moving a thin chrome lamp to one side so his view of Bo was unobstructed. "What do you want?" he asked, nodding toward a chair on the opposite side of the desk. "Why the late meeting?"

"I trust you've been well," Bo said, easing into the seat and the conversation. He had been taught by Jimmy Lee never to go directly to the matter at hand, but to take the time to judge the mood of the party on the other side of the table. "It's been a year since—"

"I'm fine," Laird interrupted, clicking the lamp's tiny bulb to its lowest intensity and pointing it subtly in Bo's direction at the same time. He knew what Bo was doing.

Laird was little more than a shadow on the other side of the desk now. "You are the family attorney," Bo began. Laird's mood was obvious. There was no need to ease into the conversation. "I wanted to let you know that I'm home from Montana for good, and that I intend to go back to Warfield full-time starting tomorrow."

"Frank Ramsey informed me of such this afternoon," Laird acknowledged, his voice giving no hint of his opinion concerning Bo's decision. "You were at Warfield today."

"Yes, I was."

"You should know that while you were away J. L. executed a new general partnership agreement at Warfield Capital."

"What?"

"The new agreement stipulates how Warfield will be run now that he is deceased," Laird continued. "J. L. was always prepared for any situation, and this is no different."

"Fill me in on the details." Bo sensed another roadblock to his Warfield return.

"The new agreement provides for a Warfield executive committee consisting of all your generation, chaired by Paul. All major issues, including the appointment of senior management positions at Warfield, will be determined by a vote of the executive committee, with the majority ruling."

"I assume you drafted this agreement."

"I did."

"Did you propose it?" Bo asked, trying to determine if Laird was friend or foe now that Jimmy Lee was gone.

"No, Paul and Teddy were responsible. Frank Ramsey had a hand in it too."

"But you didn't object to its implementation."

Laird hesitated. "In confidence, Bo, I suggested to J. L. at the time that Frank Ramsey was not the right man to be assisting Teddy with Warfield Capital. I told him that I believed Ramsey was not consistently forthright with Teddy, and that Teddy did not have a full grasp of what was going on at the firm. I said Ramsey could easily take advantage of Teddy and that made me uncomfortable as J. L.'s advisor."

"What was Jimmy Lee's reaction?"

"He thanked me for my counsel and instructed me to draft the document exactly as he had stipulated." Laird paused. "In the end, Bo, I am nothing more than a hired hand for the Hancock family." He reached beneath his desk, removed a bottle of orange juice from a small refrigerator, and opened it. "You have long overestimated my influence on J. L."

"So a three-to-two vote by the executive committee could prevent me from returning to Warfield Capital," Bo observed, ignoring Laird's comment.

Laird sipped the orange juice. Either Bo hadn't heard that Teddy had been killed, or he was doing an excellent job of playing along. "That's correct. In fact, those voting against could bar you from the premises. They could call the authorities to have you physically removed from Warfield, and be within their legal rights."

"What if the executive committee is deadlocked on an issue?"

"How could a deadlock be possible?" Laird asked.

"I assume when you said that the executive committee would consist of all my generation, you meant that Ashley would have a vote as well."

"She does."

"She may be difficult to locate."

"So?"

"So it may come down to Catherine and me."

Laird finished his orange juice and placed the small

bottle on one corner of his desk. If Bo actually believed Catherine might side against Paul, he was sadly mistaken. It would never happen that way. Catherine would always side with Paul. "Specific to your situation, in case of a deadlock, the dissenting side could not have you removed. With respect to you, or any other member of your generation, being involved on a day-to-day basis in the management at Warfield Capital, dissenters must have the majority. I buried that language deep in the document and no one had an objection at the signing," Laird added.

"No one saw it, I'm sure. If they had, there would have been an objection."

"Perhaps."

"Could I have an orange juice?" Bo asked. He had waited for Laird to make the offer, but, predictably, the offer hadn't come.

Laird reached beneath the desk and produced the bottle. "I could get you scotch if you would prefer," he said, holding the drink out.

"This will be fine."

"All right."

Bo cracked open the bottle and took a sip, weighing Laird's motivation for offering the alcohol. Laird had a hidden agenda in everything he did. He was the consummate attorney in that way. "Tell me about Frank Ramsey's contract at Warfield."

"Why should I waste my time? You already know about it."

Bo glanced up. "What makes you say that?"

"Dale Stephenson secured a copy of it for you just before his death, I believe. Isn't that right?"

"Yes," Bo admitted, "but I don't know all of the specific terms."

"You weren't supposed to contact anyone at Warfield while you were in Montana, were you?" Laird said, his manner turning confrontational. "But you violated that order."

That was the thing about Laird, Bo thought to himself. You could never determine exactly where he was coming from. One minute he was telling you how he'd buried a clause in an agreement presumably to help you, and the next he was essentially accusing you of treason for violating Jimmy Lee's gag order. "Why did my father give Ramsey a contract that involves an ownership position at Warfield? It's a tiny piece, but I don't understand why Jimmy Lee would ever do that."

Laird shrugged. "I don't know."

"Do you know that Ramsey has accepted an outside equity investor from Europe to support increasing the asset level at Warfield to somewhere in the neighborhood of two hundred billion dollars?"

Laird raised his eyebrows. "Two hundred billion? Really?"

Bo had never seen Laird show such surprise. "Yes."

"An investor from Europe?"

"Do you know who that investor is? Were you aware of this development?"

"No."

"Doesn't make sense, does it, Counselor? That investor will be subject to U.S. taxes. No legitimate European investor would ever agree to that structure. They all want offshore vehicles and there are plenty of options for them. The really scary thing is that Ramsey didn't know all of that. What the hell do you think is going on?"

"I have no idea."

"Does it make you suspicious?"

Laird said nothing.

"Did my father have you check Ramsey out before he joined Warfield?" Bo asked.

"No."

"He didn't ask you to get the Hazeltine people involved?"

"No," Laird answered, more firmly this time. "In the months before J. L.'s death there were things going on to which I was not privy."

"Such as?"

"I think mostly things that had to do with Paul's campaign."

Bo scanned the credenza behind Laird's chair. On it were two neat stacks of paper and a telephone. "Do you think Paul will win the nomination?"

Laird thought for a moment. "When you analyze the numbers, Paul is almost a lock to win it. At this point he and Ronald Baker are close in terms of delegates, but Paul will get the superdelegates at the convention as well as Reggie Duncan's delegates when Duncan concedes. I believe there has already been talk of a deal with Duncan, but, as I said, I was not allowed into that inner circle."

"Was Ramsey?"

"I don't know."

"What's your guess?"

"I never guess. You know that."

Bo leaned forward to avoid the glare from the bulb so that he would be able to observe Laird's reaction to the next question. "Now that Jimmy Lee is gone, where do you see your role? Do you even deserve a role within the Hancock empire now?"

Laird glanced up. "I know where all of the bodies are buried, Bo," he said, anger creeping into his tone. "You would be foolish to let me go. Very foolish."

Laird would make one hell of an adversary if it came down to a fight. He was a little man but he had the heart of a lion. Bo had learned during his hockey days that physical stature often had nothing to do with a man's willingness to wage war. He'd taken some of his worst punches on the ice from little guys. Given the testiness of Laird's response, Bo guessed that Laird may have thought that this question was at the crux of the hastily called meeting. Laird had seemed even frostier than normal in the foyer when he and Meg had arrived. "I didn't say I wanted to let you go. I can't speak for the others, but I wouldn't want that."

"Good."

Bo was about to ask another question when the phone on the credenza rang. Laird quickly positioned his small frame in front of the phone's caller identification screen in order to block Bo's view. Laird spoke briefly with his hand cupped around the receiver, then ended the call abruptly. Bo had been able to pick up only a word or two even though he'd strained to hear.

"What were you going to ask me?" Laird snapped.

"What about inheritance issues," Bo asked, "particularly taxes?"

"That's all taken care of," Laird answered with a slight wave of his hand. "Everything is in trust and we have worked out several attractive agreements with the feds, thanks to our connections in Washington." He checked his watch. "Was there anything else? It's getting late and Cindy had a long day with the children. She doesn't need to be entertaining Meg all night."

"Of course she doesn't." Bo finished what remained of the orange juice and placed the empty bottle down on the desk next to Laird's. He had been going back and forth in his mind all evening as he and Meg circled Manhattan on the family's yacht. Going back and forth on whether to ask this question of Laird. "There is something else."

Laird had been rising from his seat. "What?" he asked, a trace of exasperation in his voice.

"Am I adopted?"

Slowly, Laird leaned forward until both elbows were resting on the marble desktop and his hands were clasped in front of his face. "Why do you ask that?" he asked, his voice low.

"I came upon information to that effect." Bo laughed nervously. "You know how I am. I couldn't let it go as just the rantings of a jealous brother. I had to confirm or deny. I figured you were as good a source as there was on family secrets like this."

"That's why you came here tonight?"

"Yes."

"Was it Paul or Teddy who told you?"

"Paul."

Laird rapped his knuckles on the desktop. "Scum."

"So is it true?"

Laird fiddled with the lamp slightly. "Yes."

Bo nodded. He'd tried to prepare himself for an affirmative answer, but it hadn't worked. He felt his throat tightening, and he coughed several times to combat his emotion. "What about Ashley?"

"Ashley will have to ask me herself."

"So she is adopted as well?"

"I didn't say that. And, Bo, none of this affects your right to any of the fortune. J. L. was specific on that. You are as much a son as Paul as far as the will goes. Paul cannot run you out of the family now that J. L. is gone."

Bo nodded, emotion overwhelming him. "Okay, well, again I'm sorry to have bothered you," he said, his voice raspy. "I'll get going—"

"Bo, I need to tell you something about Montana."

"What?"

Laird ran his tongue across his upper teeth, thinking about the best way to tell Bo. "J. L. had a Hazeltine Security employee keeping an eye on you while you were out in Libby. We set him up in a small house down near an old paper mill. He was there to make certain you didn't get in any trouble."

Bo nodded. Jimmy Lee had mentioned this on his deathbed. "So?"

"A couple of nights ago we lost contact with him."

Bo stared at Laird for several moments. "What are you telling me, Counselor?"

"I'm telling you to watch your back." Laird raised his chin as though he found what he was about to say distasteful. "I'm not a man who lets his imagination get the better of him. You understand that I pride myself on being rational and dealing only with facts. For all I know, the Hazeltine operative will turn up drunk in a jail somewhere. That's how these things go sometimes. The type of guy who'll spend a year in Montana jerking off isn't necessarily the most reliable person out there. We do our best to hire good people, but it doesn't always work out the way we plan. . . ."

"But . . . ," Bo said, prompting Laird to go on.

"Like I said, watch your back."

"You must have some reason for—"

"No." Laird held up his hands and stood. For a moment he thought of telling Bo about Teddy, but didn't. That was a family member's job. "I will take care of J. L.'s funeral arrangements," he said, gesturing toward the door.

Ten minutes later Bo and Meg were sitting side by side in the back of a Hancock limousine headed out of New York City toward Connecticut.

"Are you all right?" she asked, slipping her hand into his.

"Fine," he assured her, smiling. "Just thinking."

"What about?"

He would tell her that he was adopted later, when he'd had a chance to come to grips with it himself. "Nothing too important." Right now he was thinking about the strange telephone call Bruce Laird had received in his study. Although Laird had tried to cover the caller identification screen, Bo had seen the numbers long enough to identify the call as coming from Catherine's cell phone. As far as he knew, Catherine disliked Laird intensely. And then there was Laird's warning. "I should be the one asking you if you're all right," Bo said good-naturedly. "You took a rough fall when I pulled you out of the way of that cab this afternoon." He and Meg hadn't discussed the incident in any great detail during the cruise around Manhattan. It had been a lovely, romantic evening, and he hadn't wanted to give her the opportunity to ask why he had taken off across Thirty-fourth Street like a wild man after a platinum blond.

"Yes, I did." She squeezed his hand. "You know, it's the strangest thing."

Bo cringed, waiting for the question about Tiffany,

wondering at the same time if Laird's warning was in any way related to her eerie appearance on Thirty-fourth Street. To the inexplicable performance he had witnessed. A man chasing her, then, only moments later, standing next to her at the corner as if they were working together. "What's strange?"

"I don't want to alarm you," she said quietly.

"Tell me," he urged.

"I was thinking about that whole crazy thing in front of Penn Station while we were on the boat tonight."

"Yes?"

"It all happened so fast I didn't have time to think about what was going on at the time."

"Tell me," Bo demanded, certain of what she was about to say.

"I'm pretty sure someone pushed me in front of that cab."

Bo turned on the seat to look at her. "What?"

"Yes, and it almost looked like the cab veered toward us as you dragged me out of the way. I know that sounds—" But her words were cut off by the signal of Bo's cell phone.

He yanked it from his coat pocket. "Yes?"

Meg watched as Bo's expression drained of emotion. "Who was that?" she asked, tugging at his arm as he ended the connection. She saw that he was battling tears. "Bo!"

"It was Paul," he answered, his voice gruffer than normal. "Teddy and Tom Bristow are dead."

Scully motioned for Dr. Silwa to follow him down the long corridor, but Silwa hesitated, uncomfortable that the unoccupied hallway seemed progressively dimmer the farther down it he looked.

"Come on," Scully called reassuringly. "It'll be fine."

"Where are we going?"

"To my office. It's at the end of the hallway."

Silwa took a couple of indecisive steps, then shuffled along behind Scully, head down, resigned to whatever was about to occur. They had him and that was that.

"This way," Scully directed, holding open a door, nodding as Silwa passed by him. "Have a seat over there," he said, indicating a guest chair on the far side of a desk as he locked the door.

Silwa cleared his throat nervously. "Why did you need to see me?"

"I have a few questions," Scully replied evenly, sitting down in the desk chair and leaning back. He could easily cut off Silwa's escape from here. "Nothing you need to be overly concerned about."

"Okay." Silwa sat on the edge of his seat, rocking back and forth. "Anything you need, just ask. I'll tell you whatever you want to know. You know I'm cooperative. I've always been cooperative, right? I've always done exactly what you've asked."

"Uh-huh." Scully pulled out a manila folder and scanned the first page inside. "It says here that Jimmy Lee and Bo had a conversation immediately preceding Jimmy Lee's death." Scully looked up. "Is that true?"

Silwa cleared his throat again.

"Don't stall, Dr. Silwa."

"No, that is not possible. Mr. Hancock was under heavy sedation. There was no conversation with Bo."

"Silwa," Scully snarled, slamming the folder down on

the desk. "I want the truth. There was a nurse in the observation room with you."

Silwa nodded rapidly, understanding that Scully had probably questioned the nurse. "Yes, yes. I'm sorry. I'm confused. Sometimes it's hard to remember everything. The days are so hectic."

"Then there *was* a conversation."

"Yes."

"What was said?"

Silwa glanced down. "I don't know," he said softly. "I was monitoring the vital signs. I knew Mr. Hancock was close to death."

"How in the hell could you let that happen? You knew what you were supposed to do. You were supposed to give him enough of the sedative so he couldn't talk. We don't know what he said to Bo."

"I gave Mr. Hancock more than the prescribed dosage," Silwa pleaded. "He shouldn't have been able to speak, let alone move," he said, remembering the way Jimmy Lee had grabbed Bo's shirt. "Any more and I might have killed him."

"You should have given him more. You should have given him whatever it took to keep him unconscious. I gave you strict orders."

"It is as I told you. There are prescribed dosages based on weight, age, and other factors. If there had been any significant deviations, I could have ended up in very bad trouble."

"Worse than you are now?"

Silwa stopped rocking. He knew it had been a mistake to come here. Somehow they had uncovered the fact that on three separate occasions he had smuggled cocaine out of the hospital and sold it, and they had threatened to expose him. He couldn't afford that at this point in his life. His oldest daughter was in medical school and he had two more in college. Besides the public embarrassment and the possibility of criminal charges if he were exposed, he would quickly go bankrupt because the school tuitions had drained his savings. He was living on credit at this point. They knew that too. They seemed to know everything about him.

"What do you mean?" Silwa whispered, terrified that he was staring into the face of death.

Scully shook his head, recognizing the mortal fear in the other man's eyes. "Don't worry, Dr. Silwa. You will walk out of here." Scully had permission to kill as he saw fit, but he had never been one to use that power indiscriminately. Not the way whoever had killed Teddy Hancock and Tom Bristow had used it. "I need you for other things."

Silwa held up his hands. "No, please. Nothing else."

"Yes," Scully said.

Silwa stood up to go. "No."

Scully rose too. "Your daughter will—"

"You leave my daughter out of this!" Silwa screamed, bolting around the desk and lunging at Scully.

Scully blocked the smaller man's attack easily, then hurled him to the floor. He was on the doctor instantly, a knee on his chest and a viselike grip constricting his throat. Silwa tried to pry Scully's hand away, but it was useless.

Just as the doctor began to pass out, Scully eased off. "Bad news, my friend," he hissed as Silwa fought to regain his breath. "Your daughter can't cut it at Harvard Medical School. She's paying a teaching assistant to pro-

vide her with advance copies of exams." Scully could see
that Silwa knew this was true. He'd probably suspected
it all along. His daughter wasn't that bright, and Silwa
had needed to pull many strings just to have her admitted
to the school. "We noticed unusual activity in her checking account, some very large withdrawals for a student.
We figured out quickly what was going on." Scully
smiled. "Point is, Silwa, if we relay what we know to the
dean, she'll be kicked out and branded a cheat for the
rest of her life. Then the little apple of your eye turns
rotten." He paused. "So you will raise no objections and
continue to do as I tell you. *Comprende?*"

Silwa nodded slowly.

"Good." He chuckled to himself. RANSACK had
proved its value again. It was working more perfectly
than any of them could ever have imagined.

CHAPTER 10

Bo hurried through the Waldorf's Park Avenue entrance, up a flight of marble steps, past two massive flower arrangements, and into the hotel's ornate lobby. He immediately spotted Michael Mendoza sitting in a wing chair to the left of the large room. "Hello, Michael," he called.

Mendoza waved. His expression was somber as he rose to greet Bo. "I'm sorry about Jimmy Lee," he said, embracing him. It was a reflex action, not the strong handshake that was their typical greeting, but it seemed appropriate today.

"Thanks."

Mendoza had called the previous night to say that he was headed to New York from the Wyoming conference and to ask if they could meet. Bo had agreed immediately. "Jimmy Lee and I made our peace before he died."

"Really?"

"Yes. I'm glad we had the chance to clear the air. He said some meaningful things to me. I was the last member of the family he saw."

"He always loved you, Bo," Mendoza said, putting a hand on Bo's shoulder. "He just never knew how to show you."

"I know," Bo said softly. "I assume you heard about Teddy and Tom Bristow."

"It's been a terrible few days for your family."

"Yes, it has." Bo saw tears welling in Mendoza's eyes.

"How is Catherine?" Mendoza asked, his voice hoarse.

"I'm seeing her after we finish here. I spoke to her briefly and she sounded strong. I'm glad, but frankly a little surprised too. Normally she doesn't hold up in bad situations."

"She was always fragile," Mendoza agreed, sitting down.

"Very."

"Well, please give her my condolences when you see her."

"I will," Bo promised as he sat down beside Mendoza. "I'm glad we had a chance to get together again so soon," he went on. "We didn't see each other for a year, now it's been twice within a few days. It's nice to have you around in a difficult time too. I've always depended on you."

Mendoza patted Bo's knee paternally. "I'm glad to be of help. How are you?" he asked, settling into the chair.

"All right, given the situation." Bo glanced around the lobby. "I went into Warfield yesterday and had it out with Frank Ramsey," he said, his voice dropping. "I told him I'd be coming back full-time. I said I'd be starting today."

"I suppose that conversation was inevitable. How was he about it?"

"Arrogant as hell, and very confident that I wouldn't be around Warfield for very long."

"Oh?"

"I found out later why he was so confident."

Mendoza's eyes narrowed. "Why?"

"A few months ago Jimmy Lee executed a new general partnership agreement for Warfield. Bruce Laird told me. There is now an executive committee of my generation, chaired by Paul, responsible for major decisions. Majority rules."

Mendoza gave a low whistle.

"Obviously Ramsey knows about the agreement and believes I will be outvoted in my bid to return to Warfield."

"Obviously."

"I assume from your reaction that you weren't aware of this new agreement?"

"No." Mendoza shook his head quickly. "I wasn't."

"I thought you might have known because Dad sought your counsel on so many issues."

"Not on this one," Mendoza assured Bo. "He probably didn't want anyone finding out before he died. You know how he was about secrecy."

Bo removed a cigarette from a pack in his shirt pocket and put it in his mouth without lighting it. For a moment he thought about asking Mendoza why Jimmy Lee had denied speaking to him on the plane out to Wyoming from Washington. But it was probably as Dr. Silwa had said. Jimmy Lee was delirious from the drugs and simply didn't remember the conversation. "Did you know that I was adopted?"

Mendoza's eyes flashed to Bo's. "What?"

"Come on, Michael," Bo said firmly. "I've seen that stalling-for-time expression on your face before. You're a damn good card player, but I've known you too long to be fooled."

Mendoza looked away.

"Michael."

"Yes, I knew," Mendoza admitted. "Did Laird tell you that too?"

"Laird confirmed it for me last night, but Paul was nice enough to be the first to break the news."

"When?"

"At the hospital just before Dad died."

Mendoza shook his head.

Bo removed the cigarette from his mouth and passed it under his nose, taking a long whiff of tobacco. "Will Paul win the nomination?"

Mendoza let out a long breath as he thought through his answer. "According to my information out of Washington he'll win unless he does something very stupid. Ron Baker doesn't have the firepower with the superdelegates and Reggie Duncan is too far behind, even though he's gaining popular support. The American people just aren't ready for a black president. It's as simple as that and it's too bad, because Duncan is a good man."

"I'm surprised. It's almost as if you'd rather see Duncan in the White House than Paul."

Mendoza held up his hands. "Don't get me wrong, Bo. I am supporting Paul in public and remaining loyal to the Hancock family even with Jimmy Lee gone. But I don't appreciate the way Paul treats people, including you. He's a user, plain and simple."

"He's got to win the election."

"I can't believe you can be so supportive after the way he's treated you over the years."

"It's what Jimmy Lee wanted," Bo said. "He made it very clear on his deathbed that I was to do all I could to help and protect Paul. I made a promise and I don't break my promises."

"No, you don't." Mendoza shook his head. "You're a good man, Bo. I don't think I could conjure up such positive sentiments about a brother like yours."

"You once thought about running for president, didn't you, Michael?"

Mendoza flicked a piece of lint from his dark gray suit. "What are you talking about?" he said.

"I overheard you and Jimmy Lee discussing it one day at the estate. It was probably six or seven years ago. You asked him for his advice, and his help."

"Yes, I did."

"Whatever happened?"

Mendoza folded his arms across his chest. "Your father was very supportive regarding my ambition, but the opportunity never materialized. With something as huge as that, all of the planets have to align, and they didn't for me."

"Are you disappointed?"

"I'd be lying if I said I wasn't, but life has worked out pretty well. I'm a senior senator of the United States of America. Without your parents' support so long ago, I'd probably be a common criminal, and that's the truth. I'll never forget what Jimmy Lee and Ida did for me."

Bo put the cigarette in his mouth for a moment, then quickly removed it. "Why would Catherine talk directly with Bruce Laird?"

"Excuse me?" Mendoza said.

"Catherine called Laird last night while I was at his apartment. I saw her cell phone number on the caller ID screen. I've been trying to figure out all day why she would call him."

"I don't know," Mendoza answered. "Why are you so concerned?"

Bo started to answer, then held back.

"Do you think Catherine is having an affair with him?" Mendoza asked.

Bo waved the question away. "No. I mean, it seems unlikely, don't you think? In the first place they aren't compatible physically."

Mendoza reclined in the chair. "It's never been my impression that Catherine cares much about physical compatibility." He chuckled. "If she did, I doubt she would have married Tom Bristow, God rest his soul."

"You and I both know that marriage was arranged by the families." Bo was silent for a few moments. "I'm very worried about the picture you showed me in Wyoming," he said, his mood turning dark as he recalled the image of Tiffany on top of him. "The one of me with the stripper." He was about to tell Mendoza how he had seen Tiffany outside Penn Station yesterday, but he stopped himself. For some reason he didn't want to relay that information yet. "And I'll bet there are more. I don't know what I'd do if Meg saw them."

"You might have thought of that before you—" Mendoza interrupted himself. "I'm sorry, Bo."

"I'll admit that it was stupid of me to let the woman in my Jeep, Michael, but I swear to you it was completely innocent. As I told you in Wyoming, I was just having a little innocent fun."

"I'm sure you were."

Bo's look turned distant. "Someone is planning to use those pictures against me."

"But who?" Mendoza asked.

"I wish I knew." Bo looked up at Mendoza. "It would

kill Meg if she saw those things. She's fought through the stories all these years."

"I'll do some checking, Bo," Mendoza volunteered. "I can call some friends of mine over at the Bureau. They'll be quiet about it."

"Thanks." He'd been waiting for that offer. "Once again you're taking care of me."

"And it's a job I enjoy, Bolling." Mendoza watched Bo turn the cigarette over and over in his fingers. "Along those same lines of taking care of you, do you think it's a good idea for you to go into Warfield right away? Maybe you should ease back into things. My God, you've lost Jimmy Lee and Teddy on the same day."

"I'll be fine."

"Sometimes people don't sense the emotional pressure they're under and they need others to point it out to them. You look very tired, Bo," Mendoza said. "This is one of those times. Why don't you wait another week before you start?"

"I told you, I'm all right."

"The place has survived a year without you," Mendoza pushed. "I'm sure it will be okay for one more week."

"What's your problem, Michael?" Bo asked, irritated. "Why don't you want me to go in there?"

"You and Ramsey can't stand each other," Mendoza replied calmly. "That and the responsibility of managing billions of dollars will be very stressful for you. That's all."

Bo stared at Mendoza for several moments. "Uh-huh."

"I'm looking out for you, Bo."

Once more Bo thought about pressing Mendoza on the conversation he had claimed to have with Jimmy Lee.

"You know, Ramsey couldn't handle a market attack if it came."

"What are you talking about?"

"Warfield has plenty of enemies."

Mendoza's baritone laugh rolled out into the lobby. "We all have enemies," he said, passing a hand through his silver hair.

"But with Jimmy Lee gone, Warfield is vulnerable to those enemies," Bo said quietly. "Before, they couldn't touch us. Now they can."

The smile faded from Mendoza's face as he straightened in his chair. "Why?"

"Jimmy Lee's network of contacts was immense. No one would have dared attack us while he was alive. If he ever found out who launched an attack, he'd crush them. I watched him do it a couple of times. He was vindictive as hell."

"What do you mean by 'attack'?"

"The Street can figure out pretty easily if you've got a significant position in something, say a particular stock, bond, or commodity." Bo thought about the night a year ago when Fritz and Teddy had been so worried about the gold position. Someone out there had found out about their situation and tried to hurt Warfield, but hadn't had the strength. "By working in concert, they can hurt you by artificially driving the price down until you have to sell, or simply not trade with you and force you to get out at a loss."

"But Warfield Capital is so big. You would be able to withstand something like that."

"We're a hedge fund and we use massive amounts of debt to leverage our investments. If the value of something in our portfolio drops hard and fast, our equity is quickly eroded and the banks and the insurance companies come looking for their money, just as they do with individuals on margin calls."

"You have your own network," Mendoza pointed out.

"Mine's stale, and it's nothing compared to what Jimmy Lee's was." Bo pursed his lips. "If Ramsey has been irresponsible with the portfolio, the Street will find out and our enemies will strike. It could be a bloodbath. That's why I have to get in there quickly. I have to be able to dig through the portfolio."

Mendoza rubbed his chin. "Have you been able to get in touch with Ashley?" he finally asked.

"What do you mean?"

"I'm sure you've tried to call her."

"Why are you so sure?"

"You and Ashley were always very close. I'm certain she would be on your side concerning any vote of Warfield's new executive committee. Now that Teddy is gone, that would give you no worse than a deadlock on anything you brought to a vote. You need to find Ashley now and get her home."

Ron Baker relaxed into his huge black leather chair, surveying the glistening skyscrapers of downtown Los Angeles from his top-floor office. "I'm very busy."

"I appreciate that," the other man said respectfully. "A presidential campaign must be grueling."

"You have no idea."

"I won't take much of your time, I promise."

"All right." The demands of a tough campaign could be pushed aside for a few minutes in the name of an attractive business proposition. The man on the other side of the desk had come to Baker's office soliciting an offer to participate with a prominent New York family in a high-profile Manhattan real estate project. Manhattan was a market Baker had never been able to crack from the West Coast, and he wanted to hear more. "The family you represent comes highly recommended by people I know in New York."

"I'm sure."

"Tell me what you want."

Joseph Scully cracked a thin smile. "I want to tell you a story."

Baker looked up from the small bag of sour cream potato chips he'd been rooting through. "I just told you I don't have much time."

"This won't take long, and I think you'll find it most interesting. It involves child pornography and an abortion."

Baker felt his mouth run dry.

"We have detailed records of certain Web sites you have visited over the last two years, and the material you've downloaded."

Too late, Baker realized what was happening. "Get the hell out—"

"Through a vast Web network and cookie technology, we have tracked your movements on that computer right there," Scully pointed to the unit on Baker's desk, "as well as the one you have at home. You have been downloading illegal pictures of underage girls. You have also been exchanging pictures with individuals who are known by federal authorities to traffic in child pornography," Scully continued matter-of-factly. "I'm willing to believe that you had no idea the girls were underage, but the public won't care. I think you know that."

"I ought to throw you out the window—"

"I wouldn't recommend that, Mr. Baker. If I don't call

my people in an hour, not only will the newspapers be filled with reports of your activities on the Internet, but there will also be accounts detailing the fact that your wife had a very secret abortion several years ago." Scully smiled triumphantly. "There was no indication that the fetus was brain-damaged or had any physical deformity that might have prevented it from growing up normally." Scully paused for effect. "You simply didn't want another child. It's safe to say that a candidate running on a platform as conservative as yours will be dead in the water soon after that kind of information is released."

"My wife was raped," Baker whispered.

"Maybe, but you never reported the crime. We checked. There is no record anywhere of her being attacked. If you use that explanation, people either won't believe you or they'll feel sorry for your wife and hate you for using her to save your campaign. It's a no-win situation."

"Who do you represent?" Baker's voice was barely audible.

"I'll let you figure that out. Meanwhile, I'll give you detailed instructions on everything you are to say and do within the next twenty-four hours." Scully stood up to leave. "By the way, the real estate transaction is legitimate. As long as you play ball, you will be a partner with the family I mentioned on the phone in that Manhattan real estate project, and you will profit handsomely."

Bo entered the antique-filled Park Avenue apartment, took Catherine by the hands, and kissed her gently on the cheek. "How are you?"

"Fine. Really okay."

Bo nodded. It was as he had described to Michael.

Catherine seemed very controlled for a woman who had just lost her husband, father, and brother. "I'm glad you're holding up."

"But you can't understand it."

"Well, I—"

Catherine pulled her hands away. "Jimmy Lee made me marry Tom Bristow. It was all in the name of greed, Bo."

"Now is no time to be bitter. We all have to—"

"I hadn't been intimate with Tom in five years. I felt nothing when I heard he was dead. I know how dreadful that sounds but it's true."

Bo gazed at Catherine. He was well aware that the marriage had soured, but until now had had no idea how badly.

She turned so that her back was to him and crossed her arms tightly over her chest. "Tom and Teddy were lovers for years, Bo." For the first time since she had received the phone call from Paul informing her that Tom and Teddy were dead, emotion overtook her and tears began streaming down her face. "For a long time I lived with it, but you can be lonely for only so long." She wept gently into her hands. "I'll probably go to hell, but I needed companionship. I needed someone to love me."

With that, she fled the room and Bo's questioning look.

Tonight's mission was out of the ordinary, but he had learned long ago not to question directives. It was a more mundane operation than he was accustomed to—he had enjoyed killing Tom Bristow and the Hazeltine Security employee—but he had learned not to complain either. They took good care of him.

He had easily penetrated Reggie Duncan's campaign

headquarters without tripping the alarm that was connected to the window through which he had entered. Now, as he stood beside a motion sensor and deliberately passed his hand back and forth in front of it, he smiled. The police would be here in a few minutes and his superiors would be pleased. Perhaps, once they had bailed him out of jail, they would give him one of those assignments he enjoyed. If not, he'd have to do it for no reason. He was becoming addicted.

Satisfied that the alarm had been tripped at the local precinct, he sat down in a desk chair to wait. When the police arrived, sirens blaring, he'd have to make it look like he was trying to escape.

CHAPTER 11

"Bring me the private equity sheet," Bo demanded, glaring at Ramsey from behind the bank of computer monitors on his desk. The private equity sheet listed, by amount and date of transaction, every investment Warfield Capital had made in a nonpublic company. Each of Warfield's ten departments, from commodities to equity arbitrage, maintained similar sheets—updated hourly by the firm's central network—so that Bo could quickly determine exactly what lay in the firm's huge portfolio. He allowed his department heads wide latitude in managing their specific portfolios, but when he noted something that seemed amiss—concentration in a particular sector or an unhedgeable security—he was quick to step in and buy or sell accordingly. Portfolio management came naturally to him, even with two hundred billion under his control. Even with a year's layoff.

Ramsey glared back from the office doorway. He had been certain that, despite Teddy's death, Paul would somehow manage to block Bo's return to Warfield Capital. Ramsey was fairly sure that Paul didn't understand the full scope of what was happening within the firm or who was pulling the strings now that Jimmy Lee was gone—as Ramsey did not either. But he knew that Paul understood quite well the critical need to keep Bo from Warfield's records. He knew that Paul understood how quickly his campaign could unravel if Bo were allowed unrestricted access to everything in the private equity portfolio. "Did you discuss all of this with Paul?" Ramsey asked.

"All of what?" Bo wanted to know. He could see Ramsey's intense discomfort, and it elated him. He had come to detest the man during his exile in Montana, but only now did he realize how much.

"This," Ramsey stammered, gesturing around the office.

In the last two days Bo had made the office his again by removing most of Ramsey's decorations—the expensive furniture and the paintings. Now papers and reports covered tables and chairs, and the six computer monitors on Bo's resurrected desk—brought out of storage yesterday—were blinking madly with financial quotes. The office no longer resembled a museum. Now it looked the way it should, Bo thought. Like the nerve center of a two-hundred-billion-dollar hedge fund. "I don't need my brother's approval concerning how to maintain my—"

"I mean working at Warfield Capital," Ramsey interrupted icily. "I'm not talking about your lack of taste."

"Four days ago you were so certain that I wouldn't be back, weren't you, Frank? You were so certain Paul would be able to keep me away from here."

"I was certain Paul *and* Teddy would be able to keep you away." Ramsey hesitated, aware that he should keep his mouth shut. Aware that Scully would be furious with what he was about to say. But he couldn't stand the smug expression on Bo's face. The hatred was mutual. "But Teddy was killed. Now he isn't around to help Paul. Quite convenient for you, isn't it?"

Bo glanced up from one of the screens. "What's that supposed to mean?" he snapped.

"You heard me."

"I heard you, but I'd better have misunderstood the implication."

"Misunderstand what you want, but let me make one thing very clear. I think the timing of Teddy's death is extremely convenient for you."

"Get out of here, Frank," Bo snarled, standing up. "Get out of here and go get me the damn private equity sheet. I'd better have it in the next ten minutes. And close the door behind you," he ordered.

Ramsey stood his ground for a moment, then darted away as he saw Bo starting to come out from behind the desk.

"Asshole," Bo muttered, striding across the office to close and lock the door himself.

When he returned to his seat, he removed a legal-size envelope from the credenza and spread the contents of the envelope out before him. The first piece of paper he picked up was a detailed memo from Michael Mendoza to Jimmy Lee, outlining a plan to alter Warfield's partnership agreement. The proposal, to be drawn up by Bruce Laird and effective in the event of Jimmy Lee's death, mirrored the new voting structure that Laird had described four nights ago in his apartment.

The words blurred in front of Bo's eyes. Michael Mendoza had proposed the structure and Jimmy Lee had implemented it. It wasn't Paul, Teddy, or Ramsey after all. It was Michael Mendoza who had been behind a reorganization of the partnership agreement that would effectively freeze Bo out of Warfield. After his meeting at the Waldorf with Mendoza, Bo had discovered the memo stuffed in a box stowed in a third-floor bedroom closet of Jimmy Lee's mansion. The box, and two others sitting beside it under a sheet, had been filled with his father's personal papers and effects, all thrown haphazardly into the three containers as if someone had been hurriedly trying to hide something.

Bo put down the memo and picked up a second piece of paper detailing all the long-distance telephone calls Jimmy Lee had made from his office on the day Mendoza claimed to have flown from Washington, D.C., to Wyoming. Mendoza had claimed that Jimmy Lee called him while he was waiting to take off from Reagan National Airport, Bo recalled, certain he was remembering the conversation accurately. His memory rivaled Laird's and he was certain Mendoza had described a call *from* Jimmy Lee, not to. Bo examined the paper line by line. There was no call from Jimmy Lee's office phone to Mendoza's cell number.

The last item he studied was a breakdown of what Warfield Capital and all other Warfield entities had paid Bruce Laird since he had resigned from Davis Polk eight years ago to join the Hancocks. The family controller had put the numbers together. Bo shook his head as he reviewed the document. Laird had been paid two hundred thousand dollars a year since joining the Hancocks. No more and no less. There had never been a raise and there had never been a bonus. "It doesn't make sense," Bo muttered to himself. Laird must have been doing very well at the high-profile Manhattan law firm before accepting Jimmy Lee's offer to come into the Hancock fold. "Two hundred thousand is nothing to sneeze at, but he would have been making much more as a Davis Polk partner. Why would he have left for this?" The intercom buzzed on Bo's desk, interrupting his analysis. "Yes?"

"A Mr. Taylor is here to see you."

"Please show him to my office."

"Yes, sir."

A few moments later Allen Taylor sat down in the chair in front of Bo's desk. He was a private investigator whom Bo had known for two decades, unrelated to Hazeltine Security. Taylor's specialty was fraud detection. He was a heavyset man with thinning dark hair, bushy sideburns, a beard, and a heavy New York accent.

"How was Europe?" Bo asked.

"Fine." Taylor was as abrupt as Laird. "I have information for you, Bo."

"That was fast."

Taylor glanced around the office warily. "Do you think it's wise to talk here?"

Taylor was as cool as they came, but today he seemed distracted. "Yes, why?"

"Just wondered." Taylor got up and went over to a stereo system installed on a bookcase near the window. Bo often listened to classical music during stressful periods of the day. Taylor flicked on a CD, then turned up the volume before sitting back down.

"What the hell is wrong, Allen? Why so secretive?"

"As you instructed, I traced the flow of funds on the new equity that came into Warfield Capital three months ago." He was still being evasive. "The two billion."

Four days ago, after confronting Frank Ramsey, and before heading for the bar on Forty-eighth Street, Bo had sat down briefly with the family controller, whose office was at Warfield. Besides the compensation records for Bruce Laird, he'd gotten all available details of the European equity investment Ramsey had mentioned during their meeting. With that information in hand, Taylor had immediately hopped a plane bound for London. Taylor had warned Bo that the process of trailing the money would take at least a week, but he had already returned. "What did you find?" Bo demanded.

"A brick wall."

"I don't understand."

Taylor shifted in his seat. "I've been tracking money for years and I pride myself on being able to locate the origin of any wire transfer. My network of back-office employees in major money-center banks all over the world is immense. It's strong in secondary cities too."

Bo nodded. Taylor was the best. He was the man Bo had called the night Fritz Peterson and Teddy had panicked about Warfield's gold position. "It's true, Allen. You've got more moles than the CIA." Taylor could confirm or refute even obscure rumors in minutes.

"But I couldn't crack this one, Bo," Taylor said. "The trail ended at a bank in Italy like an abandoned railroad spur. One minute I'm rushing along on the express train certain I'm about to find out who sent Warfield two billion dollars, and the next minute the engine comes to a grinding halt." Taylor sat back in his chair, an odd expression on his face. "It was eerie, Bo. I haven't had that experience in years. Back then it was because I didn't have the contacts. This time . . ." His voice faded.

"This time what?" Bo asked.

"Either people were too scared to talk, or they really didn't know the origin of that last inbound wire," Taylor answered. "I can't tell. I'm still working on it," he said, handing his report to Bo. "But I can't promise that I'll be able to get any further."

Bo took the report and slid it into the envelope containing the material he'd been reviewing before the intercom buzzed. "What about the other thing?"

Taylor brightened. "It turns out Bruce Laird had a little problem when your father came calling eight years ago."

"What do you mean?"

"Laird had a massive malpractice suit staring him in the face to the tune of hundreds of millions. Davis Polk needed to get rid of him quietly and it looks like Jimmy Lee was doing them a favor."

Bo nodded. Now the two-hundred-thousand-dollar salary without a raise or a bonus was beginning to make sense. "Look, I want—"

The office door burst open and Ramsey strode into the room. "Here's your damn sheet," he announced loudly, tossing the report down on Bo's desk. "Up-to-the-minute," he said, eyeing Taylor suspiciously. "Who's this?"

"That'll be all, Frank."

Ramsey waited for Taylor to introduce himself. When he didn't, Ramsey headed straight for his office to place a call.

Bo watched Ramsey rush from the office, then relaxed into his chair and rubbed his eyes. Tomorrow he would bury his father and brother.

They had nailed the guy crawling out of Reggie Duncan's Harlem campaign headquarters early this morning but, as yet, had been unable to identify him. The detective eyed the suspect sitting calmly in the holding cell of the precinct. It was strange. The man was too composed.

They had been unable to pry any useful information from the suspect during three hours of interrogation. He had been carrying no identification, just a few papers in a jacket pocket, with an address and telephone numbers, and he refused to say a word. Now he sat on the cot, smiling confidently from behind the bars of the cell, as if he hadn't a care in the world.

"Hey, look at this!" The detective's partner rushed up the hallway carrying a note.

"What is it?" the detective asked, snatching it.

"We traced the address and the telephone numbers the guy in there had in his jacket pocket," he answered, pointing at the man in the cell. "Can you believe it?"

"Jesus," the detective murmured under his breath, seeing the name on the note. "What about this?" he demanded, holding up the note so the prisoner could see the name. "Got anything to say about this? You can help yourself by being cooperative."

The man shrugged. He had no intention of being cooperative. He'd done his job and he'd been instructed to say nothing.

"We've got to make certain this doesn't get into the hands of the press until we've figured out what's really going on here," the detective warned his partner.

"I know. This thing is the fuse to a ten-thousand-pound keg of dynamite."

"Nothing to say?" the detective asked the suspect again. The suspect shook his head.

"Oh, by the way."

"What?" the detective asked, turning to his partner.

"The guy's already made bail."

The detective's eyes widened. "That's impossible."

"Why?"

"I haven't allowed him his phone call yet."

CHAPTER 12

It had been a double funeral. Jimmy Lee's and Teddy's closed dark-wood coffins were positioned side by side before the elaborate main altar of St. Patrick's Cathedral—a massive Gothic structure whose spire towered twenty stories above Fifth Avenue in the heart of Manhattan—with hundreds of mourners looking on and thousands more holding vigil outside. The Hancocks were Protestants, but out of respect for a family that had contributed great sums of money to many of New York's most important causes, city officials had persuaded the Catholic archdiocese to allow St. Patrick's, as Manhattan's most visible religious landmark, to be used for the momentous occasion.

Tom Bristow's funeral had taken place the day before in a tiny church outside Boston, near Concord. The only Hancock to attend had been Catherine, accompanied by Bruce Laird.

The two-hour service for Jimmy Lee and Teddy had been attended by senior Washington officials, CEOs of American and international industry, and a long list of Wall Street and Hollywood executives. The crowd grew so large it spilled down the cathedral's steps and out onto Fifth Avenue, washing wavelike into the street through a long line of black limousines that awaited the two caskets and the family, friends, and honored guests, and wreaking havoc with traffic.

Socialites accustomed to front-row seats were relegated to the back of the cathedral, but they didn't care because this was an event not to be missed. An event by which one's standing in society would be judged for years. The closer to the coffins the better, but being inside the cathedral was enough.

Jimmy Lee and Teddy were buried in a small graveyard shaded by majestic oak trees and surrounded by a wrought-iron fence in a remote corner of the Hancock estate. It was a hallowed site reserved for immediate family members, including Teddy's great-great-grandfather, Blanton, who had founded the Hancock dynasty with a cheap and timely investment in a Pennsylvania oil rig. The investment had paid huge dividends and allowed the family to invest further in oil and railroads, amassing a huge fortune in the process. Bo, Meg, Paul, Paul's wife Betty, Catherine, Bruce Laird, and the minister were the only people present at the burial service, besides the workmen who struggled mightily with wide canvas straps to lower the caskets carefully into graves. Catherine dropped a bouquet of black roses onto each casket and the ceremony was concluded.

The mourners rode back together to the reception at Jimmy Lee's mansion. Paul and Catherine had decided not to hold the reception at the playhouse, which could more comfortably have accommodated the throng of people visiting the estate to pay their last respects. The playhouse had always been used for festive occasions and it felt inappropriate in these sad circumstances.

For the first time the family had an ugly pall hanging

over it. The patriarch, Jimmy Lee, had been taken with little warning, and succession was muddied, though Paul had unilaterally declared himself the new leader. Teddy had been taken in his prime—which hadn't happened to a Hancock in Blanton's line for generations. And he had been taken violently in a horrible fire along with his brother-in-law. Most people attending the funeral knew that while Jimmy Lee's coffin contained his body, Teddy's coffin was virtually empty. The explosion which had rocked the Porsche at the bottom of the quarry had been so powerful and the after-fire so intense that authorities sifting through the wreckage had found only a few charred body parts that they could identify as Teddy's.

Before the limousine transporting the funeral party had slowed to a halt at a wide stone path leading from the circular driveway to the mansion's main entrance, Bo pushed open the vehicle's back door, not waiting for the dark-suited attendants who had been hired for the day. After stepping from the car, he turned and held out his hand for Meg. "Come on," he urged.

"You're in quite a rush," she said quietly as she emerged.

It had been torture for Bo to share the limousine from the graveyard with Paul. Harder still for him to mourn the fact that Teddy was gone—though he felt great guilt about this—even as the workmen began shoveling dirt onto the casket. Though not blood brothers, they had lived together as a family for many years. There should have been sorrow in his heart, Bo knew. But he could not forget how much pleasure Paul and Teddy had taken in telling him of his adoption. When they'd made it clear to him at the hospital that he was not truly a Hancock, they had reveled in the moment, and he had hated them for it.

He would honor Jimmy Lee's wish and do his best to protect Paul from whatever snakes lay hidden in the grass, but he would not relish the task.

"Are you all right?" Meg tugged on Bo's arm gently as they walked toward the mansion.

He smiled at her, overcome by the compassion he saw in her eyes. "I'm fine," he assured her.

"You look very handsome today," she murmured. "A rugged man in a crisp dark suit and a starched white shirt. Very gallant. You've always been my knight in shining armor, Bo, and you always will be." She knew he was having difficulty with the situation, and that he needed her support.

Bo had never gone out of his way to show Meg affection in public. It wasn't his style, but today it felt right. He took her hand tightly in his and, stopping on the path, kissed her forehead. "I love you," he said. "You've always been so good to me." He hesitated a moment. "Am I worthy of your love?"

"That's a silly question," she whispered.

"Am I worthy of this?" he asked, looking up at Jimmy Lee's mansion, which loomed over them. He hadn't told Meg about his adoption yet, and he wasn't certain why. Perhaps it was because he still hadn't fully come to grips with it himself, or because he was afraid of what she might think. She loved him dearly—there was no question about that—but down deep he was troubled that somehow it might alter their relationship.

"How can you even ask that?"

"Do I represent the Hancock family as well as Paul does? He is so impressive, Meg, so much like Jimmy Lee. Do people look at me and wonder, 'What happened?' "

"Stop it," she said firmly. "Stop putting yourself down. I hate it when you do that."

"What are you talking about?" A slight breeze drifted over the wide, freshly mowed lawn, blowing Meg's hair across her face and bringing the sweet smell of cut grass to them. Bo reached out and pushed her hair back. "I don't understand."

She caught his rough fingers and kissed them. "I mean that you've always felt as if Paul and Teddy were better than you."

"No, I haven't," he answered without conviction.

"Yes, you have. You've always put yourself down and at the same time tried desperately to please them. You've always been willing to be the one toiling in the background while they get all the credit. Warfield Capital is a perfect example." She shook her head disgustedly. "It's been that way ever since you were young. I've seen the home movies of you as children. It was always them against you, whether it was a snowball battle or a touch football game. And the few times you were on the same side, you were the one doing the blocking while they got the ball and scored. I hate the way they've taken advantage of your willingness to be a team player. It's always infuriated me that they've bullied you into doing the dirty work. And they know I hate it. That's why they've never liked me." Her eyes narrowed. "I'd like to say that I'm sorry Teddy is gone, but I can't. I never cared for him, or Paul."

"Meg, I wasn't aware that you—"

"I'm being honest, Bo," she interrupted. "I've held back all these years, but I won't anymore. I'm telling you what you need to hear. They've never treated you with the respect you deserve." She swallowed hard. "I'm sorry to say that on this of all days. I'm so, so sorry, but it's time you heard the truth because you need to take charge of the family. You must take control of not only Warfield but everything else too." She took a deep breath. "Catherine can't run things, she's too weak. She'd be lost, even with help from a team of advisors. Everyone knows that. Paul can't do it either. He has to focus on his campaign. It has to be you, Bo. You need to take the helm. It's your time." She touched his ruddy cheeks. "I'll help you. We'll do it together."

Bo gazed at her for several seconds, aware that the others had emerged from the limousine and were headed toward them on the path. "Why haven't you said these things before?" he asked.

"I didn't feel it was my place. But when Paul and Catherine wouldn't let you address the congregation at the funeral, I had to say something. I don't like them, Bo, especially Paul. He fools everyone with his charm, but he's evil."

Bo's expression turned grim.

"Didn't you want to say something to the people in that church?" Meg asked. "Didn't you want to say something to your father in front of them?"

"Yes," he admitted.

"Paul and Catherine didn't even ask if you wanted to speak, did they?"

He lowered his eyes. "No."

"And you didn't demand to."

He wanted to tell her why. He wanted to tell her that as an adopted child he hadn't felt it was his right to demand equal time with the blood children before the assembled mourners. That it wasn't his right to demand any time.

She lifted his chin and gazed into his eyes. "No matter what happens, I love you. You know I haven't stayed by your side all these years because of the money," she said, nodding at the huge home. "I love you because of who you are and what you mean to me. Deep down you are the most decent man I've ever known. I could be happy with you in a broken-down tenement."

"Thank you," he whispered. "But there's something I don't understand."

"What?"

"When I met you at Penn Station a few days ago the last thing in the world you wanted me to do was return to Warfield Capital. Now you want me to take control of everything. What has changed?"

"Nothing, everything. I love you as much as I always have, maybe more, but now your father and brother are gone." Meg looked up into the trees. This was difficult. She would rather have him to herself, but she knew that was impossible now. "You must take control, Bo. Without you the Hancock family is vulnerable. I don't know Frank Ramsey very well, but I know enough about him not to trust him." She hesitated. "Most of all, I want the best for you." She motioned toward the immaculately kept grounds surrounding them. "This is where you belong. You love running Warfield and you should. Just don't forget me."

"I adore you," he said, pulling her close.

"I know."

Bo saw Paul and Catherine approaching. "Let's go," he urged, taking Meg by the hand and leading her toward the mansion.

As they walked through the foyer and into the great

room, they were met by the loud hum of conversation and the scent of flowers.

"There are almost as many security people in here as there are guests," Meg said, counting the number of dark-suited men working the crowd and trying to seem inconspicuous with wires trailing from their ears down into their suit coats. She had to raise her naturally soft voice to make herself heard.

"Hi, Bo." Evan Reese strode toward Bo, a tall brunet clutching his arm as if it were a life preserver. "How are you?"

"Fine, Evan."

"My condolences. Your father and brother were great men. They will be missed."

"Thank you." Bo nodded to the young woman escorting Reese. She was several inches taller than Reese and wore a dress that was too tight and too short for the occasion. "I'm Bo Hancock. This is my wife, Meg."

"I'm Alecia."

"Nice to meet you." Bo looked at Reese. "How's the latest film going?" Reese had starred in three consecutive action films for an A-list Hollywood studio and was just finishing a fourth. A Hancock family limited partnership had financed the first film, backing Reese and immediately transforming him from an obscure actor doing bit parts in B movies and advertisements into a bona fide, twenty-million-dollars-a-script star. He was chiseled and bronzed, but shorter and older than he appeared on the screen. Nothing that good camera angles and makeup couldn't combat, Bo thought, at least for a while. "The film is almost finished, I understand."

"Yeah, we're just about done." Reese pulled Bo aside

so that Meg and Alecia couldn't hear what he was about to say. "I need to ask a favor."

"What?"

"I'm trying to get Alecia a major part in a film," he began, "but it isn't working out. She's the next Julia Roberts, I'm telling you, but for some reason nobody in Hollywood is willing to give her a shot. Maybe you could help her out like your father helped me."

Bo suppressed a smile. Meg was right. It was his time. People saw him as the successor. "We'll see, Evan. Give me a call next week and we'll talk about it."

"Thanks, I—" Evan looked away and broke into a wide grin. "Hey, Paul, how's the next president of the United States?"

"Just fine, Evan." Paul moved smoothly into the small circle of people, his back to Bo. Betty remained in the background, smiling lovingly from a short distance away, playing the role of obedient wife as she always did. "Thanks for asking. How've you been?"

Bo watched as Alecia cast her eyes on Paul. He had seen the reaction so many times. Her lips parted, there was a hesitation in responding to Paul's greeting, then she ran her fingers through her hair and tilted her head slightly to the side, smiling demurely as they locked eyes for the first time. It was so predictable. Bo saw Paul smile back—just a quick, subtle flash.

"Come on." Bo led Meg through the crowd toward one of several bars being tended by men in crisp black tuxedos. He didn't want to watch this.

"What was that all about?" Meg asked.

"That was Paul's way of showing me who he thinks is in charge."

"What are you doing?" she asked anxiously.

"Getting a drink."

"Please don't, Bo."

"What will you have, sir?" one of the bartenders asked, picking up a glass.

"Bo, pl—"

"Ice water."

"And for the lady?"

"Ginger ale."

"Yes, sir."

Bo took the drinks from the young man and turned to find Meg smiling at him. "What are you smiling about?" he asked. "You look like the cat that swallowed a flock of canaries."

She picked up a napkin from the bar and took the ginger ale. "You know exactly why I'm smiling. I'm proud of you. I know how much you love your scotch, particularly in a crowded room full of people you think are comparing you to Paul."

Bo glanced at a row of liquor bottles on the bar. She was right. It would have been easy to give in today. But since making his vow of sobriety outside the Manhattan bar, he hadn't consumed a drop of alcohol. Though it had been hard as hell, it felt good to keep the promise to himself for once. "Thanks."

"Good afternoon, Bo."

Bo turned around quickly. Harold Shaw, chairman of the American Financial Group, stood before him. AFG was the holding company for an array of financial firms, including the country's largest commercial bank, its second-largest savings and loan, one of Wall Street's bulge-bracket investment houses, an on-line brokerage firm, and a massive insurance company. AFG controlled over three trillion dollars of combined assets. In constructing the sprawling financial services concern through a series of rapid-fire mergers, Shaw had run afoul of a morass of decades-old consumer-interest regulations designed to keep the different types of entities apart. But with a combination of high-level government connections, guile, and stubbornness, Shaw had barreled through regulators. After two years of integration, AFG was a smoothly running machine constantly gobbling up smaller financial concerns all over the country without opposition from banking and insurance regulators or the Department of Justice's antitrust unit. No one got in Shaw's way at this point.

"Hello, Harold," Bo replied stiffly. Shaw was tall, angular, and hollow-cheeked, known for his terrible mean streak. He reminded Bo of Jimmy Lee, in both demeanor and appearance. Shaw and Jimmy Lee had been friends since college. "You remember my wife, Meg."

"Yes." Shaw gave Meg a cursory nod, then refocused on Bo. "What's this I hear about you going back to Warfield?" AFG's commercial bank was one of Warfield's largest lenders, with over five billion dollars of exposure to the fund.

Bo gritted his teeth, irritated at the question. "I'm needed."

"Your father and I went way back, Bo."

"I'm aware of that."

"He wouldn't have approved." Shaw had a well-deserved reputation for bluntness. "Your drinking is a problem. He and I had long conversations about this issue on several occasions, one of which took place not long before he died. There is no question that you are the most capable of any Hancock when it comes to numbers. The problem is, you're the least reliable."

"You're wrong." Bo glanced around, checking to see who was listening. "The year away helped me a great deal."

"Paul can't have you here, Bo. You could easily destroy his chances of winning the election."

"Good afternoon, Harold." Once more Paul wedged his way into Bo's conversation.

"Hello, Paul," Shaw said, smiling widely for the first time.

"Could I have a word with you, Harold?" Paul asked. Shaw glanced back over his shoulder uncertainly at Bo as Paul led him away through the crowd.

"This is getting ridiculous," Meg observed. "Paul can't leave you alone."

Bo nodded as he spotted Nick Kaplan through the crowd. Until two years ago Kaplan had operated a large leveraged buyout fund in Boston. During a difficult time for Kaplan, Bo had purchased assets with a book value of a half billion dollars from Kaplan's fund for less than two hundred million. A month later Bo had sold the assets to another fund for the half billion they were really worth. When Kaplan's fund had disintegrated last year, he had caught on with a large New York investment bank run by a close friend—poorer, wiser, and very bitter.

Bo saw the resentment in Kaplan's eyes. At the time, Kaplan had begged Bo for the two hundred million to help his fund stay afloat. Now Kaplan would never forgive Bo for Warfield's three-hundred-million-dollar profit. But that was the way of the financial world. People forgot the favor, but they never forgot the profit. Particularly when they had lost it.

"Who are Paul and Harold Shaw talking to now?" Meg asked, glancing at the pair, who had been joined by a third man.

"Jim Whitacre," Bo answered, shifting his attention.

"Who is he?"

"The chief executive officer of a company named Global Media," Bo answered. "Global is the most important information technology company in the world."

"The three of them look like they're carving up the world," she observed dryly.

"I wouldn't be surprised if they were. Global Media and AFG affect the lives of every human being in this country in one way or another, and Paul's going to be our next president. If I were to guess, I'd say they were carving up the universe, not just the world."

"How do Shaw and Whitacre's companies affect everyone?"

"Shaw is CEO of American Financial Group, the largest financial services conglomerate in the world. I've read statistics indicating that his firms have processed at least one financial transaction for every household in this country. A mortgage, a car loan, a stock market trade, an insurance policy, a credit card purchase. You name it, they do it." Bo nodded toward Whitacre. "Global Media owns long distance and local telephone lines, a satellite company, a huge cable company, an Internet portal, an Internet advertising firm, and a dominant software maker, among other things. It also does a great deal of network consulting work for the federal government, specifically for the Internal Revenue Service."

"Good God," Meg whispered.

"God should have so much influence," Bo muttered,

spotting Michael Mendoza. He watched as Mendoza worked the crowd, pausing for a moment to say something to Frank Ramsey. "What did you mean the other day when you said that Michael Mendoza didn't always have my best interests at heart?"

Meg took a sip of ginger ale. "I know you and Michael have been close for many years."

"But."

"Michael is out for Michael." Meg paused. "And I didn't appreciate the way he started seeing other women so soon after Ginny's death." She and Bo had visited Mendoza and his wife Ginny in Washington over the years, staying at their town house in Georgetown many times. Ginny had died two years ago of complications from breast cancer. "I liked Ginny very much and I thought it was terrible of Michael to date so quickly, especially such young women."

"Michael didn't see anyone for several months after Ginny's death. You can't expect someone not to want company. He didn't like being alone."

"It was only a couple of weeks after she died," Meg corrected, "and the woman was barely out of college."

"How do you know that?"

"You aren't the only one with Washington contacts." Meg glanced at Mendoza, who was coming toward them. "He considers himself quite the ladies' man."

"Hi, Bo." Mendoza took Bo's hand and shook it warmly, then kissed Meg's cheek. "Hello, Meg."

"Hello," she answered flatly, scanning the crowd.

"You look wonderful."

"Thank you."

Mendoza looked back at Bo. "And you look like someone I've never seen before."

"What are you talking about?" Bo asked coolly. He desperately wanted to ask Michael about the memo to Jimmy Lee and the telephone call that, it turned out, hadn't been made, but he would wait for a more appropriate time.

Mendoza gave Bo an exaggerated up-and-down. "Suit coat on, top shirt button buttoned, tie pulled all the way up with a fairly neat knot, fresh haircut, immaculate shave." He smiled wanly, then hugged Bo. "So now I know that it takes a funeral to get you looking neat."

Bo's expression remained emotionless and he didn't return the embrace.

"You all right?" Mendoza asked, pulling back.

"Fine, Michael."

"If the funeral comment upset you, I'm—"

"Forget it."

Mendoza stared at Bo for a few moments, trying to understand. "Would you excuse us?" he finally asked, smiling politely at Meg.

"Of course." Over the years she had become accustomed to people constantly needing Bo's time in private.

"Is there something we need to talk about?" Mendoza asked when Meg was out of earshot.

"Not now."

Mendoza nodded. "Okay," he said slowly. He pointed subtly toward Paul, who was now conferring with Catherine near the entrance to the large room. "I came over here to tell you that your brother is planning to bring the Warfield issue to a head."

"What?" Bo's eyes shot to where Paul and Catherine were talking.

"Paul is hell-bent on making certain that you don't return to Warfield. He's going to call you into a meeting in your father's study in a few minutes and put the issue to a vote."

"How do you know?"

"Bruce Laird pulled me aside as I came into the reception. He wanted you to be prepared."

"I'm ready for Paul."

"Yes, but can you beat him?"

"Catherine will vote with me."

"Are you sure?"

Bo eyed Mendoza. "I'm sure." He saw Paul making his way through the crowd. "What do you want?" he asked coldly as Paul made it to where he and Mendoza were standing.

"I need to speak with you in Dad's study."

"This isn't the time or the place for a confrontation," Bo replied.

"That's right," Mendoza agreed, stepping between them. "Bury your differences on the day that you bury your father."

"Stay out of this, Senator," Paul ordered sharply. "You have my parents to thank for everything that you are and that you have achieved. Show your respect for them by steering clear of what doesn't concern you." Paul shifted his gaze to Bo. "We're going into Dad's study, Bo, and we're going to finish this thing right now. You can come and hear what I have to say, or not. But I warn you, the security people will bar you from entering Warfield's offices from now on." Then he was off, wending his way through the crowd toward the study.

Bo watched Paul disappear into the mass of people, then went to find Meg. "I have to deal with Paul for a few minutes," he said to her over the noise of the crowd.

She nodded. "Hurry back."

"I will."

When Bo entered the study, Paul was sitting behind Jimmy Lee's desk, smiling smugly. Catherine stood behind Paul, fiddling nervously with a picture frame on the credenza. She did not look up as Bo came in.

"What do you want?" Bo asked, closing the door. The hum of conversation faded away.

Paul tapped the desk with his pen. The sound echoed throughout the large room. "I want to make you an offer."

"What kind of offer?" Bo asked, trying unsuccessfully to catch Catherine's eye.

Paul took a deep breath. "I'll give you a billion dollars of the family money to manage. You can do it on your own with no interference whatsoever from Frank Ramsey or me. You can do it from Montana. We'll hire several assistants and build a small trading room in the ranch house, if you want."

Bo removed his coat and tossed it over the back of the same chair he had sat in a year ago as Paul railroaded him to Montana the first time. "Why would I want to do that when I can manage everything at Warfield?" he asked, moving to a spot directly in front of the desk. He saw Catherine's face tense, anticipating the maelstrom.

"You aren't going back to Warfield," Paul replied evenly.

Bo leaned forward and placed his hands on the desktop. "Why are you so dead-set against having me there?"

"For the same reason I was a year ago. You aren't doing any better than you were before you left. You were drinking like a fish in Montana, just like you were here before you left. If I let you go back to Warfield, you'll screw up the portfolio and make an ass of yourself in public."

"How do you know how much I was drinking in Montana?"

"I just do."

"Had the Hazeltine boys watching me all the way out there, did you?" Bo asked, knowing the answer.

"Watching you and your redneck buddies. The ones you met every afternoon at Little Lolo's."

Bo chuckled and shook his head. "You're a bastard, Paul. I've always wanted to tell you that. Ever since that night Melissa died."

Catherine glanced up, curiosity all over her face, as Paul shot out of the chair and charged around the desk to where Bo stood. "I was going to work with you, Bo," he snarled. "I was going to try to find a solution that would leave you with some shred of self-respect, but I can see that won't be possible." He turned to Catherine. "Go find Bruce Laird," he ordered. "Let's get this thing over with."

"Why are you doing this, Paul?" Bo asked, as Catherine exited the room. "Is it that you want to break me? Do you figure that if you send me back out to Montana, I'll drive myself crazy? Drink myself to death or maybe blow my brains out with a shotgun? Do you hate me that much? Or is it that you're worried I might bring Melissa back from the dead one day?"

"Shut up!"

Bo nodded triumphantly. "That's the real problem, isn't it? That's the incident that could take you down, and I'm the only person in the world besides you that knows about it."

"I'm warning you, Bo."

"I know where Melissa's parents are, Paul. I've kept tabs on them all these years. They're both still alive." He hesitated. "And I'm the only one that knows where—"

"If it ever came out, I'd pin it on you, Bo!" Paul roared. "The press would believe you were responsible before they'd believe I was."

"But it would be more satisfying for them to take you down."

"Bo, I swear to God I'll—"

"You wanted me, Paul?" Bruce Laird entered the study, followed closely by Catherine.

"Yes," Paul answered without taking his eyes from Bo's. "Warfield Capital's executive committee is about to take a very important vote, and I want you to record it officially."

"All right."

"Point of order. Three is a quorum, correct, Counselor?" Paul asked, returning to his seat behind Jimmy Lee's desk.

"Yes."

"Catherine, Bo, and I represent that quorum."

"Yes," Laird confirmed.

"And a vote taken here is final. It cannot be revisited."

Bo's eyes flashed to Laird. "Is that true, Counselor?"

"Yes," Laird answered quietly.

"Then the vote is on the table," Paul said. "Catherine and I are permanently expelling you from the executive committee." He glanced at Catherine. "All in favor of Bolling Hancock being removed from the executive committee signify their agreement by raising their right hand and saying 'for.'" He raised his right hand quickly. "For," he said firmly. "Catherine?"

Bo glanced at her. "Don't do this," he urged.

"Catherine," Paul pushed, "vote."

"It isn't right, Catherine. Frank Ramsey will destroy Warfield. Paul doesn't understand that. You must. Please, Catherine."

"Catherine!" Paul shouted.

She glanced at Laird, then away.

"Catherine!"

"For," she murmured, raising the trembling fingers of her right hand and shutting her eyes tightly.

"How can you do this to me?" Bo whispered.

"Recorded, Counselor?" Paul asked loudly.

"So recorded."

"All opposed signify by saying 'against.' All opposed?"

It was happening again, Bo thought. In the same room at the hands of the same man. "Counselor, I need time to—"

"Opposed?"

"Counselor—"

"Let the minutes show that there is only one vote opposed to the motion. The motion is passed." Paul slammed his hand on the desk. "Bo, you are officially—"

"Not yet he isn't."

Bo, Paul, Bruce, and Catherine looked quickly toward the study door. For several seconds they were silent, wondering if the figure standing before them was real. It had been so long since anyone had seen her.

"Ashley," Bo finally uttered, his voice hushed.

She crossed the study to stand beside Bo. Then she raised her hand and looked directly at Paul. "Against," she said, her voice strong and sure.

Catherine removed her high heels and stepped into a pair of old sneakers she had left by the basement door, then slipped from the mansion and raced for the woods, praying that no one at the reception would notice her. When she reached the tree line, she stopped to catch her breath, observing the mansion from behind a large oak. There were still many people crowded on a side porch, but none of them was looking in her direction. Dusk had obscured her sprint across open ground.

She moved deeper into the woods, then pulled a flashlight from her jacket, turned it on, and found the path she had used so often as a child to get from her parents' mansion to the playhouse. Then she was off again, running through the darkness, guided by the flashlight.

He was exactly where she had instructed him to be, waiting by the lake down the hill from the playhouse's back veranda. He pulled her against him as soon as they found each other and kissed her savagely, grasping her hair tightly and roaming her body with his hands. She leaned back and allowed him to kiss and gently bite her neck, the touch of his teeth, lips, and tongue on her skin driving her wild. It had been so long since she'd been touched this way. Though she had not been intimate with Tom Bristow in years, she had never strayed until tonight. Tom had been doting in public, but he had paid no attention to her in private. Now Tom was out of the way and she was finally free to do as she pleased. Jimmy Lee was gone too, and there would be no consequences.

"It feels so good," Catherine moaned as he pulled open her dress and teased one of her nipples with his mouth.

"You hated Tom, didn't you?"

"Don't say his name," she gasped, sexual excitement coursing through her body.

"Jimmy Lee too."

"Yes," she moaned. Jimmy Lee was an evil man. Now she was exacting her revenge. "It feels so good. I've wanted you so badly."

"You just buried your husband, Catherine." The man paused momentarily, aroused by her wickedness. "How can you do this?"

"You said it didn't bother you. Don't stop what you were doing." She pulled his mouth to hers and kissed him deeply.

"Yes, but—"

"I hated him. Are you happy now? I hated him." Catherine's eyes filled with tears. "And my father didn't care." She ripped open his shirt and tugged at his belt. "Take me," she ordered. "Come on."

He stripped her clothes off. Then, as they lay on the ground, he moved between her legs, taking her nipple in his mouth again and touching her briefly before lifting her legs over his shoulders and pushing himself inside.

"Oh, God," Catherine moaned, looking up at the man as he labored over her. She discovered that she could manipulate his movements with just the slightest movement of her own. Awed by how he was so completely under her control, enjoying the power, she felt an authority she had no idea she had missed so badly. It had to be in the blood, she thought as she toyed with him like a cat playing with an injured mouse. A part of her brain told her this was the feeling of control Jimmy Lee had lived for, and now she understood why.

"You feel so good, Catherine. I've wanted you for so long."

"Good," she said, wrapping her arms and legs around his body tightly and thrusting up against him.

"Sweet Jesus." He arched his back and gazed ahead into the darkness.

Suddenly she rolled him onto his back and took him in her mouth. She felt his member swell slightly and knew that he was ready. She straddled him, momentarily holding him at her opening, then forced herself down on him, thrusting her tongue into his mouth at the same moment he entered her again. When he turned his head to the side and began to grind his teeth, she sucked hard on his neck.

"I can't stop, Catherine," he groaned.

She felt the veins in his neck bulging against her tongue, felt his entire body tensing beneath her. "It's what I want," she whispered.

When he was finished and she had collapsed beside him on the blanket, he held her tightly in his arms and began to murmur in her ear. But instead of the words of love she expected, her blood ran cold as he said, "You had Tom and Teddy killed, didn't you? Do you really think you'll get away with it?"

CHAPTER 13

Bo slowed the dark green Explorer to a stop in front of his mansion, eased his hard-soled shoes down onto the smooth stone driveway, and stretched, reaching high above his head and groaning loudly as he slid out of the vehicle. Every muscle in his body ached and his feet were killing him. It was after two in the morning and he was dead tired. The last few guests had left the funeral reception only a few minutes ago, and he had stayed to the end. He had driven Meg back here at midnight despite her protests that she wanted to remain with him at the reception. As it was, she could barely keep her eyes open on the short ride home.

He had parked the Explorer in the circular driveway in front of the mansion's main entrance. From where he stood he caught a glimpse of the lit parking lights of a vehicle sitting around a corner of the building in front of his four-car garage. He could hear the motor idling and for a moment considered investigating, then decided it was more important to check on Meg first. He hurried up the walk toward the sprawling home constructed in the middle of the woods two miles from the playhouse. Jimmy Lee had built the twenty-thousand-square-foot monolith for them fifteen years ago as a wedding present. They never used most of it, Bo thought to himself as he opened the front door. The house was a perfect symbol of how little Jimmy Lee had understood Bo and Meg's life.

"Hi, Bo."

Michael Mendoza stood in the spacious foyer. Meg was on the first step of the wide staircase, leaning against its oak banister, dressed in a sheer robe. Bo had the impression that Mendoza had been standing near Meg, then had backed off quickly as the door opened. And Meg seemed distracted. "What are you doing here, Michael?" Bo asked suspiciously.

"I wanted to say goodbye before I left. I have to be back in Washington by noon for a meeting."

"Today is Sunday."

"Days of the week don't matter in Washington. You know that."

Bo shut the door. "Where have you been for the last hour? I tried to find you at Jimmy Lee's place but no one had seen you."

"I ended up having a long conversation with Paul," Mendoza explained.

That sounded reasonable. No one had seen Paul either.

"I thought I'd try to act as mediator between the two of you," Mendoza continued, "now that you are officially Warfield's chief executive officer. You and Paul will have to develop a working relationship whether you and he like it or not, and I wanted to help him understand that." He paused. "Congratulations on your victory this evening. Ashley's timing was impeccable."

"What was Paul's reaction to your suggestion?"

Mendoza sighed. "Unfortunately, his attitude toward your return continues to be a work in progress."

"It doesn't matter," Bo muttered. "Paul and Frank Ramsey will have to deal with me now whether they like it or not."

"I'm going to bed," Meg announced, moving across the foyer to where Bo stood. "Don't be long, sweetheart," she said, kissing him on the cheek. "Please get Michael out of here," she whispered into his ear as she hugged him tightly. She pulled back and smiled politely at Mendoza. "Good night, Michael."

"Good night." Mendoza watched Meg ascend the steps gracefully. "She's a wonderful woman, Bo," he commented when she had turned the corner at the top of the long staircase.

"Yes, she is." Bo dropped the Explorer keys in an ashtray on a table by the door. "Where did you meet with Paul?"

"In that small room off of your father's study."

"And when you were finished you came here?"

"Yes. Jimmy Lee's place was pretty empty when Paul and I were done. I figured you had come home." He motioned toward the stairs. "I'm sorry to have awakened Meg, but I really wanted to see you."

"It's all right. She can sleep late tomorrow."

Mendoza tilted his head to one side and gave Bo a quizzical expression. "What's the matter?"

"What are you talking about?"

Mendoza wagged a finger at Bo. "I've known you too long, Bolling. I know when something isn't right. You weren't your usual self with me when I first saw you at the reception this afternoon." He clasped his hands behind his back. "Meg too, although I've become accustomed to her keeping me at arm's length since Ginny died. I know she didn't approve of my need for companionship."

"She and Ginny were close, and Meg's just being loyal to an old friend. You shouldn't worry about her attitude."

"I don't," Mendoza said, "but I do worry about yours. There was a tension between us this afternoon that I've never sensed before."

Bo started to say something, then stopped.

"What is it, Bo? If there's something bothering you, let me know," Mendoza urged. "We've always been able to talk things through."

That was true, Bo thought. He couldn't lose sight of how often Michael had been there for him when no one in the family had. "When we were out in Wyoming," Bo began, "you mentioned that Jimmy Lee had called while you were on the plane waiting to take off from Reagan National."

A troubled expression came to Mendoza's face. "So?"

"That was how you knew what my Jeep looked like. Jimmy Lee gave you the license plate number during the telephone call, right?"

"Yes," Mendoza said slowly, trying to anticipate where the inquiry was leading.

"But I checked the long distance account for Jimmy Lee's office telephone," Bo went on, "and there was no record of him placing a call to you on that date. He never owned a cell phone, and you and I both know that in the last few years of his life he rarely left the estate. If he called you that day, it was from his office phone."

Mendoza's mouth fell open slightly. "*If* he called me?"

"As I said, there's no record."

"Then I must have called him. We spoke on many occasions over the past few months, and excuse me if I'm confused on who called whom on exactly which day," Mendoza replied testily. "I'll be happy to provide you with records for my phone, but I'm not certain I see the significance," he said. "Is there anything else?"

"Yes." Bo reached into his jacket and produced the memo from Mendoza to Jimmy Lee about forming the Warfield Executive Committee in case of the elder Hancock's death. A structure essentially freezing Bo out of Warfield. "Here," he said, thrusting the paper at Mendoza.

"What's this?"

"It's a memo I found shoved in a box on the third floor of Jimmy Lee's place. It proposes a new executive committee structure to be implemented at Warfield Capital in the event of my father's death. The exact structure that was implemented. The structure that almost kept me out of Warfield for good." Bo hesitated. "The memo was written by you."

Mendoza glanced up from the page. "You think I wanted to keep you out of Warfield?" he asked incredulously. "Why would I want that?"

Bo shrugged. That was the problem. He couldn't figure out a motive either. "I don't know."

Mendoza scanned the memo once more, then handed it back to Bo. "I've never seen this memo before in my life."

Bo took the paper and replaced it in his jacket pocket. "You know nothing about it?" he asked hesitantly.

"Nothing." Mendoza pointed at Bo's pocket. "The entire memo is typed. Anyone could have written it. Paul could have written that to keep you off balance, then put it someplace he knew you'd look." Mendoza moved to where Bo stood and firmly clasped the younger man's shoulder. "The most difficult thing in life is figuring out who your true friends are, Bolling, because it's a real rat-fuck out there," he said. "Most people in the world are out for themselves and if you get in their way, they'll screw you. But there are those who really care about you and you should never question their loyalty. I am one of those people." Mendoza patted Bo on the back. "I forgive you for this episode. Now walk me to my car because I have to leave."

Bo nodded respectfully, already regretting his decision to confront Michael about the telephone calls and the memo. Life had been turned upside down over the past few days, and he was suddenly worried that the awful series of events had affected his judgment. Michael had always been a true friend and here he was accusing him of treason without a motive.

When they reached the corner of the mansion near the garage, they stopped beneath the arc of a flood-light. Mendoza's Lincoln Town Car—the vehicle Bo had spotted on his way in—was parked fifty feet away. Bo could see the faint outline of Mendoza's driver reading a newspaper by a map light. "I appreciate your speaking to Paul," Bo said, his voice low. "I mean that."

"You're welcome." Mendoza shook his head. "I fear Paul is at a crossroads in life."

"What do you mean?"

"There was a noticeable scent of perfume in the room off the study when I first went in there with him this evening."

"Really?"

"Yes." The floodlights glinted off Mendoza's silver hair. "I couldn't place it until now."

"The perfume?"

"Yes, it was the perfume that woman who was with Evan Reese was wearing tonight. Reese's date. What was her name?"

"Alecia."

"Right." Mendoza hesitated. "Paul better watch out," he warned. "Proof of infidelity can still be a problem in a presidential campaign. The American public still sets a high standard on that issue."

"He knows that," Bo answered, shaking his head. "He just can't seem to help himself."

"The idiot," Mendoza muttered. "The road to the White House is so clear for Paul. All he has to do is keep himself out of trouble and he'll win. People would die for that opportunity."

"That's always been the challenge for our family. We always seem to be battling our own demons, not others'. We should be supporting each other, not tearing each other apart."

"I agree," Mendoza answered curtly, still annoyed at the third degree he had faced in the foyer. "Oh, by the way, I have spoken to my friends at the Bureau about the picture we found in that motel in Libby, Montana. They're following up. They will keep their investigation very quiet."

"Thanks, Michael," Bo said hoarsely, embarrassed at how he had cross-examined his old friend.

Mendoza started to gesture to his driver, then stopped. "Oh, one more thing."

"What?"

"When we met at the Waldorf the other day, you said you were concerned about the market exacting revenge on Warfield now that Jimmy Lee is gone. I believe you called it a market attack."

"Yes, I did."

"Any indication of that this past week?"

Bo shook his head. "Nothing yet, but it's still early. People are sizing us up. I can feel it. In fact, I saw a guy named Nick Kaplan at the reception today who'd love nothing more than to see us feel pain. It's just a damn good thing I won that vote tonight. A good thing Ashley came home when she did."

"But you didn't find anything in the portfolio this past week that would lead you to believe there could be a serious problem."

"Nothing yet." Bo hadn't found anything alarming, but it would take time to be thorough. Warfield's private equity portfolio was massive and there were many ways Ramsey could mask what was really going on. "There was one odd thing."

"What?" Mendoza asked quickly.

"Frank Ramsey changed our auditors while I was in Montana. We were using PricewaterhouseCoopers, one of the Big Five accounting firms. Now we're using some no-name firm out of California."

"Perhaps you should check them out."

"I am." Allen Taylor was already working on it.

Mendoza thought for a moment. "Say there is a problem in the portfolio. What could happen? What are you most afraid of?"

"That Frank Ramsey bought a lot of something that isn't worth very much because he doesn't know what the hell he's doing." Bo gritted his teeth. "I'm worried that Ramsey has hidden the fact that he's bought the stuff and buried it so deeply that I won't find it until it's too late."

"Just how leveraged is Warfield?" Mendoza asked.

"If I can believe the reports I've been reviewing, almost fifteen to one," Bo answered. "For each dollar of equity we have, we've borrowed almost fifteen dollars. When I left, our asset level was a hundred billion. Now it's two hundred billion and we've added only a small amount of equity relative to our capital base."

"So if the value of Warfield's assets drops ten percent, then—"

"Then we're underwater," Bo finished the thought. "And that's where the problem lies. If we can't settle a transaction quickly because of liquidity problems, the market will find out and go ballistic. The result will be swift and terrible."

Mendoza glanced into the darkness. "If there's ever a problem," he said, his voice dropping, "call me at this number." He reached into his pocket and produced a card. "If for some reason you can't get me, you can speak to my aide, Angela Burns. She is at this number. Describe the problem and tell her who you are. She will be able to help in case I'm not around."

"What exactly are you talking about?" Bo asked, wanting to make certain he understood the details of what Mendoza was offering.

"If that scenario plays out and you need money to keep Warfield propped up, I can be of help."

"You mean you could find emergency funds for me."

"Exactly."

"We could be talking a couple of hundred million dollars, maybe even a billion, Michael."

"I don't care," Mendoza said firmly.

"How could you do this?" Bo asked.

"One of my best friends on the Hill is Senator Pittman from Texas, chairman of the Finance Committee."

"So?"

Mendoza took a deep breath. "Senator Pittman is very worried about the status of the largest hedge funds in this country. He believes that major ones need to be monitored more rigorously because of what we were just discussing, the leverage factor inherent in these types of investment vehicles. Not many Americans know how close our financial system came to collapsing last year when that huge hedge fund, Long Term Capital, almost went down. So many large banks had lent LTC money that when the fund's assets suddenly lost value and the firm couldn't pay up, we almost had a meltdown. Only a last-minute rescue package organized by some people at the highest levels of America's financial circles and the federal government saved this country from a very nasty situation. Senator Pittman is willing to take extraordinary measures to prevent that from happening again." Mendoza looked into the darkness again. "As I said, Pittman can make accommodations in case you run into trouble. I mean, lending Warfield money is ultimately much cheaper than facing a market meltdown, right?"

"Absolutely."

"When things have settled down, you'll pay us back."

"That's a very generous offer, Michael. I don't plan to ever take you up on it."

"I hope you never need to." Mendoza checked his watch, then waved to his driver. "Ready," he called.

"Yes, sir," the driver called back through the open window, putting the newspaper down on the leather seat beside him. He reached for the key to the Town Car's ignition.

"It's been wonderful to reconnect with you over the

past few days," Mendoza said, gripping Bo's hand. "But I don't want to feel like I'm being interrogated—"

Mendoza's words were obliterated by a massive explosion that rocked the ground beneath them. In an instant, the limousine had exploded into a massive fireball that enveloped both of them.

Harold Shaw's trip from Jimmy Lee's funeral reception in Connecticut back to his beachfront home in tony East Hampton, Long Island, had taken five hours—twice as long as it should have—because of a ten-mile backup at the Throgs Neck Bridge. The delay had been caused by a man who had ultimately taken a death plunge from the middle of the long suspension bridge into Long Island Sound. Shaw's limousine driver had chosen to detour into Manhattan, and this had turned out to be an equally bad option because construction snarled the traffic on this route. Shaw could have taken a helicopter and the trip would have been finished in less than an hour, but he was deathly afraid of flying.

Shaw hardly noticed the delay. He sat hunched in the back of the limousine, reading light on, poring over American Financial Group internal reports, engrossed in the daily business of the company he loved. He was ecstatic with the company's recent performance, and it was sweet to see such outstanding results. AFG was performing with the efficiency of a well-oiled machine, taking advantage of huge operating synergies at every turn so that Shaw could offer cheaper and cheaper financial services to America's consumers and drive his competition out of business.

The driver eased to a stop in front of Shaw's large stone house overlooking the Atlantic Ocean, then hopped out and moved hurriedly to Shaw's door. The driver was eager to return to the city. It was after two in the morning, but he had the rest of the night off and there was a party that would be going strong until noon. He had a small bag of cocaine in his coat pocket, and he planned to snort some at the end of the driveway before getting on the road. That would keep him awake for the long drive back into Manhattan.

"Here we are, sir," he said, opening the door.

Shaw hesitated a moment, struck by something he had noticed as the driver had opened the door. Something that didn't look right about the numbers. He made a note on the page to remind himself to review the issue tomorrow, then stuffed the reports in his briefcase and climbed out of the limousine. "I'll need you here by noon tomorrow," he ordered.

The driver touched his hat. "Yes, sir." He waited for Shaw to let himself into a side door of his home, then trotted back to the limousine and slipped in behind the wheel. Moments later he was tooling back down the driveway.

Shaw flicked the light switch inside the door several times but nothing happened. "Dammit!" He checked over his shoulder and saw the limousine's taillights moving swiftly away. "He wouldn't know what to do anyway," Shaw muttered to himself, fumbling through his briefcase in the darkness for his cell phone.

Shaw didn't see the shadow moving stealthily through the small entry room toward him and felt only a momentary numbness as a smooth, blunt object slammed into his neck.

The man smiled as he stood over Shaw's limp body.

They had him doing what he loved to do again and he was thankful. He had no idea why they had wanted him to break into the Harlem office and be caught, but he had done as they had asked and he had been rewarded accordingly.

Harold Shaw's body would never be found. The billionaire's disappearance would remain one of New York's great unsolved mysteries.

CHAPTER 14

Scully was having a torturous time keeping his eyes open as he guided the rented Taurus across what seemed like an endless Iowa cornfield through the half-light of dawn. All he could think of while he rushed past freshly tilled, ebony soil was that he faced at least another sixteen hours of consciousness before he could give in to the inevitable. At this point he'd been awake for three straight days, monitoring the weekend's critical events.

He had tried everything to fight off the drowsiness. He'd lowered all four windows so that fresh air blasted his face, turned the radio on full-volume, and guzzled a gallon of high-test coffee since landing several hours ago at Minneapolis–St. Paul International Airport. Nothing had worked, and when his chin bobbed on his chest and the car's right tires skidded on side-of-the-road gravel for the third time in as many minutes, he shook his head savagely and slammed the dashboard. "Dammit!" He had less than ten miles to go, but he was going to end up roadkill if he didn't wake up.

So he stuck his forefinger in his mouth and slashed the soft tissue of his upper gum with his nail. He tasted blood and right away was wide awake. Stimulating the gums, particularly with pain, awakened his body more quickly than a shot of Adrenalin. It was one of many techniques he had learned during survival training at a remote North Carolina base years ago. But the effect was only temporary, which was why he had waited until the homestretch to execute it.

Several miles down the lonely road Scully slowed the Taurus to a crawl, then turned left onto a dirt road leading off toward an oasis of trees in the distance. After a bumpy, dusty five-minute ride, he guided the car past two tall blue-and-silver Harvestore silos and an adjacent barn, in front of which were parked several tractors and two huge combines. He pulled to an abrupt halt in front of a pristine white-clapboard farmhouse encircled by tall maples. As he stepped from the car, the irritating ping of a key-left-in-the-ignition warning violated the early morning stillness.

"Hello, Scully."

Scully peered through the gray light toward a wide, screened-in porch running along the entire front of the house. "Hello," he called back. He could make out various dark forms on the porch—which he assumed were furniture—but couldn't see who had spoken. Then the screen door opened and Gerald Wallace emerged.

"You're late," Wallace announced, moving down the porch steps and striding across the lawn.

"Sorry," Scully apologized, shutting the car door. His plane out of New York had been delayed and there was nothing he could have done, as Wallace undoubtedly knew, but Scully didn't protest. Wallace was a demanding man who cared little about excuses, only results, a trait Scully admired even though at the moment he was being unjustly criticized. The country needed men of character like Wallace.

"I know the plane was late," Wallace conceded, extending his hand in greeting, "but you should have stuck a gun in the pilot's ear or something." He allowed himself a slight smile.

"That would have been subtle."

"I get tired of being subtle."

Scully chuckled as he shook Wallace's hand. Wallace was famous for his lack of patience. "Hello, Senator."

"Joseph."

Wallace was of average height and build, with thinning gray hair and a grizzled face that still bore scars from the acne of his youth. He was dressed in work boots, grimy jeans, and a red plaid shirt, sleeves rolled up to his armpits. A box of Marlboros rested atop one shoulder, held in place by the rolled-up sleeve. He wore a green John Deere cap as well as his typical pained expression—like he was constantly shitting razor blades, Scully thought.

Wallace had retired from the United States Senate two years before, after five terms and thirty years. During his last two terms he had served as chairman of the Armed Services Committee. Throughout his career he had been a key member of the military and intelligence establishments, personally responsible for ensuring that many of America's high-tech weapons were developed and deployed. Politicians of both parties had fought epic battles against him in the eighties during the days of huge budget deficits as Wallace had continued to push for massive military expenditures despite a lack of government funding. Now that America's military might had produced world supremacy, he was an icon revered on both sides of the Senate's aisle.

After retiring, Wallace had returned to his native Iowa to take over the family farm. His brother, who had run the farm for many years, had recently died, and the sister-in-law wanted to sell the property to a large corporate operator. So Wallace had stepped in and purchased her share of the land, matching the price of the corporate suitor, who wisely declined to make a higher bid. At sixty-seven Wallace still rose each morning before the sun to tend five hundred acres.

A grizzled Iowa senator retiring to a family farm had made for wonderful press, but the scenario was not quite as advertised. Rows of corn and soybeans flourished in the surrounding fields, but the property had a second, more complex reason for being. The "Nest," as it was known to a select cell of the U.S. intelligence community, served as headquarters for the Secrecy Agency, the SA, the country's most covert operation. Only ten people inside the government knew of the SA's or the Nest's existence, and only three knew of the Nest's exact location.

Scully's eyes narrowed. Wallace alone knew the identity of that other individual, whom Scully assumed was at the very top of the SA cell.

Wallace motioned toward the barn. "Take a walk with me," he ordered, his boots crunching on gravel. "How did this weekend go?"

"Extremely well."

"Give me details."

"At two o'clock this morning, Harold Shaw, CEO of the American Financial Group, disappeared without a trace. When Shaw's disappearance is made public early this week, our man, Bob Johnson, will be named acting CEO at a special AFG board meeting."

"As Jim Whitacre was named CEO of Global Media after Richard Randolph died in Korea."

"Exactly."

Wallace patted Scully on the back. "You came through on that one, Joseph. Shooting Randolph and Whitacre to make it appear as if they were both targets. I heard Whitacre was screaming like a baby while he was lying in the street."

"It was a flesh wound," Scully said, dismissing Whitacre's suffering with a quick wave of his hand. "I barely grazed him."

"All the same, it was very convincing."

"Thanks."

"He was pretty pissed off when he found out what you had done," Wallace observed, a wry grin on his face. "The fact that you had actually been aiming at him, I mean."

"Tough," Scully answered indifferently. "If he's that pissed off, he can come and tell me about it himself."

Wallace took a deep breath and gazed at the vast horizon. He had grown up on this land and had an affection for it beyond words. "Now both AFG and Global Media are free to work with Online Associates."

"Through the cutout."

"Yes. Cooperation among the three entities can be much more open," Wallace continued, "and therefore more effective. Everything is finally coming together." They reached the barn and Wallace unlocked a small side door.

"RANSACK has incredible reach," Scully observed. "The tentacles are becoming longer, wider, and more effective by the day. The operation has achieved one hundred percent penetration. Now it's simply a matter of being able to reach targets in multiple ways without specific investigations. The more information we have on certain parties the better off we are."

"How are we on capacity?" Wallace wanted to know.

"We constantly need more storage, but the wonderful thing about computers is that we can keep them in remote locations. Here, for example."

"That's all well and good, but you know as well as I do that people can still break into them and find out what we're doing no matter where they are kept," Wallace warned.

Scully shook his head. "Our people assure me that they are well ahead of any existing intrusion technology. No one can violate our systems."

"That's exactly what people out there are saying about the networks and systems we're breaking into right now," Wallace scoffed. "You're naïve if you think we're one hundred percent secure. It's a one-up proposition with computers just as it is with weapons. You build the perfect guided missile, then someone figures out a way to knock it down. Then someone else comes up with a superior cloaking device so it can't be knocked down. The cycle of escalation never ends. I spent thirty years inside the arms race—which is exactly what RANSACK is, a weapon." Wallace paused. "Except that we aren't fighting Communist insurgents or Muslim terrorists anymore. The targets in this case are ninety million households within our borders, although we can easily scale it to include the rest of the globe." His eyes took on a faraway look. "Perfect information," he said softly. "The ability to know everything there is to know about an individual. Medical records, financial situation, even sexual history. The ability to inspect every check ever written, every medical report ever issued, every cash withdrawal made, every item purchased by credit card, every service paid for over the Internet, every e-mail written or received, every Web site visited, every telephone call made."

"It's an awesome force," Scully agreed.

"More powerful than the traditional weapons I worked with most of my career," Wallace conceded. "Thank God we anticipated the end of Echelon and made provisions."

Echelon—an existing network of electronic-intercept stations and deep space satellites put in place to capture all microwave, cellular, satellite, and fiber-optic communications—was designed literally to monitor all communications around the globe. Wallace had watched as Echelon, operated by the United States, Canada, Britain, Australia, and New Zealand, came under scrutiny from consumer protection groups and nonparticipating countries. Since Echelon's technology was aging and it was unable to pick up an increasing number of communications, he realized the time had come for a new more powerful surveillance system.

"RANSACK is so much more powerful anyway, and it will be years before anyone unearths its existence," Wallace continued. "People will be so focused on destroying Echelon, it won't cross their minds that we might have developed another way to look in on their personal lives." He sneered. "Even though people know Echelon exists, the NSA won't officially admit to it for some time."

Scully laughed loudly. "They've got camera crews outside Menwith Hill round the clock now and we still won't admit to what's going on." Menwith Hill, England, was one of Echelon's largest installations. "It's amazing how fearful people are of what the government sees."

"They should be." Wallace grunted. "It's amazing how much the average person has to hide, to what lengths he'll go to hide it, and how easily he can be manipulated if the damaging or embarrassing information is uncovered." He shook his head. "It's the opposite of conventional warfare. In the face of insurmountable military opposition, people will continue to fight. They'll live like rats with bombs exploding all around them. Their resolve turns to steel. But in the face of humiliating personal information being widely revealed about them or their family members, human resolve disintegrates like sugar in coffee. Death is acceptable, honorable in fact, but public ridicule is intolerable, particularly for prominent people."

"I'm glad I'm on this side of the fence," Scully admitted.

"But, of course, the fence moves."

Scully glanced up. "What the hell does that mean?"

"It means we monitor everyone," Wallace snapped, his expression turning intense. "But I'm pleased to inform you that with no wife, no children, and no discernable vices you would appear to be untouchable, which is why we like you." He held up his hand. "Except that at this point we have the ability to plant things on or about people as well. We can fabricate very credible wrongdoings about anyone based upon an individual's personal data bank maintained in our files." He let out a long pleased breath. "Of course, it's still more effective to find an authentic skeleton in the closet. We would have to work very hard to manipulate you. Fortunately you are in the minority." He gestured at the horizon. "Most people out there are vulnerable because they have done things in their past that their family, friends, or society in general would scorn them for. That negative history allows us to manipulate policy whichever way we choose. If someone is getting in the way of what we want, we pay him or her a timely visit." He turned toward Scully. "As you have done with that bastard who would have killed the submarine project this country so desperately needs. As you have done with Dr. Silwa."

Scully shook his head. "It's so easy. They give up so fast."

"I told you, people are weak when it comes to their personal lives being exposed." Wallace ducked through a small side door of the barn and walked down a narrow passageway dimly lit by several dusty bare bulbs. "All of that computer storage capacity will cost a great deal of money," Wallace said over his shoulder, thinking about numbers now.

"Not as much as you might believe," Scully disagreed gently. He was well aware that Wallace was conditioned to think about hundreds of billions. The price tag here would run into the billions, but not by as much as Wallace assumed. "Besides, we've already moved a great deal of money offshore. The green has turned black. It's gone for good. Spirited off into the cosmos and impossible to trace. Even if someone sniffed something wrong, they'd never be able to follow the trail back to us."

"How much have we moved to date?"

"Two billion."

"On top of what we already put into the cutout last year?"

"Yes."

"Good." Wallace unlocked another door and flicked on a light. "Wipe your feet, will you?"

Scully wiped his shoes on a mat beside the door, then stepped into RANSACK's brain—an immaculate room lined with the most technologically advanced supercomputers in the world, commercially unavailable even to the few companies that could have afforded their outrageous sticker prices. Available to Wallace through his contacts at the Pentagon and his years on the Armed Services Committee. "Jesus," Scully whispered, gazing through the eerie blue light at the stacks of servers. Wallace had never allowed him in here. "This is incredible."

"Yes, and it's directly linked to Online Associates in Virginia." Wallace locked the door behind them. "Have a seat," he directed as he sat down himself in front of a console. "What about Michael Mendoza?" he asked, typing on a keyboard. "What happened to him?"

Scully sat down beside Wallace. "That was the only cluster-fuck of the weekend," he said hesitantly.

Wallace stopped typing for a moment. "What do you mean?"

"Apparently the incendiary device went off prematurely."

"Apparently?"

"Mendoza was rushed to a New York City hospital by medevac helicopter."

"But he's not dead, is he?"

Scully shook his head. "Not yet. He's hanging on."

"What about Bo Hancock? The initial report I received was that he was hit by the same blast."

"Yes."

"What is his condition?"

"He was choppered to the same hospital."

"And?"

Scully hesitated. "I received an initial report that he had died on the way, but I was informed later that the report was inaccurate. I don't know the truth yet. I'm to receive an update in an hour."

"I hope it's good news." Wallace punched the ENTER button on the keyboard. "Frank Ramsey reports that Bo has been rooting around in the Warfield private equity portfolio."

"I'm sure Jimmy Lee buried the cutout too deeply for anyone to find. It was there before Bo was sent to Montana, and he never found it."

"He wasn't looking." Wallace rubbed his pocked nose. "He could find the funding source as well, the investor link. That wasn't in place until after Bo left. That's partly why Jimmy Lee kicked him out." Wallace typed another command. "He knew Bo would never go along with the program. He's too small-minded to understand the incredible importance of what we're doing."

"So we take Bo out if the news from the hospital isn't good."

"We need to lay low for a bit. Someone might start piecing things together if Bo turned up dead too."

Scully frowned. "We'll have to do something if Bo continues to dig." He gazed at the blinking computers all around him. More than anything, he wanted to know who sat at the top of the cell. Who was running the show.

"I guess you won't need your update after all," Wallace said, pointing at a screen.

"What do you mean?"

"Bo Hancock has been upgraded from critical to stable."

"How do you know?" Scully squinted at the screen.

"It's all right there."

"That information is coming from the—"

"From the hospital's mainframe computer," Wallace explained triumphantly. "The people in Fairfax are good, let me tell you that." He typed another command. "Looks like Mendoza might make it too," he observed, as Mendoza's update appeared on the screen. "There will be some unhappy people if he does," he said, glancing at Scully.

"We'll try again. We won't miss this time. I'll give the order tomorrow."

Wallace shook his head. "You will wait for my orders before you try again. Are we absolutely clear on that?"

Scully glanced up. There had been an unmistakable sharpness to Wallace's tone. "Yes, sir."

Meg guided the Explorer into a narrow space between two economy-size cars, hopped down from the cab, and walked quickly toward a stairwell located in a far corner of the midtown Manhattan parking garage. On her way into the city from the estate she had detoured to Long Island for a few minutes to see her mother, who had caught a cold over the weekend. After leaving her parents' house for the city she had encountered unexpectedly bad traffic on the Long Island Expressway. Then she'd been forced to drive up seven levels of the garage before finding an open spot. So now she was late. As she broke into a trot, her hard-soled shoes clicked on the cement floor.

At first she believed the second set of footsteps behind her was an echo, but as she reached the stairwell and glanced back over her shoulder, she realized she was wrong. The man wasn't physically imposing, but the look in his eye brought terror to her heart. Somehow she knew he had come for her, and even as she tore down the first lonely flight of stairs, she was aware that he seemed vaguely familiar.

Meg took two and three steps at a time, racing downward in panic, but she sensed that he was gaining on her. She could hear his heavy footsteps churning after her. As she reached the fifth floor she caught sight of him to her right in her peripheral vision, then instantly felt talonlike fingers grabbing for her shoulder from over the railing. She screamed and careened into the wall to avoid him. He was only a few feet behind now.

As Meg turned at the top of the stairs on the fourth floor, her foot slipped. For an instant she hung there, balanced precariously on the edge of the step. Then she pitched forward and tumbled down, her legs unable to keep pace with her upper body. Just before her head and shoulder slammed into the brick wall on the third-floor landing, she remembered where she had seen her pursuer. He had been behind her on the sidewalk outside Penn Station just before she had been pushed in front of the oncoming taxi. Then the world went dark.

"Bo?"

Bo looked up. An overnight bag was lying open on the bed. "Hello, doctor," he said, smiling despite the dull ache that enveloped his entire body.

"What are you doing?" Silwa asked, shuffling into the private room.

"Packing."

The doctor rolled his eyes. "They brought you in here on a stretcher less than eighteen hours ago. Why don't you at least stay tonight to be safe? I'd like to run some more tests on you."

"I'm fine," Bo assured Silwa. He had no intention of spending another hour in the hospital.

"You're being—"

"Stubborn?" Ashley interrupted. "Was that what you were about to say, Dr. Silwa?" She sat in a chair by the window. "Are you surprised? Imagine, Bolling Hancock, stubborn. What a shock." She stood up. "Just say the word, Doctor, and I'll make him stay."

Bo flashed her a grin. They had spent the whole morning catching up on twenty years apart. He had missed her more than he'd realized. "Pay no attention to my sister," Bo instructed. "She talks a big game but her bark is worse than her bite. I mean, look at her."

"I may be small," Ashley warned good-naturedly, putting up her fists as if she wanted to fight, "but I can hold my own with anyone."

Bo chuckled. Five two and a hundred pounds dripping wet, Ashley had jet-black hair, dark eyes, full lips, and perfect, creamy skin. A natural athlete, she had captained the field hockey team in high school, then at Harvard. She had a feisty personality that never allowed her to let things lie. Good or bad, you always knew where you stood with her. It was a trait Bo had appreciated since their childhood. "Back off, little girl."

Ashley stuck her tongue out as she dropped her hands.

"Let me see your arm," Silwa demanded, moving to where Bo stood beside the bed.

"I told you, I'm fine."

"Let me see it. If you don't, I'll keep you here for a week."

"You can't do that."

"I most certainly can. I'll have you quarantined. I'll

explain to the state board of health that you are displaying symptoms of an exotic virus."

"You wouldn't."

"Try me," Silwa dared, rolling up Bo's sleeve. "I know you're hiding something bad."

"What do you mean?"

"This is the first time I've seen you with your sleeves rolled down." Silwa gingerly peeled back a bandage covering most of Bo's left forearm, revealing a grisly mass of burned flesh.

Ashley glanced at it, then quickly looked away. "Does he need to stay, Doctor?" she asked seriously.

"That's like asking a barber if you need a haircut," Bo cut in, reattaching the bandage with a roll of medical tape he had picked up from the bed.

"He should stay," Silwa advised.

"But I'm not going to."

"Mr. Hancock?" A nurse stood in the doorway, a wheelchair in front of her.

"What's this?" Silwa asked.

"Transportation I don't need," Bo replied. "Thank you, nurse, but I'll be walking out of here under my own power."

"Hospital rules," the woman said firmly, rolling the wheelchair into Bo's room.

"I haven't even signed a release form," Silwa protested.

"But I knew you would." Bo pulled a pen from his shirt pocket and handed it to Silwa. "Get to it."

Silwa hesitated, then moved to the end of the bed, picked up a clipboard hanging from the bed frame, and scribbled his signature.

"Good man."

"You're lucky, Bo."

"Why do you say that?" Bo asked, tossing a shirt Meg had brought to the hospital for him last night into the bag.

"Michael Mendoza is down the hall hooked up to all kinds of tubes." Silwa pointed at Bo's arm. "That burn you sustained is nasty as hell, but it isn't life-threatening. When they brought Mendoza in here, they weren't sure he was going to make it. It's still touch-and-go for him."

"Why was I so lucky?"

"The blast threw you back onto the lawn. It blew Mendoza against the side of the house. He has critical head injuries."

"Can I see him?" Bo asked, his voice subdued.

"No visitors," Silwa replied.

"Have the authorities found out anything yet?"

"I don't know." Silwa tossed the clipboard with the signed release form onto the unmade bed.

"Ready to go?" the nurse holding the wheelchair asked.

Bo checked his watch. "My wife was supposed to be here fifteen minutes ago. I don't want to leave without her. It's not like Meg to be late."

"Well, I have other patients to attend to. Can you call her on her cell—"

"Doctor!" Another nurse appeared in the doorway and beckoned to Silwa. "Please."

"Excuse me, Bo." Silwa hurried from the room.

"Look, I'll be fine," Bo said, turning to the woman behind the wheelchair. "I won't tell anyone that you—"

"Bolling!" Silwa reappeared in the doorway, a grave expression on his face.

"What is it?"

"Come with me quickly. It's Meg. She's in the emergency room."

*   *   *

They had arrived six weeks ago in a sealed brown envelope. Inside there had been no note claiming responsibility for the hideous contents—two graphic pictures which, since the day they'd been delivered, had accompanied him everywhere. Constantly buried in a pocket because he was too afraid to let them out of his immediate control. Even as he campaigned more successfully each day, they lay nestled close to his heart. As he shook hands with blue-haired ladies at auxiliary luncheons and kissed babies at hospitals. As he smiled sincerely at future constituents and promised to do good work.

Paul sat behind Jimmy Lee's desk gazing vacantly at the photographs that lay before him. He had his own study in his own home just over the hill, but he found that it gave him comfort to come here and sit in his father's chair. It gave him a soothing sense that Jimmy Lee was still looking over his shoulder and that everything would eventually be all right.

He put his wineglass down and picked up one of the photographs. It was a picture of Melissa's battered face and bruised neck as she lay on the sand, eyes wide open, her corneas a ghastly red. He dropped the picture and picked up the second one. The same image stared back at him, except that in this photograph there were hands grasping Melissa's neck. His hands. Paul could see the unmistakable brown birthmark on the third knuckle of his left hand.

Paul shut his eyes, churning in his mind, through the events leading up to Melissa's death, as he had so many times over the years. They'd been swimming in the playhouse pool when she had impulsively decided to go to the lake, pulling him through the mansion and down the hill by the wrist, both of them naked. At the bottom of the hill he'd fallen to the sand in a drunken stupor and closed his eyes for what seemed like only seconds. When he had awakened, she was facedown in the water. She must have drowned, he reasoned, but there were those marks on her neck and the blood-filled corneas. Sure signs that she had been strangled. He grimaced and looked away as the photograph began to tremble in his hand. Then he stuffed both photographs hurriedly into the top drawer of the desk at the sound of a rap on the study door.

"Come in."

Frank Ramsey entered the room.

"Sit down," Paul ordered.

"What can I do for you?" Ramsey asked, sinking into a chair on the other side of the desk.

"I want an update on Bo."

"We could have done that by phone."

"You and I will not use phones to communicate important information from now on," Paul said quickly. "Not even land lines. Do you understand me?"

"All right."

"We will arrange meetings by phone and that will be all."

"All right," Ramsey agreed again, trying to understand what was going on. Paul seemed distracted, almost to the point of panic.

Ramsey was certain that the full scope of Warfield Capital's business had never been made clear to him. Upon joining, his primary assignment had been to run the firm as Bo had, following the strategies and disciplines Bo had implemented. Ramsey would take no major risks, and under no circumstances would he allow anyone to uncover Warfield's massive investment in Online Associates, a year-old Internet-infrastructure company based in Fairfax, Virginia, just outside of Washington, D.C. That was all they had told him. It was mysterious, but he hadn't cared. The investment bank he'd been working for had been about to fire him for exceeding his trading limits and losing the firm a significant amount of money. The position at Warfield allowed him to keep his situation quiet and maintain the lifestyle to which he had become accustomed. Jimmy Lee would pay him two million a year and give him an interest, albeit tiny, in the fund. But even a tiny interest in a fund the size of Warfield could be immensely valuable.

Ramsey's immediate superior would be Teddy, but he was also to maintain close contact with a man named Joseph Scully—something that hadn't made any sense to him. Scully didn't appear to be connected with Warfield in any way and was even less numbers-oriented than Teddy. However, Ramsey had complied with his orders, working closely with Scully when Warfield had quietly transferred vast amounts of money down to the little firm in northern Virginia. And then he had learned that Dale Stephenson had somehow become aware of Online Associates.

"Have you spoken to Bo?" Paul asked.

Ramsey shifted uncomfortably in his chair. When Stephenson had turned up dead on a fishing trip, Ramsey had considered the possibility that the timing of Stephenson's accident had been no coincidence. However, he had managed to dismiss the idea that Stephenson had actually been murdered, instead allowing his judgment to be clouded by greed and the fact that his tiny sliver of Warfield Capital could be worth hundreds of millions of dollars. Now Teddy and Tom were gone, and

Bo had almost been killed last night in an explosion. "I spoke to him a few minutes ago, in fact. He called to let me know that he would be coming home to the estate tonight and into Warfield first thing in the morning." Ramsey paused. "He also informed me that Meg had had a bad fall in a parking garage on her way to the hospital."

Paul glanced up from the birthmark on his knuckle. "Is she all right?" he asked quickly.

"She suffered a concussion and a nasty cut on her head, but she will make a full recovery."

Paul nodded. "I'm glad, but I'm still very concerned about Bo's return to Warfield."

Ramsey shook his head. "Bo seems cured, Paul. I don't think you have anything to worry about. I've been watching him closely, and he hasn't been hitting the bottle. He wasn't even drinking at the funeral reception."

"That's not why I'm concerned," Paul snapped.

"What do you mean? I thought you were so worried about his late-night activities screwing up your campaign."

Paul caressed a handle of the desk drawer for a moment before answering. "You and I both know that the real reason I don't want Bo back at Warfield is that I don't want him finding out about our investment in On-line Associates," he finally said. "I don't trust him. He's looking for it, I can feel it."

"What's so important about Online?" Ramsey asked boldly.

Paul considered his reply carefully. "The company has developed a revolutionary technology. We can't allow anyone to go sniffing around down there."

"He's your brother, for Christ's sake."

"All the same, I—" There was a loud knock at the door. "Come in."

Bruce Laird entered the study. "Sorry," he said, stopping at the sight of Ramsey. "I'll wait until you're done."

"No, come in, we're finished." Paul looked at Ramsey. "I want you to stick to Bo like glue. I want to know if he's digging. Now leave us."

When they were alone, Paul pointed at Laird. "Are you having an affair with Catherine?" he asked bluntly.

"What?"

"You heard me, Counselor. Are you and Catherine having an affair?" Paul demanded again, louder this time.

"No."

Paul leaned back in his chair, suspicious of the way Laird had avoided eye contact. "Bo's been doing some digging, Counselor. He's found out about your little problem at Davis Polk eight years ago."

Laird's eyes flashed to Paul's.

"It's time to be done with him. Make it happen."

CHAPTER 15

"It's such a nice evening," Ashley remarked, gazing up through the near darkness at the tall trees towering over them as she came out onto the wide cedar deck spanning the back of Bo's house.

"Very nice." Bo was nursing a glass of water, which sat on the deck railing.

"It's gotten chilly," Ashley observed, placing her scotch glass beside Bo's water and pulling the cardigan sweater she had borrowed from Meg's closet snugly up around her neck. "How's Meg?"

"She's upstairs in our room, resting. She's still kind of out of it."

"I'm sure." Ashley had raced down to the emergency room with Bo and Silwa to find doctors already working on a gaping cut above Meg's eye. "Have you been able to figure out what happened?"

"She doesn't remember much, and I haven't pressed her on it yet, but as far as we can tell, she lost her balance going down a flight of stairs at the parking garage and hit her head at the bottom. Simple as that."

"How awful." Ashley shook her head, imagining the horrible impact.

"She's going to be all right. I've gotten a full-time

nurse, who's upstairs with her now." Bo pulled a cigarette out and lighted it. "I'm going back up there in a few minutes, but I needed a smoke."

"May I have one?"

"Sure." Bo reached into his shirt pocket again and held the pack out for Ashley. "I enjoyed this morning," he said, lighting her cigarette. "It was wonderful to catch up after all these years. I've really missed you."

"I've missed you too." They were silent for a while, watching the darkened treetops sway in the evening breeze against a starlit sky. "What's that?" she asked, pointing through the darkness at the tree line a hundred feet from where they stood. Between the deck and the tree line was a neatly manicured rose garden.

"Where?"

"It's kind of a glow through the trees."

"Oh, that's our carriage house," Bo answered. The three-bedroom house lay a quarter mile away at the end of a driveway that curled past the mansion and meandered through the woods. "We use it when we have families staying overnight with lots of children."

"Should I be staying there?" Ashley was using a guest suite in Bo's house.

"No, no," Bo said quickly. "As I said, we use it when we have families here with lots of kids. I don't care how big a place you have, it's nice to be able to send someone else's children packing when it's time to turn in."

"Agreed," Ashley said, laughing. She had often wondered how Bo would be with children. "How are you feeling?" she asked, nodding toward his arm.

"Fine."

"I don't know why I bothered to ask," she said, rolling

her eyes. "You wouldn't tell me even if that arm was about to fall off."

Bo grunted his response. She was right.

"Since when did you start drinking vodka?" Ashley tapped his glass. "I remember you as a scotch drinker like me."

"This is pure water, Sis," Bo replied proudly, picking the glass up and taking a swallow, thinking how the only time he ever drank vodka in the past was when he had to drive. "I've decided to clean up my act in my old age."

"I never thought I'd hear you say that."

"Me neither," he agreed with a wry smile.

"Have the police or the FBI found out anything about what happened?" Ashley wanted to know, sipping her scotch. "About the explosion, I mean."

"No. This afternoon I spoke to the agent in charge down at the Bureau office in Lower Manhattan, and he said they hadn't made much progress. They are fairly certain the target was Michael Mendoza, but I'm not taking any chances." Bo gestured toward the woods. "I've had our security force doubled." But the estate was so huge, even twice as many men couldn't cover everything.

"How is Michael?"

"I don't know. I called several times today but couldn't get through to his room, and the hospital wouldn't provide any information on his condition. I suppose they are trying to keep a tight lid on this thing, keep it out of the press as long as they can. After all, he is a United States senator."

"Who do you think was behind the explosion?"

Bo shook his head. "I don't know. A man like Michael Mendoza has many enemies."

"I have no doubt," she agreed.

"What?" Bo asked, hearing the unexpected edge in Ashley's voice.

"Nothing," Ashley said quickly. "Have you tried contacting Silwa? He might know what's going on with Michael."

"I tried Silwa twice and couldn't reach him. I left a couple of messages on his cell phone. I know he checks it religiously. The times I've called him he's always called me right back." Bo took a puff from his cigarette. "I hope Michael is all right." He flicked an ash and watched it dive to the ground ten feet below. "I want to thank you, Ashley."

"For what?"

"Saving my ass."

"What do you mean?"

"You were the cavalry. You got here from Europe just in the nick of time. I'm glad you got my messages."

"I could tell from your voice that you really needed me." She looked up into the trees again. "I know this sounds terrible, but I don't think I would have come back just for Jimmy Lee's funeral."

Bo nodded. Jimmy Lee and Ashley had never seen eye to eye. "And I know *this* will sound terrible," he said. "I don't care why you came back, I'm just glad you did. I'm obviously the most qualified member of our family to run Warfield. You did both of us a favor. I'll take care of your share of the wealth better than Frank Ramsey ever would." He hesitated. "Most of all, it's just good to see you."

"Were you surprised they were going to kick you out?" Ashley asked.

"I wasn't surprised at Paul."

"At Catherine?"

"Yes."

"Why?"

"I thought we always had a good relationship. I thought she appreciated the fact that I've tried to look out for her all these years. I suppose I was a fool."

Ashley hesitated. "You can't come between blood," she said solemnly. "You think you can, but when it comes down to it, you really can't."

Bo glanced up. "What did you say?"

"You heard me," Ashley said, her voice turning hoarse.

Bo turned toward her. "You mean you know?"

"Yes."

"That I'm adopted?"

A tear spilled down her soft cheek. "We're both adopted, Bo."

He stared at her for several moments. "When did you find out?" he asked gruffly.

"It was the summer before my senior year of college. I was about to take off for California with my friends for vacation. I was in the attic at Mom and Dad's place looking for some clothes and I found the paperwork." Tears were streaming down her face. "I couldn't believe what I was reading. That you and I were adopted," she said, choking on her words. "You from an agency in Florida and I from one in Texas."

Bo placed his cigarette down in an ashtray beside his glass, then took hers from her shaking fingers and slid his arms around her small shoulders. "It's all right, sweetheart."

"It tore me apart, Bo."

"And you never told me."

"I didn't want you to feel as terrible as I did. I was so

lost when I found out. It was as if I didn't really belong to the Hancock family. As if I wasn't really a part of all of this," she said looking out into the darkness behind the mansion. "Suddenly I understood the sarcastic comments Paul and Teddy had made all those years, and it hurt so badly."

Bo nodded. "I know how you felt, Sis. Exactly how you felt," he said, remembering the emotions that had ripped through him as Paul and Teddy taunted him in the corridor outside Jimmy Lee's hospital room. "It was like I had been an overnight guest all of these years."

"Yes, yes," she agreed, holding on tight, so glad to feel his strong arms wrapped tightly around her.

"Is that why you left?" Bo had wanted to ask her about this for so many years. "Is that why you went to Europe after college and never came back?"

She hesitated. "Partly."

"Partly?"

"There was another reason," she admitted, struggling with the words.

"I missed you so much," Bo said, taking a deep breath. "Maybe I knew. Maybe down deep I always realized that it was you and me against them for more than just the fact that we were the two youngest."

"And didn't look like them or think like them," she added.

"Yes," he agreed reluctantly. "So why did you leave?"

Ashley stepped back from his arms and looked away. "I . . ." But she couldn't finish.

"What, Ashley? Come on," he urged.

"I can't."

"Why not?"

She buried her face in her hands and shook her head. "I just can't."

Bo moved behind her and put his arms around her again. "We used to tell each other everything. Can't we still do that?"

Ashley caressed the back of his hand. "It's something I'm not proud of."

"Whatever it was, it happened almost twenty years ago. The statute of humiliation has run out." He kissed her gently on the forehead. "We've all had moments of indiscretion in our youth that we regret. For God's sake, look who's talking. Now tell me. It can't be that bad." He paused. "It might be important."

"What do you mean?"

"Tell me, Sis, please."

She turned slowly to face him. "Bo, I—"

"Hello."

Bo's head snapped in the direction of the voice. Through the glare coming from a spotlight affixed to an eave high above the deck, he could see Bruce Laird standing by the deck's screen door. "What do you want?" He hadn't heard Laird pull it back and step outside, and he wondered how long Laird had been standing there listening.

"We need to talk, Bolling," Laird said, his voice full of purpose.

"Can't you see I'm busy?" Bo asked angrily. But Ashley broke free from his grasp, bolted for the door, and brushed past Laird as she ducked inside. "Why have you come to my house, Counselor?" he asked curtly as Laird strode across the deck. "What do you want?"

"It's time to talk."

"We have nothing to talk about." Bo grabbed a glass

from the railing and realized as he brought it to his lips that he had picked up Ashley's drink by mistake. The scent of scotch rose tantalizingly to his nostrils and for a moment he considered taking a swallow. Just one lovely sip. It had been only a few days since he'd enjoyed the warm flood of liquor into his system, but it seemed like forever. He took another whiff and could almost taste the scotch running down his throat. "You showed your true colors in my father's study last night," he said, putting the glass down. "You made it clear where your loyalty lies when Paul tried to run me out of Warfield."

"I was doing my job as the family's attorney," Laird retorted. "I was advising you and Paul on legal matters related to Warfield Capital. Making certain that your father's wishes were carried out. That the bylaws were being adhered to properly."

"I know about you, Counselor."

Laird's posture stiffened. "What are you talking about?"

"I know about that problem you had at your law firm before you joined the Hancock family office eight years ago. And I know that several of your clients were involved in organized crime. I know that you did things you shouldn't have." Bo saw the shock registering on Laird's expression. Allen Taylor had done his job well over the past few days. "I also know that during those eight years Jimmy Lee never gave you a raise, and that he never gave you a piece of any Hancock business the way he gave Frank Ramsey a piece of Warfield." Bo paused, allowing what he had said to sink in. "Jimmy Lee didn't have to, because you were screwed. The law firm was about to fire your ass, Counselor. You would have been blacklisted. You had nowhere else to go."

"Shut up, Bo," Laird hissed. "You aren't as smart as you think."

"You couldn't stand Jimmy Lee for what he did to you all those years, could you? Couldn't stand him for manipulating you like some poor puppet. Couldn't stand the fact that he left you with nothing when he died. You have to exact retribution. That vindictive brain of yours won't let you just fade away." Bo pointed at Laird. "I believe you know a great deal more about what's going on at Warfield Capital than you're letting on. If you're smart you'll tell me right now."

"I'm warning you, Bo."

"I suppose I could ask Catherine. You've probably told her everything."

"Why the hell would I do that?"

"You've been having an affair with her for some time."

"I have not."

"Why did Catherine call you the other night when I was at your apartment? I saw the number on your phone. It was Catherine's."

"She wanted me to escort her to her husband's funeral. I felt that was the least I could do for a woman who had just lost her husband."

Caught off guard, Bo didn't know what to say. Taylor had been so certain about the affair.

"You know what I think?"

"What?"

"I think *you're* the one who knows more about what's going on at Warfield than he's letting on. You are a relentless man, Bo Hancock. I've known you long enough to realize that when you want something badly enough, nothing gets in your way." Laird spoke with cold deliberation. "You want to run Warfield, and despite stiff opposition, nothing is getting in your way."

"What are you saying?" Bo snapped.

"Teddy is gone, allowing you an opportunity which you have taken full advantage of."

"I've always taken advantage of opportunities," Bo said, moving closer to Laird, towering over him. "I see no evil in that."

"Not unless you created the opportunity yourself."

Bo's eyes narrowed. "Leave my home right now!" he yelled, pointing toward the door. "Get out."

"Paul made you an offer to manage a significant amount of Hancock money from Montana. Take him up on that, Bo, or things will turn rough."

"Forget it."

"Don't be stupid, Bo. The authorities will have many questions. If you go quietly, there will be no problems."

"What the hell are you talking about?" Bo demanded.

"Just accept the offer. That's all I can tell you. Otherwise you and Meg will be very sorry."

"Get out!" Bo roared. He took several quick steps after Laird as the other man retreated, then disappeared inside. After Laird was gone, Bo gazed up at the stars, trying to slow his pounding heart.

When he looked down, Ashley had returned to the deck.

"What was that all about?" she asked. "I heard shouting." She crossed the deck to where Bo stood. "Are you all right?"

"I'm fine."

"Tell me, Bo. Who was that man?"

"Bruce Laird, the family attorney."

"Why were you yelling?"

"There are some details of the will to be worked

out," Bo answered, pulling Ashley to him. "He is not cooperating."

"You're not telling me the truth," she murmured. "I heard what you two were saying. There was no discussion of a will."

"What were you going to tell me before, Ashley?" Bo asked, disregarding her question. "About why you left for Europe?"

She allowed her head to fall against his chest again and gazed into the darkness behind the mansion. "Why is it so important?"

He couldn't seem as if he was pressing too hard, couldn't seem as if he had another agenda. Then she might never tell him. "I thought maybe I had done something to make you leave," he said quietly. "I thought maybe it was my fault all of these years."

"No, no, it wasn't you, it was . . ."

"Was what?"

Ashley swallowed hard, hating the memories. "I had an affair with someone the summer before my senior year of college. After I got back from California. It was so wrong, Bo. I hated myself for it so much that I couldn't come back to the family after I graduated. I couldn't face everyone."

"An affair?"

"I couldn't stand the fact that I wasn't really a Hancock," she went on, the words spilling out now that she had made the admission. "I couldn't stand how Jimmy Lee had always treated Teddy, Paul, and Catherine so much better than you and me. I hated him."

The possibilities raced through Bo's mind. She would have been vulnerable and young and no one would have been blood. "Not—"

Ashley pressed her fingers to Bo's lips. "Don't say it."

Bo squeezed her arms tightly and shook her, trying to get her to look into his eyes, but she kept her gaze fixed on the dark woods. "Tell me, Ashley," he demanded, his voice shaking. "Tell me who you had an affair with."

"What was that?" Ashley asked suddenly, shaking free of Bo's grip.

"What do you mean?"

"Down there." She pointed into the woods.

Bo followed her gesture. "Where?"

"There!" She was leaning out over the railing now, pointing.

Bo searched the darkness beyond the floodlights furiously. "I can't see—"

"I thought I saw a—"

"I see it!" Bo rasped. There was a faint light bobbing through the woods, moving in the direction of the carriage house, flickering in and out of sight, as whoever was carrying it made their way slowly through the thick brush.

"It's probably just one of the security people," Ashley said, her voice wavering. "Don't you think?"

"I don't know, but I'm going to find out."

"What are you going to do?"

"Get in the house," he said to her calmly.

"Why? Do you think—"

"Get in the house," he said again, forcefully this time. Nothing could be taken for granted now. "Did you hear me?"

"Yes."

"Then go!" He scrambled over the deck railing and dropped ten feet to the lawn. As he rolled onto his injured arm, he bit his lip to keep from yelling, writhing in pain on the ground and clutching the burn. But he was on his feet quickly, tearing through the garden path toward the woods and the last point at which he had spotted the light. He plunged into the thick brush a hundred feet from the house where the lush grass ended, thorns ripping and clawing at his clothes. He pushed away branches scraping his face as he forged deeper into the woods, fighting his way to the carriage house, toward which the light was headed. He couldn't allow anyone to enter the carriage house. Then the gleam of the flashlight was gone.

Bo stood statue-still, trying to hear his quarry, trying to get his bearings among the huge trees. The driveway down to the carriage house lay a hundred yards to his left, ending at the bottom of the hill in front of the small structure's garage. A drop of perspiration fell from his forehead and trickled to his lip. He licked the salty liquid, holding his breath so he could hear, and so he wouldn't give away his position to whoever was out there. Perhaps he and Ashley had been seeing things, or, as she'd suggested, it was simply the flashlight of a security guard. However, the security people didn't typically stray far from the estate's border and the chain-link fence, which was over a mile away.

The rustling of leaves and the sound of a twig snapping caused Bo to spin to the right. The noises had seemed so close, but he knew that darkness could play tricks on the ears and the mind. He knew it could amplify some sounds and deaden others. Finally, he could no longer hold his breath and it poured in and out of him. He was sweating profusely despite the chill in the air and he wiped his forehead, easing forward in the direction of the noise. Old fallen branches and leaves crackled beneath his feet. He knew he was giving away his position, but he wanted to close the distance between himself and his quarry.

Then someone was running, as though from a pack of wild dogs. He could hear the sound of heavy footsteps pounding over leaves.

Bo lunged forward, dodging trees and fighting his way headlong through vines and thorns. He slammed into a small tree obscured by the darkness, absorbing the collision with his injured arm. He screamed in pain as rough bark met the exposed burn, and tumbled to the ground, clutching his arm, then battled to his feet, aware that the wound was bleeding. He could hear the intruder racing away and he lurched forward again.

Then suddenly he was down once more, hurled to the ground by something that had loomed up out of the darkness. He scrambled to his knees, twisted around, spotted the form coming at him again through the gloom, and slammed his shoulder into his attacker's legs. A body tumbled over him, and Bo was on the attacker instantly, pinning the struggling form to the ground with his considerable weight, thrusting his uninjured forearm into the man's throat.

Their faces close, Bo could make out the man's features. As the attacker's face came into focus in the darkness of the woods, Bo could hear the sound of crashing footsteps growing faint. "Blackburn!"

"Bo!" Sheriff John Blackburn's voice croaked, with Bo's forearm pressing hard on his throat.

Bo got to his feet. "What the hell are you doing, Sheriff?"

"Someone was hanging around the carriage house," Blackburn gasped. "I surprised them and chased them out here. I didn't expect it to be you. What the hell were you doing sneaking around?"

"It wasn't me." Bo helped Blackburn get up. "Come on!" He turned and headed in the direction of the carriage house. Catching the intruder was out of the question at this point. The person had too big a lead. He or she could melt into the forest and never be found. The priority now was protecting Meg.

Scully tossed his backpack over the ten-foot-high chain-link fence, then clutched the fence and began to climb. He had lost his bearings in the woods and Bo and the idiot who had bolted from the carriage house had come close to catching him. Too close. Wallace would have lost his mind if Scully had allowed himself to be apprehended on the Hancock estate.

Scully reached the top of the fence, gingerly negotiated his way over razor wire curled on top, and jumped for the ground, landing in a pile of leaves beside his backpack. He'd simply been performing reconnaissance under cover of darkness in case they needed the information later, and he'd almost been caught. He breathed a sigh of relief, then headed away from the fence, aware that the Hancock security force would soon be passing this spot on scheduled rounds.

"What the hell happened?" Bo asked as he and Blackburn broke through the underbrush onto the small lawn that surrounded the carriage house.

"I looked out the upstairs window and saw somebody over there by the truck," Blackburn answered, pointing in the direction of the Explorer. "He had a flashlight and he was looking at something. I thought maybe he was security so I didn't do anything right away. Then he started edging around toward the back of the house. I went downstairs to confront the guy but he took off as soon as I opened the door, so I chased him. I lost him, then I saw a light up toward your house. I guess he got disoriented and risked turning the light on to get his ass out of here."

"Ashley and I must have seen that same light," Bo observed. "We were out on the deck."

"So you chased him."

"Yes."

"I thought you were him. Sorry."

They reached the front door. "It's all right," Bo assured Blackburn, just glad that the man had been willing to fly East on such short notice. "I want to make certain Meg's okay."

Bo trusted no one at this point, no one but Blackburn and Meg. Not even Ashley. He'd lied to his own sister about Meg being upstairs in their mansion.

Blackburn tapped on the front door, then opened it a crack. "Katie," he called softly. He pushed the door open and reached for the light switch but couldn't find it. "Come on," he whispered to Bo. "I think the switch is right here." He searched once more, found the switch, and then the room was bathed in light. Blackburn's wife stood before them, eyes closed, fingers wrapped tightly around the pistol he had left her. It shook wildly in her hands, barrel pointed at them.

"Jesus!" Blackburn raced across the room, grabbed the gun from Katie, and embraced her. "It's all right! It's us, Katie. For God's sake, it's us!"

"Thank the Lord, John," she cried, grabbing him. "I didn't know who you all were. I thought you might be the man you saw outside."

"It's all right," Blackburn said gently, comforting her.

"Meg is awake," Katie said, wiping away her tears. "She's coming around."

Bo raced up the stairs and burst into the bedroom where he had brought Meg several hours ago. She was lying on her side, smiling at him. She hadn't regained consciousness at the hospital, but Bo had spirited her away behind Silwa's back, not certain that he would be able to protect her in the city. Bo was sure that Meg hadn't accidentally fallen down the stairs, and he feared that whoever had pushed her would be coming to finish the job. He had spoken to the man who had found Meg on the stairwell landing and the man had claimed that someone had run from the scene.

Bo knelt down beside the bed and took Meg's hand. "I love you so much."

"I love you too," she said weakly. "Bo—"

"Just rest, sweetheart. Don't try to talk."

"Bo, listen to me," she said, mustering as much strength as she could.

"What? What is it, honey?"

"I was being chased down a stairway, Bo. He was after me." She paused for a breath. "I think it was the same man who tried to push me in front of the cab in front of Penn Station the other day."

Bo nodded slowly. Here was confirmation of what he had suspected. Meg wasn't safe. None of them were.

"I'm so scared, Bo."

"It's all right. Nothing's going to happen to you. I've asked Sheriff Blackburn to help me. He's here for you as well. He's come all the way from Montana."

"John is here?" she asked, trying to lift her head.

"Yes," Bo said, easing her gently back down on the

pillow. "Katie is here too. But please try to rest, Meg. That cut on your head is serious."

She pulled him close. "I have to tell you something, Bo."

"What?" he asked as she pressed her face against his neck.

"It's about Michael."

"Michael Mendoza?"

"Yes."

"What?" Bo's eyes narrowed. "What is it?"

"Michael made a pass at me the other night," she gasped, her voice unsteady. "When you came into the foyer and I was standing there on the staircase, he had just tried to kiss me. Thank God you showed up when you did."

Bo pulled back and gazed into her eyes. "I can't believe it."

"I couldn't either."

Bo stroked her hair, careful not to touch the bandage covering one side of her forehead. The blood was pounding so hard in his brain that Meg's face was blurring before him. "Get some sleep, sweetheart." He saw that she could barely keep her eyes open. For a few moments he continued to stroke her hair. Finally her eyes flickered shut and her breathing became regular. When Bo was certain she was asleep, he pulled the covers carefully up to her chin.

"I'll stay with her, Bo," Katie whispered, approaching the bedside. "John needs to talk to you."

He nodded and joined Blackburn in the hall outside the bedroom. "What is it, John?"

"I've got some news for you."

"Yes?"

"Remember you asked me to get an identification on

that John Doe we pulled from the accident in Montana that night? The guy who was in that car that flipped over?"

Bo nodded.

"His fingerprints came back. His name was Dale Stephenson."

CHAPTER 16

Catherine smiled pleasantly at the young man behind the hospital's front desk. "I'm here to see Michael Mendoza," she announced.

The man continued tapping casually on his keyboard a few moments longer before finally looking up. "Michael who?"

"Mendoza. Michael Mendoza. He is a United States senator from Connecticut."

"Michael Mendoza?"

"Yes," she answered, quickly becoming exasperated. "He was admitted to this hospital early Sunday morning. He was flown here from Connecticut by medevac helicopter after being involved in a serious accident. I'm here to see him. He is a very close friend of our family."

"You must be mistaken." The man shook his head. "There's no one at this hospital by that name. Perhaps Mr. Mendoza was taken to another hospital here in Manhattan."

Catherine leaned over the counter and checked the computer monitor sitting on the desk in front of him. "How do you know, you didn't even check?" She straightened up and pushed her long hair over her ears triumphantly.

The man gazed at her intently for a few moments, then nodded. "As you like." He exited the word-processing program, then tapped Mendoza's name into his computer and waited several seconds. "Nope, no one here by that name."

"But he *was* admitted here early Sunday morning." She understood that people were trying to keep Mendoza's name and any word of the explosion out of the newspapers. "Correct?"

"No, he wasn't," the man said firmly. "If he had been, I'd see it on the screen. I can access admittances up to a year ago right here from the desk. I'm afraid you've made a mistake."

Catherine took a deep breath, trying to remain calm. "You look tired. Have you been here all night?"

"Yeah, I've got the graveyard shift this week." He glanced at his watch. "Two o'clock to ten o'clock. Fortunately I've only got thirty minutes left." He rubbed his eyes. "Then I can go home and get some sleep."

"Well, thanks for your help," she said appreciatively.

"Sure. Sorry I couldn't give you more information."

"That's all right." She smiled warmly, then turned away and headed back to the parking lot. He was lying. There was no doubt in her mind.

Half an hour later Catherine spotted the young man coming out of the emergency room area. Duffel bag slung over his shoulder, he walked between two ambulances, lights still flashing. "Hello, there," she called as he reached for the driver's-side handle of his beat-up Chevy Chevette.

He looked up quickly, hand over his chest. "Jesus, you scared the hell out of me."

"I'm sorry." She moved in front of him and alongside the door so he couldn't open it. "I didn't mean to."

He glanced around nervously. "What do you want?"

"Tell me where Michael Mendoza is," she demanded.

The man rolled his eyes. "I told you several times. No one by that name was checked into the hospital early Sunday morning." He attempted to open the car door, but Catherine refused to move out of his way.

"Look, I'm Catherine Hancock Bristow," she said, "Jimmy Lee Hancock's daughter."

The man looked up, eyes wide. "Oh? God, you are," he said, suddenly recognizing her.

"Senator Mendoza was injured on our family estate early Sunday morning. I know for a fact that he was brought to this hospital."

The man puffed out his cheeks, uncomfortable with his situation. "Well, yes, he was."

"Is the Senator still here?"

The man checked the parking lot again carefully. "I'm not supposed to talk about this. I could get into a lot of trouble."

"I won't tell anyone how I found out." Catherine dug into her pocket, produced a thousand-dollar bill, and held it out. "Now, is he here?"

The man gazed at the bill longingly. "No, he isn't."

"But he was admitted?"

"Yes."

"And?"

The man's eyes flickered around the parking lot one last time. He started to say something, then stopped.

Catherine reached down, took the man's hand in hers, stuffed the bill into his palm, then closed his fingers tightly over the money. "Now, tell me where he is."

* * *

Bo stepped onto the Lexington Avenue subway train from the platform at Grand Central just as the doors closed. This was the No. 6 train and it was headed north toward Harlem making all local stops. Bo reached for an overhead handle, checking each face carefully as the train lurched from the station. The Lex line platform at this station served both the local and express tracks, and at the last second he had darted away from the express train's open doors and across the platform to the closing doors of the local. He'd felt a little foolish for making the mad dash and for being suspicious of even the elderly lady huddled in her seat at the far end of the car clutching her purse, but at this point he couldn't be too careful. Only fifteen minutes ago, in his office at Warfield, he had found out that Harold Shaw, CEO of the American Financial Group, was missing from his Long Island home.

Satisfied that no one in the train car was overly interested in him or trying too hard to look as if they weren't, Bo struggled toward the front of the train as it thundered ahead, grasping handles as if he were swinging from tree limb to tree limb. When he'd made it to the front of the swaying car, he pulled back the door, stepped out onto a small platform to a deafening roar, yanked open the door of the next car, and hauled himself inside. He repeated the process once more and made it to the lead car just as the train was pulling into its next stop, at Fifty-first Street.

Bo stood at the back end of the car and watched four passengers board. As the train began to pull out of the station, Bo made his way forward. "Hello, Jack," he said loudly over the sound of clattering wheels, sitting down beside a white-haired gentleman in a gray suit—the last person to enter the car at Fifty-first Street.

"Hello, Bo." Jack O'Connor was a tall, barrel-chested, fifty-four-year-old Irishman who headed global commodities research for Stillman & Company, one of Wall Street's largest brokerage houses. During his thirty-two-year career at Stillman, O'Connor had worked in several areas of the firm, including its corporate finance and mergers and acquisitions departments. A native of working-class Queens, he had dedicated his life to Stillman and was now a senior member of its six-person management committee. He was the only member of that committee without an Ivy League degree.

"Thanks for meeting me on such short notice," Bo said.

O'Connor answered gruffly. A financial analyst by training, he was accustomed to letting his numbers do most of his talking. "You said it was important."

"It's very important." Bo checked the car once more. "First of all, let me say that my family appreciated you and your wife attending the funeral on Saturday."

"It was an honor to be invited and to sit so close to the front of the church." O'Connor raised both eyebrows. "Frankly, I was surprised at that."

"My father was always fond of you. He always knew you to be a man of integrity. So do I."

"I appreciate that. Having a relationship with Warfield Capital has helped my career immeasurably," O'Connor said. "For a poor boy from Queens to be the point person for the Hancock family is incredible. Honestly, without it, I wouldn't be where I am today."

Over the last twenty-five years, first Jimmy Lee then Bo had directed tens of millions of dollars of business to Stillman through O'Connor. Bo had also consistently purchased huge amounts of securities—both stocks and bonds—using O'Connor's trading floor. "I do business with people I trust," Bo said. "You are one of those people."

O'Connor looked down, surprised by Bo's directness. "It seems like it's always been your family doing things for me. I've often hoped that there would be an opportunity for that to go the other way."

Bo nodded. Jack understood what this meeting was about, and he had just opened the door. Now it was time to fill him in on the details. "I appreciate your willingness to help."

"What do you need?"

When the train was deep into the Bronx—cars elevated above the streets now that it had made its way out of Harlem—O'Connor leaned back, shut his eyes, and ran his hands through his snow white hair. "I don't know if I can do this, Bo."

"I've never asked you for a favor, Jack. The family has never asked you for a favor."

O'Connor glanced into Bo's piercing eyes, then away. "You know how much I want to oblige, but it's—"

"Is it that you don't trust me?" Bo asked directly.

"No, no, it's just that—"

"Then I don't understand," Bo interrupted. "Your firm won't be hurt."

O'Connor nodded. "I know," he said softly.

"No one other than the two of us will ever know about this conversation. I assure you of that."

O'Connor nodded again. "Yes, Bo. It's just that I don't feel right about this. This is not how I saw myself repaying your family's kindness."

"I can't tell you everything that's happening, Jack. Believe me, it's better that you don't know, but suffice it to say that you will be doing a good thing. I know that is hard to believe, given what I've asked of you, but it's true."

"I only wish I could talk to someone else about what you're proposing. One confirmation, that's all." O'Connor didn't glance into Bo's eyes this time. He didn't have the courage. "I trust you, but what you are talking about is terribly drastic. It could spin out of control on you. And I don't understand why you'd want this to happen to Warfield."

CHAPTER 17

Fritz Peterson burst frantically into Bo's office, tie pulled down and top two buttons undone, his hair a mess.

"In the future I'd appreciate your knocking when my door is closed," Bo chided, sipping calmly on a cup of black coffee. "And pull yourself together, will you? You look like shit and it isn't even seven in the morning."

"We're in trouble!" Fritz yelled, ignoring the rebuke.

"What do you mean?"

"The traders over at Stillman are shutting us out. They've told my people that they won't enter into any transactions with us as of this morning. Stocks, bonds, commodities, everything. No trades, end of discussion."

"Why not?"

"They say they have information leading them to believe that our capital reserves have been depleted, and that we're having trouble executing our buys. They claim we failed last night on a big bond transaction with them, and senior managers on all Stillman trading floors have scratched us—across the board."

"That's ridiculous!"

"That's what I told them, Bo, but they wouldn't believe me, and you know how fast word like this spreads on Wall Street. It's viral. One minute we're a triple A credit, the next we can't even get a credit card from a guy on the street corner. Traders from other firms are already calling to find out what's going on because the Stillman traders are spreading the word to everyone about our fail on the bonds last night. Somebody from *The Wall Street Journal* even called. We're telling people that the rumor is completely false," Fritz stammered, "but it's getting choppy out there. We're going illiquid on the buy side, which leaves us totally naked. I can't hedge anything at this point. My ugly ass is hanging out there in the wind for everyone to see. Our people are panicking."

"My God," Bo whispered, checking one of his computer screens. There were already several reports on Reuters and Bloomberg citing a possible funding problem at a large family-run hedge fund. "Sell fifty million dollars' worth of gold immediately!" he shouted.

"What?"

"You heard me."

"Are we really having problems?" Fritz asked unsteadily. It hadn't occurred to him that Warfield Capital would ever face a serious financial challenge. "Bo?"

"I told everyone that Ramsey would bring down this firm," Bo muttered to himself, picking up a file from his desk and hurling it against the far wall. "He's leveraged us to the hilt, and we're paying the price. Now that Jimmy Lee is dead we're being attacked, and we're defenseless because people have figured out what Ramsey's done. We've got so many enemies after all these years." Bo put his head in his hands. "I knew this would happen." He looked up at Fritz. "We've got to raise cash, Fritz."

"Don't you know someone pretty high up over at Stillman?" Fritz asked anxiously. Bo's shaky reaction to his news from the trading floor was causing Fritz to wonder if things were suddenly crashing in around them. He knew full well how fast financial markets turned on the weak, and he knew there would be no mercy. In these instances, people raced for cover and grabbed whatever they could get their hands on in the process. "Can't you tell them to back off? Aren't they our friends?"

"What?" Bo asked, not focused on what his head trader was saying.

"Use your contacts over at Stillman," Fritz urged. "We've sent millions of dollars of business their way over the past few years, for Christ's sake. Call in a favor."

Bo shook his head dejectedly. "It won't do any good. My father screwed one of their senior partners on a land deal up in Connecticut last year. Bruce Laird was the front man but the bastard at Stillman knew it was Jimmy Lee who was behind the whole thing, and he's been waiting for this opportunity." Bo slammed his fist on the desk. "That bastard sat less than fifty feet from my father's coffin in St. Patrick's Cathedral last Saturday, and now he's dropping a neutron bomb on Warfield."

"Bo—"

"Just sell the gold!" Bo yelled. "Get me some cash to work with. Don't stand there staring at me, get on the phones. Minutes are critical."

"We'll have to actually deliver the securities or the commodities before anyone will pay us at this point. Firms won't take our word on anything. At least not until we've beaten back this rumor."

"I don't care, just do what you have to do. Now get the hell out of here!"

"But, Bo, I—"

"Get out!"

Fritz backpedaled through the office, his mouth open. "Can't our house banks put together an emergency line?"

"Not fast enough to do us any good. Now get your ass back to the trading floor!"

When Fritz was gone, Bo grabbed his wallet from the desk's top drawer and pulled a small piece of paper from a compartment behind the cash pocket. On the paper was the telephone number Mendoza had given Bo just before the explosion. Bo dialed the 202 area code quickly.

A female voice answered on the first ring. "Hello."

"Hello, is this Angela?" Bo asked, remembering the name Mendoza had mentioned. There was no answer, only dead air. "My name is Bo Hancock and I'm in charge of Warfield Capital," he continued, his voice low. "Michael Mendoza instructed me to call this number in case of an emergency. He said you would know what that meant."

There was another long silence at the other end of the phone.

"Hello."

Still nothing.

"Look, I've got a big problem here, and I need Michael's help," Bo barked into the receiver, frustrated at the lack of response. "I need at least half a billion dollars immediately to keep us afloat. Michael told me to call him if I ever needed help!" Bo shouted desperately. "We're old friends."

"Give me a telephone number where I can reach you at any time," the voice at the other end of the line finally responded.

As soon as Bo had finished speaking, the line went dead. He hung up immediately, then rang Frank Ramsey's extension.

"Warfield Capital, Mr. Ramsey's office," a woman answered politely.

"Beth?" Beth was Ramsey's executive assistant.

"Yes?"

"It's Bo." Bo checked his watch. It was ten minutes past seven. Ramsey typically made it to the office no later than six-thirty in the morning, a half hour after Bo arrived. "Let me speak to Frank."

"Mr. Ramsey is not coming in today, Mr. Hancock. He's ill."

"What?"

"Yes, he called a few minutes ago to let me know."

Bo slammed the phone down and charged for the door.

Fifteen minutes later he jumped from a cab in front of Frank Ramsey's Fifth Avenue apartment building, just as Ramsey was coming out, suitcase in hand.

When he saw Bo, Ramsey flung the suitcase at him and took off across Fifth Avenue into Central Park.

"I just need to talk to you!" Bo shouted, racing after Ramsey.

Ramsey paid no attention, sprinting past early-morning joggers and people walking dogs, down toward the Friedsam Memorial Carousel, constantly checking back over his shoulder as he ran, a wild expression on his face.

Bo dodged a German shepherd on a long leash, then a woman pushing a baby stroller, straining to keep sight of Ramsey as the younger man tore past the carousel toward the lush softball fields beyond. Crisscrossing the softball diamonds were four-foot-high, temporary fences erected by the Central Park Conservancy to deter people from using the freshly seeded fields until the season began in May. Bo smiled to himself as he ran. Ramsey was headed straight into a horseshoe-shaped enclosure formed by the one of the fences.

Too late, Ramsey saw his predicament. But instead of turning back, he attempted to hurdle the fence. For a moment it appeared that he would clear the fence, but at the last second the toe of his shoe caught the top of the fence, sending him sprawling to the ground on the other side. He was up quickly, desperately trying to escape, but Bo was over the fence and on Ramsey like a big cat, pinning him to the soft turf.

Bo grabbed Ramsey by the neck and cocked a fist in the air. A year ago Ramsey had lied about Bo and a woman in a bar to get his chance to run Warfield, Bo remembered. Lied to have Bo removed from the firm and sent to Montana. "Why did you lie to Jimmy Lee about me and that woman, Frank?" he shouted. "Was it just so you could run Warfield?"

"They made me do it, they made me do it!"

"Who?"

"All of them. Jimmy Lee, Paul, Teddy," Ramsey spluttered. "It was a setup, Bo, a charade. I'm sorry."

"Damn you."

"Don't hurt me, Bo," Ramsey pleaded, holding his hands in front of his face. "I don't know anything," he whimpered. "I swear to God I don't know anything."

"Shut up, Frank!" Bo ordered, slowly relaxing his fist and dropping his hand. He wanted to pummel the man, but there was a much bigger picture to worry about right now.

"You were right, Bo. I didn't know what I was doing in the job," Ramsey mumbled, shaking his head. "It got away from me. Fritz called me around six this morning and told me about the Stillman problem. Two hundred billion is so much money, but I thought we had the capital reserves. I thought I could handle it. I don't understand why Stillman shut us out. It isn't right. Scully's going to kill me. *You're* going to kill me."

"I am not going to kill you, Frank. Just tell me where the money came from," Bo demanded, trying to assess the validity of the terror he saw in the other man's eyes. Ramsey seemed to feel his life was in genuine danger.

"I didn't want this," Ramsey blathered. "Sure I had some problems before I came to Warfield, but I wasn't a—"

"Shut up!" Bo yelled again, grabbing Ramsey by his lapels.

Ramsey suddenly stopped babbling and stared up at Bo childlike.

"Now, tell me where the money came from, Frank," Bo demanded evenly. "Whose money is it?"

"What money?"

"The two billion we talked about last week. The new equity into Warfield."

Ramsey squinted, as though trying to remember.

"The day I came to see you at Warfield," Bo prodded. "The day my father died."

"Oh."

"Remember now?"

"Yes."

"Whose is it?"

"I don't know."

Bo squeezed Ramsey's lapels, choking him. "Tell me!"

"I don't know," Ramsey gasped. "They never told me."

"Who are 'they'?"

"Teddy."

"And?" Bo tightened his grip. "You said 'they.'" Ramsey struggled wildly for a moment, but Bo brought one hand to his throat, cutting off his oxygen. "I wouldn't recommend trying that again," he warned, allowing Ramsey to breathe once he had stopped struggling. "Now tell me who else is involved."

"A guy named Joseph Scully."

"Who is he? Who does he represent?"

"All I know is that Scully has an office on the ninth floor of the building across Park Avenue from Warfield. I have no idea who he represents. They never told me." Ramsey shut his eyes. "I shouldn't be telling you this, Bo. I'm just a cog in the machine. I was supposed to run things the way you had and keep my mouth shut. For that they were going to make me very rich."

"Where were you going when I pulled up in front of your building two minutes ago?"

Ramsey hesitated.

"Frank!"

"I was leaving, Bo. I was getting out. I didn't sign up for all of this. There's too much strange stuff going on. First Dale Stephenson dies in some accident out West, now Teddy and Tom are dead. Nobody's safe."

Bo saw the terror in Ramsey's eyes again. "Why don't the assets match the liabilities?" Bo asked through clenched teeth.

"What are you talking about?"

"I've been through all of the department sheets many times, and I can't find two billion dollars."

"Huh?"

"Two billion is missing," Bo repeated angrily. "Evaporated into thin air. The sheet says it's supposed to be in one of our Chase accounts, but it never made it and there's no record of where it went. I called our relationship officer at Chase. He was as mystified as I was. And I don't think the amount is a coincidence. Two billion, Frank. The same amount as the new equity you alerted me to."

"Hey, I didn't alert anybody," Ramsey said quickly, his eyes opening wide.

"You did," Bo said firmly, sensing an opportunity. "You told me all about it the day I came to Warfield. If you don't cooperate with me I'll let them know that you were the one who put me onto it."

"No, please," Ramsey begged.

"If you don't start coming up with answers, I'll make everybody understand that you've been working with me all along."

"God, no," Ramsey implored.

Bo grabbed Ramsey again. "Why was I sent away to Montana?"

"They didn't want you digging in the portfolio," Ramsey replied. He was perspiring heavily.

"Who didn't want me digging?"

"Paul and Teddy. And Jimmy Lee. They were afraid you might find . . ."

"Find what?" Bo demanded.

"I can't tell you."

Bo grabbed Ramsey by his necktie, jerked him up from the ground into a sitting position, and slammed his mouth with a right. Ramsey hit the ground heavily, groaning for mercy. "I'll do that again," Bo threatened, grabbing Ramsey by the tie once more.

"Ernie Lang," Ramsey moaned through blood oozing from a split lip.

"What?"

"Warfield's computer guy."

"What about him?"

"Tell Lang to look for something called RANSACK in the network," Ramsey gasped. "Tell him to dig deep. He can tell you much more than I can if you give him that code."

Bo stood up quickly. RANSACK. The word Jimmy Lee had whispered in his ear just before taking his final breath. Bo had had no idea at the time what that could mean. "Get out of here, Frank," Bo snarled. "Go back to your apartment building, get your suitcase, and get as far away from New York City as possible. Go to a small town, change your name, fade into the background forever. Forget your desire to be rich. That's the best advice I can give you. Because if you don't and you make yourself easy to find, you'll end up like Dale, Teddy, and Tom."

Bo stood by the same chair in the Waldorf lobby where he had met Michael Mendoza only a few days before, waiting expectantly, worried that somehow she had become caught up in what was going on. His whole body relaxed out of relief when he spotted her. "Ashley," he called quietly.

She hurried to where he stood, then dropped her suitcase and hugged him tightly. "What's wrong?" she asked. "Why did you want me to come to the city so quickly?"

"Before I can answer that, I need to ask a question of my own."

She said nothing, but looked up at him curiously.

"Last night you were about to tell me why you left for Europe after college and never came back."

Her eyes dropped to the carpet.

"Please tell me now," Bo said.

They'd been apart for years, but she still recognized that tone in Bo's voice. He would not be denied an answer this time. "This is still hard for me to talk about."

"I understand," he said compassionately, "but I really need to know." He had called Ashley two hours ago, insisting that she pack her bags immediately, get to the train station near the estate without alerting anyone, and meet him here. He had already gotten her a room under a false name. She wouldn't be going back to Connecticut. Very soon it wouldn't be safe for anyone there. "You said you had an affair when you were very young," he pushed. "When you found out we were adopted."

"Yes." Tears filled her eyes. "He was my first. It lasted only a week, then he wanted nothing to do with me. I was nothing more than a conquest for him," she said sadly.

"Who was the affair with?"

She covered her eyes. "I'm so terrible."

"No, you aren't," Bo said gently, pulling her close. "Tell me, Ashley."

She took a deep breath. "It was Michael. Michael Mendoza." She put her hands to her face. "Ginny was always so nice to me and that's how I repaid her. I'm terrible. I'm so ashamed."

Bo pulled Ashley to his chest and wrapped his arms around her. "It's all right. Michael is the one who ought to be ashamed."

Ron Baker stood at the podium beneath white-hot lights, shielding his eyes as he looked out at a sea of reporters. He was already sweating profusely despite the fact that he had taken his place behind the microphone only a few moments before. "Can I have some quiet?" he pleaded over the hum of speculation circulating among the press. There had been no advance word from Baker's campaign staff as to the nature of the announcement. "Please!" Slowly the room settled down. "Thank you. I will read a prepared statement and answer no questions." Baker reviewed the words on the index cards one more time. He was nervous as hell. "For personal reasons, I am withdrawing my bid to become my party's nominee for the office of president of the United States," he said, his voice rising as reporters began shouting questions. "From this day on I will do whatever I can to help the candidacy of Reggie Duncan. I believe Mr. Duncan will be a strong leader of this country. He has earned my support, and yours. Thank you!" Baker tried to ignore the pandemonium as he trotted for a door held open by two aides.

Three thousand miles away, in Manhattan's city hall, the detective—backed by a number of high-ranking local and federal law enforcement officials—tapped the microphone in front of another large throng of reporters. Just like the reporters attending Ron Baker's news conference, these people had no idea what was coming. However, their sources had told them that the announcement, to be made by a joint task force of the New York City Police Department and the Federal Bureau of Investigation, would be a blockbuster.

"For the last several days," the detective began slowly, "we have been conducting an investigation into what we had originally believed was a routine break-in and robbery attempt at the offices of Reggie Duncan's campaign

headquarters in Harlem. Several nights ago we apprehended a man fleeing those offices." The detective took a
deep breath. He knew what he was about to say would
touch off a firestorm. They had considered trying to keep
a lid on the investigation for at least twenty-four more
hours, but experience told them that someone would
leak the information soon. It was simply too hot, and
they wanted to make certain they were controlling the
flow of information. "It turns out that the man we apprehended was on the payroll of Paul Hancock's campaign. He was—" But the detective's voice was drowned
out in a roar of chaos as the press began screaming questions and at the same time madly dialing cell phones to
report what they had just heard to their offices.

The detective shook his head as he watched members
of the press strive to be the first to report the incredible
news. Then his expression turned grim. Over the last two
days he had received information definitively linking the
man they had arrested outside Reggie Duncan's office to
Paul Hancock. Detailed information from an anonymous source. It had been too easy, he thought, as if
someone inside Hancock's campaign was trying to take
the candidate down.

"Ernie Lang."

"That's me. What the hell do you want?" Lang asked
without looking around. He was Warfield Capital's chief
technology officer and he was hunched over a keyboard
entering the last of a pile of sensitive financial information into the firm's network. His lair was a large, windowless room located one floor below the firm's trading
floor and executive offices. "I don't have time to be interrupted," he added loudly, spinning his chair around

toward the voice. "How the hell did you get in here any—" He stopped cold. "I . . . I'm sorry, Mr. Hancock. I certainly didn't expect to see you down here."

Bo smiled reassuringly. "No need to apologize."

"What can I do for you, sir?" Lang asked nervously.

Bo closed and locked the door. "Everything concerning Warfield's portfolio is on our network, correct?" he asked, taking a seat beside Lang, scanning the room to make certain they were alone.

"Yes."

"How up-to-date is the network?"

"Up-to-the-minute," Lang said proudly, delighted by the chance to show off in front of one of the Hancocks. "The system is tied directly to the trading floor as well as the other departments. As soon as an investment is made, I know about it."

"Good." Bo put his hand on the young man's shoulder. "What we're going to talk about tonight is extremely confidential. Do you understand what I'm saying?"

"I think so."

"Let me be perfectly clear so there are no misunderstandings later."

Lang nodded. "Okay."

"I am going to ask you to perform what I believe are several fairly simple data-mining requests. You will not discuss what we talk about with anyone. It's as simple as that, got it?"

"Yes, sir."

"Are we *crystal* clear on that?"

"Yes."

"One more thing."

"What?"

"Can we perform these data requests transparently?"

"You mean—"

"I mean, can we log on without creating a record? I don't want anyone to know we went into the system."

The young man nodded slowly. "It will take some doing, but I can go back in when we're finished and erase our tracks."

"Good." Bo nodded at the keyboard in front of Lang. "First of all, I need to see if a wire transfer has arrived at one of our Chase accounts."

"That's easy. We're directly linked to Chase's computer." Lang tapped on the keyboard, flashing through several screens. "Here's a list of all our accounts over there, Mr. Hancock. Which one do you want to examine?"

Angela, Mendoza's aide, had called Bo on his cell phone only a few moments after he'd let Frank Ramsey up off the ground in Central Park. As Bo watched Ramsey jog away, she'd confirmed that she was wiring Warfield five hundred million dollars as he had requested. "That one," Bo said, pointing at a string of numbers on the screen.

"Jesus," Lang exclaimed as the account detail appeared on the screen.

Bo smiled to himself. There it was. A half-billion-dollar deposit. "Now I need you to locate a specific investment in our portfolio."

Lang hesitated. "Excuse me, sir, but you can do that from the personal computer in your office. The network is set up so that you and Mr. Ramsey can get to everything," he explained. "You and he are the only ones with that kind of universal access, except for me, of course. I'm happy to help you, but you can review from upstairs all assets and all liabilities including a full list of institutional investors

who are funding us. We've been over that before," he said
deferentially, not wanting to irritate Bo.

"I know that, but I'm having trouble finding one investment that I'm certain is in the portfolio. It isn't
showing up on my screen when I search."

"Perhaps it's been sold and you weren't informed,"
Lang suggested, tapping on his keyboard to bring up the
system's main menu. "Once investments are sold, you
wouldn't be able to access them on-line. After an investment is sold, the record of its being a Warfield asset is
stored in a data bank off-line. I'd have to dig it up for
you, but that wouldn't be hard."

"I don't think it was sold."

"What kind of investment is it? What sheet should I be
reviewing? Can you tell me that?"

"The private equity sheet."

"That's sector Q," Lang muttered to himself, entering
a data request. Moments later an alphabetized list of
names appeared on his screen. "Here we go. What's the
specific name of the investment?"

"RANSACK."

In a seventeenth-floor corner office overlooking the
sprawling Tysons Corner Mall in northern Virginia, an
automatic e-mail registered on Scott Trajak's personal
computer at Online Associates. If Trajak had received
the message instantly, as he was supposed to, he would
have notified his contact immediately and Bo wouldn't
have made it back to the Hancock estate that evening.
As it was, Trajak had fallen ill with a bad spring cold
and had taken the day off to recover from a burning
sore throat and nausea. To knock himself out he'd taken
a double dose of powerful cold medicine, and so he

didn't hear his cell phone or his home computer—both of which were connected to his office computer—alerting him that an unauthorized user had inspected the RANSACK file at Warfield Capital.

Not until tomorrow morning would he understand what had happened.

CHAPTER 18

Paul sat slouched in Jimmy Lee's study chair, a bottle of whiskey and a half-full glass on the desk before him.

"How much have you had?" Bo asked, standing near the door. Paul hadn't looked up as Bo opened the door and walked into the room.

"What do you care?" Paul's voice was subdued and his speech slow.

Bo's eyes flickered over the honey-hued liquor behind the black-and-white Jack Daniel's label.

"You're here to gloat, aren't you?" Paul asked, reaching for the glass. His natural confidence seemed shattered, as if today had been a very bad day.

"What are you talking about?"

"Don't toy with me. I'm sure you've heard about the break-in at Reggie Duncan's headquarters. It's being broadcast over every radio and television station in the country, even as we speak." Paul took a long swallow of whiskey. "But you probably didn't need to hear it from a newscaster, did you?" he asked, peering at Bo suspiciously over the rim of his glass.

"What are you talking about, Paul? What's going on?"

Paul nodded. "Okay, I'll play your little game." He slowly lowered the glass to his lap. "Late this afternoon a joint task force of the New York City Police Department and the FBI announced that several nights ago they'd apprehended a man trying to escape after breaking into Duncan's headquarters. The man was carrying sensitive information he had stolen from Duncan's offices."

Bo crossed the study to stand in front of the desk. "Go on," he said.

"I'm sure you know the rest."

"Go on!" Bo demanded.

Paul swirled the ice in his glass and took another sip. "When they took the guy down to the precinct for questioning, they found a name scribbled on a piece of paper in his pocket. The name was Ray Jordan—my campaign treasurer." He shook his head. "The guy made bail an hour later. The person who came to the precinct tried to use a check drawn on one of my campaign accounts to put up the bail money. When the cops wouldn't take the check, he produced cash on the spot."

"Have you talked to Jordan?"

"Jordan denied knowing anything about what was going on."

"It's obvious that you've been set up."

Paul clapped slowly several times, spilling whiskey in his lap. "Of course I've been set up, little brother, but it doesn't matter. I've already been crucified by the press and the public. The damage is done. I'm Tricky Dick all over again. Reggie Duncan will be the party's nominee."

"Why Reggie Duncan?"

Paul chuckled. "Very good, Bo. Playing this one all the way out. Acting like you haven't heard that Ron Baker has dropped out of the race and pledged his support to Mr. Duncan."

"I haven't had time to listen to anything today, Paul. I've been trying to hold our family's fortune together."

Paul glanced up. "What are you talking about?" he asked, his head wobbling slightly from the alcohol he had been consuming for the last two hours.

"Warfield Capital had a liquidity crisis at seven o'clock this morning. Stillman shut us out."

"I don't believe it." Paul sat up in his chair and placed the glass back on the desk, a stunned expression on his face.

"Believe it. We failed on a fifty-million-dollar bond transaction with Stillman last night and they spread the word around Wall Street that we weren't good for our bids," Bo explained. "At that point the market shut us out across the board. Reuters and Bloomberg were screaming about our problem by seven-fifteen and it was a very long day."

"How could that be?" Paul whispered. "Aren't we worth ten billion dollars or something? How could we fail on a fifty-million-dollar transaction?"

"Your friend Frank Ramsey put Warfield into some very bad investments. They lost value quickly over the last few months and depleted our capital reserves in the process."

"Oh, my God." Paul reached for the Jack Daniel's and refilled his glass. "Are we going to make it?" he stammered. "Will Warfield survive? I mean, is it critical?"

"Yes, it is, and I honestly don't know if Warfield can survive. I have implemented several emergency measures and raised over half a billion dollars in cash, but Ramsey made several huge investments that are totally illiquid, including a two-billion-dollar transaction with a firm down in northern Virginia. We have tens of millions of dollars' worth of hedge maturities coming due every hour. We could run through that five hundred million very quickly if people gang up on us." Bo paused. "I'm very interested in that northern Virginia firm, Paul."

Paul took a long swallow of whiskey and looked away.

Bo leaned over the desk. "What has been going on at Warfield Capital for the last year? I know now that I wasn't sent to Montana because you and Jimmy Lee were worried about me screwing up your campaign. I know that was a red herring."

"I have no idea what you're talking about," Paul said, defiant to the end.

"Tell me, Paul!" Bo shouted. "What has been going on?"

Paul slumped down in his chair again.

"Paul!"

"It's so complicated."

"Tell me," Bo demanded once more, teeth gritted.

Paul gazed at his glass for several moments. "Politics is all about information, Bo."

"Everything is about information, brother. Now talk."

"Jimmy Lee wanted to make certain I won the election," Paul mumbled. "He wasn't going to take any chances."

"So?"

"So with the cooperation of certain influential people he erected an information-gathering system. We collected all kinds of nasty skeletons." Paul took a long swallow of whiskey. "Several people who were going to run against me in the primaries didn't because we had very damaging information on them. Through back channels we made it clear to them that we'd release the information if they tossed their hats into the ring. We didn't want them to have a chance to even get started."

"What about Baker and Duncan?"

"We had information on Baker too," Paul replied. "That's why he dropped out of the race today. We had evidence of him visiting child pornography sites on the Web, and we knew that his wife had an abortion, which would be devastating for a conservative platform candidate. We told him we'd use all of that against him. We let him in the race up until now because there had to be somebody real running against me or we wouldn't get any publicity. The press wouldn't pay any attention because they'd figure the race for our party's nomination was over, and the other party would get all the ink. We knew the information we had on Baker was so damaging that he'd drop out as soon as we laid it on him. We were right."

"Jesus Christ. What about Duncan?"

Paul shook his head. "We have nothing on Reggie Duncan. We never figured it would be necessary to have anything on him because we thought he'd never have a chance to win. He was an afterthought until today. He's black, for Christ's sake. When we did look we couldn't find anything. He's clean."

"Who are the 'influential people' who helped you and Jimmy Lee?"

"I don't know."

"Tell me!"

"Jimmy Lee and Teddy handled all of that," Paul said, his voice low. "Jimmy Lee didn't want me knowing. I was introduced to a man named Joseph Scully, but he's my only contact."

Scully. The same name Frank Ramsey had mentioned. "Who did Scully represent?"

"I don't know. I told you, Dad didn't want me involved in all of that."

Bo moved around the side of the desk so that he was standing beside his older brother. "You're finished, Paul. It's over."

"Yes," Paul said softly. In the top drawer of the desk—slightly ajar—he could just make out the pictures of Melissa's ashen face, and the polished wooden handle of a .38 caliber revolver. "It is over."

"You will resign from Warfield Capital's executive committee effective immediately," Bo continued, "and you will sign a binding document agreeing to give me complete authority over the fund as well as all business matters related to our family. It will be irrevocable. Catherine will sign the same document. You will make certain that she does. Do you understand?"

Paul was silent.

"Paul!"

"You'll still have to deal with Ramsey," Paul observed. "He's got his share of the Warfield pie. It's a minuscule piece, but he'll always be a problem."

"I doubt it. Frank Ramsey is gone."

Paul looked up. "Gone?"

"Ramsey called in sick early this morning. When I got to his Fifth Avenue apartment building, Ramsey was leaving, suitcase in hand." Bo eyed the bottle on the desk. Suddenly he had a strong yearning for alcohol, any alcohol, even sour mash whiskey. He ran the tip of his tongue along his lower lip. "I have alerted the authorities that I want Ramsey apprehended."

Paul covertly slid the desk drawer shut, aware that Bo might be able to see inside from where he stood. Then he reached for the bottle and pushed it toward Bo. "Go ahead, little brother."

"No."

"Come on." Paul produced a glass from another desk drawer, placed it in front of Bo, then poured whiskey until the glass was half-full. "Don't you want to celebrate your victory?"

Bo's eyes shifted to Paul's, requesting clarification.

Paul smiled sadly. "Just a little more than a week ago you were tucked away safely in Montana with no influence on the family at all. I was the alpha son and you were nothing. Now you control Warfield, the family, and me. You are going to permanently remove me from Warfield's executive committee and I have lost my bid for the nation's highest office. What I have been living my life for since I was ten years old. You've won and I've lost."

"Let me remind you that only a short time ago you tried to remove *me* from Warfield's executive committee." Bo picked up the glass, brought it to his lips, and inhaled. Saliva flooded his mouth. Like Pavlov's dog, he thought.

"Drink, Bo," Paul said softly. "Have a taste."

Bo inhaled the fumes from the glass again.

"It all goes back to that night, doesn't it? The night of my thirtieth birthday."

"It goes back further than that," Bo assured Paul.

"The night Melissa died," Paul continued.

"The night you killed Melissa."

Paul shook his head. "You killed her, Bo."

"What the hell are you talking about?"

Paul pulled the top drawer open, removed the two photographs of Melissa, and dropped them beside the bottle. "I was passed out that night, Bo. I was so drunk I couldn't stand up. I couldn't have killed her."

Bo snatched the pictures and stared at the image of Melissa's dead face, then at Paul's hands wrapped around Melissa's neck.

"Why would I have taken pictures of myself killing her?" Paul asked. "You know I wouldn't have. You know that's ridiculous."

"If you didn't take them, how did you get them?"

"They were delivered to Bruce Laird's office. He brought them to me."

"He saw them?"

"The envelope was still sealed when he gave it to me. There was nothing inside but the pictures. No note, no return address, no nothing," Paul explained. His eyes narrowed. "Why did you kill her, Bo? So you'd have something to hold over me at that critical point when you really wanted to ruin my life? Did you hate me that much growing up?"

"Oh, I hated you," Bo admitted calmly, "but not enough to kill someone."

"But now it's over for me anyway," Paul rambled on, intoxication overtaking him, "so you killed Melissa for nothing."

"Shut up."

"Just like you killed Teddy and Tom."

Bo put the glass back down on the desk. "You've gone insane, Paul. Your world is crumbling around you and you've lost your mind."

"Why would I take those pictures if I killed Melissa?" Paul asked again. "It doesn't make any sense. You, Melissa, and I were the only ones at the playhouse that night."

"You've lost your mind."

"You always knew that Dad cared more for Teddy and me. You knew it and you hated it, didn't you?"

Bo hesitated. "Yes, I suppose I did."

"Down deep you've always wanted to be the one who ultimately had control of the family. Always wanted to be the one who ended up with everything," Paul continued. "Even now that you know you're adopted. Probably even more now."

Bo shook his head. "You killed Melissa and you know I had nothing to do with Teddy's or Tom's death."

"I don't know anything of the kind," Paul said, standing up suddenly so that the desk chair fell over behind him, clattering loudly to the floor. He reached into the drawer, grabbed the revolver, and aimed it at Bo, both hands clasping the handle tightly.

Bo slowly backed off several steps, then froze. "Put that thing down. Somebody might get hurt," he said, watching the pistol shake in Paul's hands.

Paul brought the gun higher, aiming it at Bo's chest. "That's the idea."

Bo inched forward.

"Stay where you are!" Paul warned. "I swear to God, Bo, I'll shoot you."

"You don't have the guts."

"I detest you," Paul hissed, bringing the gun even higher. "I don't know why they adopted you."

Bo gazed down the barrel of the revolver, pointed directly at his face now. "I'm sure you do detest me, but you detest yourself more."

For several moments Paul stared at Bo, then his upper lip began to tremble and in one swift motion he brought the barrel to his own right temple. "Damn you, Bo."

"No!" Bo shouted, lunging forward as Paul pulled the trigger.

A s she had many times before, Catherine stole through the darkness up the path toward the farmhouse nestled in the rolling hills of Middleburg, Virginia. For many years this had been a place of refuge for her. A place she could come for consolation and compassion. She had fantasized that it would also be the place where she would make love to him for the first time, but it had never been that way when she had visited him after the long train rides. He had always been a perfect gentleman—until the night of the funeral reception.

She felt her heart rise into her throat as she made it to the back of the house and stole up the creaky wooden steps. From her jeans pocket she retrieved the key. Guided by the dim rays of a tiny flashlight attached to her key ring, she slid the key into the lock. As she did, she shut her eyes and thought about what had happened down by the lake. How her passions had exploded after all these years and how she wanted him again so badly.

Catherine pushed open the door, moved swiftly to the alarm pad on the wall, and entered a code. As the loud beep faded, the back foyer's overhead light came on and she turned to her left. For a moment she gazed at him. Then she ran to him and threw her arms around him. "Why did you do all of this, Michael? Why did you make me think you were at death's door?"

Mendoza caressed her shoulders and nuzzled her sweet-smelling hair. "I had to," he said softly.

"You didn't call me."

"I wanted to."

"But you didn't."

"I couldn't."

"Why?"

"I can't explain now. You just have to trust me." He kissed her gently. "How did you find out I was here?"

"I bribed a nurse at the hospital," she explained, feeling safe now that she was in his arms. "I love you, Michael."

"I love you too," he said tenderly. "How about a drink?"

She nodded. "Yes, a glass of wine would be nice."

"Come on," he said, leading her away from the back door.

As they turned the corner into the living room, two men clad in black uniforms and ski masks appeared before them. Catherine attempted to scream, but one of the assailants was on her instantly, forcing a foul-tasting rag far down her throat. As her ability to struggle drained from her body, she had a fleeting glimpse of Mendoza being pinned to the floor by his attacker, an expression of utter shock on his face.

CHAPTER 19

Bo raced down the long driveway toward his mansion, whipping past the tall oak trees which were swaying wildly in the gale. The spring storm had swept up the Atlantic seaboard into the Northeast a few hours ago, but was just now beginning to unleash its full fury on Connecticut, pelting the Explorer with buckets of rain and hail.

Bo had waited two hours for the police and the paramedics to finish at Jimmy Lee's place, and it was now almost midnight. The bullet had ripped away part of Paul's skull, but as far as the paramedics could determine, hadn't pierced his brain. Bo's last-second lunge had deflected the gun barrel toward the ceiling, where the slug had lodged after burrowing through Paul's scalp, creating a momentary bright red halo around his head. Bo's white shirt was spattered with dark, dried blood.

Paul had remained conscious after collapsing to the floor. Blood dripping steadily from his head, he lay with his hand clasped tightly in Bo's. Over and over, he swore on Jimmy Lee's fresh grave that he hadn't killed Melissa, even as the paramedics tended his wound. Paul would survive, the paramedics had said, eyeing him nervously as he rambled on about Melissa. The wound was serious but not fatal.

After the ambulance had pulled away, a detective had asked pointed questions about exactly what had happened in Jimmy Lee's study. Bo had answered the queries curtly but directly and the detective had reluctantly allowed him to leave.

A flash of jagged lightning crackled above the mansion as Bo skidded to a halt at the edge of the driveway, jumped from the car, and headed toward the front door through the wind and rain. Protected by the porch roof, he guided his key into the lock. As he pushed the heavy door open, he happened to glance to his right. One foot on the sill, he stared into the darkness. He had an eerie sensation that he had seen the silhouette of someone standing at the corner of the structure. Another bright flash illuminated the grounds, but this time he saw nothing.

Bo stumbled inside and made certain the front door was secured behind him. He hurried to the basement door, flipped on the lights, and headed downstairs, taking several steps at a time. He raced down a long corridor past several closed doors, finally stopping at the last one on his left. "John!" he shouted, pounding on the door. "Blackburn!"

"Yes," came the muffled reply.

"Open up."

"I need to hear the—"

"Churchill!" Bo interrupted with the agreed-upon code word. The lock clicked and he burst into the room, rushing past Blackburn, who leaned into the hallway and checked both ways before returning his gun to his shoulder holster and relocking the door.

Meg sat in a chair across the room. Her eyes alit at the sight of Bo at the door.

"You look terrible," he teased with a smile.

"I don't feel so great either," she admitted feebly.

"Is Katie all right?" Bo asked Blackburn.

"Yes, she's on a plane back to Montana. I spoke to her just before she boarded. She's fine."

"Good."

"I appreciate your friend Allen Taylor escorting her to the airport," Blackburn added.

"Not as much as I appreciate you staying here with Meg," Bo replied.

Late last night, at Blackburn's urging, they had moved Meg from the carriage house to the mansion, Bo carrying her to his Explorer as Blackburn, gun drawn, covered them. Meg was still weak from her fall in the parking garage, but Blackburn didn't want her staying in one place too long. After the episodes at Penn Station and in the garage, it was clear that someone was after Meg, and Blackburn's law enforcement training told him that they needed to avoid being a stationary target in order to remain one step ahead of the hunter. Bo had agreed.

Bo knelt down beside Meg. "You seem stronger," he said, checking the bandage above her eye.

"I'll be all right. I'm a pretty tough woman. I may not look like it, but I am."

"I know."

"I have to admit that right before I hit the wall, I didn't think I'd be waking up. You know, that terrible feeling you have right before something bad happens when you're still all right but you know you aren't going to be in a second and there's nothing you can do about it." She slid her hand into his. "The very last thing I thought about was you, Bo," she said, her voice trembling. "About how I'd never see you again."

"It's all right, sweetheart, I'm here now. John and I will take care of you." Bo looked over his shoulder at Blackburn, who had turned around and was adjusting his holster, trying to give them the illusion of privacy. "We ought to get her out of here right away," he said. "To someplace safer. I think she'll be able to handle a move now."

"I agree," Blackburn said.

"Is that all right with you, Meg?" Bo asked, turning back toward her. "Do you feel strong enough to move?"

"Yes," she said, wiping a tear from her cheek.

An earsplitting clap of thunder exploded directly above the mansion, causing all three of them to duck down instinctively.

"Damn!" Bo shouted. "That was close."

"Hey, what was that?" Blackburn called out.

"Thunder, John. Jesus!"

"No, I heard something else." Blackburn had already drawn the revolver. "It came from out in the hallway."

"Are you crazy? How could you hear anything over that?"

"It was like a door opening and closing." Blackburn held up his hand. "There! There it is again."

Bo had heard it this time too—it sounded as if someone was systematically searching the rooms along the corridor. He glanced up at a small window, near the ceiling, that opened onto the area below the deck in back of the mansion.

Blackburn stepped away from the door and aimed his gun at it. "Might be security people," he muttered, "and it might not."

"We aren't going to stick around and find out," Bo said, helping Meg to her feet as gently but as quickly as possible. He pushed the chair she'd been sitting in against the wall beneath the window, then jumped up on it and pulled frantically on the window lock. "The damn thing probably hasn't been opened in years," he muttered, smacking the lock hard with the base of his palm. Finally, it popped open. He pushed the window up and held his hand out to Meg. "Come on!" he urged, helping her up on the chair beside him. "Hurry, sweetheart."

"Outside?" she asked fearfully.

"That's the only choice we have."

With what little strength she had and aided by a boost from Bo, Meg struggled through the narrow opening, then scrambled beneath the deck toward the lawn, her fingers digging into rain-soaked earth as she pulled herself along.

"Come on, John!" Bo whispered hoarsely over his shoulder, hoisting himself up. He scrambled through the opening, then turned and, on his hands and knees, stuck his head back into the room. Blackburn remained motionless, both hands clasped around the revolver's handle, barrel pointed at the door. "Come on!" Bo said again.

"Get out of here!" Blackburn hissed back without taking his eyes from the door. "I'll be all right."

"You won't be all right. Now is no time to play hero."

"Go!"

Bo glanced over his shoulder. Through the darkness he saw that Meg had paused to wait for him. His eyes raced back to Blackburn, who still stood defiantly in the room, gun pointed at the door. The man had children back in Montana, Bo thought. Two young sons who would not become orphans if he could help it. "Dammit." He pulled himself back through the window and plunged eight feet to the floor, his cell phone tumbling from his pocket and skittering into a far corner. He regained his feet instantly, ignoring the shooting pain in his shoulder and the burn on his arm. Above the roar of the storm he could hear people in the corridor twisting the doorknob frantically and banging on the door. He raced to Blackburn, grabbed the gun from his hand, and pushed him violently toward the window.

"Get out of here!" Bo yelled.

A shotgun blast from the hallway obliterated the knob and half the door, spraying tiny pieces of wood and steel across the room and barely missing Blackburn's lower legs as he pulled himself through the window.

The explosion knocked Bo down, but he was up again quickly, unloading the revolver's chamber at the destroyed door even as he once again used the chair as a springboard and lunged for the window. As he hoisted himself onto the soggy dirt beneath the deck, he felt a screaming pain in his calf, like a swarm of hornets stinging all at once. Pellets must have grazed his leg.

Blackburn pulled out the .22 caliber pistol he kept in a holster affixed to his calf and aimed it down into the room, squeezing the trigger six times in rapid succession. He clipped one of the men who had burst into the room in the thigh and killed the other instantly with a clean shot to the head.

Bo dragged himself to where Meg lay. "Are you all right?"

She nodded, shielding her eyes from another flash of lightning.

Bo and Blackburn helped her to her feet. The three of them emerged from beneath the deck and dashed ahead, the men steadying her against the violent gusts of wind as they ran.

"You okay, Bo?" Blackburn yelled.

"I wouldn't be," Bo gasped, "if you hadn't played Tonto." The burning in his leg was brutal. He grabbed Blackburn's arm and pointed as another jagged bolt illuminated the grounds. Several men stood on a slight rise to their left, guns draped over their arms. "We've got to make it to the woods." As they struggled toward the line of trees, Bo looked skyward apprehensively. "Gotta pray for no lightning in the next few—"

The next-second flash was the brightest of the storm, slamming into a tree above their heads and splitting it in two. Sparks, shredded leaves, and limbs showered the three. Bo threw himself on top of Meg as a huge limb slammed to the wet ground beside them, a sheared-off branch impaling the turf a foot from where Blackburn was sprawled.

Through the leaves of the downed tree, Bo saw them coming—at least five men, sprinting toward where he, Meg, and Blackburn lay. He dragged Meg to her feet and guided her into the woods, pushing her the last few yards. "Cover your face," he shouted as they tumbled into the thick underbrush, Blackburn just behind them.

They were up again quickly, scrambling and rolling together through branches and vines that tore at their flesh and snagged their clothes. Bo could hear the pursuers yell as they hit the first line of underbrush, like an advancing infantry line encountering the first enemy rifle volley. "Come on." He took Meg's wrist and pulled her forward.

Deeper into the woods the underbrush thinned and progress became easier, as it would for the pursuers too,

Bo knew. He veered right, wiping water from his drenched face. He glanced over his shoulder and saw flashlights bobbing up and down behind them.

"Keep going, Meg," Blackburn urged from behind when she slowed down. "You've got to keep going."

"I'll try," Meg gasped, practically dropping to her knees on the muddy ground. "But I'm so dizzy."

Bo glanced back once more. The flashlights were spreading out behind them to cover more ground. One was coming directly at them, visible off and on as the man weaved around trees, less than a hundred feet away. "Carry her, John," Bo rasped. "Straight ahead no more than a hundred feet. I'm going up," he said, pointing toward a tall tree.

Blackburn scooped Meg up in his arms and stumbled forward.

As the pursuer passed beneath him, Bo dropped from the tree he had climbed, knocking the man to the earth. The man's rifle exploded as they struggled, a hot blast of steel barely missing Bo. Then Bo caught the man flush on the point of his chin with his right fist, and the man collapsed, unconscious.

Bo scrambled on his hands and knees across wet leaves to where the man's flashlight lay and hurled it like a grenade. It caromed off a tree thirty feet away and came to rest on the ground, still illuminated. He raced back to where his pursuer lay, slammed the man with another hard right to the jaw to make certain he didn't regain consciousness anytime soon, grabbed the rifle, and hunched behind a tree, watching four more flashlights bobbing toward the one on the ground. The other pursuers had been alerted by the blast even over the din of the storm and had spotted the beam of light. A moment later lightning sliced the sky wide open, and Bo saw the squad of men beginning to fan out again.

Bo dragged the unconscious man beneath a bush to hide him, then rushed ahead to where Blackburn and Meg lay curled against a tree. He knelt down beside her. She was shivering, more from fear than cold, although the temperature felt like it had dropped ten degrees in the last half hour. "Here," he said to Blackburn, shoving the rifle into his hand. Then he lifted Meg in his arms and began moving forward. The storm's intensity was fading and they needed to get out of here or face certain discovery.

Bo knew the estate as a hunting guide knows his territory. He was quickly able to put distance between them and the hunters by locating a familiar dry streambed and using it as a path.

"Where are we going?" Meg murmured, her head on his shoulder.

"To a safe place." He struggled along, doing his best to avoid rocks that could cause him to stumble. The rain had stopped and an eerie mist was rising from the forest floor. It was visible in the dim moonlight that filtered down through a canopy of young leaves.

Thirty minutes later Bo had reached his destination— a cave that had been a childhood hideout. He had identified the spot by the huge egg-shaped rock which lay in the middle of the streambed. It was the way he would find the cave when he'd come out here as a child.

"Can you stand up?" he asked. He looked up the side of the ravine to the cave's entrance.

"Yes. I'm sorry you had to carry me," she whispered, leaning against a tree for support as he put her down gently. "I couldn't have gone any farther back there."

"I know," Bo said. He turned to Blackburn. "This is

the plan. There's a cave about thirty feet up the side of the hill," he said, gesturing upward. "It doesn't offer much in the way of creature comforts, but it'll be dry and, most important, safe. You and Meg will stay in it while I go for help."

Meg too followed Bo's gesture up the steep bluff through the moonlight. She could barely make out what appeared to be a tiny opening in the hillside. "You want us to stay out here in the middle of the woods?" she asked, her voice rising.

"Trust me. You'll be safe in the cave with John. It's much better that I go for help on my own. If they find us out here, we won't be able to evade them if John and I have to carry you." He nodded toward the moonlit sky. "There's too much light now. They'd track us down easily if they spotted us. And I'll be much faster on my own."

Bo glanced up at the top of the bluffs. It had turned peaceful now that the storm had moved off. The only remnants of its onslaught were a few lingering rumbles from far away. He took a deep breath. The night air carried the springtime fragrance of blossoms and the pungent odor of cedar and pine.

"What is this all about?" Meg asked, putting her arms around Bo and pressing her face into his wet shirt. "Why are people chasing us?"

"I'm close to finding out, Meg, but I'm not sure yet."

"Are they after me?" she asked, her voice shaking.

"No," Bo said firmly. "They're after me." Suddenly, exhausted from the exertion, she went limp in his arms, and he scooped her up once more.

It took them ten minutes to scale thirty feet to the narrow ledge in front of the cave opening. Bo entered first, forced to crawl through the fifteen-foot tunnel on his belly. When he reached the cave's main chamber, he removed a small flashlight from his pocket and scoured the space. The cave was damp and it smelled heavily of mildew, but it hadn't changed much since the last time he'd been in it so long ago. Satisfied that Meg and Blackburn would be safe here, he crawled back out.

"Take my hand," he said calmly to Meg, who stood on the sliver of a rock ledge clutching a root, eyes shut tightly, her body pressed to the side of the bluff.

"It's dark in there," she said, her voice trembling.

"I realize that."

"Do you have a flashlight?"

"Yes," he said, pressing the small light into her hand. "Come on."

She grabbed Bo's arm and allowed him to help her into the opening. "Don't let go of me."

"I won't," he assured her. Slowly they worked their way along the short passage to the main chamber. Blackburn followed.

"You keep the rifle," Bo said to Blackburn. "There are still four shells in it. I checked. Anybody comes in here without calling your name first, don't ask questions, just shoot."

Blackburn nodded. "Don't worry."

"Good." Bo helped Meg sit down against the wall across from the opening. He knelt and brushed her wet, matted hair from her face. "I wouldn't use the flashlight a lot," he suggested. "I don't know how much juice the batteries have left and I wouldn't take the chance that someone sees light coming from the cave."

"Okay." She shuddered at the thought of the men who were looking for them.

"I'm going to go."

"Okay," she said again, already missing him.

"You'll be fine," Bo said, starting to move toward the passage. "John is a good man."

"I know." She looked up. "Bo."

"Yes?"

"Please give me a hug."

He turned and slipped his arms around her shivering frame. He held her tight. "It will all work out. Soon we'll be back together and safe."

"Promise me you'll come back."

"I promise." He began to pull away, then hesitated. "I love you, Meg."

She kissed him deeply, then pulled back. "I love you too. You are my life."

"I'll see you soon." With that he was gone.

Bruce Laird fell to the ground, sucking air into his lungs madly. He was in top physical condition for a man in his forties, but he'd just sprinted two miles over difficult terrain and perspiration was pouring from his body. As he lay prone and raised the night-vision glasses to his eyes, he could hear the others crashing through the woods toward him. They hadn't been able to keep pace.

Laird scanned the face of the bluff quickly but saw nothing, just shades of gray and green. Then a slight movement caught his eye. He pulled back to it and focused in quickly. It was a man pulling himself to the top of the bluff. The man struggled to his feet and then limped away into the black forest.

"Dammit!"

"What's wrong?" One of the men had dropped beside Laird, panting from exertion.

"Bo's getting away." Laird allowed the glasses to fall to the ground, pulled out his cell phone, and handed it to the other man. "Here, call out," he ordered. "Tell the others he's heading northwest. You need to get people cruising state road number seven."

The man took the phone. "This may not be secure."

"Fuck it," Laird responded. "At this point it doesn't matter." He gestured back over his shoulder. "I'm going to take the other two men and go after Bo. You find out if he hid his wife in the cave. Do you see the opening?" he asked, pointing across the ravine.

"Yes."

Bo had told Laird about the cave at a party once after several drinks. Told Laird about discovering it as a child. Laird had found it himself one day during a lonely walk after being berated by Jimmy Lee for a mistake on a document. Now he grabbed the other man's arm as the man began to stand up. "Be careful as you approach that thing. Bo Hancock is a very resourceful man. He may have left you a surprise or two."

CHAPTER 20

Scott Trajak was exhausted. He was still fighting the effects of a terrible spring cold and today had turned into an eighteen-hour workday. He'd arrived at the office at six this morning with a raw throat, a one-hundred-one-degree fever, and an upset stomach, and it was almost midnight now. He'd been about to leave for home at seven o'clock when he'd received a call on the secure line in his office from Gerald Wallace demanding another Level Blue investigation. Level Blue meant that Wallace needed all information available on the target immediately. A federal judge in Florida was about to rule that local police hadn't had probable cause when they'd brutally forced their way into a suburban Miami home and stumbled onto a major drug operation—not just a local crack house as they had originally assumed. Wallace and his cronies—whoever those people were, Trajak thought grimly—were afraid that the judge's ruling would inhibit law enforcement's ability to search and seize for years to come. Unscrupulous lawyers would use the precedent-setting case to keep the forces of justice from using surprise as a tactic.

For the last five hours Trajak had worked Online Associates' computers and all of the immense resources available to him through Global Media, the American Financial Group, and their affiliated networks to uncover something Wallace could use.

Uncover something he had. Multiple cash withdrawals by the Florida judge over the past two months in a section of Miami known to be frequented by prostitutes, as well as a single use of the judge's debit card at a shop called Adult Pleasures. It was the same old story, Trajak thought, as his bodyguard moved into the elevator ahead of him and pressed the button for the lobby. The judge was married, with three children, and was considered a pillar of his community. Wallace's people would approach the judge and present him with the information, probably embellishing it with a story that they had a hooker who was willing to identify him as a John with whom she'd had sexual relations. They'd threaten him with exposure, then give him what Trajak called "the choice." Toe the line or face the music. So far, everyone had cooperated. Trajak had no doubt that the judge would choose the same course of action, falling in line to rule that police indeed had reasonable cause to attack the house in the quiet neighborhood with a twenty-five-member SWAT team (two innocent children had been killed in the ensuing gun battle), and allowing the trial of the four suspected drug traffickers who had survived the attack to proceed.

The elevator doors opened and Trajak followed his bodyguard through a marble-walled lobby and out into the warm spring night toward a waiting limousine. On-line Associates' small offices were on the top floor of the four-story building located directly across Leesburg Pike from the entrance to the Tysons Corner Mall, just outside the Capital Beltway fifteen miles west of the White House.

The bodyguard pointed a remote control device attached to his key ring at the vehicle and pressed a button. Lights flashed and locks popped open. The extensive protective measures were standard operating procedure— per Wallace's strict orders—that Trajak usually saw no need for. But today he knew that someone had breached Warfield's computer and found RANSACK. There had been a warning on his screen this morning indicating the violation, the first ever of its kind. "Thanks," he muttered, easing into the backseat while the bodyguard held the door open. Though it seemed unnecessary, he had to admit that it was nice to be driven home after a long day. At least there were some perks to working with these bastards.

Invasion of privacy wasn't ethical, but they had him over a barrel, just like they did all the others. He'd been about to go to prison for ten years on a wire fraud charge when they had made a deal for him, allowing him to go free as long as he was willing to use his considerable computer skills to their benefit. As they had made clear, the deal could be rescinded at any time and he'd end up being some ape's bitch in the big house. Trajak was youthful-looking and frail, and during the negotiations Wallace had described in graphic detail what the young man could expect during his incarceration if he ever did anything to violate the security of Online Associates or RANSACK.

"Thanks, Bud," Trajak said to the bodyguard. He touched his throat gingerly. It was even sorer now than it had been this morning.

"I'll have you home in a few minutes, Mr. Trajak."

As the bodyguard closed the limousine door, Bo emerged from behind a column at the building's entrance and raced through the darkness toward the hulking man. At the last moment Bo lowered his shoulder, slamming the bodyguard's legs against the rear of the limousine, sending him sprawling across the trunk. In one deft motion Bo grabbed the man by his hair and thrust his forehead against the vehicle three times in rapid succession. The bodyguard crumpled to the ground beside a back tire, unconscious.

Bo scanned the area quickly for security personnel—the first floor of the office building was home to upscale retailers including Tiffany and Hermès—but he saw no one. He reached quickly inside the bodyguard's coat, pulled a .38 caliber revolver from the man's shoulder holster, and raced to the other side of the car as Trajak thrust the door open.

"Hold it right there, Trajak," Bo ordered, aiming the gun into the other man's face.

Trajak lifted his hands in the air automatically. "Who are you? How do you know my name?"

"This afternoon I asked your receptionist who ran the show. Answer, Scott Trajak."

After leaving Meg with Blackburn in the cave, Bo had hiked through the woods to a county road and hitched a ride from a passerby to Greenwich. There he'd rented a car and driven to northern Virginia, arriving early this morning. He had tried Blackburn's cell phone number every half hour of the journey. There had been no response.

"What do you want?" Trajak asked nervously.

"Answers."

"To what?"

"Online Associates and something called RANSACK."

Trajak shivered. This was the nightmare scenario. One he had scoffed at each time Wallace had warned him about being careful. "I don't—"

"Don't move," Bo interrupted, training the revolver on Trajak as he leaned down and searched the young man for a weapon. He found only a cell phone, which he shoved in his pocket. "Help me with this guy."

Trajak nodded, eyeing the barrel of the revolver. Now he understood why people did exactly as they were told in such a situation.

Bo moved back around the vehicle to where the bodyguard lay. The man was just regaining consciousness. Bo leaned down and slammed his chin with the butt of the revolver, knocking him senseless once more. He rooted through the man's pockets, found the limousine's keys, popped the trunk, and, with Trajak's help, lifted the huge man up and tossed him inside, slamming the trunk closed after him.

"Here," Bo said, throwing Trajak the keys. "You drive."

"What?"

"Go on," Bo directed, gesturing toward the driver's seat. "We aren't going far." He followed Trajak with the gun until the younger man opened the driver-side door and slipped in behind the steering wheel. Then Bo jumped into the car, keeping the gun trained on Trajak. "Let's go."

Carefully, Trajak eased the limousine forward and, at Bo's direction, steered it to a parking lot on the far side of the building.

"Give me the keys," Bo ordered.

Trajak turned off the engine and handed Bo the keys.

"Follow me out," Bo said, opening his door and stepping onto the asphalt. He was aware that if Trajak was allowed to exit by his door, he might bolt. His prisoner had had time to think about an escape plan now. "Come on," Bo urged, checking the parking lot for anything suspicious.

Trajak slid across the bench seat and got out beside Bo. He had no intention of putting up any resistance. "Don't hurt me, please."

"I'm not going to hurt you," Bo assured him, pointing the nose of the revolver into his face, "as long as you answer all my questions. Now come on." He grabbed Trajak by the back of the collar and pushed him along roughly, trotting behind him until they reached the car Bo had rented. "You're driving again." Bo pressed the rental car keys into Trajak's hand. "Hurry."

Moments later they were headed west on Leesburg Pike away from Washington, pushing farther into northern Virginia. "Just stay on this road until I tell you," Bo ordered, glancing at the strip malls and car dealers rushing past.

"Okay," Trajak agreed, his voice shaking.

Several minutes later they crossed the Dulles Toll Road, a wide swath connecting Dulles Airport to the Capital Beltway, and the scenery turned from strip malls to forest. Two miles past the toll road, Bo ordered Trajak to turn right, constantly looking back to see if they were being followed. Tall trees arched over them now and the terrain became hilly as they sped north on the winding road toward the Potomac River. By the time they'd reached Georgetown Pike, roughly paralleling the south side of the Potomac, the forest had become thick.

"Left here," Bo ordered as Trajak eased to a stop at the intersection. He was scrutinizing a map of the area.

Trajak obeyed.

Bo's eyes searched the darkness ahead of them. "Turn off the road here," Bo directed as they crossed a bridge spanning something called Difficult Creek.

"Where?" Trajak asked, squinting into the darkness beyond the headlights, trying to see what Bo was pointing at.

"Here!" Bo shouted. He had found the abandoned fire road this afternoon.

Trajak slowed and guided the rental car onto a narrow, rutted path, stopping a hundred yards into the dense forest, where Bo felt they were safe.

"Turn off the engine."

Again Trajak obeyed.

"It's come-to-Jesus time," Bo said quietly as the noise of the engine faded.

Trajak gripped the steering wheel with both hands and allowed his chin to fall to his chest. "What does that mean?" he asked, his voice hushed.

"I told you, I'm not going to hurt you as long as you answer my questions," Bo said.

Trajak nodded, unconvinced.

"Tell me about Online Associates."

Trajak glanced at the gun. He had been told many times that if he were to compromise the security of the operation, he would experience a punishment far worse than his prison sentence.

"Come on," Bo urged.

"We're just a small Web consulting company," Trajak answered. "We offer a complete e-commerce solution for firms that are just beginning to offer products and services on the Internet."

"Don't give me that crap."

"There are only fifteen of us," Trajak whined. "We're barely funded. Christ, I had a helluva time making payroll last month."

"Then why are you being driven home in a limousine by a guy the size of Texas who was carrying this thing?" Bo demanded, nodding at the gun.

Trajak hesitated.

"I drove by your house in McLean today too," Bo continued. "Very nice. Hardly the digs of a man who can barely fund his company."

"How did you find out where I lived?"

"I have a friend who works for an airline. I had him run your name through his company's frequent flyer program. Your address came up right away." Bo raised one eyebrow. "That and your ticket history. You sure fly to Iowa a lot. What the hell is in Iowa?"

"Nothing," Trajak said defiantly.

Bo leaned forward on the car seat and pointed the gun menacingly at the young man's chest. "Answer my questions."

Trajak shook his head. "I can't," he said quietly. "They'll kill me."

"Who will?"

"I won't tell you."

Bo cocked the trigger. "I'm warning you."

"You can warn me all you want but I won't say anything."

Bo stared at Trajak for several moments, then shoved open his door with his shoulder. In the dim moonlight, he moved to the trunk of the car and pulled out a length of rope. "Come on!" he shouted, thrusting open the driver-side door and dragging the thin man onto the ground.

"What the hell are you going to do?" Trajak screamed, looking wild-eyed at the rope.

Bo placed the revolver on the car's roof, then dropped to his knees beside Trajak and rolled the man onto his chest. Trajak struggled but Bo overpowered him easily, yanking his hands behind his back and lashing them together at the wrists before running the rope up Trajak's back and looping it around his neck several times.

"What the hell are you doing to me?"

Bo said nothing as he dragged Trajak to the back of the car and tied the rope to the bumper.

"Oh, God, don't," Trajak pleaded. "Please!"

Bo returned to the front of the car and started the engine, spewing exhaust into Trajak's face. He could hear Trajak screaming and choking. Then he jumped from the car and raced back to where Trajak lay whimpering. "You ready to talk?" he barked.

"Yes, yes."

"Then tell me what RANSACK is."

Still Trajak hesitated.

"Why has Warfield Capital poured almost two billion dollars into what you describe as a little operation that can barely meet payroll?"

Trajak glanced up into Bo's eyes. "Who are you?" he asked, tears spilling down his soft cheeks.

"Bo Hancock. I run Warfield and I want to know what the hell's going on."

"Please, I can't tell you."

Bo stood up. "I promise you I'll have no problem getting behind the wheel and dragging you all the way to the Potomac."

"All right, all right!"

"Talk!"

"It's an intimidation network," Trajak admitted. "I gather personal information and my superior uses the information to scare his targets into doing things his way."

"What kind of information?"

"Sexual deviance, drug use, infidelity, tax fraud. You name it, I find it."

"How?"

"Through the network."

"What network?" Bo demanded.

"I have complete access to all individual records at two very large companies."

Bo caught his breath. "Let me guess. Global Media and AFG."

"Yes." Trajak struggled against the rope binding his wrists. "How the hell did you know?"

"Just keep talking."

"Through the network I can access all individual records. We have also developed technology that enables us to follow people all over the Internet."

"You place cookies," Bo said. He knew enough about the Internet to understand that codes could be attached to URLs, or Web addresses.

Trajak shook his head as he lay on the ground. "No, I can follow you individually. We can identify your specific e-mail address, then match that address against a list of names and home addresses we keep on computer file. I can know everything about you even if you are one of the few people who aren't touched by Global Media or AFG, because there are always transactions going on between AFG and other financial institutions. I can get to you through AFG. People have no idea how easy it is."

"And you needed the two billion for . . . ?"

"For infrastructure. Computer storage, servers, et cetera."

"My God."

"Yes, I can know more about you than you know about yourself."

Bo untied the rope from the bumper, then loosened it from around Trajak's neck. "Who is your superior?"

"Untie me all the way first," Trajak demanded.

"Tell me."

"Untie me!"

"You aren't in a position to negotiate."

"You don't think so, huh?"

Bo studied Trajak through the gloom. "What do you mean?"

"That bodyguard you threw in the trunk of the limousine is supposed to check in with somebody every fifteen minutes. If he doesn't, they come looking for me. He forgot to once and they were in my office ten minutes later."

Bo glanced back down the fire road. "They'll go to your home and the office."

"They'll come right here, asshole. You have maybe five minutes before they're swarming up that dirt road."

Bo's gaze snapped back to Trajak. "How would they know?"

"I've got a homing chip surgically implanted in my leg. They did it to me when they hired me. It isn't very high-tech, but it will lead them right to me. I'm not lying! They'll kill us both!"

Bo's eyes narrowed. Trajak could be bluffing but what he was saying made sense. And the man didn't look as if he was bluffing. He looked terrified.

Bo picked Trajak up, tossed him onto the rental car's backseat, jumped in behind the wheel, and gunned the car backward down the fire road, swerving crazily from side to side as he tried to steer the car through a gauntlet of trees, guided by only the red hue of taillights. As he skidded out onto Georgetown Pike, he could see head-lights coming at him through the back window. The other car was just crossing the bridge over Difficult Creek. He slammed the car into gear and jammed his foot on the accelerator. "Come on!" he shouted. The car seemed to be reacting in slow motion, wheels spinning on the dew-slick asphalt.

Finally it lurched forward, but now the headlights of the other car were directly behind him, darting to the left and right as the driver tried to pull alongside. Bo jerked the wheel to the left, slamming fenders with the other car. "Who's your boss?" he shouted to Trajak, watching the other car lag back after the impact.

There was no answer, just a groan as Trajack was hurled onto the floor of the car when Bo slammed on his brakes, then hit the accelerator again.

"Tell me, dammit!" Bo shouted. "We're in this thing together now. Your best bet right now is to throw in with me."

"Gerald Wallace!" Trajak shouted back.

"Senator Wallace?"

"Yes."

Bo checked his side mirror. Whoever was in the car behind them was gaining ground quickly. "No wonder you've been going to Iowa."

"Yes, no wonder."

"Who is Wallace's boss? How high up does it go?"

"I don't know any more than what I've told you."

A hundred yards ahead was a traffic light and the top of the long hill they had been climbing since pulling out of the dirt road. Bo checked his rearview mirror for a split second as they crested the hill. Suddenly a pair of high beams appeared directly in his path and he jerked the wheel to the right to avoid a head-on collision, grazing the oncoming car and hurtling off onto a side road at the intersection. For several moments it appeared that the car would plunge into a gully by the side of the road. It hung on the edge for what seemed an eternity, but at the last second the tires grabbed hold of the roadway and leapt ahead, fishtailing several hundred feet before he could straighten out the front wheels.

"Dammit!"

"What's wrong?" Despite the fact that his hands were still tied behind his back, Trajak had managed to get back up on the seat and into a sitting position.

"I don't like this," Bo answered, keeping the accelerator pressed to the floor.

"Don't like what?" Trajak shouted, leaning against one side of the car to keep his balance as they raced forward.

"We're going downhill."

"So?"

"The Potomac is ahead of us somewhere and this road doesn't look big enough to have a bridge." A sign flashed past. "Shit, I was right. Look at the damn sign."

"What did it say? I couldn't read it."

"It said that the park closes at dusk!" Bo shouted. "This road leads to a state forest or something. It's a dead end." Then he saw a small darkened ranger station bisecting the road ahead and a sign detailing the cost of admission to the park. "Four bucks for passenger cars!"

"I can't get to my wallet right now!" Trajak yelled back. "I hope you understand."

"Get down!" Bo ordered as they hurtled toward the white pipe gate obstructing the road beside the ranger station, leaning down into the passenger seat at the last moment.

The pipe slammed into the windshield, shearing off the roof of the car.

Bo rose up from the passenger side covered with tiny pieces of broken glass. "You all right?" he asked, wind whipping past his face.

"Just great!"

Bo skidded to a halt in the parking lot. It made no sense to try to go back up the hill. He could already hear vehicles racing through the forest toward them. He jumped out of the car, then leaned into the backseat, dragged Trajak out, and frantically untied the rope. "You're on your own now."

"Don't leave me," Trajak pleaded, brushing glass from his hair as he scrambled to his feet.

"You've got a homing device in your leg. I'm getting as far away from you as I can."

Trajak reached out and grabbed Bo strongly by the shoulder. "I understand. Thanks for untying me. You didn't have to do that."

Two sets of headlights raced past the ranger station as Bo bolted to the left and sprinted past a Plexiglas-encased map of the area toward a hospitality center. Then he was beyond the wooden structure and running down a dirt path into darkness, aware that the headlights were following him. His pursuers had leapt the curb of the parking lot in their vehicles and were racing after him down the walkway.

Bo darted left down a smaller path and over a foot-bridge, then turned left again, racing through bushes that grabbed at his clothing. He held his arms up and forged ahead blindly, wishing he hadn't forgotten to grab the revolver from the top of the car back at the fire road. Then he heard a great roar and came to a sudden stop, balanced for a moment on a rock ledge that seemed to fall away straight down into nothing. In the moonlight he could make out the Great Falls of the Potomac stretching out before him, the spring thaw from the combined Potomac and Shenandoah Rivers thundering over the rocks below.

Bo gazed into the darkness. It was seventy feet down to the swirling mass of white water. He started to turn back toward the path, but he could see the flashlights of his pursuers bobbing toward him.

He took a deep breath and jumped. Instantly the air was rushing past his ears, then his feet hit the frigid water and he was in the midst of chaos, fighting for a breath. A swirling current dragged him down, cartwheeling him over and over to the bottom, where a huge rock caught him flush in the chest. He blacked out momentarily, then the current sent him shooting up as if he were riding the crest of a large wave so that his entire body burst through the surface and he sucked life-sustaining oxygen into his lungs.

All at once the water turned calm and he was floating in a quiet pool. Slowly he swam toward the trees and dragged himself up onto the bank, exhausted, unconcerned that his pursuers might find him. He had been swept downriver at least a half mile and they would have no idea where he was. He crawled back about thirty feet into the woods, where night-vision glasses wouldn't be able to spot him, and collapsed on the ground, spent.

Ten minutes later he pulled himself to his feet, bracing his body against a large oak tree. He had a long trek ahead. He tried to get his bearings. If this was the Maryland side of the river, he thought, that would put even more distance between him and the people who had been chasing him.

Suddenly a flashlight beam shone directly in Bo's eyes, blinding him. He turned to run, but a rifle butt slammed across the back of his head and Bo dropped to the ground unconscious.

The man who had struck Bo chuckled as he bent down and inspected his shoulder in the beam of the flashlight. "I guess Trajak wasn't lying to us," he called to his partner. "The tracking device is right here on Hancock's shirt at his shoulder, just like he promised."

CHAPTER 21

The hood was removed by someone behind him and for the first time in several hours Bo was able to breathe freely without drawing velvety material halfway up his nostrils. When the handcuffs were gone, he clasped and unclasped his fists several times to get the circulation going in his hands again.

Michael Mendoza sat behind Jimmy Lee's desk in the mansion's study, calmly smoking a cigar. "Hello, Bolling," he said smoothly in his deep voice. "Sorry about all the rough stuff, but I had to make certain I got to you before you did something rash. I wanted you to have all of the facts."

Bo sat in a chair in front of the desk. "Something rash?" he asked, watching the man who had removed the hood and the handcuffs exit the study. Now they were alone. "Like what?"

"Like calling the FBI or the Justice Department."

"Why would I have done that?"

Mendoza shrugged. "Maybe you wouldn't have." He puffed on the cigar. "But I wanted the opportunity to lay it all out for you first, just in case." He nodded at a scotch bottle on the desk and two glasses beside the bottle. "Have a drink," he offered.

Bo gazed at the bottle. "No, thanks," he finally said. "You're looking awfully fit for a man who is supposed to be clinging to life by a thread."

Mendoza chuckled. "There was a lot going on so we decided it wouldn't be a bad idea for me to look like a target as well. Just in case we needed to throw somebody off the trail."

"*We* decided?" Bo repeated. "Other than Gerald Wallace, who is involved?"

"Did Trajak tell you about Wallace?" Mendoza wanted to know.

"Yes."

"Well, I still consider him a loyal guy," Mendoza muttered, more to himself than Bo. "He put a tracking device on you at Great Falls so we could find you. And I imagine you can be a pretty effective interrogator when you want to be."

"Who else is involved, Michael?"

"Several others, but I sit at the top of the cell. Only Wallace knows that I run the operation. And now you, of course."

"Which is basically an information network," Bo said, standing up to stretch his legs. He'd been sitting for several hours, on the trip up from Washington to the estate in the helicopter. He moved to the window overlooking the lake and peered into the light of breaking dawn, then turned back to face Mendoza. "Is that right?"

"Yes."

"A Big Brother infrastructure that allows you to conduct constant and widespread surveillance on the American people. A surveillance system that can be used as a weapon of intimidation when you so require by mining the data warehouse of individual files you're probably storing in computers all over the country."

"That's exactly right," Mendoza admitted. "And it's a damn effective operation."

Bo moved back toward the desk. "In fact, RANSACK allows you to make policy by circumventing the political process."

Mendoza smiled at Bo's casual use of the top-secret project's name. "In many cases we still use the political process."

Bo sat down before his old friend once more. "You mean you intimidate the process. You make people do what you want by scaring them, people like politicians and judges who are unfriendly to your way of thinking."

"We *facilitate* the process and enable those who have the wrong ideas to see the light. It can take years to enact legislation in our society because of all of the damn checks and balances built into the system. Justice is constantly impeded by bleeding hearts and whistle-blowers who don't understand the bigger picture. RANSACK has addressed all of that inefficiency, and we don't use our power indiscriminately. We let things function normally for the most part. We pick our spots and act only out of necessity.

"We've talked about it so many times, Bo," Mendoza continued. "About how often the guilty go free because we in this country seem to have a fascination with protecting the criminals, not the victims. About how a democracy is such an inefficient form of government."

Bo nodded. They had discussed and agreed on that fact many times. "What you're doing sounds good in theory, but you know as well as I do that actually practicing that kind of vigilantism is an entirely different matter. We've talked about that too."

Mendoza took a deep breath. "Let me give you an example of why we need RANSACK, Bo. Not long ago we discovered that a defense contractor executive, just this one guy, had decided on his own to shut down a top secret project only weeks from completion. It was a new attack submarine the navy badly needed. The guy had decided to blow the whistle on some insignificant overbilling by his superiors. He was going to testify to the overbilling in front of a congressional committee, and you know what would have happened, Bo. They would have delayed the project, maybe even shelved it, over a measly twenty million bucks. I know twenty million sounds like a lot of money, but in a multi-trillion dollar budget with world peace hanging in the balance, it's a pimple on the ass of an ant. Now we will have that attack submarine and it will prove itself invaluable. Without RANSACK, who knows what would have happened?"

"Where does it stop?" Bo asked.

"What do you mean?"

"When we had these discussions, that was the point we could never agree on. How far does this type of thing go? Immense power concentrated in a few people's hands can easily spin out of control. Look at your history books. It has happened time after time down through the centuries."

Mendoza took a long puff from his cigar. "That's one of the reasons I want you involved, Bo," he said softly. "That's what all of this is about. I know you will always act as a voice of reason. I've known you for more than forty years, and I have more confidence in you than I have in anyone other than myself. You always do the right thing, and you have more courage in your little finger than most people have in their entire bodies. I saw it on that mountain the day you saved my life, and you were just a teenager then."

Bo hesitated. "You want me involved?" he asked, his eyes widening.

Mendoza nodded. "I want to bring you into the inner circle. I want you to run Warfield Capital as a legitimate business and take control of the family empire. At the same time I want you to run cutouts through the firm for us. For those of us at the highest levels of the U.S. intelligence structure."

"Cutouts?"

"Like Online Associates," Mendoza said. "Warfield will make the investment so that the government can never be linked to anything. We spin the money through a maze of money-laundering systems, then bring the cash into the private sector through an offshore vehicle that appears to be controlled by European or South American investors."

"Like you did with the original two billion into Warfield."

"Yes."

"And the five hundred million that came in after that."

"Yes." Mendoza pointed the cigar at Bo. "I'll give you a lot of credit on that one. You had me over a barrel and you knew it. You knew I couldn't afford to have Warfield fail. You knew I'd send the money to prop you up."

On his way back to the mansion after putting Paul in the ambulance, Bo had called Allen Taylor. Taylor had confirmed on the call that the additional five hundred million Warfield had received that morning had ultimately been routed through the same Italian bank that the first two billion had come from. The two billion Ramsey had alerted Bo to the day Jimmy Lee had died. Once again, Taylor had been unable to follow the money any further back than Italy, but it didn't matter to Bo. He had confirmed what he needed to know.

"If Warfield had gone down, the federal regulators would have crawled all over the firm and dug through everything in detail," Bo pointed out. "All of our records and all of our investments. They might have found Online Associates, and RANSACK might have been exposed. At the very least, damaged, and you couldn't have that."

"It was a helluva bluff, Bo," Mendoza agreed. "I thought about not sending the money, but my people checked out the Bloomberg and Reuters stories about Warfield being in serious trouble and the information was confirmed. Warfield had failed on a transaction with Stillman and the markets went crazy." He puffed on his cigar. "How did you manufacture that whole thing?"

Jack O'Connor had been hesitant to honor Bo's request, but in the end had acquiesced. The fail on the fifty million in bonds had been arranged quietly and O'Connor had instructed his traders not to deal with Warfield at the open. Finally, O'Connor had called contacts at Bloomberg and Reuters to exacerbate the problem and accelerate the effect. "That was easy," Bo said, not wanting to give away O'Connor's identity. "And once a rumor gets started on Wall Street, it's harder to stop than a nuclear reaction."

Mendoza tapped an inch-long ash into a tray beside the scotch bottle. "Well, it was a nice piece of poker playing."

"Where did the money actually come from?" Bo asked, curious how Mendoza could so easily and quickly manipulate such an immense amount of money.

"The Energy Department," Mendoza replied, allowing Bo the kind of high-level information that would make him feel right away like a part of what was going on. "Energy has a huge budget with the least amount of oversight. A little-known and closely guarded Washington secret," he added.

"So you want me involved?" Bo asked, interested in where Mendoza was headed with all of this. "I assume I'm not the first civilian allowed inside."

"We do this kind of thing quite a bit, though rarely at this level," Mendoza admitted. "You'd be surprised how many CEOs and general counsels of large corporations allow us to run cutouts through their publicly held corporations. It's very effective." He gestured toward the window. "As we expand our network, we'll need to make more investments related to RANSACK. Warfield gives us a perfect platform from which to do so. We can do things quietly and quickly."

"Why did Jimmy Lee agree to set this thing up through Warfield in the first place?" Bo asked.

"First of all, he was a patriot. Your father understood the need for this kind of operation immediately. Second, he wanted Paul elected president."

Bo smiled. That was the real reason. Jimmy Lee would never have done anything purely for the good of the country. There always needed to be a return on his investment. "So the understanding was that he would allow you to use Warfield as an investment vehicle in return for information on Paul's political opponents."

"Yes."

"Other than Jimmy Lee, who within the family knew about RANSACK?"

"Teddy."

"Not Paul?"

"Paul knows very little. In case the thing ever blew up in our faces, Jimmy Lee wanted Paul insulated."

"What about Bruce Laird?"

"He never knew anything about RANSACK. Paul told him only that it was imperative that you not be allowed back into Warfield, and he asked no questions. At the end Paul convinced Laird that you were attempting to get rid of him because you'd uncovered his problems at Davis Polk, which is why Laird tried hard to get you to accept Paul's offer to manage a billion of the family's money from Montana." Mendoza chuckled. "He did, however, turn out to be quite a hero. He and a crew of men rescued Meg and your friend John Blackburn from a cave on the estate last night. Rest assured, Meg is fine. She is with her parents on Long Island as we speak."

Bo's shoulders slumped and he felt himself choking up. He had not stopped thinking about Meg through everything. He'd truly believed that she was safer with Blackburn in the cave, but he had second-guessed that decision thousands of times since. "That was Laird who was chasing us?" Bo asked, trying to hide the emotion overcoming him.

"Yes," Mendoza confirmed. "Laird happened to see our people breaking into your mansion and quickly rounded up estate security. When you came out from under the deck with Meg and Blackburn, it was the estate security staff chasing you. They were trying to save you, not hurt you. But you couldn't have known."

"But it was your people who broke through the door in the basement?"

"Yes."

"You killed Teddy and Tom Bristow, didn't you?" Bo asked. "Once Jimmy Lee was gone you saw the opportunity to consolidate power."

"Teddy, yes, but we didn't kill Tom Bristow," Mendoza replied, his voice dropping. "Teddy took care of that for us."

Bo glanced up. "What?"

"Teddy and Tom were homosexuals. They were partners, though they kept it very quiet. Yes. We think that once Teddy saw he was going to be running Warfield, he panicked, understanding that his relationship with Tom made him vulnerable."

Bo was silent for several seconds, trying to comprehend what Mendoza was saying. "Tiffany was working for you, wasn't she," he finally said.

"Yes, I was trying to find out if you intended to come back to Warfield. Jimmy Lee had mentioned to me that you were becoming very restless out in Montana and I was worried, so I manufactured my trip out there under the cover of being keynote speaker at the Jackson Hole trade summit. Tiffany planted a microphone in the dashboard of your Jeep and when you told her that you were definitely coming back, we went into action. I knew that if you ever discovered what was going on at Warfield without me having the proper opportunity to explain everything to you, you'd notify the authorities. It's one of many things I admire about you, Bo. You are the most honest man I've ever known."

"So that's why I was sent to Montana. To get me out of the way."

"And because Jimmy Lee was worried about you screwing up Paul's campaign. Both factors were at work. No one has ever questioned that you were the right person to run Warfield. Now you can do so with no constraints."

"Then you did write the memo to Jimmy Lee suggesting the change in Warfield's general partnership structure."

"Yes," Mendoza admitted, "and if Paul had done even a half-assed job of hiding your father's personal papers, you never would have known. Not that it matters now."

Bo pointed at Mendoza. "You had me attacked and drugged in the Jeep. You had the pictures taken of me with Tiffany in the motel."

Mendoza nodded.

"Are there more than the one photograph I've seen?" Bo asked hesitantly.

Mendoza let out a sigh. He had hoped to avoid this discussion. "Many more," he said softly. "Some extremely graphic ones too. Ones that would make Meg's stomach turn if she ever saw them," he warned sternly. "But let's focus on more important issues, of which there are many. There is a great deal more to tell—"

"Did you go after Meg?" Bo interrupted, his voice hollow. "Were you behind the attacks at Penn Station and the parking garage near the hospital?"

Mendoza puffed on the cigar.

"Michael!" Bo shouted, standing up.

The study door swung open quickly. The man who had removed the hood and handcuffs appeared in the doorway. "Everything all right, sir?" he asked gruffly.

"Fine," Mendoza answered. He waved his hand. "Leave us."

The man glanced menacingly at Bo, then shut the door.

"Sit back down, Bo," Mendoza ordered, waiting until Bo had complied before speaking again. "This gets to the heart of the matter, my friend."

"What do you mean?"

"Don't you think it would have been easier for me simply to have you killed and let Frank Ramsey continue to run Warfield, than go through all of this? Ramsey was a puppet, a man I could control very easily, and you were a damn bull in a china shop. I could have had you capped so easily that night in Montana and been done with you. It would have been so much cleaner than bribing Tiffany and taking those pictures, and losing sleep knowing that you were closing in on what was going on at Warfield. Don't you see how much easier that would have been for me?"

"I suppose it would have been." The thought had occurred to Bo several times.

"I love you like a brother, Bo. I couldn't kill you."

"But you could kill my wife."

"No." Mendoza pursed his lips. "However, I made you think she was in danger to distract you and make you vulnerable. I could have killed her in that parking garage, but I didn't. I wanted you to recognize that you needed to back off, but you didn't. You kept charging forward. I should have known you would. It's what I love about you, and what I hate." He leaned forward on the desk, gritting his teeth. "RANSACK is the most important intelligence initiative our government has ever embarked upon, and I have allowed our personal relationship to cloud my judgment. Gerald Wallace has questioned my commitment to RANSACK several times because of my decisions regarding your safety. But make no mistake, Bolling, I will not let that happen again. I have pictures in my possession that would destroy your marriage to Meg, and from this point on I would not hesitate to use them or to use excessive force if necessary to protect the sanctity of the operation." He leaned back slowly in the chair. "But there is no need for all of that, Bo," he said, his voice softening. "Come and be my partner, not my adversary. RANSACK represents an incredible opportunity to clean up this country once and for all. You know down deep you believe strongly in what I'm doing. You hate seeing criminals go free as much as I do. You hate seeing the bleeding hearts win."

A long silence ensued, both men deep in thought.

"What about Dale Stephenson?" Bo finally asked.

"He went to Montana to warn you about what was going on. Somehow he found out more than he should have. We killed him," Mendoza admitted matter-of-factly, "then told people he had died in an accident in Colorado." Mendoza tapped the desk. "I'm not proud of some of the things I've had to do, Bo, but to make RANSACK a reality I agreed to go to any lengths necessary to succeed. Dale was a good man and I'm sorry about what happened to him. I'm sorry about Richard Randolph and Harold Shaw too, but—"

"But you had to have your people in charge of Global Media and AFG," Bo finished the thought.

"Of course we had to have our people in charge. It's terrible and I spent a great deal of time trying to figure out a better way, a solution in which men did not have to die. But they did have to die, and I'm comfortable that ultimately I have followed the honorable course of action to protect my country. Sometimes individuals have to be sacrificed for the good of the colony."

"What will happen now that Jimmy Lee is gone?"

Mendoza cleared his throat. "As I said, I want you to run Warfield and take control of the Hancock family empire. If not, I will appoint someone who will do exactly as I direct. What I have sacrificed for this operation will not be in vain."

Bo's face contorted. "How the hell would you appoint someone?"

"Catherine and I are to be married. Through her, I will control the family if you choose not to."

"Are you mad?"

"I couldn't be more sane." Mendoza laughed. "Right now Catherine is being 'held captive' at my farmhouse in Middleburg, Virginia. She thinks we both are. The truth is that I wanted her protected through all of this and the best way to accomplish that was to make her think she had been taken hostage. You never know what may happen to your loved ones at critical times in this business," he said, raising an eyebrow. "When this is over, we will marry. I want you to be our best man."

Bo shook his head in disbelief. "But remember the new partnership agreement you had put in place. Ashley and I could always—"

Mendoza held up a hand. "Don't push me, Bo."

Bo fell silent, understanding the not-so-veiled threat. "When did you and Catherine become close?" he asked.

"I have always admired Catherine," Mendoza answered, "ever since she was young. When I found out about Teddy and Tom, I informed her. I discovered then that she had always hated Jimmy Lee as much as I did," he said, his expression turning steely.

"Jimmy Lee gave you everything," Bo said incredulously. "How could you have hated him?"

"Your *mother* gave me everything," Mendoza retorted. "Ida was the one who rescued me from the orphanage after I escaped from Cuba. Ida was the one who invited me to spend time at the estate when I was young. As you've said yourself, Jimmy Lee was quite a bigot. In the early years he referred to me in private as 'the little spic welfare case.' He didn't think I knew about that. I loved your mother, Bo, but I hated Jimmy Lee." Mendoza leaned forward and poured Bo a drink. "Here, you look like you need it."

Bo glanced down at the glass. "I don't understand," he said slowly.

"Jimmy Lee used me the same way he used Catherine. When he figured out that I was intelligent and that people gravitated toward me, then he took an interest in me. He paid for the finest education money could buy, then he bought my way into the Senate, just as he bought Paul's way into the Connecticut governor's office. When I became a senator, he used me. It was no coincidence that Jimmy Lee knew about major Senate decisions before they were announced. Before anyone else knew about them. He made incredible amounts of money using the information I fed him." Mendoza's expression turned grim. "When I asked Jimmy Lee to help me run for president, he turned his back on me." His voice intensified. "I'm eminently more qualified to run this country than Paul, but your father put the kiss of death on my chances by calling his high-powered friends and telling them lies about me. He never knew that I'd found out about what he had done."

"So in return you destroyed Paul's campaign."

"Yes!" Mendoza snarled. "I arranged for that break-in at Reggie Duncan's campaign headquarters. I arranged for Ron Baker's destruction and for Baker to throw his support to Duncan." He laughed aloud. "Baker still has no idea who really fucked him." Mendoza's voice turned calm again. "I'm glad to see a black man on the doorstep of the White House. He's a much better man than Paul Hancock."

"I agree," Bo said quietly, picking the glass of scotch up off the desk. He took a small sip, savoring the taste and the warm feeling that coursed through him instantly. "Who took the pictures of Paul's hands around Melissa's neck?" he asked, knowing the answer.

"I did," Mendoza replied. "I hated Paul then as much as you did. Almost as much as I do now. He's a worthless bastard, wouldn't you agree?"

Bo took a longer swallow of the scotch. "Yes."

"My only regret is that he didn't kill himself the night before last right here in this room," Mendoza said ruefully, glancing up at the hole in the ceiling where the slug had buried itself. "But he's only a shadow of his former self now. Without Jimmy Lee and Teddy to support him, you and I will be able to manipulate him any way we choose."

"You're right." Bo guzzled down what remained of the scotch. "So you saw Paul kill Melissa that night?" he asked quietly.

Mendoza leaned forward and refilled the glass, then filled the second one on the desk. "No, Bo. I killed her," he admitted finally, his lip twitching slightly as he said the words. "I hate Paul more than even you can imagine. And she was so very expendable."

For a long time they were silent. Then Mendoza picked up his glass, rose to his feet and nodded for Bo to stand as well. "To Warfield," he said, touching Bo's glass.

"Yes."

"To RANSACK as well."

Bo hesitated. "To RANSACK," he finally said, pressing the glass to his lips and drinking, exhilarated by the taste. He had missed the feeling of intoxication so badly.

EPILOGUE

When you dump two hundred billion dollars' worth of anything into a marketplace, you don't get full price. You don't have to be a Nobel Prize–winning economist to figure that out. When it's the federal government doing the dumping and the product is financial securities, you don't even get wholesale. At first the feds tried to sell off Warfield's assets quietly, but financial vultures have a better scent for blood than great white sharks and the thing quickly turned into a chaotic auction. From what I read, they got a hundred and forty billion for everything, but it was probably even less than that. The Hancock fortune was reduced to smoldering ruins and several huge financial institutions—Warfield lenders— came close to bankruptcy. Global Media and AFG were sold off piecemeal.

I played along with Michael Mendoza's proposal to run the family empire for almost three months. I'm not much on patience, but in this instance I realized I had to be very careful about what I was doing. I knew that if I rolled over on Michael, my case would have to be air-tight, and that even the Justice Department wouldn't be able to protect me afterward, though they'd tell me they could.

It wasn't an easy decision, let me tell you. I knew I'd be destroying the Hancock name, as well as the lives of family members, Warfield employees, and friends who'd had nothing to do with RANSACK. But I knew if I didn't go to Justice, I'd be destroying much more than that.

One thing I regret is that I've never had a chance to talk to Ashley about what I did. Two weeks after the funerals she returned to Europe to resume her life. We talked every day by telephone after she left, right up until the day I went to the Justice Department. I never talked to her about my plan because I couldn't risk a wiretap, or risk putting her in danger by letting her know what I was going to do. I hope she supports me. I think she does. Someday, when everything calms down and it's safe, I'll go see her in Europe. Until then I'll feel good about the ten million dollars I got her before I detonated Warfield. I miss her every day.

What you have to understand is that I always trusted Michael Mendoza. Really trusted him. He'd always been the big brother that neither Paul nor Teddy had been. I can't emphasize that enough. Michael and I were that close.

Over the years we had talked so many times into the early morning hours over a good bottle of port about the pros and cons of democracy. About how criminals seemed to get away with things more often than they got caught. About how ridiculously bad the legal system had become. And about how bleeding-heart elements had no idea what they were doing when they championed liberal causes. But in the end, I knew where RANSACK could lead, and it frightened the hell out of me.

I realized that evening in my father's study that some-where along the way—I'm not sure where—Michael had truly lost his perspective, and his mind. It isn't easy when you make that call about someone, especially a person you're as close to as I was to Michael. It leaves you feeling the way you do after waking up in the middle of the night from a really awful nightmare. And at first you aren't certain you're accurate in your assessment, or right in what you're doing. Maybe it's you that isn't all there, not the other guy.

But in the weeks that followed, I came to find out that I was absolutely correct. Michael hadn't seized on an opportunity, he'd created one. Turns out, Dr. Silwa had actually poisoned my father after being blackmailed by RANSACK. We confirmed that when we exhumed Jimmy Lee's body under cover of darkness and performed a second autopsy. I had this strange feeling about the whole thing and I was dead on. When we confronted Silwa with the test results, he crumpled in front of our eyes. It was almost like he was relieved that he didn't have to sneak around anymore wondering what they'd order him to do next.

Frank Ramsey turned up dead one day outside a small Oklahoma town. He joined Teddy, Harold Shaw, Richard Randolph, the Hazeltine employee who had been watching me in Montana, Dale Stephenson, and Tom Bristow as RANSACK victims. I'm sure Tiffany ended up dead too, but I never heard.

The Ramsey thing scared me. If they could find him in Oklahoma, no one was safe anywhere.

"Anything to drink, sir?"

The man behind the bar seems friendly enough, but I don't trust anybody these days. "Diet Coke."

I haven't had liquor since that night in Jimmy Lee's

study. It's been six months now. This time I think I've licked the thing, but you never know for sure.

God, I love New Orleans. You can really get lost here. They had offered me the Witness Protection Program, but I knew that was a joke. I'm sure the Justice boys meant well, but they didn't know who they were dealing with. Mendoza would have ripped the WPP computer apart with his capabilities like a chain saw going through microwaved butter, and located me in a New York second. No thanks.

So I went out on my own. I stashed ten million bucks around the country in fifty different banks, something in every state in case I stopped by. Mendoza will look because he knows I would have taken care of myself, but he won't find anything. I learned a thing or two along the way as well. I also took a bunch of diamonds with me. They're the best if you're ever on the run. They're lightweight, untraceable, and readily marketable. A little free advice for you.

As promised, Michael made certain Meg saw all of the pictures of Tiffany and me in the Libby motel after I disappeared. She filed for divorce immediately. I'm sure Michael was happy about that.

The woman is very pretty and I notice her right away at the far end of the bar. We have an instant attraction. Maybe she likes my ruggedness or the short ponytail coming down from under the white skimmer hat I've taken to wearing these days. Whatever it is, she comes and sits down next to me. Sort of sidles around nervously for a while, but pretty soon she's on the stool next to mine. She has short, dark hair beneath a baseball cap pulled low over sexy eyes, but it isn't her physical beauty to which I'm so instantly attracted. It's this aura. This vulnerability that turns on my urge to protect like a switch on the wall.

"Hi, Bo."

"Hello, Meg."

I haven't seen her since the night before I rolled over on Michael. I told her everything that night, even showed her the picture of Tiffany and me that Michael had given me out in Wyoming. It didn't faze her one bit. She believed me right away when I told her I had been set up, and was fully prepared when fifty-seven more showed up in her mailbox after I left. I told her I was adopted that night too and that didn't faze her either. She said she'd always known and not because I looked different from Teddy and Paul. She said it was because I was such a different person than those bastards. She actually used the word "bastards," which I liked.

I told her to wait three months before she came to this dive in the French Quarter. I knew Michael would be watching and listening. We haven't spoken since that night, but I had no doubt she would be as punctual as always. We have a bond no one can understand.

"I'm scared, Bo," she says, taking a sip of my Diet Coke.

"Don't worry, nothing can happen to us now," I say, gazing at the woman I've missed so deeply. I kind of like this new look of hers—the cropped brunet hair.

"I did it with a pair of scissors at the airport," she says, touching my leg.

"It looks good."

"I love you," she whispers.

"I love you too."

I know Michael will never figure out how I could throw it all away. He thought I couldn't live without the money and the luxury, but he never really knew me, as close as we were, because ultimately his mind didn't work like mine. I'm a pretty simple guy when it comes down to it. All I really need is Meg, and now I have her back again.

I heard years later that people speculated I had destroyed the family and our fortune because I had some deep-seated bitterness over being adopted, but that wasn't it.

It was a matter of honor. And that was all.

The exhilarating world
of point–and–click stock market trading
takes a lethal turn
in Stephen Frey's newest thriller

THE DAY TRADER

Coming in hardcover from
Ballantine Books in January 2002.

Read the first chapter now . . .

CHAPTER 1

I'm not a religious man, but I make the sign of the cross over my heart just in case. The way I do every time I start. After all, the next few seconds could change my life forever.

Employees aren't supposed to use company Internet access for personal reasons, but lots of us violate the policy and no one's ever been fired for it. Jesus, they only pay me $39,000 a year to be an assistant sales rep for retail paper products in the mid-Atlantic region. So, the way I see it, I deserve a perk or two along the way. I've dedicated eleven years to this company, but my wife and I still live paycheck-to-paycheck, even though she has a full time job too.

Images flash across my computer screen, and I quickly reach the home page of the on-line brokerage firm I use to trade my small stock portfolio. As I enter the information required to access my account, adrenaline surges through me, like it always does when I get to this point. It's as if I've bought a lotto ticket when there's a fifty million-dollar jackpot, and I have that lucky feeling tingling in my veins.

My fingertips race across the keyboard as I close in on my target, so I pause for a sip of coffee and a deep breath.

The deal is only a few screens away, and I'm addicted to the anticipation—so I prolong it. It's one of the few things I really look forward to these days. This morning, as I guided my rusting Toyota through the bumper-to-bumper northern Virginia traffic and thick summer humidity, I had a premonition that today would be different. That something was going to interrupt my daily grind. But I've had that feeling before.

> Name: Augustus McKnight.
> Password: Cardinal.
> Account Number: YTP1699.

There's a sharp knock and my eyes shift to the office doorway. Standing there is my boss, Russell Lake, vice president of all paper product sales. Russell is a slender man with thinning brown hair, a full mustache and a pasty complexion. He leans into my cramped office, one hand on the doorknob, peering at me over wire-rimmed glasses. And I stare back like a boy caught digging in the cookie jar just before dinner.

"Good morning, Augustus."

I can tell by the intensity in Russell's eyes that he's trying to figure out what I'm doing on my computer, but I've positioned it so someone standing at the door can't see the screen. "Hello," I say warily. You never know what he's up to.

"Up with the eagles this morning?"

"What do you mean by that?"

"It's only eight o'clock," he says sarcastically, tapping the cracked crystal of the same Timex he wore the day he interviewed me more than a decade ago. He's always been sarcastic. That's just the way he is. "Aren't you usually just crawling out of bed about now?"

I'm in by 7:30 almost every morning, sometimes earlier, but there's no point in arguing. Like most bosses, Russell has a convenient memory.

"What are you working on?" he asks.

"Cold fusion."

"Very funny," he says, moving into the office. "Now tell me the truth."

I'm tempted to flick off the computer, but that would be a dead give-away I'm doing something wrong. "I'm updating a sales report for central Virginia," I say, hoping he doesn't walk around to my side of the desk. "Nothing exciting."

"Checking your stock portfolio again?"

Russell blurs before me. "What?"

He settles into a chair on the other side of my desk, an annoying smile tickling the corners of his mouth. "I know all about your day trading." He snickers. "You're on that computer at least two hours a day doing research, checking quotes and placing orders." Russell removes his glasses and cleans the dirty lenses with his striped polyester tie. "I'm willing to look the other way at a little indiscretion, but sales in your region are way down. A couple of weeks ago senior management wanted to know what was going on. I defended you as basically a good employee, but I had to tell them about your stock market addiction."

"Dammit, Russell! Why'd you screw me like that?"

"Don't blame me, Augustus," he says coldly, replacing the lenses on his face. "You've got to start accepting accountability for your actions if you want to get anywhere around here. That's always been a problem for you."

"How do you know what I'm doing on my computer anyway?"

"I monitor the network."

"So you've been spying on me?"

"Spying is such a nasty way to put it," Russell replies smugly. "I prefer 'monitoring.' "

"You've been watching me without me knowing. That's what it comes down to."

He raises his eyebrows and grins smugly. "Now you know."

"That sucks."

"You shouldn't be using company property for personal reasons," he retorts.

"Lots of other people do."

"Other people get their work done on time. Besides, the company has a right to protect its assets."

"And I have a right to protect my privacy."

"Last year, you and everybody else around here signed a waiver permitting us to monitor your Internet activity," Russell reminds me, "including E-mails. This shouldn't come as any surprise."

Now that he says it, I do remember signing that waiver. It didn't seem like a big deal at the time, but it's come back to haunt me.

"Are you day trading right now?" Russell wants to know.

I hear a different tone in his voice. There's curiosity as opposed to warning, with a hint of goodwill too. But Russell is skilled at convincing people he's reaching out when he's really digging, so I have to be careful.

"Come on," he urges when I don't respond right away. "I'm interested."

I've been caught red-handed, but if I'm cooperative,

maybe he'll cut me a break. "I'm not actually day trading," I say cautiously. "Real day traders execute hundreds of buy and sell orders every day. I'm not doing that."

"What *are* you doing?"

"I'm buying a few shares here and there and holding them for the long term." My entire portfolio is worth less than a thousand bucks. I won't be retiring on it, but I get a kick out of knowing that when prices go up I've made money without lifting a finger. "Once in a while I get in and out within a couple of days," I add. "But not very often."

"So give me an example. Like what are you doing right now?" he asks, gesturing at the screen.

"Checking my account. Last night I E-mailed my on-line brokerage firm about an IPO they're involved in."

"An IPO?"

"An initial public offering," I say deliberately. Russell knows almost nothing about the stock market. He's told me he puts most of his money in a bank account earning a boring four percent a year. He hates it when the market goes up and loves it when it dives. "The company's stock is scheduled to begin trading on the NASDAQ at 9:30 this morning. I was checking my account to see if I had won any of its shares in a lottery my firm was running yesterday."

"What do you mean, 'lottery?' "

I've spent a lot of time over the past few years learning all I can about financial markets by reading the *Wall Street Journal*, studying business school textbooks I've borrowed from my local public library and doing research on the Internet. It feels good to show off a little of what I've learned. "The big brokerage houses sell shares of going-public companies to their preferred clients," I explain. "Clients like insurance companies, mutual funds, pension funds and a few rich individuals."

"The haves," Russell sniffs. He's from a working class family, like me.

"Brokers sell shares to those preferred clients at a price they think will rise during the first day's trading," I continue, ignoring Russell's resentment.

"Ensuring them a profit."

"Right. The brokerage houses want to make sure the preferred clients are always happy so they can count on them for the next deal, and the next and so on."

"It's a stacked deck," Russell mutters. "An insider's game you and I will never get to play."

"That's mostly true," I agree. "In the past, small-share-lots were around, but you had to know somebody at the company or the brokerage house to get your hands on them. You really did have to be an insider. Now there's a chance for me to get them too."

"How?"

"That's where the lottery comes in. Because of all the Internet trading, the big Wall Street firms that lead IPOs have recruited on-line brokerage firms to help them sell shares to the general public. On-line brokers serve regular people who may have only a small amount of money to invest, but, when added together, they control a lot of cash. Like big firms, the on-line firms give their best customers first crack at most of the shares they have. But, as a marketing gimmick, they make a small part of their allocation available to all their customers by running a lottery. The lottery gets lots of people interested. Even if they don't win any shares in the lottery, the little guys do their best to get them in the after-market as fast as they can."

"Which helps drive the price up on the first day of trading," Russell reasons, "just like the big Wall Street firms want."

"Exactly."

Russell leans forward in his chair and rotates the monitor so he can see the screen too. "And you participate in these lotteries?"

"Sure. As long as you have an account," I explain, nodding at the screen, "and money in the account to cover the share purchase if you win, you can play."

"How long have you been doing this?"

I can tell Russell isn't asking questions to build a case against me. He could do that simply by tracking my network activity. He wants to learn how to play the game. "Six months."

"Ever won?"

"No," I admit. "They don't make many shares available in the lottery. Like I said, it's mostly a marketing gimmick designed to spark interest in the stock."

"Ever *heard* of anyone winning?"

"No."

Russell laughs harshly. "No one like you ever wins at this game, Augustus. It's all a big con. They're trying to make you think they care about your business. But they really don't."

That thought has occurred to me before.

"Well?" he asks.

"Well what?"

"Aren't you going to check to see if you won?" He wants to see my disappointment because he's the kind of man who finds comfort in the despair of others. "Go on."

I move the mouse so the flashing white arrow is on the appropriate spot and click to my personal page. Instantly, a summary of my account—a detailed description of the few shares I own—appears on the screen, but at the bottom of the page is a blinking message I've never seen before. A message instructing me to click on it. The text is surrounded by exclamation points and turns rapidly from red to white to blue with firework graphics exploding all around it. Usually this message is a dull black and white. Usually it informs me that I haven't won any shares—again.

Russell leans across the desk and points. "What does all of that mean?"

"I don't know," I say, unable to hide my grin. "Looks good though, doesn't it?"

"Click on it," he orders, an edge in his voice. As much as he takes pleasure in another's disappointment, he hates his own envy.

I glance at the ceiling, cross my heart one more time, then guide the flashing arrow down to the message and click.

Suddenly the entire screen is exploding, and in the middle of the chaos is a box with words congratulating me on winning five hundred Unicom shares. It informs me that the IPO price will be $20 a share and that my account has already been debited $10,000, plus commissions.

"My God," Russell exclaims. "Where did you get ten grand?"

According to Wall Street's experts, Unicom could finish today's trading at $100 a share, maybe even $200.

The era of every dot-com IPO soaring into the strato-sphere right away is long gone, but Unicom has been tagged a can't-miss-kid by the Street's All-American ana-lysts. It has developed an amazing, next-generation wire-less technology, and the huge telecommunications firms are pounding on its Silicon Valley door to steal a peak in-side the kimono.

Elation rushes through my body. In a few hours my ten thousand could be worth fifty thousand, maybe even a hundred.

"Augustus, I asked where you got ten thousand dol-lars," Russell demands, irritated.

"Calm down. I haven't saved that kind of money working at this place." I know that's what he's worried about. "It's my inheritance."

On her death-bed last Christmas my mother in-structed me to dig in the back yard beside the porch. There I would find something helpful, she said. I was skeptical because during her last few years my mother's brain was racked by Alzheimer's. But in the fading light of a cold January dusk I followed her instructions and a few inches down into the icy soil my shovel struck metal. Inside a shoe-box-sized container lay neat stacks of hun-dred dollar bills, flat and crisp, as though she'd individu-ally ironed each one. I stood there in the cold for a long time, gazing at the money in the rays of a dim flashlight, overwhelmed. Apart from the money in the tin box, my mother had little else. The equity in the house barely cov-ered her funeral.

My mother's last request was that I not tell my wife what I found in the yard. That I use the "something helpful" for myself. Mother never liked Melanie.

I've kept this money in a very safe savings account

since I dug it up, afraid that if I invested it in anything else I might lose it. I earned almost nothing in interest, which was frustrating, but the bank had an extremely strong credit rating which gave me a great deal of comfort while I waited for the right opportunity. Now it looks like my patience has paid off.

"What does Unicom do?" Russell asks impatiently.

"It has developed a state-of-the-art wireless application," I explain, eager to show how thoroughly I've done my research. I've tried to talk to Melanie about the market many times, but she doesn't share my passion for it. In fact, she doesn't share my passion for much of anything anymore. These days most of our conversations seem to dissolve into a predictable set of questions and answers. "And they've invented a codec, a compression-decompression device, which brings real-time interactive television to desktop computers regardless of a user's hard-drive capacity or Internet connection. Now people won't need a server the size of a living room or a T-3 hookup to make two-way desk-top television work. It's revolutionary."

Russell air-mails me an irritated look. I know it annoys the hell out of him to think that I'm up to speed on concepts like byte compression, hard drive capacity and bandwidth connections. Things he knows little about.

"You need to focus on why paper towel sales are down at the big supermarket chains in Maryland," he warns, standing up. "Not on technologies that have nothing to do with your job." He turns back when he reaches the door. "Listen and listen to me good, Augustus. I want half of everything you make on that Unicom stock today, and I want it in cash by the end of the week. Otherwise you're fired."

* * *

When I get home Melanie is waiting for me in the small foyer of our cookie-cutter three bedroom ranch-house, arms folded tightly across her ample chest, one shoe tapping an impatient rhythm on the scuffed wooden floor.

"Where have you been?" she demands before I've even shut the door.

"The Arthur Murray school of dancing. I know how you've always wanted to learn that ballroom stuff, and I was going to surprise you for your birthday, but—"

"Augustus!"

My attempt at humor isn't going over well. "Mel, I—"

"Dammit, Augustus, it's late and I'm in no mood for this."

At thirty-three—the same age as me—my wife remains a beautiful creature. The same long-legged blond I fell for in eleventh grade. The same girl I followed to Roanoke College and married a month after graduation with a few family members and friends looking on. To me, she's still every bit as pretty as she was the day of our wedding. "Something came up at the last minute." I smile mysteriously, but she doesn't seem to notice.

"I can't count on you anymore, Augustus. You tell me you're going to do one thing, but then you do something else. You told me you'd be home by six and here it is after eleven."

"You said you had to stay late at the office again tonight, so I thought you wouldn't care if I went out." My smile fades. "And you've been working later and later over the past few months. I wasn't sure you'd come home tonight at all."

"I don't appreciate that," she snaps.

Melanie is an executive assistant for a Washington, D.C., divorce attorney named Frank Taylor, and I've always suspected that he has more than just a professional interest in her. During the past few months she's been wearing lots of perfume—sometimes heavier when she gets home at night than when she leaves in the morning. She's been dressing more provocatively too, and working late several nights a week, sometimes until one or two in the morning. Even a few Friday and Saturday nights recently. I finally tried talking to her about it last week, but she flew into a rage right away, then accused me of silly macho jealousy and stalked off. But it occurred to me later that she never actually denied anything.

Melanie won't look at me. "I have to talk to you."

Her eyes are puffy, as though she's been crying. "What about, sweetheart?" I move forward to comfort her but she takes a quick step back and buries her face in her hands. "What is it, Mel?"

"Oh, Augustus," she murmurs sadly.

I wrap my arms around her and hold on tightly, even as she struggles to turn away. I work-out almost every day in the make-shift gym I've set up in our basement and, at six-four and over two-hundred-twenty pounds, I easily control her slender frame. "Easy, honey."

"Let me go, Augustus."

"Not until you tell me what's wrong."

"Let me go!" she yells, her arms starting to flail.

Suddenly her fingernails rake the side of my neck. I've never seen her like this before. "Calm down, Mel."

"Get your hands off of me!"

"Stop it."

"You don't understand me!"

"Of course, I do. You've had a long day and you're exhausted," I say sympathetically, controlling my anger despite the fact that my neck feels like it's on fire where she scratched me. "And you're sick of me telling you that we can't afford anything."

"You've been drinking," she says, her tantrum easing. "I smell scotch on your breath."

"I had a few drinks with a friend. That's all."

"A female friend, I'm sure."

Melanie has never accused me of cheating before. In fact, I didn't think she cared anymore. "I was with Vincent." Vincent Carlucci and I have been friends since I was ten years old.

"I've seen how women look at you, Augustus," she says wiping tears and smudged mascara from her face, "and how you look back."

"I've always been faithful to you, Melanie."

She slumps against me like a rag doll, arms dangling at her sides, face pressed to my chest. "I can't do this anymore," she sobs.

"You're right. You can't keep up this pace anymore," I agree, slipping my palms against her soft, damp cheeks and tilting her head back until she's looking up at me. I smile down at her confidently, feeling better than I have in years. I've scored big in the stock market and she's going to be impressed. "I want you to stop working, Melanie. I want you to sleep late in the mornings and pamper yourself."

"What are you talking about?" she asks, grimacing as she glances at my neck.

"You don't have to work anymore. It's as simple as that."

"We can barely make ends meet as it is. From what

you've told me, sometimes we don't. How could we possibly survive without my salary?"

"You let me worry about that."

She stares at me for a few moments, then closes her eyes and shakes her head. "Did you think I was talking about my job when I said I couldn't do 'this' anymore?" she asks softly.

"Of course." In that awful moment I understand what she really needed to talk to me about tonight. "Wasn't it?"

"No."

"Then what did you mean?" My voice is hollow, almost inaudible.

She cups her mouth with her hand. She says nothing, but she doesn't have to. The look in her eyes says it all.

The first few moments of lost love are terrible. I gaze at her helplessly, and it's crushing to see how sorry she feels for me—pity is such a useless emotion, only making matters worse for both of us. Melanie wants to be with someone else. Over the years I've heard the whispers from her family and friends that I'm a disappointment to her. Now she's finally listened to those whispers and given in to her desire to be with someone else. "Melanie?"

"We don't have any children, Augustus," she sobs, "and so little money. It won't be hard to split things up."

"It's your boss, isn't it?" My rage erupts. An awful, mind-numbing fury that spreads like wildfire from my brain to my eyes to my chest. I've tried to be understanding about the late hours, the new wardrobe full of short dresses and lacy blouses, the matchbooks from expensive Washington restaurants on her dresser, even the hang-up telephone calls I endure on weekends. Her indifference to me. But I can't take it anymore. "It's Frank

Taylor!" I shout. "You're having an affair with your God damn boss. I knew it! Taylor's made you all kinds of ridiculous promises and you've decided to take a chance."

"This has nothing to do with Frank!" she shouts back. "It has to do with me. I need a fresh start, Augustus. I'm drowning in our life. I have to save myself. If I don't do it now, I never will."

"He's tempting you with houses, cars. Jewelry. I know it."

"Wouldn't that be awful if he was?" she snaps.

"You bi—"

"It's not true!" she snarls, teeth clenched. "But do you blame me for wanting those things?"

"Melanie, come to your senses," I say, swallowing my pride. "It's going to be much better for us from now on. I promise."

"You've been saying that for eleven years. I'm not willing to wait any longer." Tears stream down her face, but they're tears of rage, not sadness or compassion. "I'm sick and tired of being married to a man who accepts being ordinary," she says, gesturing angrily over her shoulder at the inside of our modest home. "I want someone who wants success as much as I do."

"Let's not kid ourselves. You want money. That's all you've ever wanted."

Her eyes fill with tears again. "How can you say that to me?"

"Because it's true, and you know it."

She drops her face into her hands. "Let's just end it," she begs pitifully. "Please."

I stare at her, wishing I could take back those words, even if they are true. "Mel, come on."

"I'm sorry, Augustus. I'm so sorry, but I want a divorce."

"This is crazy," I say, taking her gently by the arms. "Stop it."

"Let me go."

My heart sinks as I realize that this is not passing drama. She's serious. "Oh, God," I mutter, looking down. Both of Melanie's wrists are marked by painful looking purple bruises. "What have you done to yourself?" I murmur, looking up into her beautiful, anguished face.

She yanks her arms from my grasp and runs away down the short hall without answering.

"Wait, Mel. I hit it big today in the—" But the slam of our bedroom door cuts me off.

For five minutes I stand in our foyer, unable to comprehend what has just happened, my emotions ricocheting from dejection to rage. Finally I stumble to the kitchen and ease into a chair at the scarred wooden table where Melanie and I have eaten so many meals together. My eyes come to rest on a note pad lying beside the sugar bowl and a stack of unpaid bills. In Melanie's looping script I see that Russell Lake has telephoned four times this evening. I'm supposed to call him back no matter how late it is.

I touch my neck where Melanie scratched me, then bring my hand in front of my face. My fingertips are stained with blood.